Amanda Cinelli was born into a large Irish-Italian family and raised in the leafy green suburbs of County Dublin, Ireland. After dabbling in a few different careers, she finally found her calling as an author when she won an online writing competition with her first finished novel. With three small daughters at home, she usually spends her days doing school runs, changing nappies and writing romance. She still considers herself unbelievably lucky to be able to call it her day job.

USA TODAY bestselling, RITA®-nominated and critically acclaimed author **Caitlin Crews** has written more than one hundred books and counting. She has a Master's and a PhD in English Literature, thinks everyone should read more category romance, and is always available to discuss her beloved alpha heroes. Just ask! She lives in the Pacific Northwest with her comic book artist husband, she is always planning her next trip, and she will never, ever, read all the books in her 'to-be-read' pile. Thank goodness.

THE BUMP IN THEIR FORBIDDEN REUNION

AMANDA CINELLI

WEDDING NIGHT IN THE KING'S BED

CAITLIN CREWS

MILLS & BOON

First published in Great Britain 2024
by Mills & Boon, an imprint of HarperCollins*Publishers* Ltd,
1 London Bridge Street, London, SE1 9GF

www.harpercollins.co.uk

HarperCollins*Publishers*, Macken House, 39/40 Mayor Street Upper,
Dublin 1, D01 C9W8, Ireland

The Bump in Their Forbidden Reunion © 2024 Amanda Cinelli

Wedding Night in the King's Bed © 2024 Caitlin Crews

ISBN: 978-0-263-31992-7

01/24

This book is produced from independently certified FSC™ paper
to ensure responsible forest management.
For more information visit: www.harpercollins.co.uk/green.

Printed and Bound in the UK using 100% Renewable Electricity
at CPI Group (UK) Ltd, Croydon, CR0 4YY

THE BUMP IN THEIR FORBIDDEN REUNION

AMANDA CINELLI

MILLS & BOON

CHAPTER ONE

ISABEL O'SULLIVAN STARED at the chubby-faced babies in the photos that lined the Swiss fertility clinic's testimonial wall and felt her chest tighten with excitement. Today was the day. By this time next year *her* child's picture would be up on this wall too, accompanied by her own smiling face full of maternal joy.

She was finally going to be a mother.

Well, she would be on her way to becoming one if the doctor would hurry back from whatever emergency she'd been called out to.

Izzy had arrived at the glossy marble front desk perfectly on time two hours ago. First they'd struggled to find her charts, and then a series of phone calls had had to be made while she sat out in the waiting room. Now, with every passing minute, she just couldn't shake the feeling that something wasn't quite right.

The clinic was decorated more like a hotel than the plain, sterile hospital where she had done her preliminary check-ups back home, but still she felt nausea threaten, as it did for her in all medical situations. She tried to get comfortable on the examination bed, smiling as her brightly painted toes poked out from the end of the sheet.

A bubble of emotion clogged her throat as she remembered how carefully her best friend Eve had painted the tiny flowers and bumblebees on each toe the night before.

'Because, babe, you're much more terrified of bees than hospitals, so they're bound to cancel each other out.'

Their friendship had once been the closest thing to family that either of them had ever had, after their shared experience of growing up in the Irish foster care system. But Eve had a little family of her own now, with her wife Moira getting ready to give birth to their first child any day.

Izzy was determined to prove that she could do this alone. That she was ready.

A nurse re-entered the room. The same one who had first instructed her to undress an hour ago and then stood completely stone-faced while Izzy awkwardly joked about preferring to be taken out on a date before she got naked. There had even been a loud *tut* when Izzy was taking off her scuffed biker boots, whilst trying to maintain some level of privacy over her plus-sized curves.

She hadn't thought she'd needed to dress for the occasion, but judging by the similar looks that had been thrown her way in the waiting area, her graphic rock band T-shirt and comfy leggings ensemble was a little out of the ordinary from the clothes of their usual clientele.

She had smiled boldly in the other women's direction, resisting the urge to ask if there was an official dress code for being artificially inseminated with your dead husband's sperm.

After her short-lived marriage to Singaporean playboy Julian Liang she was more than a little familiar with the icy stares that came from not fitting in to the expectations of his social circles. As always, she refused to let it faze her—not when she had managed to make it to Zurich today against all the odds, with Dublin Airport in chaos due to an arctic weather system wreaking havoc across Europe.

But the nurse was not stone-faced now. If anything, she looked a little nervous as she flipped through a chart and looked furtively across to where Izzy quietly swung her legs from her perch on the cold examination table.

She tried not to react when another nurse entered, his face a mask of polite calm even as he leaned in to whisper furiously to his stern-faced colleague. Both shared what Izzy could only describe as *a look*, and began flipping through the forms that Izzy had painstakingly filled out weeks ago online.

She stiffened, her mind expecting a blow even though she knew there weren't any errors. Being dyslexic made written tasks challenging for her, but she knew that she had proofread everything twice with her assistive software.

When Julian had finally confided in her about his possible reproductive issues, after several months of trying for a baby, and had asked her to consider going down the IVF route, she'd thought it wonderful that he was willing to do anything to have a child with her. She'd had no idea that her husband had been freshly out of rehab when he'd eloped with her, and had been using her in a last-ditch attempt to stop his father from cutting him off from his inheritance completely.

Even after she'd found out the truth he'd been filled with promises and pretty words as he'd presented her with plane tickets and the address of a luxury chalet where they would stay during the procedure.

He'd said he was drunk that night he finally admitted the truth, of course. That she was *crazy* to think such a story could ever be true. But for Izzy it had been the first thing he'd ever told her that made complete sense. Suddenly she'd seen the previous year of her marriage for what it was, and walking away had become an act of salvation rather than cowardice.

She wasn't crazy. She never had been.

It had been easy to put the idea of ever having a family of her own out of her head as she'd fought for the courage to begin the process of divorce. But then, before she'd been able to do so, he'd died. His overdose had been ruled as likely accidental, but they would never truly know.

She hadn't loved Julian. Not really. Not the way she'd believed she had when she'd agreed to marry him after only two weeks together. He had been charming, and exciting, and she had been reeling from finding out that her contract as a nanny in a position that had begun to feel like home wasn't being renewed. And, yes, perhaps there had been a little rebellion at play, considering that Julian's egomaniac racing driver best friend had been to blame for her sudden joblessness.

Since dropping out of school at sixteen she'd had all sorts of jobs, from simple waitressing gigs to a wedding singer, and even a face painter in a travelling circus. She had never been able to understand how anyone was happy to pick just one career; she wanted to try all of them. And so she had, accidentally landing her first nannying gig when a wealthy family had spied her face-painting at a kids' party and taken a shine to her.

Moving around the world from family to family had been an exciting way to see the world at first, but soon it had become her normal.

The position with Astrid Lewis, the PR manager for one of the Elite One class racing teams, Falco Roux Motorsport, and her young son Luca had only been meant to be temporary, but she had clicked with little Luca and his powerful single mum, and her two-month contract had turned into an entire year.

Travelling around the world, attending the glamorous motor races and caring for an adorable toddler had been a dream job, but she had got too attached.

Abandonment, even if only perceived, had always been her biggest trigger. It was the lonely, small part of her that still bore wounds from being moved around so often as a child. She closed her eyes, hating the fact that this pro-longed waiting period had brought back all these difficult memories on what was supposed to be a wonderful day.

It had been two years since she'd become a widow at twenty-five, and she had spent that time trying to stay in one place for the first time in her life and doing the kind of soul-deep recovery work that she'd always run from.

She'd bought a house. The first one she'd ever had of her own. Sure, it was a rundown little cottage that she'd had to spend the past year renovating with her own two hands, but it was hers, and she paid the mortgage with her book illustration work. She'd always loved drawing and was grateful that she'd found a career in it after Astrid had let her go.

But taking this final gift that Julian had given her— his sperm, still stored at this clinic—was a once-in-a-life-time opportunity for her to give herself the dream she'd always longed for. She was going to create a little family of her own and, best of all, nobody would be able to take it away from her.

With the warm, invigorating glow of that reminder, she closed her eyes to begin her practised calming regime of inhaling and exhaling in slow sequence. She was supposed to imagine that she was blowing the sounds away with each exhalation and breathing in an oasis of calm with each inhalation…or something like that. But the sound of faraway voices was fast intruding upon her oasis with what sounded like an increasingly fraught argument.

She huffed out a breath, cursing herself for believing that her therapist's deep breathing techniques would work on her deeply ingrained hyper-alert ways.

Another chorus of voices sounded, right outside the examination room's door now, and Izzy sat up impatiently. Evidently she was cursed when it came to actually getting this treatment today.

'Ms O'Sullivan's is the sole name on this account. We weren't aware that any further action was necessary.'

Izzy felt her entire body deflate. Further action? Had Julian not fully paid off the account? He had always been terrible with money.

She closed her eyes, mentally calculating how much money she had in her savings and hoping that it would be enough to straighten things out. She had only just entered her fertile window, so even if they had to wait for a bank transfer she could arrange to stay in town for a couple more days.

She could come back tomorrow. She could sort this out.

She inhaled another deep breath and prepared to get up—only to find herself frozen in place as a familiar voice sounded out in the hallway, raised above the others.

'Tell me which room she is in. *Now*.'

The icy demand was laced with the kind of cool threat that she had only ever heard from one man before in her life. But there was no way *he* would be here, in Switzerland of all places. You couldn't conjure someone up simply by thinking of them.

She swung her legs over the side of the table, just managing to cover her lower half with the sheet as the door was pushed open.

Her view was mostly obscured, but from what she could see a handful of clinic staff had formed a concerned crowd around a broad-shouldered figure. The sour-faced nurse had moved to stand guard in the doorway, a blush high on her cheeks as she attempted to appear stern and immovable. But just as quickly as she'd begun frowning she looked up—and promptly melted back against the doorframe.

'Sir, you can't just…' The nurse visibly fawned even as she tried to remain stern, her voice high with excitement and nerves as she continued, 'I mean… I'm such a huge fan. But only assigned partners are permitted in this area, or people who are known to the patient.'

'She knows me.'

The man stepped into the room, his dark gaze instantly landing on her.

'Don't you, Isabel?'

Izzy froze at the sound of her name on motor racing legend Grayson Koh's perfectly chiselled lips. For the briefest moment she felt a ridiculous urge to run to him—the one familiar face she'd seen since being stuck waiting in this posh, frigid place all morning. But then she remembered that while they might technically know one another, they had never been friends. Even if for a while she'd thought they might be.

It had been two years since they'd stood shoulder to shoulder as Julian's remains were loaded onto the Liang family's private jet. Two years since Grayson had told her she should never have married his best friend in the first place—right before he'd offered her money to stay away from the Liang family entirely.

She instantly felt her blood pressure rise.

True to form, Grayson ignored everyone and remained singularly focused upon where she sat, frozen on the edge of the examination table. His eyes seemed to burn with urgency as he scanned her half-clad form, his eyes coming to rest upon the neat trolley by her side, filled with sterile implements and tubes.

For a man famous for his icy control, on and off the racetrack, his expression flickered with a sudden wildness that she had never seen before.

When he spoke, his voice was a dry rasp, his throat straining as he seemed to struggle to form words. 'Am I too late…have you already done it?'

'That's none of your business.' She subconsciously guarded herself with folded arms, feeling her pulse throb at the base of her throat. 'W-why are you here?'

She hated how weak her voice sounded, with an audience of doctors and nurses watching their little exchange. His shrewd gaze seemed to follow her every move, missing nothing and giving nothing in return. She shivered, feeling thoroughly exposed.

'The insemination.' His eyes narrowed upon her. 'Has it already been done, Isabel?'

She flinched back. Embarrassment and anger began to creep in where her surprise had held her immobile. It was so typical of Grayson Koh to barge into *her* private appointment and make her feel as though *she* was the one who had done something wrong. His look of stern disapproval was one she had become quite used to whenever she'd been visiting the racetrack with his young godson in tow. The fact that she'd had an unbearable crush on him back then was now unthinkable.

'Who do you think you are to barge in here and make

demands?' she asked, putting as much steel into her voice as she could muster, considering her entire body had already been under stress and she was close to fainting.

Of all the times that Grayson could have shown up in her life, it had to be today. It had to be here.

She had seen emotion on his face that day in Dublin, when he had appeared in the hospital only hours after Julian's death. He wasn't as ruthless as the media portrayed him. He was simply effortlessly aloof, notorious in his sport for his calm confidence and bravado. He was infinitely sure of himself and his ability as a legend in the world's most fast-paced sport.

He had always looked devilishly handsome in his sleek racing suit and trademark gold helmet, but now...freshly retired and rocking a shirt and formal trousers...he was still the most beautiful person she'd ever seen up close. It was an assault to the senses just looking at him.

The news of his recent retirement had been shocking, and impossible to avoid in the news, but as always she'd forced herself not to think too much about it. Not after the way he'd spoken to her on the day she'd laid her husband—his best friend—to rest.

She had wondered if Grayson blamed her. After all, if Julian hadn't followed her to Dublin, and insisted upon remaining there while he attempted to woo her back as his wife, maybe he wouldn't have relapsed. But of course no one else knew Julian's secrets.

Perhaps that was why Izzy had given him more chances than she ever would have given anyone else. She had recognised the struggle in him. It had been the same lonely emptiness that she had seen in her friends who hadn't made it very far once they'd all aged out of the foster care system. She'd always had Eve back then, at least.

Grayson stepped through the doorway, closing it behind him. 'You didn't think to consult me before travelling here? Did you really think that I wouldn't find out?' he asked, levelling her with a cool stare.

'Why on earth would I need to consult you?'

She readjusted the sheet on her lap, hardly believing this moment was happening for real. Maybe she had fallen asleep on the examination table and this was all just some weird, very messed-up dream.

'If you're here on behalf of the Liang family, I have already signed every legal waiver known to man. I know full well there will be no inheritance for Julian's child, just as there was none for his widow.'

'*Julian's* child? Why would you think that you were...?' A horrified expression transformed Grayson's handsome features. 'My God. You have no idea, do you?'

'No idea about what, Grayson? You barge in here, to a private examination room, like the hounds of hell are at your feet. And you expect me to simply know what I've done wrong?' She inhaled a sharp breath, needing her worst fears confirmed. 'Did you...did you pay for the treatment on Julian's behalf, or something? Have you rushed here just to make a scene of informing me that I'm in your debt? Or are you here to tell me you won't pay for it at all?'

Grayson cursed under his breath. 'You think that I'd rush out of a meeting in Monaco and break every speed limit to get here over a supposed *debt*? I came here to close the account. To put a stop to it all just as I should have done long before now.'

Cold seeped into Izzy's chest, snuffing out all the hope that had fuelled her through this hellish day so far. What kind of terrible luck had she accrued in her lifetime that the one person standing between her and the only thing she wanted was *him*? In the year she'd spent travelling alongside the Elite One racing teams he'd made it clear how much he disapproved of her with a series of icy stares and cold shoulders. He hadn't deemed her fit to be his godson's nanny, and now he was trying to stand in the way of her having a child of her own.

'You can't do this, Grayson. I'll cover the cost myself somehow,' she said, her voice dripping with a mixture of shock and fury.

But if he stood against it she knew that with his financial power and influence she'd never be able to go ahead. And even if she wanted to pay for it herself, she knew she couldn't afford the entire bill.

He continued to stare daggers at her, his nostrils flaring as though she'd just kicked him in the gut.

'This damned place…the whole agreement…' He cursed, dragging a hand over the light stubble on his sharp jawline. 'All this time…and you didn't even *know*?'

Izzy raised a palm, unable to listen to his imperious tones a moment longer. She was absolutely furious, and so very done with how people seemed intent upon judging her and assuming the worst of her today.

'Oh, I *know*. I know that I've wrestled with this decision for the past two years and that I came here today to carry out Julian's last wish…for me to have a child. Those were the last words he spoke to me the day before he died—other than telling me to call *you*, of all people. You can't just…cancel this, like it's a bank account. Like it's *nothing*.'

The last word came out perilously close to a sob, and Izzy felt the swift scald of tears prickle her eyes.

She bit down hard on her inner cheek, refusing to unravel here, in this place. She just needed him to leave. She needed him to disappear and for everything to go back to the plan that she had so carefully lined up. She'd taken the next week off work. It was a new year. It was a fresh start. She had finally felt fully in control of her path forward—and now here was Grayson, standing in her way.

'It's not nothing to me,' he said, his hard features blazing with some strange emotion as he took a step towards her. 'Isabel, we need to talk—'

'*Get out*!' she said with a growl as she hopped off the table. 'I don't want to talk to you. You may have the wealth and authority to cancel my plans at will, but this is a private examination room you've just barged into.'

Grayson froze, looking briefly down to where her bare legs and feet poked out from the bottom of the sheet she'd hastily wrapped around her waist.

'Of course,' he said abruptly, turning away from her. 'Take a moment to dress. I'm going to go and speak with the doctor. And then…then we can discuss our situation.'

Had he seriously just referred to this as *their* situation?

She didn't bother to correct him. Didn't bother to say anything else at all. She just pushed him out of the room and closed the door behind him with a snap. Once she was alone, she leaned forward, pressing her forehead against the cold wooden panels.

Her breath came harder.

She looked around at the implements on the trolley and felt the dizziness come closer. She needed fresh air. She needed to get outside…to breathe… Get away from Grayson Koh's dominating presence. Once he was gone, maybe then she would be able to figure this out.

She inhaled another deep breath, trying to ignore the rising panic in her chest as she pulled on her clothes as fast as she could.

* * *

Grayson hadn't bothered to wait for the doctor to open her office door, instead storming in and placing his hands down heavily on the woman's desk by way of greeting.

'Mr-Mr Koh…' the doctor stuttered. 'I've been informed of the situation, and I must issue my full apologies. The account has already been nullified and your sample has been sent to be destroyed.'

'Good,' he growled. 'Now I'd like to know how this almost happened in the first place.'

'Well, Ms O' Sullivan had already booked for the insemination before the death of her husband, so it was simply listed as a pause—'

'She doesn't know it's my sample,' Grayson gritted. 'I'm pretty sure that violates something in your damned terms and conditions.'

The doctor sat upright. 'That's impossible. She signed the contracts.'

'It's clear that she doesn't know the sample is mine.'

Grayson emphasised each word through gritted teeth, closing his eyes against the memory of her staring at him in confusion when he'd questioned her decision to come here without his knowledge. He'd assumed her dislike of him was the reason she'd never openly addressed the deal he'd made with Julian, against all his better judgement.

'My wife desperately wants a child,' his friend had begged, *'and it's your fault I can't give her one.'*

Even today she had spoken of her plans, her hopes… and he was the villain in her story once again.

Guilt rose in his stomach.

'She thinks she's being inseminated with a donation from her late husband today. Not mine.'

The woman stood up, straightening to her full, impressive height. 'That's a very serious accusation, Mr Koh. We take meticulous measures to ensure that all parties are fully briefed before we carry out treatments involving donors. I can assure you—'

A thought suddenly occurred to Grayson. 'Are they briefed in writing?'

'Well, in this case, yes. Considering she resides in Ireland, today was Ms O'Sullivan's first in-person visit.'

Isabel had never openly discussed her dyslexia, but his young godson had told him about his nanny's fancy phone apps, and upon watching more closely, he'd noticed all the ways she overcame her challenges himself. Not that he'd spent a lot of time watching her, of course. She'd just always seemed to be around during that season. Everywhere he'd turned there she'd been, filling up the space with her laughter and smiles.

The doctor was pacing now, using a sheaf of papers to fan herself, as though she too had just realised how close they had come to having a woman accidentally inseminated by the wrong man.

'Your voicemail this morning simply said we must delay the appointment.' She winced. 'I thought perhaps it was a payment dispute...'

'You are quite aware of my public standing? Do you think that I would simply disclose such sensitive information in an email? No. I've had to drive across Europe in a snowstorm. Praying that I would get here in time because every flight from Monaco was cancelled.'

Every moment of that drive had been agony, and he had arrived to find his friend's widow on an examination table...unknowingly readying herself for a procedure that had the potential to intertwine their lives for ever.

There was a reason why he had told Julian he could no

longer give his blessing for his donation mere days after giving it. It had been that moment when he'd first imagined Isabel O'Sullivan pregnant with his child.

Grayson closed his eyes and inhaled a shaky breath, pinching the bridge of his nose. If he'd got here just half an hour later that very well might have been on its way to happening.

The thought struck at something dark and greedy within him. A feeling he'd tried to bury for three years now, since the scandalous elopement that had made Izzy Julian's wife. He'd practically sent her running into his best friend's arms when he'd shattered that careful distance between them with an illicit kiss in his darkened garage, then selfishly asked his friend Astrid not to renew her nanny's contract just so that he could secretly be free to pursue her.

It made sense that she had no clue that Grayson had been a part of this arrangement. He should have known she'd never have agreed to accept such personal, long-lasting help from a man she'd made it clear she would never trust again.

Julian had never shown even the slightest interest in marriage and children before meeting Isabel, preferring instead to live the life of a playboy bachelor. Grayson had assured Julian that he would never claim paternity of the child. It had been the least he could do after Julian had revealed to him that his infertility was due to the racetrack accident that had left him unable to drive ever again.

They had both been young drivers then, filled with ego and the desire to win a much-coveted seat with an Elite One racing team. But as the son of a housekeeper and a chauffeur, Grayson had needed to toe the line and earn billionaire Peter Liang's patronage to avoid being forced out of the sport entirely. Even if it had meant quite literally driving his best friend off the road.

Grayson closed his eyes at the familiar tightening of emotion in his throat that came whenever he thought of Julian. Their parents had been close friends, despite Grayson's parents being their long-time employees. The Liangs had been kind to him, even paying for him to join Julian at a private school in England, where they had both started their careers on the karting tracks. Of course his relationship with Julian's father was what had driven a wedge between the two friends in the end.

Damn Julian's lies. Damn him. It was unbearably cruel that Isabel had lost her husband in such an abrupt fashion. Had she thought of this child as her last link to him?

'I need you to come with me and explain the situation to her,' Grayson said, straightening to his full height and unbuttoning the top button of his dress shirt.

When he had received his bank's notification that payment for the procedure had been initiated by the clinic, he had raced out of an important meeting about an upcoming charity race in Singapore.

'Of course.' The doctor nervously cleared her throat. 'I just need to assure you that this has never happened before.'

Grayson realised the clinic's employees were likely quaking at the idea of potentially major legal ramifications. But of course he wasn't the party who had been wrongfully treated.

'I will take full responsibility if she wishes to sue, or if she wishes to wring my neck—whatever it takes. I just need you to help me talk to her.'

'Absolutely.' The doctor fanned herself again, her face turning a deep pink hue as she called a nurse in from the hallway. 'Gianni, we will need to get Ms O'Sullivan into one of the nicer consultation rooms.'

The nurse frowned. 'She walked out a short while ago.'

'She…what?' Grayson felt his blood pressure spike.

'She seemed quite upset,' the nurse said quietly. 'She mumbled something about needing some air, but then I heard her car skidding out of the car park.'

'In this weather?' the doctor asked, appalled. 'Conditions mean we're actually closing early for the weekend. The airports and train stations are all closed too. She can't have gone far.'

Grayson cursed under his breath, launching himself out into the hallway and striding towards the exit doors. He had no intention of returning on any other day. And Izzy wouldn't be returning either—not once he'd explained everything to her.

CHAPTER TWO

IZZY FOCUSED ON getting her tiny rental car uphill in the heaviest snowfall she had ever seen.

One call to try to get an earlier flight home had quickly informed her that the airport had grounded all flights for the remainder of the day, due to the severe weather conditions.

Her eyes burned with tears she refused to shed. Crying didn't get anything accomplished when the world pulled the rug out from beneath you—she had learned that pretty fast as a child. She preferred to be practical and focused, pushing through challenging times until she had a solution.

But this... She had no idea how to make it right. She didn't have the kind of money that it would take to foot the bill at the clinic herself, and there was no way she would crawl to Grayson for charity. His loyalties would always be with the powerful Liang family—the people who had refused even to acknowledge her marriage to their son and publicly decried her as an opportunist.

Just a few more miles and she would be at the address detailed in Julian's letter. The place where she had envisaged herself resting after her successful appointment—not running to in order to nurse the overwhelming waves of disappointment coursing through her.

She bit down on her lower lip until it hurt, refusing to let herself break apart. She just needed to get out of the snow and then she could begin to attempt to unravel the mess of her perfectly laid plans.

Judging by the speed of the growing snowdrifts, she would be staying up here for the night, at least. A prickle of unease slid down her spine as she realised how isolated it was on this winding mountain road. Her car had already slid perilously close to the guardrail a couple of times, despite the well-treated Swiss roads.

The chalet couldn't be much further from here, could it? The map on her phone showed her destination was around the next curve in the mountain, but the road seemed to be rapidly becoming a sharp incline.

When a small lay-by appeared on the curve, she pulled to a safe stop, deciding she would rather walk the next few kilometres safely than continue to risk the drive. She should have stayed below in the town and tried to find a hotel room for the night.

Cursing, she grabbed her small overnight backpack and began trudging uphill, suddenly thankful that she'd thought to wear boots in lieu of canvas sneakers. These were surely waterproof, at least.

Her leather coat did little to protect her neck from the icy winds, though, and she discovered the hard way that her boots were built more for fashion than functionality. Damp trickles of water soon leaked through to her thin cotton socks, and she was pretty sure if she didn't get indoors soon she'd turn to ice.

By the time she reached the heavy gate at the top of the lane her breath was coming in bursts and she was shivering violently.

In Ireland, a snowstorm like this would shut the entire

country down for days—but she'd thought a place like Switzerland would be accustomed to freezing weather conditions.

Finally she spied a sleek white access panel, and hastily pulled out her phone to get the code that would unlock the electronic gate system. After multiple failed attempts, thanks to her overly stressed mind, the system beeped and the gate opened to reveal a stunning chalet crafted in glass and natural wood.

It was split across multiple levels and carved into the face of the mountain. At the moment the snow fully obscured what she would guess was a panorama of spectacular views from the front. Through the hedging on her right she could see steps leading up to the next level, where she possibly might find a front door, but she was freezing, and her thighs burned from the uphill climb.

Had Julian thought that he would bring her here himself? Had he wondered if it might lead to a reconciliation, despite her telling him over and over again that their marriage would never recover from his lies and manipulation?

She pressed the code into another panel on the wall and watched as one of the heavy garage doors slid upwards on invisible hinges. Eager to get out of the snow, she walked inside quickly, groaning in relief at the comparative warmth of the dark basement space. She didn't need to adjust to the darkness for long, as automatic lighting switched on in slow motion, revealing a cavernous workspace that smelled of engine oil and rubber. Rows of cars spread out before her, some of them fully built, while others were suspended and surrounded by high-tech equipment.

She wandered along the rows of vehicles, searching for an exit from the garage, and finally found one towards the end. It required yet another code, of course, because clearly whoever owned this place was obsessed with security.

She was infinitely grateful as she opened the door and felt much warmer air envelop her as she made her way up a staircase.

To call this place a chalet seemed absolutely absurd, for the formal entryway she now stood in was more like the entrance to a boutique hotel than a mountaintop retreat. The entire floor was decorated in warm oak and polished stone, offset with sleek furnishings and textiles that gave hints of burnished gold and strategic accents of red. Her eye was drawn to the stunning glass floor-to-ceiling hearth that dominated the main living space, bracketed by a plush L-shaped red velvet couch.

She roamed the opulent upper floors in a haze of confusion, noting that each bedroom had a four-poster bed larger than any she had ever slept in in her life, and looked out upon spectacular sweeping views of the valley below.

She felt like an intruder, and just being there made her every nerve stand to attention. But it was clear from the storm outside that she would need to stay the night. Despite her misgivings, she forced herself to sit down on the red-cushioned sofa downstairs, and let her head fall back against the plush headrest.

The prospect of being potentially snowed in at a strange place was not a big deal for a girl who had grown up knowing she might be shipped off to another foster home at any given moment. It steeled her, that thought. Reminding her of how she'd forged her way out of the difficult life she'd been told she should expect as the daughter of a troubled teenaged runaway. She'd refused to become another statistic—the victim of a broken system like her beautiful birth mother had been. She was strong. She would not let the events of today throw her.

She was still going to have a child, somehow. She might not know the exact details just yet, but she was not going to allow one man to cow her into giving up.

The image of Grayson towering in the clinic doorway was still burned into her mind. She hadn't seen him once since the day he'd left to accompany Julian's remains to Singapore. She had not been invited to the Liang family's private ceremony there, and he had seemed angry to find out that she didn't intend to fight them and ensure she was adequately settled financially.

She'd been disarmed by his kindness over those two days. He'd even organised for her to stay in his hotel suite in the city while they dealt with the funeral arrangements. She'd been awash with grief and he had been comforting and attentive, ensuring that she ate, and even sleeping on the sofa in her room when she had nightmares.

She hadn't had the energy to feel awkward, even considering the last time they'd seen one another had been the night before she'd left Singapore on Julian's yacht. Neither of them had ever addressed that kiss, but it had remained burned into her memory ever since. Just as the awful day that had followed had too.

After receiving nothing but Grayson's stony silence for the duration of her short marriage, whilst they'd grieved together she'd begun to believe, for a moment, that maybe she'd been wrong about him. Maybe he wasn't the cold, ruthless egomaniac that he was so often portrayed as in the press. In those quiet moments as they'd stood side by side in the crematorium, he'd even held her hand.

Her husband had known that it was Grayson who had first captured her attention when she'd begun attending the Elite One races. He'd known that it was her hurt at learning Grayson had asked Astrid not to renew her contract that had led to her hasty agreement to travel to Bali on Julian's yacht.

She wasn't entirely oblivious to the reasons behind her own actions. She knew that she had some lingering issues with forming secure attachments to people. It had taken Julian's death for her to finally begin doing the necessary work to heal that part of herself—hence why she had got to the point where she finally felt ready and able to move on to the next part of her life. To start a family of her own, nurture her own roots, and settle down for the first time in her life.

Astrid had lost her previous nanny in the midst of the frantic run-up to the new Elite One season. Luca, her two-year-old son, had been obsessed with motor racing, and the godson of legend Grayson Koh. Izzy hadn't known what to expect after essentially joining a group of people who clearly knew each other very well, but everyone had adored Luca, so by extension she was welcomed by the Falco Roux crew with open arms.

Well, most of the Falco Roux crew.

From first glance, Grayson had been cold towards her. His strong personality was a well-known fact, mostly attributed to his preternaturally ferocious drive and talent. It didn't help that he was possibly the most handsome man she had ever set eyes on, and she did nothing but babble nervously in his presence.

He'd seemed to dominate every room he entered, with his shrewd gaze and chiselled jawline, and on the few occasions she had seen him smile her heart had pumped painfully in her chest. Yes, she had developed quite a crush on him over the following months, as she'd spent time in relative proximity to him.

She'd learned quickly that life on the road during the season was hectic and isolating, so the Falco Roux crew treated one another as friends, eating meals together and blowing off steam on their off days.

Grayson had been suspicious of her easy acceptance into the fold, and had even begun to linger around her and Luca in his off time. Astrid had been curious as to why he was calling in to visit his godson more often than he usually did. Izzy had known it was likely that he disliked her wild hair-colour changes and was afraid her free-spirited attitude would ruin his tiny protégé.

Until that kiss.

She was sure that no one knew about the illicit kiss she'd shared with Grayson after the last race of the season, but afterwards, Astrid had begun to behave oddly around her. At the party on their final night in Singapore, before their planned return to London, she'd revealed that she would not be extending Izzy's contract after all.

After that emotional equivalent of a bucket of cold water being thrown over her Izzy had been only vaguely aware of Astrid hugging her, gushing that she had some connections for selling her book illustrations if she was interested. Izzy remembered pasting on a bright smile and flinging herself into enjoying the rest of the party as much as she possibly could.

Copious amounts of alcohol later, she'd found herself being consoled in Julian Liang's arms. He'd been so easy to talk to, so adventurous and free with his compliments and open thoughts.

When Julian had asked her to travel to Bali with him the next day, just as friends, Izzy had jumped at the chance to run away from yet another painful rejection. He had told her everything she wanted to hear—that he had been falling for her over the few times they had met over the previous year, that he had decided he wished to settle down and start a family…and the rest was history.

They had been married a matter of weeks later.

Apparently Grayson had called him a few times, utterly furious. It hadn't been a surprise to Izzy that people had believed *she* was the one taking advantage of charming, fun-loving Julian Liang. And even less of a surprise when no one had believed her when she'd eventually discovered the painful truth behind their sudden elopement.

Julian had been on his way to bankruptcy, and had decided the fastest way to force his wealthy parents to cut him in on his future inheritance was via the promise of grandchildren.

She froze, suddenly processing that she'd been staring up at a large impressionist-style painting of an eerily familiar gold motor racing helmet. The cold efficiency of the layout had set off some hidden warning in the back of her mind that she'd been ignoring before. She stood up, looking around her for something to prove the increasing sense of recognition wrong. But sure enough, the more she actually looked at her surroundings, the more evidence she saw everywhere.

The walls and shelves were mostly bare, except for a glass case that contained a row of golden trophies. She moved closer to look at the inscription on one of the bases and jumped back as though burned.

Julian had sent her to Grayson's home.

After having already hidden from her the fact that he had let Grayson pay for the insemination, Julian had also just handed his friend's private security codes to her.

None of this made sense—but she wouldn't be staying around to find out why he'd done it.

She had just grabbed her bag and run into the foyer when the front door burst inwards. Snow swirled, framing the broad silhouette of the last man she wanted to see.

'How the hell did you get up here?' Grayson growled, his voice a furious echo.

'I walked,' she said, determined not to squirm.

'In a blizzard? Do you have no care for your own safety? When I realised that you'd attempted to drive...' He inhaled sharply, rubbing a hand against his chest. 'You abandoned your car on the side of the road. I thought you had been...'

Izzy looked at him. He thought she had been hurt. His heavy breathing, the frantic look in his eyes... It wasn't anger. It was...concern.

'This was the address in my information pack. I wouldn't have come here if I'd known that this place was yours.' She blurted out the words, moving cagily around him towards the still open door. 'Don't worry. I was just leaving.'

'Don't go.'

She ignored his command, hoisting her bag over her shoulder and walking out into the icy air. The snow was falling so thickly now it had already formed a fluffy blanket upon the car Grayson had arrived in. It was a heavy-duty SUV—much better to scale the mountain roads than her tiny rental hatchback had been. But driving downhill would be easier, surely?

She had no other choice. Because staying up here alone with him was not an option.

She heard his footsteps crunch through the snow in her wake.

'For God's sake, Isabel, stop running from me. There are things we need to discuss...things I have to explain.'

'I don't need you to explain. You chose to come here and ensure that my appointment was cancelled without even giving me the option to pay the bill myself. What's done cannot be undone. You can just stay up here in your beautiful ice palace,' she called back, trying not to be alarmed at the sound of his heavy steps pounding closer. 'It's perfectly matched with your personality after all.'

Proud of herself for that parting line, she picked up her pace as much as she could manage, trying not to feel alarmed at the depth of the snowbanks that now lined the road. She couldn't have been up here any longer than an hour, and yet the world outside had been transformed from a white wonderland into more of a Snowmageddon situation.

Her senses screamed at her to retreat, to go back inside, but she never had been good at backing down from her own impulsive decisions. It was a double-edged trait. Once she committed, she followed through. Not out of willpower or determination, but out of pure, unfiltered spite.

She had barely left the driveway and had taken no more than a few steps along the downhill slope of the lane when her boots began to lose their grip on the frozen ground. A vision of herself sliding down off the edge of the mountain came into stunning focus in her mind, and the utter foolishness of this endeavour crashed down upon her.

She was fighting to keep her balance, just managing to keep one foot stubbornly in front of the other, when she felt hands clamp down upon her shoulders.

Grayson's face was a mask of tightly controlled irritation as he spun her around to face him.

'Do you despise me so much that you'd risk falling to your death?'

His breath steamed in the frozen air and the heat of his

strong hands seemed to scorch her even though she wore three layers. Almost as quickly as he'd grabbed hold of her, he let her go. She swayed a little on her feet, but refused to let him see how unsteady she felt.

It was a bone-deep shakiness that wasn't just because of the weather. She felt…inconvenient. And immature. As if she had been left in the dark about some important fact. She'd thought she had all her plans in order, that she knew exactly what came next, but now it felt as if those plans had been swept out from under her, leaving her adrift and vulnerable. It was a feeling that triggered all her darkest fears.

'I just need to get down to my car,' she said weakly.

'It's likely buried in a snowdrift by now,' he gritted, taking her by the hand and abruptly cursing. 'You're freezing. We need to get back to the house. Let me say what I need to say, and then I'll stay out of your way until the blizzard passes, if that's what you want.'

She debated fighting him, but the snow was still falling in thick blankets—more than she had ever seen in her life. Far from feeling like a winter wonderland, it felt… scary. As if, if she stood still for long enough, it might bury her too.

After a moment's pause she began walking ahead of him back up the steep hill, refusing to take his hand as they trudged towards the chalet.

Once she was standing back in front of the giant fireplace, watching as he set about lighting it and getting them both steaming cups of some kind of herbal tea, she felt panic crawl in her chest.

Until this snow cleared she was trapped here with him. No place to run.

He stood on the opposite edge of the hearth, stirring his tea slowly, as though he was afraid he might scare her again. As though he had gleaned just how jumpy she was around outward displays of anger...how they made her heart race as if she was a small child all over again.

'I'm going to talk now, and you are going to listen. Understood?'

He took a few deep breaths, looking briefly towards the still-open doorway of the living room that led back to the foyer, but not moving to close it.

'There are things you don't know about the clinic. Things that I assumed Julian had explained to you.'

'Is it about the money to pay for the procedure?' she prompted.

'No. Not about the money.'

Grayson closed his eyes, pinching the bridge of his nose with one hand, and for a moment she thought he looked absolutely tortured—which made no sense. This was a man who did not show weakness or discomfort. Ever. Perfection was his brand, for goodness' sake. And yet right now she could tell that something was very, very wrong.

Her heartbeat drummed loudly in her chest, and she held her breath in her throat as she took a seat back on the red couch. Reflexively she reached out for her tea, cradling it in her hands as though it might provide her with some kind of comfort in the face of whatever terrible secret or new detail this man was about to reveal to her.

So much of her marriage had been built on deception and dishonesty—she honestly didn't know if she could take any more. But if therapy had taught her one thing it was that she was resilient, and that was something to be proud of.

Grayson paced to the window, then back to the open fire. She had seen him like this before, unable to stand still when he was talking. It seemed to impede his focus somehow. Clearly whatever he was about to tell her required his full concentration.

'Isabel, the sample at the clinic…it wasn't Julian's.' Grayson met her gaze. 'If I'd arrived too late today…if you'd already gone through with the insemination and it had resulted in a child…the baby would have been mine.'

CHAPTER THREE

OF ALL THE potential reactions that Grayson had considered while he'd been driving up the mountain, preparing to reveal the truth, he hadn't expected cold indifference.

He had taken a lucky guess that she would seek shelter in his chalet, knowing that had been part of Julian's original plan. Now he inwardly cursed, staring down at the stony-faced woman on his red velvet sofa. Her fresh-faced beauty and luscious curves were still as perfect as ever, but her spirit was dimmed.

The Isabel he'd once known had always been very fast and free in her responses—the first person to laugh or grumble in conversation. But now, instead of shouting at him or bursting into tears, she seemed to be crumbling in upon herself, piece by piece.

She'd made no move to question what he'd told her, so he kept going. He told her about the text Julian had sent to him, asking to meet up. How Julian had told Grayson his marriage was in trouble, because Isabel wanted a child and Julian couldn't give her one because he was infertile. He told her how he, Grayson, was the reason for that, and so his guilt had led him to agree to be the sperm donor, waiving all rights to paternity.

When she still didn't respond, he opted to give her

some space to process everything. He moved away and set about calling various authorities, only to confirm that they were, in fact, snowbound for the foreseeable future. All the main transport links were closed, and people were being urged to stay indoors until tomorrow afternoon at the very earliest.

Isabel, obviously having heard most of this via his side of the aggravated phone conversations, asked which bedroom she could use to rest in, and when he showed her promptly disappeared behind the heavy wooden door with a final-sounding click. He hovered in the hallway, wanting to ensure she was okay, but he also remembered his promise to leave her alone once he'd said what he needed to say.

He'd done that. He'd explained himself... So why didn't he feel any better?

An hour passed and still nothing but silence came from her room, while the snow continued to fall hard and heavy outside.

Usually he paid a management company good money to have his residences ready at all times, as with his international schedule he never quite knew when he might need to stay in any of the properties he owned around the world. But, of course, with the current weather that had not been possible today. Still, the freezer still contained some choice cuts of meat from his last stay, and the larder held a decent assortment of jars and dried foods. He wasn't a chef, by any means, but he could rustle up something decent when needed.

The words seemed to be frozen in his chest as he thought over everything that had been said. The fact that Julian had intended to have Isabel carry another man's child without her knowledge was utterly unconscionable. But the fact that he himself had never even thought to speak with Isabel before agreeing to Julian's request made him complicit as well.

He had simply assumed that it was what Isabel wanted. He had even made sure to have legal documents drawn up that would prevent her from claiming financial benefits from him in the event that her marriage to Julian failed.

The knowledge that all he had considered was the risk to himself shamed him anew.

But the one thing he hadn't considered at all back then was the effect it would have on him once he'd allowed himself to envisage Isabel carrying his child. He had done his very best not to think of it, even in a hypothetical sense. But in the days immediately after he completed his part in the agreement, something had changed.

He had picked up the phone to call Julian numerous times, to tell him everything was off and to risk the friendship that they had rekindled. But every time he'd thought of the words he needed to say to end the deal he'd remembered that he was the reason why Julian was in this position at all.

Julian had told him how badly Isabel wished to have a child, and how he had initially lied to her about his own infertility, thinking it would stop her from marrying him. He'd said that now they had decided to go ahead with sperm donation they both wished for their donor to be someone they knew.

That had been the story he'd been told. But now, linking together all the small bits of information he'd discovered over the past couple of years about his oldest friend, he didn't know what the truth was any more.

He knew that Isabel was not a fool, but he also knew how manipulative and selfish his friend had been when he was at his worst. Julian had commented on Grayson's behaviour around Isabel more than once, noticing his lack of focus whenever she was with them. He'd known that Julian had been cut off financially from his family, that his addiction was spiralling once again, and he'd refused to lend him any more money, widening the rift between them.

It was his fault that Isabel was in this situation. If anything, he'd wounded her and sent her off into Julian's arms like a perfectly presented gift.

He brooded for the rest of the afternoon and until the late evening, when finally Isabel emerged from her bedroom in search of food. He watched as she gathered up some crackers, then walked over to the windows to stare out mournfully at the conditions outside.

'Can I make you more tea?' His words came out roughly, and snappier than he'd intended, making her brows rise.

He forced what he hoped was a neutral expression to his face, not wanting to continue the frosty silence that had settled between them. They were going to be stuck here for the night, judging by the weather reports, and possibly for the next day also.

'I think the situation calls for a little more than tea, don't you?' she said. Her voice was detached, and still devoid of her usual energy and emotion.

He stood motionless as she made her way over to the ornate drinks cabinet on the opposite side of the room. She ran her fingers over each bottle, lightly tinkling the glass, finally coming to rest upon the neck of a top-shelf whisky. Not the choice he would've imagined for the smiling Irish girl he had only ever seen drink soda with a straw, like a teenager.

She poured herself a generous amount, then tilted her head back and proceeded to down it in one gulp.

'That's not a good idea.' He walked across to her and slid the bottle very firmly away from her reach.

'Give it back,' she said, and there was a little more fire in her tone now.

'Not until we talk this through soberly.'

'What exactly is there to "talk through", Grayson?' Her eyes narrowed on him, and her purple-tipped fingers gripped the crystal glass she held in her hand. 'Would you like to discuss the fact that Julian's lies almost resulted in me unknowingly carrying your baby? Or would you like to discuss the fact that you actually agreed to his mad proposal in the first place?'

'I told you—I agreed to it believing that you knew all about it.'

'And you thought that I wouldn't want to speak to you about it myself? Ask you what your intentions might have been?'

'It's no secret that I caused the accident that led to Julian's early exit from motorsport. But it's not common knowledge that his injuries resulted in him being told he would never father a child. For years I tried to find a way to make it up to him, and he finally came to me and gave me that chance. My part was to stay anonymous.'

'So it was some kind of penance?' She stared at him, her expression filled with ire.

'After I'd agreed I barely lasted a week. I called him the night he died. I called him and told him that I couldn't go through with it. And then he went out and overdosed.'

'All this time…did you think that was why he did it?' She shook her head sadly at Grayson's solemn nod. 'Well, that was the same night I told him I wouldn't go through with it either. So I guess that makes us quite the pair, doesn't it?'

Grief and regret burned shamefully in his throat. He held back the torrent of excuses on the tip of his tongue, the cleverly worded arguments that would extricate him from his guilt. Because as he looked at this strong, beautiful fireball of a woman imploding before his eyes he knew that now was not the time for any of that. Now was the time to remain silent and let her be.

Even if that meant allowing her to reach out and grab the bottle of whisky from his hands.

She filled her glass and then popped earbuds in her ears. He could only vaguely make out the sound of some kind of heavy rock music—her genre of choice, he remembered, along with bubblegum pop and show tunes.

He remembered far too much about this woman for his own comfort.

He watched as she downed another two glasses of his whisky, but thankfully seemed to rethink having a fourth. She kicked off her boots and swayed gently from side to side as the music took hold of her, and he was powerless to look away, telling himself that he remained seated where he was simply to ensure that she didn't get hurt.

She was blowing off some steam and, truthfully, he had nothing else better to do.

He moved away, into his office. He had already gone through his more urgent work emails, and fired off a few of his own relating to the annual charity Legends race, which was being held in his home country of Singapore next month, in honour of him being the latest racing legend to have retired.

It would be the ideal time for him to unveil his business plans going forward, as he moved from being a shareholder in Verdant Race Tech to being its CEO.

Verdant was an exciting sustainable-energy-focused

auto engineering firm. He'd been a shareholder since the company's infancy, ten years ago, having seen their potential for innovation across the entire motorsport industry and beyond. His plan was to launch his own team in next year's Elite E—the highly competitive league that used the world's fastest electronically powered cars.

He had also founded the Boost Academy—a global motor racing initiative that provided a springboard for disadvantaged youth.

He hadn't been home much recently, with his work so often taking him around the world. But now, since his retirement, he wouldn't have the same level of engagements from week to week. His restlessness had been one of the factors that had been tempting him to accept one of the countless offers he'd received to return to the sport. To end his career on a high.

The Verdant factory and headquarters were currently set up in Monaco, to capitalise on it being a hotbed of talent for motorsport professionals, but he'd kept his own role remote while he'd been competing.

He had set up the business to be flexible on purpose, after learning the most up to date methods from his successful corporate friends. And over the past two decades, since the very start of his racing career he'd learned what to do and what never to do. He knew better than anyone the corruption and malpractices of the wealthy elite.

He'd kept his lifestyle in check, ensuring that he never lost sight of what his parents had raised him to be, even after they were no longer around to see it. But his ethics and business practices were a separate entity entirely from his image…his persona as racing legend Grayson Koh.

Julian had always called his wife Dizzy—their little joke, he'd said. It had never felt like a joke to Grayson.

He's thought it unnecessary and demeaning to Isabel. But then again everyone said he took things too seriously. He couldn't relax…have some fun.

So Isabel had never truly met the real him—not really. She had only ever seen the driver, the personality that he'd adopted as part of his drive to dominate his sport. It had been a necessary role for him to play, for he had discovered from an early age that when he won, when he performed at his absolute max, he was accepted by everyone—unlike when he'd just been a nerdy kid with working-class parents.

Elite One was an expensive sport, and Julian's father liked winners. So the legend had been born. He'd always had a temper on the track, and the impatience, the cold arrogance he'd shown in interviews, had grown with him as he'd risen up through the various Elite platforms, finally reaching the pinnacle that was Elite One.

When he had been behind the wheel or on the podium he had felt powerful. He hadn't even noticed that the powerful persona he'd adopted had begun to seep into his day-to-day life until eventually he'd rarely let his real self take the reins at all.

A loud splash sounded from the other side of the door, jolting Grayson from his thoughts. He looked down at his watch and realised he had been in his office far longer than he'd intended.

Quickly, he made his way back into the main room—only to find it empty. The doors to the partially covered balcony were spread wide open, letting in the chilly night air, and when he stepped out he was met with the sight of Isabel sliding her partially clothed body into the hot tub.

He reached it just as she submerged herself, up to her waist, and cursed as he saw her shivering violently. Before she had been wearing only a black wool jumper and skinny jeans with rips in the knees—not exactly warm winter attire. But she had since stripped down to a simple black camisole, and he had briefly seen matching black lace-edged panties. Not that he had been looking.

He had long since trained himself to stop looking at Isabel O'Sullivan.

He cleared his throat loudly to announce his arrival, satisfied when she jumped a little and crossed her arms defiantly over her ample chest. She was clearly absolutely freezing, and likely already regretting this ridiculous venture. The covered terrace was purpose-built for the winter months, but even with the heated tiles and steaming water the air was still cold if one was not fully submerged. Most of all, she was very clearly drunk. This was a most unsafe activity.

'Don't be a spoilsport,' she said, pushing his proffered hand away with far more strength than he would've expected.

She moved down another couple of steps and let out little groans of pleasure as the water splashed up over her chest. Grayson closed his eyes for a moment, frozen when her throaty sounds hit him directly in the stomach, then travelled lower.

His body had always been treacherous around this woman. Even before she had married his friend he had been forced to pretend she didn't exist to avoid the thrall she held over him.

'You've had too much to drink,' he said, trying to ignore the delicate outline of her erect nipples through the sodden black material of her vest top.

'I'd argue that I haven't had nearly enough.'

She sighed, dipping her head into the water. The movement sent Grayson's heart pumping through his chest as he dropped to his knees, then reached forward to grab her by the shoulder and pull her back up to the surface. His shirtsleeve was absolutely soaked, and her eyes were filled with mirth as she unleashed a spout of water from her mouth directly into his face.

'You're done here,' he growled, guiding her towards the edge so that he could fish her out.

The ridiculous woman was going to end up drowned if he left her in there any longer.

'You're not my keeper,' she said, eyes blazing.

The alcohol had apparently loosened the fury that she'd held back earlier, but to be honest he far preferred it over her cold indifference. She was a passionate woman, and she'd often been the loudest one in the room, always talking, moving and smiling. He shouldn't care—it wasn't his place… But it felt wrong to see her in any other way than as the tornado of passion she usually was. So if making her angry was what was necessary, he would take that hit.

'Stand up, Isabel. *Now.*'

He stood back and folded his arms, using the same cold expression and commanding tone that he had perfected over two decades in Elite One. The tone that had once got his contract terminated by a corrupt billionaire team owner, penalty-free, and that on countless other occasions had taken journalists to task when they'd dared to ask questions that invaded his privacy.

Isabel simply rolled her eyes at him.

He exhaled on a growl, easing down into a squat position as he debated just hauling her out by that pretty blonde ponytail. Sure, she'd be furious, but at least she'd still be conscious and breathing by morning.

'I can't leave you in the hot tub alone after you've been drinking. It's not safe.'

'Not safe if I'm alone?' she asked, mimicking his gruff tone. 'I think I know a way we can solve that problem.'

He spotted the spark of mischief in her eyes a second too late, and suddenly she was in front of him, her hands wrapped around his shirtfront. One quick tug was all it took for him to lose his balance and slide into the water.

He didn't quite fall so much as slide slowly. But by the time his feet hit the bottom and he'd regained his equilibrium he was submerged to the waist, with bubbling froth rising up to hit his chest.

Isabel laughed, sliding to the opposite edge of the tub to evade his potential retaliation.

'I'm fully dressed, for goodness' sake,' he growled, feeling the warm water permeate his bespoke suit trousers and handmade leather loafers.

'Would you have agreed if I'd *asked* you to strip off and hop in?' she asked sweetly.

'You know the answer to that.'

He sighed, unbuttoning his shirt and peeling it off his wet skin. He left his trousers on, to keep some semblance of decency between them, feeling her eyes following his movements intently as he unclasped his antique watch and laid it down safely, away from the edge.

'Is your...? Is the watch okay?' she asked suddenly.

'Thankfully it avoided the same fate as my shoes.'

He narrowed his eyes upon her, seeing that all trace of mirth had been replaced by a look of guilt. She knew how much the timepiece meant to him, he realised. She knew because he had told her himself one day, as they sat side by side while Luca served them imaginary tea. She'd asked, and he'd surprised himself by telling her the truth.

It was the last gift he'd ever received from his father, before his death. He wore it every day, eschewing the flashier designer brands.

'I know that I'm having fun, so this must be unbearable for you,' she said dreamily, leaning her head back to twirl her hair in the water.

'You think I find fun unbearable?'

'I *know* that you find fun unbearable. Well...unless you're playing with Luca. Or with your fast cars.' She frowned, looking up at the sky through the plate glass roof that covered the length of the wraparound terrace. 'Maybe you just find *me* unbearable. I suppose my own particular brand of chaos must be less than appealing for Mr Perfection.'

'I'm far from perfect, Isabel.'

She looked at him, and her eyes seemed to heat every spot of his face and chest as she scanned him with interest.

'You just got thrown into a hot tub and your hair hasn't even moved out of place. It's inhuman. I'm convinced you're a vampire, or something.'

She tilted her head to one side, considering him for far longer than anyone else would dare. For some reason that action alone had him wanting to laugh, but he was deeply conscious of the fact that she was still in shock, and that this strange, almost humorous interlude was simply a result of her teetering on the edge of her control and trying to find some kind of solace.

And if he had to indulge in strange conversations about vampires to stop her from doing anything more chaotic than jumping fully clothed into a hot tub, then so be it.

'Actually, no...you'd be more of an animal shape shifter, I think.' She assessed him shrewdly. 'King Grayson...a powerful warrior...renowned for the speed and strength of the lion that he transforms into at will. I'd draw your eyes first...'

'You know my track nickname, I see.'

'Everyone knows who the Golden Lion is.'

Who he *was*. He felt tempted to correct her, and felt a flare of irritation at the reminder of that vague sense of loss he had felt over the past few months since his retirement. The irksome worry that without his racing persona he didn't know who he was or how to behave.

He'd walked away from Elite One because he'd achieved everything he'd set out to and the timing had felt right, but the boardroom was a vastly different environment, and he could no longer hide behind a racing helmet.

In order to show his belief and passion for what Verdant was capable of he had to show more of himself...and therein lay the problem.

He reached out to hold her upright as she leaned her head back against the edge of the tub. 'Why don't we go back inside?' he asked.

Her eyes snapped open, pinning him with their pale green depths. Like cat's eyes, he had always thought. Shrewd and all-seeing...giving nothing away of what thoughts might lie beneath.

'I don't need to be minded,' she said, her gaze showing another hint of that fury he had seen earlier. But just as quickly she closed her eyes and tilted dangerously backwards again.

Grayson was upon her in a moment, hoisting her bodily against him and deciding it was better to simply risk her anger than it was to continue with this madness.

He wasn't prepared for her to run her hands up his wet sleeves.

'I always wondered what these arms felt like without

the racing suit… The night we kissed you were all covered up. They're even harder than I remember.'

Her reminder of that night caught him unawares, sending a rush of heat deep into his gut and lower, hardening him into an embarrassingly swift erection.

He tried to shake it off, thankful that he was so practised in burying his reactions to this woman. Still, he couldn't quite stop himself from asking, 'Do you think of that night often?'

She narrowed her gaze. 'Do you?'

They remained in a silent stand-off for a full minute, neither of them willing to give in. He slowly became aware of her hard nipples, pressed tight against his chest, and froze for a long moment, shocked and unable to move. Or at least that was what he told himself as he remained still and allowed her curious hands to slide up his biceps and link around his neck.

He told himself to stop her. That she'd had an emotional upheaval. That this would make everything so much worse between them.

He closed his eyes, praying she wouldn't move and press against the evidence that he was very much affected by her, and that thoughts of the one night he'd allowed himself to taste her lips and wound up having to stop himself from making fast, passionate love to her in a darkened Falco Roux garage lingered.

'Okay, it's time to get you to bed,' he said briskly.

'To…your bed?' she asked, her eyes widening.

'To *your* bed. To sleep,' he corrected her, cursing his own stupidity at not taking that damned whisky bottle away sooner. She was absolutely sauced.

'I don't want to sleep. I'm still furious with you, you know.'

She looked up at him, her expression suddenly more serious and more lucid than it had been before.

'I know. I'm sorry,' he said sombrely.

Even if she didn't remember this conversation tomorrow, he would. And he would apologise again and again until she believed him.

She stared at him, wet curls framing her beautiful face as she chewed on her lower lip. 'I can't stop wondering… if everything had gone ahead today…if you'd been too late…what would you have done?'

A vision of Isabel, radiant and round with his child, crashed into his mind just as wildly vivid as it had been before. Only now the real woman stood before him, awaiting an answer that he couldn't give.

Because how could he admit that he'd already wondered what that child might look like without revealing that his primal reaction to the idea of such a reality had been the reason he'd had to back out of his agreement with Julian in the first place?

'I'd have honoured the agreement, of course,' he answered quietly.

'And your paternal rights?' she asked. 'Would you still have waived them?'

'If you'd asked me to, of course,' he lied.

She instantly raised one brow. 'You know, Grayson… you made a deal with Julian. You could make one with me too. We could both have what we want.'

Her words struck him squarely in the chest, spreading along his veins like wildfire. No. He couldn't have what he wanted—not when it came to Isabel and her picket fence dreams. He had long ago accepted that he was much too selfish and career-obsessed ever to be a good husband or father.

'You're young. You can remarry—'

'I'll never remarry.' She cut across him. 'I'm scarred enough after my one experience of trusting a man with my heart. Even the thought of dating makes me feel slightly ill. That's why I made the decision to come here. I want to have a child and focus all my energy on making each day the best it can be. No threat of relationship drama or heartbreak.'

'You'll change your mind,' he said, partly to her, partly to himself, to push away the dangerous lines of thinking her words were opening up inside him. Lines that were perilously close to a deeply rooted yearning he hadn't truly acknowledged until just now.

'Ugh…don't say things like that,' she said loudly, then hiccupped and swayed a little in the water. 'I'm well aware I'm tipsy, but I do know my own mind, Grayson.'

'Of course. I didn't mean that to sound dismissive. I do, however, think it's time for you to go inside before we both freeze,' he muttered, gathering her tightly against his chest.

'Put me *down*.' Her fist pummelled his shoulder for the briefest of moments—until he grabbed it and held her still. He stood up, the cold air hitting his lower half and making him inhale with shock. She obviously felt the frigid cold too, her body immediately beginning to shiver and gooseflesh spreading across the pale curves of her upper arms.

'Hell, it's freezing!' she gasped, clinging onto his neck with renewed force as she tried to mash the entire front of her body against his for warmth.

Grayson ignored the effect of having Isabel's partially nude wet body touching almost every surface of his own and focused upon grabbing one of the robes that hung near the doorway. He managed to wrap it around her without dropping her, despite her repeated protests at being managed by him.

By the time he'd walked her step by step up the stairs her head had grown heavy on his shoulder and her speech more slurred. He knew all too well the bone-deep tiredness that often came after an adrenaline rush, and she had certainly been put through it today. Even his own heartbeat still hadn't quite returned to normal.

Focusing on practicalities, he carried her the rest of the way up to the guestroom and laid her down softly in the centre of the four-poster bed. She still wore her damp underwear under the robe, but for now it would have to do.

He would not be able to tolerate her having any less clothing on than she already wore.

She moved in her sleep, nuzzling her face into his forearm and sighing softly. He backed away, but remained in the doorway for far longer than he'd intended, wondering how things might have been if he hadn't messed everything up so royally. If he hadn't pushed her away after that kiss in Singapore...

CHAPTER FOUR

IZZY AWOKE TO sunlight filtering in through the windows. Her head felt fuzzy and her mouth dry, but she hadn't drunk that much last night, had she? Groaning, she remembered how good an idea it had seemed to jump into the hot tub in her underwear...then pull Grayson in with her.

So maybe she had drunk a little too much.

She remembered talking and talking, the words coming out of her mouth against her will, until Grayson had pulled her out of the tub. She remembered pressing her face against his heartbeat and closing her eyes—and absolutely nothing else after that.

Groaning with embarrassment, she went straight to the bathroom and set about freshening up. She showered and donned her most comfortable leggings and oversized jumper combo, complete with hand-knitted wool socks that reached halfway up her calves, with tiny tassels on their edges.

She contemplated hiding in the bedroom until the snow melted enough for her to make her escape, even though the scent of something delicious had been wafting under her bedroom door for the past twenty minutes and her rumbling stomach had her on the verge of desperation.

She placed her ear to the bedroom door, listening for sounds of her cranky playboy host. Maybe she could just slip out to the kitchen and grab some supplies from the cupboards?

As she was wrestling with her indecision a knock sounded firmly on the door, making her let out a little yelp. Remaining firmly still, she clapped a hand over her mouth and waited, hoping that he would assume she was still asleep.

'I can hear you overthinking through this door.'

'No, you can't,' she blurted on reflex, then cursed aloud.

She thought she heard him chuckle softly as she pressed her ear to the door once more.

'We need to talk.'

She felt her insides quake at those words and the potential meaning beneath them. Her memories of what she had said last night were swishy, as if she was looking at them through a carnival mirror, but she remembered a few of the choice phrases she had uttered. Had she actually suggested that he make a deal with her? And asked him if he'd ever thought about their kiss after practically swooning over his biceps?

What on earth was wrong with her?

Yes, she had been fairly tipsy, but she had been hurting as well. She had been angry, and devastated that her hopes had been dashed, and it had brought up something impatient and furious within her that she had never experienced before. That and the way he had looked at her...

That didn't quite make sense either. Surely her drunken memory had embellished that spark of heated interest in his gaze?

Thank goodness she hadn't done anything worse than get him soaked in his own hot tub. That kind of embarrassment was something she knew she would most definitely not come back from. Because one thing was for certain: Grayson Koh was not interested in her. He never had been.

'*Isabel.*'

His voice held an edge, and she heard the thud of one of his hands upon the doorframe. Not an angry thump, more of a prompt.

He never had been one to wait around. When Grayson Koh wanted something, he got it immediately. Maybe it was better that she got this awkward conversation over with. With any luck the weather would turn soon, and she would be able to leave and forget all this had ever happened. Maybe once she was home she would be able to figure out what her next step should be.

'I'll be down in a moment,' she said, hoping he couldn't hear the slight tinge of sadness that had accidentally crept into her voice.

She thought of the one tiny white babygrow that she had been unable to stop herself from buying the day after she'd made her appointment at the clinic. She wasn't superstitious, but she knew some people thought that buying things for a baby early was bad luck. Perhaps this entire venture had been doomed from the start.

Yes, it would have been wonderful to have had a child. And, yes, she knew that she would have made a wonderful mother... But the idea of trawling through pages of donors and trying to select a father based on a few tiny details just felt too overwhelming. And even if she could afford it—which she couldn't—there would be the effort of actually trying to get through an appointment at another medical setting without fainting into a puddle on the floor.

As a single woman, self-employed and up until last year having spent most of her life without any fixed abode of her own, she knew that her chance of being approved for adoption was unlikely.

It was a strange feeling...having accepted a new path in

her life and now having everything completely changed. But, really, was she all that surprised? Any time in her life that she had ever begun to hope for a better future things had always had a way of taking a turn for the worse. But she would figure it out—she always did. She worked best alone, after all.

The chalet's main living space looked very different in the early-morning light, with warm sunlight streaming in through the high windows. She looked down and shivered as she realised the snow had reached up past the basement level overnight. But the blizzard had passed, and you might almost be fooled into thinking you looked out at a peaceful winter painting.

Inside, the fire had been lit in the large wood-burning stove and the long dining table had been set for two at one end. Pitchers of orange juice and water lay in the centre, along with bowls of dried cereal and what she rather hopefully prayed was her favourite chocolate spread.

But upon dipping a spoon in and taking a taste, she grimaced.

'What on earth is that?' she said, half to herself.

'Sugar-free vegan cacao spread.'

Grayson appeared in the doorway of the kitchen, a white cotton tea towel slung over one shoulder as he mixed something in a bowl. To her surprise he was wearing dark jeans and a wine-coloured sweater, a more casual outfit than she had ever seen him in outside of his racing jumpsuits.

'It's all I've got, I'm afraid.' He winced. 'The last time I was here it was during race season, so I was in full training mode.'

'Ah, so you've embraced a more slovenly lifestyle in your retirement?' she said drily, trying and failing not to remember the rock-hard feel of what that 'full training mode' had created beneath his wet shirtsleeve the night before.

Get it together, Izzy.

'I didn't say that...' He walked back into the kitchen. 'I only work out twice a day now, if that's what you mean?'

Twice a day? She coughed on a mouthful of orange juice, earning what she thought was a dry chuckle from the kitchen, though she couldn't be sure.

He looked quite serious when he returned a moment later, laying down two plates of pancakes. Gluten-free, sugar-free protein pancakes, as he quickly informed her, producing some bowls of partially defrosted chopped fruit as a topping.

'I understand the need for strict nutrition as an athlete. And, honestly, these taste great...' She took another bite for emphasis. 'But a life without any sugar? You poor man.'

As they ate they kept the conversation safe, speaking only of his new business ventures and her illustration work and how they were both lucky to be able to work remotely.

She was immensely grateful for his unspoken decision not to address the things she had said to him in the hot tub. She had been angry and hurting—always a dangerous combination for her self-control. She hadn't meant any of it, and it wasn't as if she would have accepted if he had offered to go ahead with the deal he'd made with Julian. That would have been absolutely crazy.

Grayson raised his coffee cup to his mouth, his eyes meeting hers as he sipped. She didn't know why, but she felt the moment was suspended in time, and the sudden tension in the air made her stomach tighten.

He leaned forward, strong forearms corded with muscle flat on the surface of the table. Her eyes drifted downwards for a split second before she pulled them back up, mindful of maintaining a businesslike distance between them. She had worked near him for weeks before, in close contact, but of course back then she hadn't known what it felt like to have his strong hands sliding along her bare skin like they had last night.

He cleared his throat and she realised he must have spoken while her thoughts had wandered again.

Dammit, Izzy, get it together.

'Can you repeat that?' she said, her voice strained and high-pitched even to her own ears.

'I said, I have a proposition I'd like to discuss with you.'

'Okay…'

She resisted the urge to squirm in her seat, wondering if his proposition had something to do with her skiing down the mountain to the nearest hotel. She wouldn't blame him if he wanted her gone as quickly as possible. She had behaved terribly. Yes, it was understandable, considering her shock at his revelation, but she just wished she hadn't chosen to process those feelings with whisky, that was all.

'Isabel, focus.'

She sat up straight, the deep timbre of his voice sending a shiver down her spine. Her treacherous touch-starved spine.

'Last night…'

Isabel covered her face with her hands. 'Grayson, please. I hoped we could just move on from last night and chalk it up to emotion and alcohol.'

He watched her for a moment, his thumb and forefinger making a slow swirling motion on the surface of the marble tabletop.

'So when you said that you longed for a child, without

the drama or heartbreak of a relationship...that wasn't really you talking?'

'I don't know...' she lied, knowing full well that it had been her.

She had been drunk, but she had not blacked out. She remembered the feeling of her anger rising within her, of just wanting her plans to be back in place. Needing the world to make sense again, the way it had the day before when she'd had everything clear.

'You suggested I consider making a deal with you,' he said, his expression calm, yet serious, as though they were discussing stock prices.

'Of course I wouldn't really suggest such a thing.' She groaned, hiding her face behind her hands as she felt herself blush. 'That would be unfair and...wrong.'

'I happen to disagree.' He stood up, walking to the sideboard at the edge of the dining space to pick up a slim tablet. 'Your words last night made me realise a great many things. Most of all that my biggest mistake was not ensuring that you were present when my agreement with Julian was discussed. I'd like to correct that now—if you're open to it.'

Izzy felt her jaw sag a little, and her heartbeat definitely doubled its pace as he walked to her side and placed the device before her. A contract was open on the screen, and with one tap of his finger a computerised voice began to read the document aloud.

She sat frozen as she processed the phrase *pre-conception agreement*, followed by the mention of both their names and some very official-sounding jargon surrounding their future efforts to procreate.

The document covered everything, putting all major decisions under her primary control while simultaneously recognising Grayson as the child's father and affording him the relevant rights. Once the voice began to delve into heavier legal jargon she pressed the pause button, and looked up to find Grayson staring at her, awaiting a response.

'You can't honestly be serious about this?'

'I thought this ten-page contract which I had my lawyers draw up in the middle of the night might be a clue as to how serious I am.'

'Grayson, you rushed all the way here to stop me from going ahead with the insemination. You made it very clear that it was not what you wanted.'

'I came here to put an end to the deal that I made with Julian. A deal made without my ever speaking to you about it first. And as I rushed here…not knowing whether you had already gone through with it or not… I thought of the possibility of you carrying my child. Thought that if I were too late I might already be on my way to becoming a father. And my reaction to the idea of you pregnant with my baby…it wasn't a negative one. I've seen you with my godson, Isabel, and I know any child would be lucky to have you as their mother.'

Izzy stared at him, pretty sure that if her jaw dropped any further it would fall to the floor like a character in one of her favourite old cartoons.

'A baby? But you're an eternal bachelor. A playboy.'

'I am a bachelor. A devoted one, at that.' He sat back in his chair. 'But a playboy? That makes me sound like some rich waste of space, running around throwing supermodels on and off his yachts.'

'That's not how you spend your downtime?'

'Well, for one, I don't own a yacht.' He raised a brow. 'And when it comes to women… I had one serious relationship in my very early Elite One days and quickly figured out that I'm not cut out for domestic bliss. Not surprising, considering my family life was far from traditional or happy.' Grayson shook his head. 'But last night I realised that, strangely, we both want the same thing. To have a child without the messy relationship that usually comes along with parenthood.'

Izzy nodded, her hand unconsciously rising to press against her chest, as if to try and hold in her frantic heart-beat. She was rapt. She couldn't look away from his sombre face and the emotion in his eyes. She had rarely seen him smile, so closed off was he. And yet here he was, baring this part of himself to her.

'So, Isabel…what do you say? Would you like us to create a beautiful child together?'

She fought the urge to burst into laughter. 'This is just utterly nuts on so many levels.'

'You don't think that you and I would make a beautiful child?' He raised a brow.

'You know exactly how handsome you are—that's not the thing I'm questioning here. I'm questioning the very idea of two people who can hardly stand one another coming together to create a child.' She stood up and paced the length of the table, then paused, laughing awkwardly at her own phrasing. 'Of course, I don't mean *coming together*… Obviously you mean taking the artificial route.'

'No.'

Izzy froze, whirling around to stare at him, where he still sat perfectly still and calm, one hand idly stirring more sugar into his coffee.

'No?'

'I remember you told me you have a fear of medical settings. I'm not very fond of them either, and artificial insemination seems like a lengthy and uncomfortable process. As you know, I value efficiency. With that in mind, my proposal would be for us to use the more traditional method of creating a child. One that would involve us getting into bed in the literal sense. We would start immediately. Today, ideally, going by where you are in your current cycle.'

Her brain seemed to hiccup as she picked over his words slowly, as though every phrase were sending her closer and closer to a panic attack. 'You can't possibly mean that we would *sleep* with one another?'

'There wouldn't be any sleeping involved. Not if we plan for it to work quickly.'

One dark brow quirked as he stirred his coffee again, completely at ease in himself, as though he were proposing they go skiing rather than have sex.

She opened her mouth to speak and then thought better of it. When she looked back in his direction he seemed to have stiffened, his back ramrod-straight as he brushed an imaginary speck of dust from the table.

'You mentioned that we are two people who can hardly stand one another,' he said. 'However, despite my distance, I've never claimed to dislike you. Quite the opposite, in fact. And, of course, our chemistry won't be an issue, judging by the way you kissed me that night in Singapore.'

She stiffened. '*You* kissed me first!'

Grayson stood up, taking his coffee cup across to the kitchen area. 'My point is that we clearly find each other attractive. It's a win-win.'

Izzy stopped herself from asking him to clarify that last statement, watching as he moved towards the office area that branched off the living room.

'I've emailed you a copy of the contract for you to take

some time and think it over. Of course you can simply refuse, if you already know your answer.' The corner of his mouth twitched, as though he believed it incredibly unlikely that would be the case.

Izzy stood alone at the long dining table, feeling like a soda bottle that someone had shaken and shaken until she was fit to burst with so many thoughts bubbling to the surface.

Despite the effect it had had on her, she'd brushed off that kiss between them as a moment filled with adrenaline that he likely regretted.

He'd been injured in his final race of the season and forced to retire his car early, but he'd still won the overall championship. Such was the wild unpredictability of Elite One racing. She'd gone to congratulate him, finding him alone in the darkened garage as all his team mates had been up at the podium celebrating. One minute she'd been hugging him…the next they'd been kissing as if their lives depended on it. His hands had been everywhere, his mouth devouring hers. He'd been like a man possessed.

Then they'd heard some of the others, coming to look for him, and he'd simply cursed under his breath and… walked away.

She didn't know how long she'd sat alone in that dimly lit garage before she'd finally mustered the courage to walk back out and join the celebrations.

The next day, Astrid had let her go.

So he found her attractive… It was likely meant as a compliment but, coupled with how he was proposing this potential lovemaking between them as part of a pragmatic business arrangement, she had a feeling she shouldn't let it go to her head.

There wouldn't be any sleeping involved.

What exactly had her life become that she'd heard such a phrase coming from one of the world's sexiest men, right after he'd informed her that he'd like to start trying to put in a baby in her? Immediately.

Izzy covered her face with both hands and felt that she was blushing again. She walked to the patio doors, sliding one slowly open in search of some cool air, trying to calm down her raging heartbeat. She didn't know how long she stood there, staring out at the snow-capped trees, but after a while she could no longer hear Grayson's voice coming from the office area.

The thought of him walking out here to continue their discussion while she was literally burning up at the thought of agreeing to it was just not okay. Perhaps a more confident person might have stood her ground and prepared to discuss the finer details of this proposal, but while she prided herself on being a modern woman, Izzy had always been an absolute prude when it came to talking about sex.

She was awkward, and *it* was always awkward, and the very thought of having to ask him to explain step by step exactly what this was going to involve made her cringe so hard that before she knew it she'd bundled on her coat and ventured down the back stairs into the snow. She needed some time to think, to make sure she wasn't overlooking a potential misstep in all of this. She wasn't running away...not really.

Izzy felt the pressure within her chest increase until she feared that she might actually split apart, right there in the snow. The cold air was almost painful as it entered her lungs in swift gasps. Was she actually considering his offer? She didn't need to ask herself that question twice, because from the moment he had spoken, something had lit up inside her like firework. *Hope*. Hope that she had told herself not to feel.

But the way Grayson had laid it all out just felt right. Not typical or conventional by any means, but…inexplicably right. It was as though her intuition had taken one look at that ridiculously detailed pre-conception agreement and then rolled over onto its back and said, *Okay, let's get pregnant, Izzy*.

The realistic part of her knew that it was absolute madness to consider such an arrangement with a man who was so uptight. Let alone the fact that his proposition of them doing it 'the old-fashioned way' would involve a lot more than just learning not to fight with one another… they would actually have to have sex.

Sex with Grayson Koh was something she had definitely imagined during her short-lived crush three years ago. He'd always had a kind of enigmatic charisma without even trying to be personable. His very presence seemed to engage her—and not just because of his perfectly defined abs and smooth, chiselled jaw.

No, for her, Grayson's appeal lay in how ridiculously competent he was at everything he did. She was convinced the man could decide to build a space rocket and he would complete it on time and under budget. She couldn't help it. To her, as a walking chaos gremlin herself, witnessing his sharply focused expertise as he discussed his job was more heady than any effect his athletic physique might have.

She closed her eyes, telling herself that it was just the ovulation hormones making her instantly imagine that physique all hot and sweaty and pressed up against her. She hadn't had sex in years. She and Julian hadn't been intimate with one another after the first couple of months of their marriage, and she hadn't even tried to entertain the idea of dating since his death. Her husband's issues with addiction had often led to difficulties in the bedroom, which had affected his mood, and her confidence, and... Yeah, her sex life had been pretty much subpar up to this point.

She had a feeling that sex with Grayson would be anything but subpar.

But sleeping with him was only a temporary means to a much more permanent end. If she did this, he had made it clear that he would not be an anonymous donor—he would be their child's parent. He would be her baby's father.

She waited for an internal shift towards resistance at that idea—after all the soul-searching she had done to arrive at her decision to become a single mother by choice, surely this was a backward shift?

But he had used words like 'want' and 'chemistry'... words that had touched upon that tiny little spark of hope that lived within her chest.

The little spark that she had tried so hard to keep under control. Because it tended to blossom at the first hint of nourishment.

She would never do something so foolish as to dream of a happy ever after, like she had done in her marriage. She wouldn't even dream of any relationship with her child's father beyond platonic co-parenting. If she did this, she would be accepting an equal partner in a team of two. She wouldn't be alone in this—not all the time anyway. And she wouldn't have her child wondering who its father was and if it hadn't been wanted, the way she had wondered for most of her teenage years.

She felt as if she stood on a precipice, gazing down at uncertainty, black and swirling below.

CHAPTER FIVE

WHEN GRAYSON ENDED his call and found the living space empty, Izzy's cup of tea unfinished and abandoned on the coffee table, he got a bad feeling. Looking out at the snowy slopes to the rear of the house, he thought he could see the distinct impression of two delicate-sized footprints from poorly insulated footwear stumbling off in the direction of the hills.

Before he could think, he put on his heavy ski coat and ventured out after her. As he followed her footprints down the long, sloping garden to the rear of the chalet, he prayed she hadn't gone through the treeline and out onto the mountain beyond. His chest tightened at the thought of her losing her footing in those ridiculous boots and sliding down into danger.

But when he reached the edge of the garden and looked towards the treeline, he spied her sitting on a rock, a safe distance from any potential danger.

He stopped, exhaling hard as she turned to face him. 'Do you have a death wish?' he heard himself growl, his own fear destroying all his tact, as usual.

But he didn't care. He had seen far too many people make poor decisions when they were in shock or under pressure. She wasn't used to this terrain, and the swiftness with which one could get into difficulty here.

'I just needed to clear my head.'

She crossed her arms over her chest defensively, eyes narrowed into pinpoints, spitting green fire. In comparison with the lifeless disillusionment he had seen on her face yesterday, her anger was quite a welcome sight.

Isabel was not made for small, shy emotions. She was made to feel everything at full throttle, like an emotional engine of the highest power. Whereas he had always felt cold, reserved, and tightly wound up. He was certainly feeling wound up now. She had almost run off the side of a mountain at the first mention of him taking her to bed.

'Is my proposition so unappealing that you'd prefer the risk of falling off a snowy cliff?'

'Don't exaggerate. I just walked down to the end of the garden path.'

'In the aftermath of a blizzard,' he said, reaching forward to extend his arm for her to take. As expected, she shook her head and stood up—then immediately slipped and lost her footing on the incline.

'You wouldn't keep slipping if you were wearing appropriate footwear for the weather,' he said grumpily, grasping her hand and holding her tightly against his side.

Her eyes narrowed up at him, incredulous.

'You can glower at me, or we can try and actually get back into the warmth before you get frostbite. Your decision.'

If she had considered shooting more fire in his direction, she restrained herself, remaining stubbornly silent as she attempted the short uphill trek back to the chalet. He felt that he was giving her footwear entirely too hard a time, considering he did actually like them. The boots suited her style, and her tough-as-nails personality. But he was angry with them for not protecting her feet appropriately, hence his snark.

He couldn't seem to control his emotions at all around this woman.

It was an unusual feeling, considering he was so completely in control of himself at all times, and had essentially made it part of his persona. In his world, where smooth reflexes and perfectly calculated turns were the difference between life and death, Izzy O'Sullivan was an unexpected obstacle on the track. Every single time.

When they reached the deck she could have let go of him and walked easily enough by herself. But he had wrapped his other hand around her waist, and neither of them made any move to pull apart—which was entirely fine with him. Without a word, he marched them both upstairs and directly into the large master bathroom.

'I can get changed myself,' she said, teeth chattering between every syllable.

He held up one of her hands to the light, hissing at the blue tinge to her skin and lips. 'Just let someone take care of you for one second, would you?'

Her mouth turned into a stubborn line, her eyes dropping towards the floor. Apparently tough love was the way to make her accept help. He would have to file that discovery away for later.

Assuming there even was a later, after he had thrust his half-baked proposition at her without warning.

He had never been a patient man; it was possibly one of his greatest flaws. The moment he decided he wanted something, he took action. And perhaps that was an admirable quality out on the tracks, or in the boardroom. But it wasn't quite so effective when it came to this fiercely independent woman.

He busied himself turning on the shower to full blast and ensuring that the temperature wasn't too hot for her. She hadn't been out in the cold for long, but the sub-zero conditions up on the mountain affected different people in different ways. While Isabel had certainly spent her fair share of time in hot climates, when she'd travelled with them for that Elite One season, he knew for a fact that she despised the cold. She was not an avid winter sportsman like he was. But, far from feeling superior, he felt nothing but anger at this damned snow for making her shiver and shake.

'I'm going to help you get undressed,' he said, keeping his voice as neutral as possible. 'Your hands are quite clearly numb, and your feet probably are as well.'

'So your solution is to help me get naked and get in the shower?'

'I'm not going to look, obviously.'

'Obviously.' She stared at a point above his head while he set to unbuttoning her coat and pulling it down her arms. She chewed on her bottom lip before speaking again. 'If we went ahead with your ridiculous proposition you would have to look at me.'

Surprise held him still for a long moment as he processed the mental image her words evoked. Shaking himself back into the moment, he allowed his gaze to rake slowly down her still clothed body.

'You think that would be a difficulty for me?'

A rosy blush appeared high on her cheeks. 'I don't know what to think when it comes to you, Grayson. I never have.'

He raked a hand through his hair, not quite sure how to verbalise his response without sending her running for the hills. How could he tell her that his offer was not just about them making a child together. That it was also about appeasing his own burning curiosity and putting to bed—quite literally—the need that he'd had since the moment he'd first laid eyes on her. The purely physical, burning lust that had shamed him when he'd realised how very innocent and idealistic she was.

The fact that he had avoided her so effectively said nothing about her and everything about him and his own lack of control around her.

But here he did not need to exercise that control…

Not if she said yes.

Not if she agreed to this wild arrangement where he would be required to perform…

And perform he would. He would not stop until he was sure that he'd done his very best to fill her with his seed in every position imaginable—that much would be an absolute promise. But, more than that, he would make sure that the memory of how he'd got her pregnant would haunt her long after the deed had been done…

Izzy fought with her own curiosity and confusion as Grayson remained silent while he finished helping her to undress, before turning around and leaving the bathroom, as promised. She stepped into the shower, soon warming up, and closed her eyes as she tried to process the labyrinth of the conversation between them.

She had learned long ago not to waste her time trying to make people like her. Most of the time you couldn't change their minds anyway. And, sure, perhaps Grayson had never been openly hostile towards her—but he had never tried to get to know her. Not to mention the long, narrow-eyed stares he'd thrown her way whenever she was talking to others, or being chatty and sociable, as though her very existence irked him.

When she'd told Eve about it, during one of their long phone conversations, her friend had laughed and said it was probably some ridiculous form of repressed attraction. A theory that Izzy had instantly squashed, because he was a world-famous racing driver, for goodness' sake. The idea that a man like him would ever need to repress any desire he had was laughable when she had witnessed women quite literally throwing themselves in his direction almost every time he was out in public.

But even if it *had* been the case—which it most definitely hadn't—she would never have rewarded such childish behaviour. She hadn't tolerated being teased by the boys in primary school, and she most certainly wouldn't tolerate it from a fully grown man, famous heartthrob or not.

But she was going to agree to his deal. She just needed to tell him as much without completely losing her nerve.

Without another second of waiting, she got out of the shower, walked to the opposite side of the bathroom and opened the door to the master suite.

He had showered too—that was the first thing she noticed. The scent of his lime soap was heavy in the air and tiny droplets of water still clung to the edges of his jet-black hair. He had shaved, his jaw now clear of the shadow that she had noticed this morning. The entire length of the room separated them, and yet she thought that she could feel the exact moment when his eyes raked along her towel-clad form.

'Don't say anything,' she said quickly, taking another step forward, bridging the gap between them and praying that her bravado wouldn't wear off and leave her speechless and silly in such a crucial moment. 'Just…let me get this out first. And then you can do your usual thing.'

'My usual thing?' One of his dark brows rose instantly in defence.

'You're good at this…the contract talk. The way you raised the subject, it sounded like something from a boardroom rather than a proposal for us to create a child together. To sleep with one another…'

She closed her eyes, feeling her words tangle together in the way they usually did when she urgently needed to get a point across. Typical that her mind was a swirling vortex of thoughts and words just when she needed peace, and that in the moment she actually needed it to work everything went radio silent. She pressed her lips together, opening and closing her mouth a few times, before gulping in defeat.

She heard Grayson's footsteps move a little closer towards her, but she couldn't quite force herself to look up for fear of the pity she might see in his gaze. She didn't want this to be a moment of pity—she needed them to be equals, so that she could actually accept his offer. So that she could feel empowered by doing so.

All those words had seemed right on the tip of her tongue when she had been alone in the bathroom, staring at her own reflection, but now that she was here, and he was looking at her in his usual handsome brooding way… She felt like that same little girl who had always been overlooked and rejected and made fun of. Logically, she knew that was ridiculous. Logically, she knew that she was an adult. But that was the funny thing about trauma. It didn't care for logic.

'Can I just say one thing?' he asked, and his tone was

not mocking or impatient, but tinged with a softness that she was not accustomed to hearing from him.

Izzy nodded, crossing her arms over her chest and trying not to focus on how very vulnerable she felt, standing in his bedroom in a towel while he was mostly dressed and looking a lot more poised than she did.

'I'm sorry if my wording seemed businesslike. I thought that was the best approach at the time. Truthfully, I didn't think much at all before laying it all out there.'

He ran a hand through his still-damp hair in a way that should have made him look unkempt, but didn't. The man seemed to exist in permanent male model mode—it was ridiculous.

'I'm not any more relaxed about this than you are,' he said. 'I'm just a little bit better at putting on a mask of indifference.'

She stared down at her ridiculous bumblebee toenails. 'You must wear that mask a lot, then. Because I don't think I've ever seen you look anything other than completely calm and in control.'

'I just asked my best friend's widow if she would like to be the mother of my child… I'm probably feeling the furthest from calm and in control than I ever have in my life.'

It should have been a sombre statement. It really should. But as Izzy took in this reminder of their situation, of the link between them, she had to press her lips together to stop herself from laughing aloud.

'You find that funny?' he asked, sounding confused.

'Oh, come on.' She let out another thoroughly inappropriate gasp of laughter. 'It's so utterly ridiculous. This entire thing… It's positively Shakespearean.'

He looked away, but not before she got a glimpse of what she would have bet money was a half-smile of his own. She cleared her throat, chasing away the last of the giggles, and faced him once more.

'Okay,' she said simply. 'I want to do this with you. I… I agree to your terms.'

'You do?'

'I'd already decided I was going to say yes when I was out in the garden. I just… I had to work myself up to actually saying it out loud.'

'Is that so?' He took another step forward. 'It would have been nice to be informed then. Especially as I practically dragged you back from said snow-covered garden when I thought you were running away from me.'

'I wasn't running away. I was thinking.'

'You couldn't have done your thinking indoors and away from sharp mountain drops?'

'You are so ridiculously bossy.' She shook her head, trying not to wonder if he was this bossy in bed.

'I am,' he said, jolting her from her thoughts.

It took her a long, mortified moment to realise that he was referencing her first statement and not reading her filthy mind. At least…she didn't think he was.

Izzy looked up to find him looking at her, his gaze narrowed. The air was thick with tension, and she felt awkward and thoroughly out of her depth now her initial pep had gone after her walking in here and telling him her answer.

'So… How do we go about this?'

She sat down on the end of the bed, trying to hide her shaking hands by sitting on them and crossing her ankles in a way she hoped was elegant and ladylike.

Grayson tilted his head to one side, surveying her. 'If you'd read the contract, you'd have seen that it includes my most recent health screening results.'

She nodded. She had seen that and greatly appreciated it. 'I don't have the results to hand, but the clinic had me do some tests too and I'm all clear,' she said.

'I'll take your word for it.'

Izzy inhaled a fortifying breath and forced herself to meet his gaze without dissolving into tears or more of those panicked giggles. 'You said we would start immediately if I said yes. And I think we should. Just to...to get the awkward part over with, you know?'

He didn't move, and didn't speak for a long moment, but she could hear the sound of him grinding his teeth. A muscle ticked in his jaw rhythmically as he seemed to think over her words.

'You make it sound like a chore to tick off a list. Like doing the laundry or taking out the trash.'

'I don't mean to be offensive. I'm sure you're quite good at this under usual circumstances. I just mean that this isn't a typical situation for either of us, so there's no need for us to...'

'To pretend that we're enjoying it?' he offered helpfully when she tailed off.

She exhaled a harsh breath. 'I just mean that I don't expect a big seduction or a prolonged performance. We should be practical.'

'This isn't a fertility clinic.' His eyes seemed to glitter darkly, and his lips were a harsh line—as though he were about to dish out some kind of punishment for an unknown infraction she had just made against him. 'But we can skip the seduction and pleasure...if that's really what you want?'

'Practical would be best,' she heard herself say.

If he was surprised by her answer he didn't show it. He simply stood with hands on his hips, staring down at her in his usual imperious way. To all intents and purposes, they might well have been conversing over a boardroom table rather than across his luxurious king-size four-poster bed.

Izzy gulped.

The corner of his mouth quirked slightly and he took another step closer. 'Do you expect me to lie you down right here and just get the job done?'

Izzy squared her shoulders. 'I think that would work best for me, yes. That is…if that's okay with you.'

He was quiet for a long moment, his brows knitted together in thought, before his charming smile was back in place.

'You are in control here, Isabel, so if you want the business performance… I'll will give you the business performance.'

Izzy swallowed past the lump in her throat as he took another step forward until the barest few inches separated him from where her knees rested on the edge of the bed. It was completely clear that this was to be an agreement between them, with no emotions, no feelings. So why did she suddenly feel as if she was missing something important? As though for the briefest moment he had been waiting for her to object.

After all her soul-searching over the past day, she didn't think she could take it if he changed his mind again so soon. But then again it was probably better that he changed his mind now than after they let things get any further and she became more attached to the idea of having him as her child's father.

Even just allowing herself to think of him that way… It felt so right.

This arrangement that he'd proposed was the best of both worlds, and all she had to do was get him through this part. The baby-making part of their arrangement. She could hide her attraction to him and she could school her reactions, she was sure of it. She would do whatever it took.

CHAPTER SIX

IZZY HAD LEARNED long ago that if she gave herself too much time to think she got frozen up. So she knew, like taking a sticking plaster from a wound, there was no sense in prolonging an uncomfortable situation. It was easier to just pull it off.

She was about to have sex with a world-famous motor racing legend and she had tiny yellow cartoon bumble-bees on her toenails.

'Something funny?' His voice was low, and seemingly calm, but his eyes didn't stray from where they were raking over her bare legs.

'I laugh when I'm nervous. Sometimes I make jokes too… Bad ones.'

'Inappropriate footwear and inappropriate jokes? I would expect nothing less from you.'

'If you mention my boots one more time, I swear I will…'

His hands moved down to his belt, unbuckling it slowly, and her words died on her lips.

'You will…?' he prompted.

'Well, I was going to say I would walk out of here right now, but that's not really going to happen, is it?'

He paused, a serious expression transforming his face. 'You can walk out of this room at any moment. Now…

ten minutes from now…no matter what. You change your mind, we stop immediately—understood?'

She had been referencing the whole snowbound situation, but still she felt something release in her chest at the acknowledgement that even though she had signed their agreement she could always walk away if it became too much. She'd had to resist running from this room multiple times already, but now, as she stared at the very prominent evidence of his eagerness to fulfil the physical part of their bargain, she felt that she would stick around just a little longer.

'The same goes for you,' she breathed, hating how wispy her voice sounded to her own ears, but needing him to know that she wanted him to feel he could stop, too, if he was having second thoughts.

There was nothing typical about what they were about to do. She wasn't quite sure how he usually operated, with the long line of beautiful dates who had adorned his arm at various events, but for her sex meant something and it always had.

She had tried to separate herself from it—had tried to have one-night stands like some of her other nanny friends had. But being a nanny was a high-pressure job, with very little room to make friends or go on dates while on contract, so really it had been no surprise that she had got to the age of twenty-four without ever having had sex.

Then along had come Julian, with his charm and his declaration of true love, and she had been head-over-heels in lust. The first few times they had attempted to make love had been disastrous, with her nerves and Julian's ego taking a bruising. So it had been easy to blame herself for their non-existent sex life when he had disappeared on week-long yacht parties mere months into their marriage.

It had only been once they had separated and she had begun seeing a therapist that she'd realised how abnormal all of their marriage had been. Julian had basically wanted a fake wife to placate his parents, and he had found himself an easy target.

Grayson's husky murmur of her name pulled her from her thoughts, and she looked up to find him staring down at her with an expectant look on his face.

'I'd like to start now, please,' she said.

Her sweet little *please* ripped through Grayson's tightly wound control, the politeness of it coming from her plump pink lips almost more than he could bear.

She'd like to start now. Right here, on this bed, she would like him to begin creating their child.

He'd made his offer as businesslike as possible, and, in truth, he was more than prepared for the arrangement to proceed with no passion whatsoever, if that was the way it was destined to be. But after almost an entire year spent lusting after this woman, only to watch her elope with his best friend, he had more than his fair share of pent-up desire that he would very much like to slake.

And, judging by the darkening of her eyes when he had mentioned just how thorough he intended to be, he didn't think he would be alone in feeling that desire. Not one little bit.

Carefully, he took the final step, bracketing her knees with his own. In this position, she would have to tilt her chin all the way up to look at him. The sight of her this way... It lit up his treacherous mind with illicit images. For too long he had denied himself any fantasy of those lips, but now he leaned down, taking her chin in his hand and tilting her face up even further, so that she would have to stretch forward to meet his kiss.

He kissed a path along the side of her throat, and the taste of her skin was like hot syrup drizzling down over the sweetest plum cake. He wanted to devour her whole. But he held back, keeping the kiss level, allowing her to get used to him.

He felt her hold her breath for a split second before she gave in, the barest moan escaping her throat. The sound of it destroyed some long-held dam within him and his control slipped by the barest inch, heat sweeping along his veins like wildfire.

He had mere seconds to savour his victory before she was clawing at his chest, pushing at him frantically, as though she feared he might not stop.

With one movement he created space between them and waited.

'Why would you…? What are you doing?'

'I was kissing you,' he said roughly, resisting the urge to lean forward and continue where he'd left off. But he could tell she was determined to keep him at a distance. If he pushed again now, she'd only pull back even further.

She remained still, her eyes studiously avoiding his and her delicate hands braced against the front of his chest.

'No kissing,' she whispered.

She abruptly lay back on the bed, as though she were trying to do it quickly, so as not to lose her nerve. And with every prim tug that she gave to her robe to cover herself his confidence lessened. His fantasy of unwrapping her slowly and savouring the delicious revelation of her nude skin before tasting every creamy inch no longer seemed within reach.

Suddenly he felt less sure about his decision to partake

in this arrangement. This morning everything had seemed so simple. He would have his cake and eat it too. He would have the child he longed for, while also getting a taste of this maddening woman he knew he could never let himself have for real. But now, faced with her determination to hold him at arm's length, he wondered if perhaps he was only digging the knife in further by having her this way without truly having her at all.

Whenever he'd allowed himself to imagine taking her she had felt what he felt, and she had been longing for it just as much as he had. But this real version of Isabel was distant and determined to keep their arrangement under control, and he had to respect that—even if he knew that she had wanted this too, once. He had seen it in the way she'd looked at him whenever they'd been alone together. He had felt it on the night that they had almost given in to that desire before fate had stepped in and ruined everything in the grandest way possible.

His intuition had never steered him wrong in his entire life. Not on the track, not with his business endeavours, and not even with his one disastrously failed relationship. When his gut told him something, he listened and he took control. And he won—every time. But Isabel needed to be in control here, and he needed to tell himself that he was just going along for the ride. He would take whatever she gave him and it would be enough. It had to be.

He spread her thighs wide, praying that she would be wet enough to take his girth. He usually took pleasure in the prelude to sliding inside a woman, but she had made it more than clear that she didn't want him to do that.

As he placed himself against her entrance, the feeling of her hot bare flesh was so intense it sent a shiver of pleasure up his spine, almost undoing him before he'd even begun.

He groaned, and when he spoke his voice was strangled as he fought to hold himself still. 'I need a moment… I can't—'

She stiffened, turning her face away from him. 'It's okay. You tried.'

'I tried?' Grayson frowned down at her, taking in her awkward posture and her refusal to meet his eyes. 'You think that *I'm* the one having difficulty here?'

She stubbornly kept her head turned away from him, her chest still rising and falling fast and her cheeks flushed rosy pink. 'Aren't you?'

'Isabel… If you think that I'm not fighting off every instinct that's within me to take you right now, to open you wide and accept everything you're offering me…'

'I don't understand…'

He realised that she didn't. Isabel had absolutely no idea that he'd been about a second away from an embarrassing release, simply after that first touch of his erection sliding against her soft skin.

So soft… So painfully perfect and surpassing every one of his dreams…

Suddenly his insistence on completing their deal 'the old-fashioned way' felt less like an indulgence and more like an exercise in torture. The most painfully perfect torture he had ever endured. But he didn't want to endure it. And he didn't want her just to endure it either. He wanted her to enjoy it.

'My research told me something very interesting about increasing the chances of conception…' he said, increasing the pressure of his pelvis against hers. 'Would you like to hear it?'

'Yes…'

That single word came out almost like a moan, hardening him even further, but he remained still, resisting the urge to thrust against her like a rutting animal.

'We're far more likely to be successful if it's not just me who…reaches the finish line.'

'Did you just use a racing pun in lieu of the word orgasm?'

'Is orgasm the word you'd prefer?' he asked, with as much patience as he could muster with her staring up at him, green eyes wide and uncertain.

'I… I don't know.'

For a woman who always seemed so self-assured in her day-to-day life, this lack of confidence in the bedroom set off alarm bells in his mind. He fought against the anger he felt in his chest at whatever had happened to make her feel this way. She was trying to deny her own needs, minimising herself to a mere spectator, and he wouldn't have it. Not with him.

'There's no rule to say we can't be practical and still enjoy this, Isabel. And I think you'd enjoy me making you come…very much.' He inhaled a breath of her delicious scent. 'I could take it nice and slow with my mouth…or I could get you there fast with my touch. Whatever you want. Let me get us both there.'

She inhaled a swift breath, her pretty pink lips pursing as she turned away. When her gaze finally returned to his, her pupils were wide and her lids heavy. His words had created that reaction. Could it be that she'd enjoyed a little dirty talk…? Interesting. Very interesting…

On the track, a millisecond's delay in reaction had the potential for disaster. He was a master at observing that and reacting under pressure. But he didn't think he'd ever felt more pressure than at this moment. It should be simple, he told himself. It was just business, after all. Right?

Perhaps it was selfishness, or bravado, or his own ego, but he needed Isabel to enjoy this. He needed to know that his attraction hadn't been one-sided all those years ago. If he had any chance of laying his own fixation to rest, he needed this to be right.

He met her gaze head-on as he trailed his fingers down her stomach, emboldened when she didn't look away this time. 'You said you don't want me to kiss you and I won't...' he said, his voice a husky whisper. 'But I can't promise that you won't beg me to.'

'I don't beg,' she said roughly, gasping as his fingers finally reached their destination.

'I'll remember that,' he murmured. 'I don't need to kiss you to get you there. I'm quite thorough. And when I set myself a goal... I like to win.'

CHAPTER SEVEN

IZZY COULD FEEL her heart beating in every point of her body. Grayson was barely touching her, and yet it felt as if he was everywhere. His mouth almost touched the sensitive skin beneath her ear and she fought not to groan aloud. His teeth grazed its sensitive shell for a split second and she felt her entire body shudder against him, her hips moving upwards of their own accord.

He let out a thoroughly masculine growl of approval, his own hips pressing back against hers. The delicious hardness of him was right there, pressing against her upper thigh, and she thought that she might convulse into flames upon the spot.

'This is better,' he murmured against her ear. 'Do you like your breasts to be played with?'

'Um…yes, please.'

'So polite, Isabel.'

His breath fanned against her neck, his eyes meeting hers for a split-second before he trailed his hand down the centre of her chest and parted her robe.

She was in a haze, in some kind of dreamlike state where nothing made sense, and the most handsome man on the planet was undoing the tie of her robe as though she had just given him the keys to a bank vault.

She looked at him and realised he had frozen at the sight

of her naked breasts, bouncing free from their silk cover. He liked her breasts—that much was certain. He wasn't a good enough actor to pull off that kind of reaction. The realisation that he hadn't been lying when he'd said he was attracted to her was both unsettling and intensely erotic.

He didn't wait for another breath before encasing one entire nipple with his mouth. No gentle teasing or nuzzling. As though he knew it was exactly what she wanted. He sucked and laved the sensitive tip, kneading one breast with his hand while his wicked mouth teased a slow, sensual torture upon the other.

A loud moan echoed in the darkened room, and it took her a few moments to realise that the sound had come from her own throat. She froze, embarrassed, immediately wishing that she hadn't agreed to his ridiculous mention of an orgasm. It would take too long, it wasn't necessary, and she needed this to be done with.

Unable to speak such words aloud, she settled for guiding him with her hands as best she could, until he got the message and positioned himself firmly between her thighs. Like this, there was no denying the power of his muscular frame against her own much softer curves. They were so different, worlds apart, and yet when he finally pressed his length against her none of that seemed to matter.

His expression was stark when she looked up at him, his jaw tight as he entered her in one slow thrust. He moved slowly, filling her and then retreating, with smooth, shallow thrusts that sent stars bursting behind her eyelids.

Izzy inhaled a soft gasp at the instant build-up of pleasure in her core with every flex of her inner muscles around his hot length. He paused, angling himself upwards before his next thrust, and Izzy fought the urge to cry out as he rubbed against that perfect spot deep inside her. Her hips moved of their own volition, needing more and more of whatever magic he was working between her thighs. But as another raw moan escaped her lips she froze again.

Keeping her distance seemed utterly laughable in the face of the pleasure he was wringing from her body after just a few short minutes. It was far too much…and yet nowhere near enough. Was this how sex was supposed to feel? This intense, insatiable hunger?

'You still with me?'

A hand reached up to touch her cheek, jolting her from her spiralling thoughts. Grayson's dark eyes pinned her in place, his strong hand coming to brace just below her jawline. For a moment she thought he might try to kiss her again, and she both wished he would and wouldn't all at once. She felt as if the world had turned upside down and she was no longer in control.

'Tell me what you need,' he said, his body poised like a statue above her.

His hard length was still buried deep inside her, but he didn't move an inch as he awaited her response. She couldn't hide herself away—not from Grayson. He easily held himself in check, his patience and strength evident in the stillness of his rippling muscles.

You might think that driving a car around a racing track would lead to you being able to look whatever way you wanted, but that wasn't the case. Elite One drivers were among the fittest competitors in the world. And she had this driver all to herself in this snowed-in cabin. It would be anyone's dream. And yet here she was, trying to talk herself out of the physical reaction that she was having with him.

Maybe he was right. Maybe they should use their mutual attraction to their advantage. It didn't have to be clinical. Maybe she should take this as a chance to explore the things she'd always been afraid to ask for before.

'I need you to...go a little...harder, maybe,' she said, gasping when he seemed to grow harder inside her.

'Like this?'

He withdrew slowly, tightening his grip on her hips before sliding back home with one sharp thrust. Izzy gasped and saw stars.

'Or like this?'

He spread her thighs wider, angling one arm on the headboard above her before repeating the motion with even more effort.

With a gasping, 'Yes!' Izzy scored her fingers down his smooth chest, earning a loud growl of appreciation.

There was no more talking after that. She was lost to the sensation of being possessed by him as he found that spot within her once more and refused to let up until she was crying out in the most powerful climax of her entire life. She vaguely heard his words of praise as he continued to move inside her, seemingly determined to hold off on his own release.

'This is what you need?' he demanded, his thrusts slowing as he sought her gaze. 'This is what you want from me? Show me, beautiful... Take it from me.'

It took her a moment to realise what he meant, and then she was moving, angling herself up against him and meeting him thrust for thrust. She was stunned as another climax began to build inside her, but she was determined to hold off. The pleasure of moving against him was so intense. He growled as he found his release, spilling himself into her with a shocking heat that sent her hurtling straight into another orgasm.

Breathless and exhausted, she was only vaguely aware

of Grayson propping a pillow under her hips, murmuring something about her not moving for a while.

That would not be a problem, she thought, catching her breath, considering her entire body was boneless. And then the sleeplessness of recent days caught up with her and she drifted off peacefully to the sound of Grayson's wry chuckle.

Grayson's morning workout had taken twice as long as usual for him to complete, so consumed was he by the effect last night had had on him. His punishing twice-daily strength training sessions had been the only thing keeping his sanity intact since he'd found himself stepping away from competitive motorsport after two decades. But today, with every mile he ran on the treadmill in his high-tech home gym, he had to fight not to go in search of Isabel and ask her for a repeat performance.

Accepting the end of his Elite One career had been a complex process. Much harder than he had anticipated, as he had learned to cope with less travelling from country to country across multiple time zones and climates, and no more hectic testing and racing schedules, not to mention never-ending sponsorship commitments and press appointments. It felt like going through withdrawal. But his drug had been the rush that came from constantly being on the go.

Now he'd retired, he suddenly had as many days off as he wanted. It had been welcome for a few weeks, but after that boredom had set in. And because of his natural competitive spirit, it hadn't take long for him to begin looking for fresh challenges.

He hadn't known what to expect from Isabel this morning, after she'd come apart for him last night, but this little game of cat and mouse was not it. Although, really, was he surprised?

She had all but admitted to being celibate these past few years, and he'd responded by taking her fast and hard as if they were teenagers having a quickie.

He closed his eyes, remembering the feeling of sliding into her for the first time...watching her try not to react to him. Her efforts had been in vain, as he'd known from the start. She'd softened under his touch like butter, and he'd devoured her like a starving man offered his first meal. Feeling her perfect body respond to his touch, hearing her little sounds as he'd filled her all the way that first time... It had been too much, and it had been over far sooner than he'd been ready to accept.

Then afterwards he'd felt completely undone. He'd wanted nothing more than to slide into bed alongside her and doze, until they were both ready for round two, but she'd made it quite clear his job was done for the day. It had been a rude thump back to reality and he had responded in his usual bullish fashion. He would be avoiding himself too, if he were her.

The problem was, if she wanted to get pregnant she would have to come and find him eventually, before her three days of optimal fertility were up. Their chances would only increase with the frequency of their lovemaking, after all.

He paused the treadmill. Yes, that was something he definitely needed to remind her of...immediately.

After taking the world's fastest shower, he pulled on a pair of loose grey sweatpants, opting to wait a moment before putting on his T-shirt. It might be shameless, but if her open adoration of his body was the only arsenal he had in this battle of wills he was going to use it. He hadn't earned his reputation of being ruthless without reason, after all.

He prowled along the lower floor, seeing no sign of blonde curls or long legs.

There were too many levels in this house—too many rooms for her to hide in.

But the sweetest aroma wafted on the air, coming from the main living space, making his mouth water instantly. The kitchen was tucked behind the formal dining room, and as he neared he could hear soft humming.

She had her back to him, and a large mixing bowl balanced in the crook of her arm as she stirred with a wooden spoon, round and round. She didn't hear him come in— she was far too busy singing along to something playing in her earbuds, her hips swaying softly from side to side as she worked.

Isabel was not a natural singer. He had found that out one sunny summer afternoon when Luca had asked them both to sing nursery rhymes with him. She had joked that what she lacked in actual ability, she more than made up for in pizazz. Her off-key crooning had sent his godson into fits of laughter, and he'd only barely managed to hold his own stern expression in place. Of course his lack of reaction had only encouraged her to sing louder, her pink cheeks matching the bright streaks of colour that had accentuated her riot of blonde curls at the time.

He frowned at the memory, remembering how carefree she had been. How she'd made him wish he could be the same.

Somewhere over the past few years she'd lost that fire. He wanted it back.

He waited for her to turn, to catch sight of him in her peripheral vision, and sure enough her entire body stiffened. Gone was the dancing and the swaying, and back came that damned distance.

'Sorry, I should have asked before I went digging around in your kitchen.'

'Don't apologise. Not when it makes my house smell like this.' He stepped further into the kitchen, seeing that she had laid out three full trays of circle-shaped biscuits. 'Were my healthy protein pancakes not to your liking?'

She smiled, ducking her head as she looked at the first batch of cookies on the cooling racks. 'You may be used to a boring athlete's regime. I, however, still require a daily dose of sugar for my sanity.'

'Boring?' He gasped, placing a hand playfully over his heart.

'Perhaps disciplined is a better word. Discipline is necessary, of course. But I firmly believe that nothing tastes better than what you think is forbidden. Especially when it comes hand-frosted.'

She lifted up one of her finished confections and, sure enough, he saw the plain circle had been transformed into a tiny snowflake. As he watched, some of the icing dribbled onto her fingers and she licked it off. He exhaled on a slow hiss, feeling himself instantly become hard.

'Want a taste?' she asked innocently.

She had no idea.

He moved at lightning speed, grasping her wrist and sliding his tongue slowly from the centre of her palm up towards the tip of her fingers. The taste exploded on his tongue and he groaned, fighting the urge to bite into her flesh. Not a hard bite…just a little one. He had a feeling she'd like it too.

A barely audible moan escaped Isabel's lips as he tested

his theory, scraping his teeth gently against her skin as he worked a second path back down.

'I meant the cookies...' she breathed, still not making any attempt to remove her hand from his grasp.

'I know.'

With a herculean effort, once he'd finished cleaning the sticky icing from her fingers, he removed his lips... and waited.

'I'm pretty sure you just seduced my hand,' she whispered. 'How is that even a thing?'

'You offered me a taste and I took it.' He held her gaze. 'Besides, I agreed to forgo seduction, remember?'

'That felt pretty close to seduction.' She licked her lips. 'You're not playing by the rules.'

He popped the remainder of one deliciously frosted cookie into his mouth with another groan, and felt deep satisfaction when her pupils widened at the sound.

'You said nothing tastes better than what we think is forbidden? I say that when we make the rules, we get to decide when a situation requires breaking them.'

'What rule would you break first?' she asked curiously.

'You know which one.' He took a step closer, narrowing the distance between them until her amply curved bottom was pressed up against the kitchen cabinets. 'Tell me to seduce you. Tell me that while you're here in my bed for the next three days you're mine. Let us both take all the pleasure we want from each other. The pleasure you deserve, Isabel, if you want it.'

Her eyes closed at his words. 'I want it...'

'Then open your eyes and touch me,' he demanded, needing to know that she was there with him in this. Needing to know that when he took her this time, she would be giving in to the craving just as much as he was.

She trailed her hands down his bare chest, taking her time as she caressed his skin inch by inch. When she began to explore his erection through the thin material of his sweatpants he cursed under his breath and stilled her exploration, lifting her up until she was perched on the kitchen workbench.

'Can I kiss you this time, Isabel?' he asked, framing her face with his hands.

She hesitated, chewing on her lower lip. 'I think I'd like to keep that rule, if we can?'

He nodded once. Disappointed, but not entirely surprised, considering how he'd behaved the first time he'd kissed her all those years ago. How quickly he'd lost control and then abandoned her.

How could he tell her that he had carried his regret about that night for the past three years? That it was like an ache in his bones, accompanying him through every day? He'd behaved badly...shown her exactly why he was the wrong man for her...and all the while he'd foolishly hoped she'd see through the act. That she'd *see* him and feel some level of what he felt.

No, it hadn't been a simple attraction. There had never been anything simple about what he felt for Isabel.

He skimmed his fingertips over every inch of her, avoiding the perfect lips he craved. He nipped at her skin with his teeth, removing each item of her clothing in a slow torture, and making good on his promise to show her *exactly* what it meant to be seduced.

By the time he finally slid a finger into her slick folds she was plump and begging for release. He obeyed, taking another firm bite from her shoulder as she screamed her climax and collapsed backwards against the marble countertop. Grayson spread her wide, sliding into her molten heat as he stared into her pleasure-drunk eyes and wondered if *enough* was a concept that would ever apply to this woman.

He needed to show her that in his bed…in his arms… she was *his*.

He needed to make her crave him.

His own orgasm built swiftly, his hips pistoning hard and fast as he worked to give her every last drop of his release. Closing his eyes as he came, he resisted the urge to claim her lips as he wanted to. To break down all her walls and demand more. But that wasn't fair. He wouldn't fool himself into thinking that they could have anything more than this, but he could ensure she was satisfied.

Taking her by the hand, he guided her to his bedroom, where he thoroughly intended to keep her until their deal was completed. Two more nights was what he had, and two nights was all he would take. But he would make the most of every damned second.

CHAPTER EIGHT

FOR TWO WEEKS Izzy threw herself into work. The fantasy novel illustration package was the kind of thing she had grown used to being able to complete with minimal issues. But every day she grew more and more distracted and restless.

It was strange that for all the months when she and Julian had, as she now knew, been fruitlessly trying to conceive a child, she had been hyperaware of her body's signs, counting down each day on her calendar with a borderline obsessive frequency. But that since her plane had landed in a snowy Dublin and she had driven herself home to her tiny cottage to sit alone in the silence, she had only been thinking of one thing.

Grayson.

The few days she had spent in his chalet, in his bed, in his arms…

It had changed something within her.

Once she had realised that her marriage to Julian was a sham, she had been relieved at the idea of never opening herself up to anyone. Why on earth would she? Why would she risk her heart being broken by someone she loved?

Not that she would ever be so foolish as to fall in love with Grayson, of course, but she at least trusted him enough to create a child with him. She'd trusted him with her body, with her pleasure. People talked about *risking* one's heart, or *falling* in love, as though romance was some kind of extreme sport. For Izzy, trusting someone felt much more dangerous than loving them. Unrequited love could break your heart, but trusting the wrong person could ruin your entire life.

The enormity of how her life might be about to change had been weighing heavily upon her mind—so much so that she had almost completely blocked out the idea of their efforts actually working. But now the day had arrived and her period was due. She hadn't been able to muster the energy to walk into her local chemist and procure a pregnancy test, knowing that in such a small town it would lead to people asking questions that she wasn't quite ready to answer.

Eve and Moira had welcomed a healthy baby daughter shortly after Isabel's return, so she'd opted not to fill her friend in on the updated details of her own baby-making efforts. But yesterday a care package of sorts had arrived, containing chocolates and a full packet of pregnancy tests ready to go.

Grayson had been in contact a handful of times since they'd parted ways in Zurich, when he had scolded her for not accepting the use of his private jet. Such a wasteful luxury, she had told him, scandalised that he owned one but not entirely surprised. She had told him that she would be testing today and that had been it, really.

It shouldn't hurt that their communication was based solely around her potential pregnancy, but her brain and her heart couldn't seem to reach an agreement on that.

So the day had arrived, and with it the moment of truth. She slid open the simple packaging and read the instructions. Nothing about this was glamorous…nothing at all…

She performed each action with an almost detached efficiency until there was nothing left but the four-minute wait that would seal her fate.

She was pacing the bathroom when the sound of the doorbell rang out across the cottage. Looking at her watch, she frowned, knowing that the post was never delivered on a Sunday and she had no unexpected guests here, ever, such was her position on the outskirts of town.

A tall, dark shadow was barely visible through the smoked glass of her front door, and she felt her heart begin to beat a little faster. One peek through the peephole had her scrambling to open the door before she'd even had a chance to breathe.

Grayson stood in her tiny portico, his collar turned up against the light Irish rain that had created a dull mist along the rolling hills behind him.

'You're here...at my house...' Her words were a stunned whisper even as she fought the urge to smile. Because Grayson was here, on her doorstep, looking as gorgeous as ever. And, fool that she was, she had missed the sight of him.

'I thought perhaps you might like company...in case there's cause for celebration.'

Izzy felt her chest deflate a little at this reminder that he was not here for her, he was here to check in on his investment. It felt rather cruel to refer to their potential child in such businesslike terms, but the alternative was to romanticise their situation—and that was not an option. Nothing had changed. Even though for her it had felt as if it had for a moment back in his bed.

She ushered him inside her narrow hallway, scrambling to push her hastily discarded muddy Wellington boots out of sight. As if on cue, the scrambling of paws sounded and Sasha came running at full speed to greet their guest.

'No, Sasha, down!' she chided, easing the over-eager dog away from Grayson's perfectly pressed slate-grey trousers. 'Sorry, it's my elderly neighbour's dog. I her walk sometimes. She still hasn't quite mastered the art of the polite greeting.'

Grayson chuckled and got down into a crouch to scratch Sasha behind her ears. Izzy could do nothing but stare. He looked so impossibly handsome at that moment it threw her for a loop, and her brain stuttered to a stop.

For a man so feared for his ruthlessness, it seemed he was gorgeously soft with small creatures of all species. He'd hidden this softness away so tightly, always concealing it beneath that formidable racing driver persona. She wondered what else he hid of himself, and if she would ever truly know the father of her future child. Because she knew without a doubt that with every tiny piece of himself that he revealed, the more she wanted to see. And that was a real problem for their platonic parenting arrangement.

She sagged back against the wall a little, praying that he would say something predictably cold, just to set the world back to rights again. But, alas, Grayson stood up and took a look around her tiny cottage and smiled. Not just a tiny ghost of a smile, either. The man had *dimples*.

She was pretty sure she felt the final barrier around her heart drop, shattering on the ground around her at that revelation.

'It looks exactly how you described,' he said, walking further into her cramped living room and touching a few of the tiny statuettes that she'd placed above the fireplace. 'You said you did all the work yourself?'

She had said that, hadn't she? During their last night together in the chalet they'd stayed up talking until dawn. She'd found herself telling him about her childhood, and about what a big deal it had been, buying her first home after essentially being homeless for most of her life.

'It's no fancy ice palace or Monte Carlo villa, but it's home.'

'I see now why you found my decor lacking,' he murmured, sliding his hand along the bookshelves, where she kept a mixture of her favourite fantasy novels and some of her most prized artwork. His hand stilled over one of her childhood drawings she'd managed to keep, his fingers tracing over the messy crayon lines.

She'd told him about her childhood habit of drawing a huge house on a hill, with four square windows at the front and one big red door. Every time she'd been moved to a new place she'd drawn that house and imagined herself living in it with a family of her own. She'd learned that her imagination could be a place of solace. That she could create her own world by opening a book or taking out her crayons. Art had been her sanctuary, and she still tried to hold that knowledge close every time she embarked upon a new project.

'I didn't say it was lacking, did I?' She hid a smile behind her hand, turning to walk into the kitchen.

He followed closely behind. 'You didn't. But I bet you were thinking it…weren't you?'

'I wouldn't dream of insulting your delicate ego that way, Mr Koh.' She laughed good-naturedly, letting out a long exhalation of breath before turning back to face him in her tiny kitchen. 'But mostly I'm panicking over what on earth I can offer you to drink. I don't have fancy coffee or artisan pastries.'

'You don't need to offer me anything, Isabel.'

'I'm Irish—these are the rules. So I'm going to make tea—proper tea, unlike the tripe you served up in Zurich—and then we can look at the...' She froze, planting one hand quickly upon her forehead. 'The test!'

She heard him follow along behind her as she raced into her tiny bathroom and grabbed the white stick from the vanity unit.

'I've already done it... I was waiting for the results when you arrived.'

'Do you want me to leave?'

Izzy shook her head. 'This is as much a big deal for you as it is for me.'

She took a deep breath, unwrapping the test from the cocoon of toilet paper she'd left it in. Nerves swooped around her stomach like butterflies. This was it. This was the moment when she would find out if they had created a child together. And if they had then there would be no need for them to continue seeing one another outside of routine doctor's appointments until the baby was actually born.

That was the plan, she reminded herself.

She placed the white stick on the counter in full view of them both, then exhaled the breath she'd been holding as she processed the two little words in plain text on the screen.

Not Pregnant

Grayson stood by her side, but she didn't dare look up at him. Not when a riot of emotion had unleashed itself within her chest, making her hands shake.

She suddenly wished she'd been alone, as she'd always been before when doing these tests. She'd only ever had to deal with Julian's disappointment via text or passive aggression, even though she now knew that had all been fake and manipulative, as she'd never have got pregnant by him.

But before the voices within could begin telling her

what a mistake this entire venture had been, Grayson met her gaze in the mirror. She couldn't quite make out the emotion blazing in his eyes, but he certainly didn't look disappointed with her, or angry.

'Well, that's that, then.' Izzy forced a smile, turning to face him. 'It didn't work.'

'It didn't work *this time*,' he said, that shrewd gaze seeing far too much. 'I'll have to try a little harder on my next visit.'

She felt heat rush through her at his words and the image they evoked. It made no sense; she should be upset that she wasn't pregnant. She waited for the familiar wave of inadequacy to come, but instead she was horrified to realise what she was actually feeling was...*relief.* Relief that for one more month at least she would be the only woman in Grayson Koh's bed. And that made her more confused than ever.

She knew in that moment, with all her heart, that she was most definitely in trouble.

If Grayson had already been unsure of why he'd travelled all the way to Ireland, when Isabel had said she'd be quite content to send him the test results via text, then he was even more unsure as to why he'd insisted on taking her out to lunch.

The wet and winding Irish country roads proved to be a surprising challenge to navigate in the clunky rental car that he'd managed to nab at the last minute. But Isabel was comfortable in the passenger seat, laughing as she instructed him to drive far away from her small town to avoid any local busybodies asking questions about her famous guest.

If any of the other Elite One drivers could see him

now—oh, how they would laugh. He imagined driving these roads in one of his own cars, with the wind whipping Isabel's curls around her face. The image his mind conjured was so clear and so *right* that it shocked him for a moment, and his jaw clenched almost painfully.

Thoughts of her had consumed him with increasing frequency as he'd awaited news of their baby-making results. Of course a selfish part of him was happy that he would have another chance to bed her for three nights, as per their agreement. He'd already begun to plan where those three nights might take place. But the more he tried to place his attraction to her in that perfectly labelled box, the more his mind seemed intent upon wanting something else.

He looked across to see Isabel staring serenely out at the passing green fields and wondered how today might have gone if the test had been positive. If the 'business' part of their arrangement had already been completed and they'd moved on to the part where he'd see her only for doctor's appointments and then as per their arranged co-parenting schedule.

His jaw tightened as he pulled up where Isabel indicated.

'The food here is good, but not very fancy...'

Isabel bit her lower lip, looking suddenly unsure as they stepped out of the car and gazed up at the thatched roof of the mountainside pub.

'I said that I wanted to experience authentic Irish cuisine.'

'Okay, just try not to draw too much attention to that handsome face of yours. I'm starving, and I don't fancy having to wait hours for you to sign autographs.'

'Why do I suddenly see why Luca always instantly fell into line around you?'

'Strict boundaries with a heavy dose of empathy. It works.'

'Lead the way.'

He tried hard to ignore the sudden tightening in his jeans as she swirled and sashayed those glorious curves ahead of him into the warm pub.

The interior was just as quaint and fundamentally Irish as the exterior, with polished stone floors and a high fireplace dominating one end of the large open dining space. Posters and memorabilia covered almost every spare inch of wall space, showing advertisements from times long past and famous Irish musicians and poets. It was a renowned tourist spot, apparently, as evidenced by the busy air of the place and the myriad languages he could hear being spoken among the tables as they walked through.

He had only ever visited Ireland twice before, on fleeting press trips, and he had loved the people's lack of interest in celebrities then just as much as he did now.

The flow of music and chatter around them formed a charming cocoon as Isabel guided him through the traditional Sunday lunch menu. They started with a creamy vegetable soup, served with freshly baked Guinness bread and possibly the most delicious butter he had ever tasted in his life. It was golden in colour and slightly salted, and he was pretty sure he moaned a little as it hit his tastebuds.

Izzy tried to hide her smirk behind her napkin, but he saw it and answered it with his most stern expression, which only made her smile even wider.

Next came tender thin slices of roast beef, dressed in a rich gravy and served with creamy mashed potatoes and steamed garden vegetables. The presentation was no-fuss, the flavours simple, and yet he enjoyed it more than the food at some of the most highly rated Michelin star restaurants he'd eaten in. It helped that there were no judgemental gazes upon him as he ate, no unwritten society rules that he might inadvertently overstep. These were normal people, enjoying a relaxing meal with loved ones before the working week began anew.

He thought it was much the same as the way his own life had been before his driving career had skyrocketed, but he could hardly remember it now.

'Now, tell me again that Irish cuisine isn't a thing?'

Isabel was sitting back, patting her stomach with satisfaction. She smiled at him, her eyes sparkling in the pub's dim lighting, and he felt something tighten in his stomach in response.

'I stand corrected.'

His smile was forced now, but if she noticed his sudden tension she didn't comment. He was glad, because he couldn't explain it himself.

They both declined dessert, having planned to follow the signs for a scenic walk along the mountainside—only for the skies to open out of nowhere, soaking them both to the skin by the time they ran back to the car.

The Irish weather was just as temperamental as the feisty blonde beside him. He had already seen blistering sun and hail today, and he had barely been in the country more than a few hours.

The drive back to Isabel's cottage passed with her telling him about her latest book cover commission, for a young adult fantasy novel filled with monsters and magic. She lit up when she spoke about her work, and the new techniques she'd had to master in order to get it just right. He got the impression that she was a perfectionist with her craft and that no one pushed her harder than she did herself—something he could definitely relate to.

When they arrived at her home, he found himself walking her to her door despite her protests. She paused on the doorstep, fiddling for a moment with her keys. It reminded him of the kind of awkward first date aftermaths he'd seen in teen comedy films.

'I'm glad you were here today.' She spoke softly, staring out at where the sun was beginning to lower on the horizon. 'I know your schedule is crazy. There was no need for you to come all this way for nothing.'

'It wasn't for nothing. And I don't do anything that I don't want to do, Isabel.'

He hesitated, not quite wanting to reveal exactly how much he had been haunted by thoughts of her over the past couple of weeks. How his mind had been invaded and his body overheated at the mere hint of the memory of their few nights together. He knew he wanted more time with her than just the bare minimum, but that was the one thing they'd both agreed not to do.

He had entered into this arrangement with the perfect balance of control and distance. Isabel would be the ideal mother for his child, with no risk of divorce or drama. Every moment he spent with her like this was a risk that she would begin to view their relationship as something more, and that would be disastrous for both of them.

He checked his watch, knowing that he needed to get to the airport soon or risk having to reschedule his flight to Singapore.

He had thought he was taking control of his desire, slaking his lust for her while still benefiting from their orderly deal. He'd wanted to make her crave him. But in reality it was probably the other way around.

'I hope that your new love affair with Irish butter made

up for it just a little,' she said. 'I don't think I've ever seen someone eat it directly from the packet before.'

'I'm debating having a crate ordered, so I can take it with me whenever I'm travelling.'

She laughed, but something in it sounded a little hollow. 'You still do quite a bit, even now you're retired, right?'

He nodded.

She bit down on her lower lip, considering her words for a moment. 'Grayson, I need you to know that if you've reconsidered our arrangement at all—'

'I haven't.'

'I know you haven't *now*, but conceiving can take a while for some people, and—'

'Have I done something to make you doubt our agreement, Isabel?' he asked, taking a step closer to her in the cramped porch.

Up this close, he could see the tiny flecks of gold in her hazel eyes, and the dash of freckles on her nose and cheeks. She stared up at him, her pupils widening in the way he remembered. He wondered if she was just as turned on as he was right now...just as aching for release.

'Of course not. You were... You've been amazing.' She inhaled sharply, rosy dots appearing on her cheeks. 'I mean, you've been very thoughtful and patient, and I'm happy to try again, as we agreed.'

She blushed again, and he felt a flash of heat in his abdomen. Was she already anticipating it? Was she also secretly thrilled that they weren't 'one and done', as he'd promised her so confidently?

He'd never been so relieved not to win at something—not that it was a race. The way they'd made love back in that snowbound chalet had felt more like an exercise in endurance. He'd felt aches in his body for days afterwards, every twinge reminding him of how he'd wrung every ounce of pleasure from her eager body. How she'd opened to him completely and trusted him to show her true pleasure.

He reached out, the barest touch of his fingers on her jaw, to guide her eyes back to him. 'You were amazing, too.'

Isabel leaned in, surprising him with the softest kiss on his lips. The first she'd given him since that one night three years ago.

It was like being bathed in sunshine, and the heat spread along his skin instantly, warming him to his bones. He hadn't even realised he was cold. But just as quickly as she'd leaned in, she stopped and pulled away.

'Sorry, I just…'

He pulled her right back to where she belonged, swallowing whatever apology she'd been prepared to offer with a kiss of his own. But while her kiss had been soft and sweet, his was filled with raw hunger and demand.

She'd told him no kissing, and he'd obeyed. But now that she'd broken her own rule all bets were off. He held her right where he wanted her, her soft waist bracketed between his hands, as he plundered and took with sensual ferocity. Punishing her, punishing them both with everything they had agreed they couldn't have together. This wasn't about their deal—this was about them.

When he finally raised his head and looked down at her he was satisfied that she looked just as affected as he felt. They stared at one another, breathless in the fading evening light. She exhaled a long breath, but didn't look away. Her pupils were blown wide with desire, her lips swollen from his.

He reached out, running a fingertip along the damp

flesh of her lower lip, and she shivered. 'Tell me to walk away again…and I will,' he said.

'I know.'

Her admission was all the permission he needed to gather her up into his arms. He'd never seen kissing as more than a prelude to lovemaking. But he could have kissed Isabel O'Sullivan for hours, right there on her doorstep, in full view of the street. Let the neighbours gossip. He didn't care about anything right now other than getting this woman to the nearest bed.

He needed her complete attention. He didn't think he could bear any more of her smiling deflections—not when he felt as if every inch of his carefully crafted armour had been ripped apart. She had got under his skin with her steadfast refusal to be impressed by the trappings of fame and wealth. She was everything that he had studiously avoided for decades, while he'd kept his focus where it needed to be, but now he'd had a taste of her and he had no idea what anything meant any more.

All he knew was that he wanted more.

CHAPTER NINE

ISABEL WAS ONLY vaguely aware of how she and Grayson got through her front door and along her cramped hallway while kissing one another as if they were on their last breath.

One of his hands was in her hair, holding her in place, while the other soothed along the side of her neck. His mouth was hot and frantic on hers, his lips and tongue working a delicious rhythm upon her control.

She was the first one to pause, gasping for air, while Grayson simply growled a protest and continued his path of sensuous torture down her neck.

'Isn't this breaking one of our rules?' she forced herself to ask.

'Not my rule.' His voice was a husky murmur against her skin. 'And you broke it first.'

She had, hadn't she? She knew there was a reason why it had seemed important to kiss him, but as Grayson seemed intent on driving her wild with his sinful mouth she couldn't seem to muster any resistance at all. In fact, she urged him on, with her fingers in his hair and her body writhing under his expert touch.

This was what she'd denied herself back in the chalet. This intense sense of connection was what she'd known she needed to hold at bay. But she could no more tell him to stop now than she could deny herself air. His hands moved to grip her by the belt loops, pulling her flush against the very hard evidence of his arousal.

'Sorry.'

He froze, angling himself away from where Izzy had been more than ready to have him. Pressed hard between her thighs.

'Don't be...' she breathed. 'I liked it.'

Her words seemingly placated him, but still he didn't grind against her like she wished he would. He retained a maddening distance away, keeping their contact to slow, drugging kisses. When she took him by the hand to lead him towards her bedroom, he stopped and lay her down on the sofa instead. Where they kissed some more, still fully clothed.

It was simultaneously too much, this deep kissing, and not nearly enough. Surely what they had done in Switzerland should have felt ten times more intimate? Ten times further across the invisible line drawn between them in the sand? But this moment...whatever this was...felt like something new. What had happened between them before had been a part of their arrangement. Using their mutual attraction to their advantage, as Grayson had said.

But this... She had no idea what they were doing here. No idea why he had chosen to spend basically an entire day in her very non-glamorous area of Ireland, eating pub food and running through the rain. Her head swam with confusion and wonder, and her long-buried inner romantic scrambled to find meaning in his actions.

'Grayson... You don't have to be careful with me, if that's what you're worried about. I'm here. I want this.'

He stared down at her for a long moment, his expression thoroughly unreadable in the lamplight. His hand cupped her jaw, his fingertips sliding slowly along her sensitive skin. 'I didn't come here for this.'

'We don't have to do anything.'

'No, believe me, there is nothing I want more right now. Nothing I have fantasised about more for the past two weeks... I just mean I'm not expecting you to do anything you're not comfortable with. Just because we've done this before.'

That tiny romantic within her came roaring to the surface, punching her fists to the sky with hopeful optimism. He had thought about her. For the past two weeks he had been haunted by their time together just as she had. He wasn't unaffected. She had no idea what any of that meant for them, for their arrangement, for anything... But right now Grayson was kissing her because he wanted to.

There was no chance of them creating a child tonight. If she was to make love with him right now it would be just that—two people finding pleasure in one another's bodies, bringing each other to the dizzying heights of climax simply because they desired it. Because they desired each other.

She pulled him back down to her, taking his mouth in a kiss that was far more assertive and dominating than any of her others. She felt bold, ablaze with heat, and hungry for this man. She wanted him so damned much.

And, yes, while she might have had him many times in their snowbound chalet, she had never before had the knowledge that even if they hadn't had their agreement he would still be there. That she would be the woman he chose to have in his bed right now. And although they might not currently be in a bed, she had him here on the sofa, looking at her like that... She didn't plan to waste a single moment.

'I need to know what you're thinking,' he growled.

'I'm thinking that we're both wearing far too many clothes.'

'Is that so?'

She made a murmur of agreement and he rocked against her, his hardness against her soft core sending bolts of electricity along all her nerve-endings.

Her T-shirt was pulled over her head less than gracefully, and she barely had a moment to catch her breath before Grayson's mouth was on her breasts.

'There you are,' he growled, his lips latching on to one hard peak.

'Did you just address me…or my breasts?'

'They made quite an impression on me last time.' He looked up at her, his smirk lopsided.

He took his time wringing pleasure from her, with slow strokes of his tongue on her skin and his fingers working magic between her legs. He had learned what she liked very quickly, and he had retained all that information, systematically bringing her to a bone-shattering orgasm in less than two minutes. He looked up at her, and the smile on his face was one of complete satisfaction.

The rest of their clothes weren't so much removed after that as ripped from their bodies with a complete lack of patience. She was pretty sure she heard buttons ping onto the wooden floor as she impatiently pulled his shirt front apart.

His dark chuckle turned quickly into a growl of approval as he finally sank down on top of her naked form. She was breathless, and wanting, and yet she still had a moment of stunning clarity, gazing up into his beautiful face and seeing his expression soften as he finally entered her. With each slow thrust she felt herself begin to come apart all over again, but she didn't want to be alone this time. She wanted him right there with her.

'Come one more time for me, Isabel,' he urged. 'I need to feel you.'

So she did. She came on a silent scream, glorying as he roared his own release and came to rest in a heap on top of her.

Neither of them moved for a long time, their ragged breaths mingling into one until the chilly night air began to make her shiver. She was vaguely aware of Grayson carrying her into her bedroom, perhaps with the intention of going to sleep, only for her hands to begin wandering the moment they both lay under the covers.

'You're insatiable.'

He chuckled, but didn't stop her in her explorations. He simply lay back, watching as she set about showing him just how insatiable she was. She teased and worshipped him with her mouth until he lost patience and pulled her on top of him, where she rode them both slowly to the peak all over again.

Grayson slid out of bed just before dawn to the sound of his phone ringing from somewhere on the other side of the cottage. He hissed under his breath as he bumped into numerous surfaces in the dark, finally finding the device in the pool of clothing he'd discarded earlier.

He winced at the bright light of the display, sobering when he processed the name of the caller.

'It's early, Astrid,' he rasped. 'I hope this is important.'

His close friend and PR manager's cool tones filtered down the line. 'It would be afternoon if you were in Singapore as scheduled, Grayson.'

'I made a last-minute change to my travel plans.' He

kept his tone light, not offering up any details, but trying not to lie either. 'It was a personal matter. I haven't missed any important events.'

There was a long pause on the line—a sign he knew only too well meant that either bad news was incoming or he had royally messed up and she was calling to tell him off. He guessed at the latter.

'Is this "personal matter" the reason why social media has been abuzz with rumours that you're currently zipping around the Irish countryside with a mystery woman? My phone hasn't stopped ringing.'

Grayson stilled. 'Are there photographs?'

'Just some very grainy ones of you in a pub. I'll send the link.'

The photo came through instantly—a side profile of himself smiling. Other than a flash of blonde curls, Isabel was mostly obscured by the wingback chair she'd been seated in. He hadn't seen anyone taking pictures, but of course there would have been someone who recognised him. He wasn't that naïve, was he?

He leaned forward on his knees, looking around at the cosy living room that Isabel had worked so hard to transform. He knew all too well how quickly his presence could bring the hounds right back to her door. And yet he had still chosen to come here, selfishly wanting to see her again.

'Well? What am I telling them?' Astrid asked.

He rubbed an agitated hand across his face, his voice coming out as much more of a growl than he'd intended when he answered. 'Tell them nothing. No comment. I'm on vacation.'

'You know that won't make it go away...' A pen clicked in a slow, steady rhythm in the background. 'First you race out of those meetings in Monaco and refuse to tell anyone where you're disappearing to. Now you're off on an impromptu sojourn around Ireland...'

Grayson scowled at the knowing tone in his friend's voice. Astrid hadn't made her way up from being a personal assistant to become the most in-demand PR manager in motorsport for no reason. She still worked for Falco Roux, but she'd agreed to continue to represent him after he'd retired. She knew damned well that he was hiding something. It was her job to keep a handle on some of the biggest egos in motorsport; she had honed her skills and could smell a lie a mile off.

'Sometimes I value my privacy in these things, Astrid,' he said, ignoring the pang of guilt in his gut at such an obvious deflection. But at least it wasn't a lie.

'Okay...' He heard the confusion in her voice, laced with just a little hurt. 'Well, I suppose I can deflect the questions for now. But you know that not turning up to these public appearances will only lead to more speculation. And we can't afford that right now.'

'I know.' He pinched the bridge of his nose. 'I'll be there.'

'Just let me know if you're bringing anyone along to these events,' Astrid said, her tone calm now, bordering on cajoling. 'Privacy is fine when you can get it, but you know that some good press wouldn't hurt right now, Grayson. You'll have to share details of your mystery lady eventually.'

Grayson felt his gut tighten as he disconnected the call, realising that in all his negotiations with Isabel they hadn't really discussed how they would navigate the public nature of his life. She had said she wished to remain separate from his world, yes. But what if that choice was taken from them?

Astrid was right. He couldn't bank on keeping his connection with Isabel private for ever. Not once they'd had a child together and he was flying back here frequently. But he wasn't about to jeopardise her trust by putting anything about them in the spotlight just yet. Whether she wanted to step back from the scrutiny of the public was for her to decide.

'Is everything okay?'

Izzy's sleep-husky voice came from the doorway behind him and Grayson jumped as though burned. The room was dark, but he saw the way she stood a little more stiffly than usual, as though she wasn't quite sure what she'd walked in on.

'Just a call from Astrid,' he said, noticing that she still didn't relax. If anything, she tensed even further.

He inhaled a breath of her cotton-fresh scent, taking in her sleep-mussed hair and the oversized superhero T-shirt she must have thrown on before coming to find him. She looked cute as a button—and yet all his filthy mind could drag up were images of how fast he could have her naked and screaming out his name beneath him on this sofa. He hadn't heard that particular sound anywhere near enough times to satisfy him yet...

'Is something wrong?'

Isabel interrupted his X-rated thoughts, her eyes not quite meeting his as she fiddled with the hem of her T-shirt.

'She was calling because I was supposed to be on a plane to Singapore last night for a charity race.'

She looked up, staring down at him. 'Grayson...you should have gone.'

'Do you regret asking me to stay?'

'No. Of course not,' she said quickly. 'I just mean... We said we wouldn't let this arrangement impact on anything else. Your career comes first.'

Her practical words should have soothed the restlessness within him—so why did he find himself pulling her closer, until his thighs bracketed her knees?

'That wasn't the only reason Astrid called. Some photos of us having lunch at the pub yesterday have appeared on social media. Don't worry, you aren't visible,' Grayson said slowly. 'But she wanted to know if she could spin my mystery woman…for good press.'

Isabel stilled. He felt her body tense under his hands, her weight shifting as though she intended to move away. For a moment he contemplated pinning her in place, but in the end he let her go. Sure enough, she was on the other side of the room in an instant.

'I said no, of course,' he added, cursing himself for how terribly he was handling this.

'Okay.' She nodded, her arms wrapped around herself.

'Is it?' he asked, standing up and clearing the distance between them with rapid strides until he was close enough to touch her again. 'Because you look very much not okay right now.'

'I didn't think this part through,' she said, her voice weak and wispy. 'The fact that you're *you*. How idealistic it was of me to think I could keep my life private if you're a part of it.'

Grayson closed his eyes, hating himself for this oversight almost as much as he hated whoever had posted that picture of them online. But she was right. It was completely unrealistic to think they could avoid this ever happening again.

'I'll understand if you want to reconsider our deal,' he said.

'No,' she said quickly, a few curls shaking loose from her messy hair. 'I don't want to do that… I just think that maybe we both need to think a little more practically.'

'I can protect you to a certain degree, but I cannot guarantee your privacy any more than I can guarantee my own.'

'But we can control how we appear to the media,' she said thoughtfully. 'How we spin it, I mean.'

'That's my reality. That's not something you or our child should have to deal with.'

'That's the reality I'm signing on for, whether we've planned for it or not. Surely it's better to get ahead of any scandalous story with our own version? For the press, for our friends? We're going to be co-parents for a long time… I'd prefer to tell our child that its parents had a short-lived fling rather than have to disclose the strange truth of this arrangement, wouldn't you?'

'A fling?' he said slowly.

'A *fake* fling,' she clarified, taking a deep breath. 'I could come to Singapore with you and we can pretend to be together while I'm there.'

A whole week of having Isabel in his arms and in his bed? Where did he sign up?

He prepared himself to heartily agree to her new proposal, but then he noticed the anxious look on her face. Instantly he got the feeling that whatever she said next would be decidedly less fun than the sex-filled montage that had taken over his imagination.

'Grayson…last night we came a little too close to breaking all the rules of our agreement.' She set her shoulders, taking another deep breath before delivering her final edict. 'If I come to Singapore with you, there can be no more sleeping together outside of our arrangement.'

CHAPTER TEN

THE MOMENT IZZY had uttered her agreement, Grayson began making calls. Izzy's suggestion that she book her own flight and follow along in a few days was met with a look of abject incredulity.

Ignoring the pit of growing panic in her stomach, she showered and dressed, then pulled out her small purple travel case—just like she had done countless times back in her nannying days. She had developed the perfect last-minute travel wardrobe over years of being on call to busy jet-setting families. A few day dresses, suitable for the humid Singaporean climate, some walking shoes, and the one evening dress she owned, black and reliable.

She held it up in the morning light, catching sight of the distinctly frayed hem, and frowned. She'd poured all her funds into renovating her home, and she hadn't really needed to update her wardrobe. Especially not so that it was suitable for being thrust suddenly into the spotlight on the arm of a world-famous racing driver. It wasn't ideal, but it would have to do.

She turned to find Grayson standing in the hallway, watching her pack, with his phone still pressed to his ear.

'She'll need dresses for events too,' he said to whoever was on the other end of the line, his eyes scorching her skin with the ferocity of his slow, lingering perusal. 'Set up some private appointments.'

'Grayson…' She reached for the phone, embarrassment heating her cheeks.

He placed his hand over the phone briefly. 'Isabel. Let me spoil you.'

She escaped into her bathroom to finish dressing, trying to ignore the calming murmur of Grayson's husky voice as he finalised the rest of their travel plans and a busy event schedule.

He continued to field a series of calls on the short drive to the airport, and she was reminded that things moved quickly in the international motor racing world.

The private jet was luxury such as she had never encountered. From the moment they had arrived at the small airfield just outside Dublin, she'd felt as if she'd stepped through a looking glass into another world. She'd considered herself accustomed to the ways of the kind of wealthy families she'd worked for. She'd occasionally even travelled business class with Astrid and Luca, as it had been easier for the little boy to sleep on long-haul travel, but now, as she was guided along the length of seating areas and bedrooms on this jet, she had to consciously stop her mouth from dropping open.

The jet was more like a penthouse hotel suite than a form of air travel. It came complete with a five-person crew, a gourmet meal service, full-sized beds and luxurious leather seats that most definitely would not require her pinching her sizeable hips against her neighbour's armrests. Each seat was placed at a comfortable distance from the next, with its own television screen and everything else one might need to keep track of business in the sky.

She felt Grayson's eyes follow her as she moved down

to the private bedroom cabin, sitting down on the queen-sized bed to test its firmness with a little bounce.

'It's exactly like a normal bed,' she said, resisting the urge to sprawl out on what felt like million thread count sheets.

'Were you expecting rocks?'

'I thought planes had weight limits and stuff. I've only ever seen one of these on TV.'

'I find it hard to believe you never travelled like this with Julian.'

She ducked her head, the reminder of Grayson's assumptions like a chilly breeze upon her excitement.

'I paid for all the flights we took myself, before I moved back to Ireland. I only found out he was cheating on me because he used my credit card for a first-class flight to a yacht party in Miami. He hated flying commercial, but he had no money, so...'

She shrugged, realising that she had said far more than she'd meant to. Speaking of his best friend like that...it felt like a risk to the fragile truce they'd entered into. But she was done with lying about the past, when it had taken so much energy for her to move past it.

Grayson's expression was stark. The silence between them was heavy with tension as he visibly struggled to speak. 'He was lucky to have you. Even if he didn't appreciate it at the time.'

'If he was raised in this kind of luxury, I can see why it would be hard for him to fly any other way. Still, I've got to point out that sleeping in a bed in the sky without being strapped in just seems utterly reckless. I assume they *are* actually used for sleeping?'

'It's like being in any other bed, Isabel. It can be as safe or as reckless as you wish.'

She processed his words in her mind slowly, bringing up a vivid image of Grayson's long, toned body covering hers while the clouds swept past the windows and the white noise of the jet's engines muffled the sound of her moans...

Izzy bit down hard on her inner cheek to stifle a very real groan to match the fictional ones in her mind. Grayson was still watching her far too closely, and she prayed he wouldn't see her blush as she tried to shoo away that image.

But just as quickly as he'd followed her, he retreated to the cockpit, to speak with the two pilots, giving her space to set up her things in a seat across the aisle from him and buckle in for take-off.

If she had felt any worry about being tempted to join the mile-high club it was swiftly quashed when Grayson announced that they would be making a stop in London to pick up a few of the other drivers who were competing in the charity race.

The first, a British former champion in his fifties, now a well-known sports commentator, came on board with his wife and their two very shy and awkward teenaged sons. The reason for their shyness became apparent when the second driver who embarked directly behind them turned out to be a stunning brunette in her early twenties.

Isabel already knew who Nina Roux was—like most of the world did. Her family's Monaco based racing team and its financial woes had been all over the news lately. The historic Monegasque car brand, which had been bought out by a playboy billionaire and rebranded as Falco Roux, had nabbed Grayson as their main driver for his final few seasons, and had been none too happy when he'd made his shocking retirement announcement.

After some polite small talk, the three drivers predictably segued into a discourse on racing, leaving Izzy to strike up a conversation with the teens and their mother. It turned out one of the boys was an avid fantasy reader, and Izzy was all too happy to show off some of her work until the time came for everyone to buckle in for take-off again.

To her surprise, at the very last moment, Grayson slid down into the seat beside her.

'I got carried away talking shop and almost forgot about my nervous flier.' His gaze was soft as he enveloped her hand in his and brought it to his lips for a gentle kiss.

'You didn't have to...' Her words died away as she looked up to find they were being watched closely by their companions.

Right, we're playing the part of a couple here.

Her stomach clenched at the reminder that this week would have plenty more of this.

Grayson remained perfectly attentive and charming throughout the remainder of the flight, only just drawing the line at following her into the bathroom. A fact that was noticed by the other two drivers, who looked on with rather bemused smiles.

'I never thought I'd see the day the Golden Lion would become housebroken,' the older man remarked loudly, when Grayson could be seen pouring her tea and fetching a blanket for her cold feet. 'Hats off to Miss O'Sullivan.'

'They make me sound like a pussycat.' Grayson raised an amused brow in her direction, his hand coming to rest on her thigh in another mark of firm possession. 'Tell me, my love, have I lost my edge so soon?'

'You're still quite ferocious, darling, I'm sure.'

The endearment had slipped past her lips, setting her pulse skittering into a gallop. Grayson's answering smile made her heart beat even faster—so much so that she had to stand up with the excuse of needing the bathroom.

It took another ten minutes for her to calm herself enough to return to the cabin, where she discovered the lights had been lowered for sleep and Grayson had set up their seats to recline side by side.

It was going to be a long flight.

By the time the pilot announced their descent into Changi International Airport, Izzy had managed two long naps in between some work on a mock-up of her next illustration project to send off to her client over the coming week. Her monthly cycle was always at its worst on the second day, and she was certainly feeling its effects.

The others disembarked ahead of them, eager to make their way to their various hotels and recharge. The warm air was heavy and fragrant in her lungs as she made her way from the jet to the sleek chauffeur-driven car that awaited them on the Tarmac. Grayson had said that one of his press officers would join them, to brief him on his schedule for the next few days. But neither he nor Izzy had been prepared for Astrid Lewis to step out of the car.

'I decided to come and greet you both myself and save us an awkward public reunion.'

Grayson visibly flinched, looking briefly back to where Izzy stood, frozen at the bottom of the jet's stairs.

'Let me handle this,' he said in a low tone, his hand briefly touching her cheek in what she knew he meant to be a comforting gesture.

The touch, intimate as it was, only served to deepen the smug smile spreading across Astrid's lips.

'You didn't actually think you could keep this a secret from me?' Astrid said, her heels clicking as she strutted slowly towards them, pointing one red-tipped finger in Grayson's direction. 'I knew something was up the moment you went tearing out of that meeting in Monte Carlo. There's only one other time I've seen you lose your cool like that.'

Izzy caught a small glimpse of Grayson's almost panicked expression before Astrid shook her head with a laugh and redirected her attention to her.

'Izzy…you have no idea how glad I am to see you here.' Astrid spoke directly to her. 'I've wanted to call you to apologise so many times. I should never have let you go. I understand that you probably hate me…but I'd like to try to make amends.'

'I don't hate you. You just did what you thought best at the time.'

'And I apologise again. This time in advance. I may not be able to contain my excitement.'

Her excitement?

Izzy fought to retain a neutral expression as her former boss bypassed Grayson and enveloped her in the kind of hug that she'd only ever had from Eve in the past.

The embrace lingered, and when Astrid finally pulled back she thought she saw the tiniest glimmer of moisture in the other woman's eyes.

'Be warned: Luca will not be able to contain himself.'

'Luca is here too?' Izzy said, her voice a breathless whisper, feeling one step away from a full-blown panic attack.

This was too much, too soon, and she was completely underprepared. Grayson, on the other hand, had plastered a serene smile on his face as he accepted a hug of his own from his PR manager.

Izzy had wondered at the closeness between the two of them when she had begun working for Astrid, but had quickly realised that their friendship was like a family bond. Astrid had described to her Grayson's care towards her and Luca when she had been cast out from her own family as a young single parent. Really, that should have been Izzy's first clue that Grayson Koh was not the man he seemed to be from his public persona.

'He wouldn't dream of missing Uncle Gaga's big Legends race. He's back at the hotel,' Astrid said, her eyes never leaving Izzy's. 'If you want to see him, of course. I don't want to assume…'

Izzy held back the lump in her throat as she thought of the little boy she had cared for for almost an entire year. He would be nearly six now. She had always prided herself on keeping a professional distance from her young charges. Being almost a part of someone's family, in the role of nanny, it could be easy for the lines to get blurred. From the beginning of her time with Astrid and Luca it had been so easy to see herself as more than just a member of staff. But in the end she had been the one to get hurt, and reminded of the reality of her place in their lives.

'I would love to see him,' Izzy said now, hearing the small break in her voice. 'I've missed him so much.'

Astrid pressed her lips together, her own training in the public eye far too iron-clad for her to do something so silly as to cry. But still, the slight tremble in her lower lip as she looked away was all the confirmation that Izzy needed to know that she wasn't the only one feeling the emotion of the moment. That she'd been missed, as she'd missed them both.

'Right, now that's all cleared up….' Astrid smiled at them both, a gleaming pristine smirk that meant business. 'Let's discuss our plan to launch this fairy-tale to the press!'

Grayson should have predicted that Astrid's plan would be in part a punishment for his recent evasion over his private life. She accompanied them to his modern mansion in the affluent Sentosa Cove district and quite literally set a timer, giving them precisely thirty minutes to freshen up and return to the car for their first scheduled event.

He'd had plans to talk to Isabel about their living arrangements while they were here, and to discuss her preposterous wish for them to refrain from sex until the next window in their contract agreement. But when he entered his guest bedroom and looked at her face, unguarded and thoroughly exhausted, he realised that he wanted nothing more than to send her to bed—to sleep.

While it was bright and early here in Singapore, it was the middle of the night in Dublin, and he couldn't be sure how well she had slept on the flight.

She instantly refused his suggestion, of course, and their first stop was a private press conference, where Grayson was booked to formally announce his intention to launch his own team in the next year's season of Elite E. It was a move that not many could have predicted, considering he'd never discussed his interest in the engineering side of the sport, nor his part ownership of Verdant Race Tech.

When the conversation moved on to his personal life, with some questions about how his retirement was going and the recent photographs of him and his mystery woman he found himself freezing up.

Isabel sat in the back corner of the room, beside Astrid, out of the line of fire from the journalists awaiting every titbit of new information.

He was supposed to be saying what he had agreed with Astrid, but suddenly his old persona returned with full force, clamping down and freezing out every personal question that was thrown his way with ruthless efficiency. He saw Astrid's brow furrow, and the small shake of her head warning him that this was going badly. He knew he needed to return to their plan, but he was strangely powerless to stop himself.

By the time the press conference ended, and he was ushered out through a side door into the green room, a thin sheen of sweat had erupted upon his brow. His heart hammered in his chest, and he reached for the closest glass of ice water, gulping it down in an effort to regulate the riot of feelings within him.

'What on earth was that?'

Astrid burst into the room, her face a mask of thinly veiled shock and irritation. Isabel followed closely behind, her expression one more of pity than anything else. He didn't know which bothered him more.

Like always after these conferences, he simply wished to be left alone. He hated this part of his career and always had—the intrusions and demands upon him, the media waiting for the tiniest glimpse of weakness so they could exploit it.

'Could we have a moment alone?'

The request came from Isabel, and to his surprise Astrid simply dipped her head and retreated from the room. But not before delivering a tight-lipped warning that they had ten minutes before the car left for the next interview, of course.

Grayson paced the room, his hands in his pockets. For a moment Isabel simply watched him, grabbing her own glass of water and sipping delicately. Then she cleared her throat, capturing his attention, and motioned for him to take a seat alongside her.

'Is this some kind of misguided attempt at chivalry?' she asked. 'Or is there something else going on here that I need to know about?'

'You've seen what it's like out there. You know about the pieces that were published about you when you were with Julian. I can't do that to you again.'

'I think that's my decision, don't you?'

'Of course I know that it's your decision.'

'The entire reason I came here is to create the illusion of a normal relationship between us, Grayson. So that when…if…a pregnancy is announced, there's no big scandal. The press always want what they can't have. They already know something is being kept from them, so surely controlling the narrative with our own version of the truth is better than them following us around looking for gossip?'

He shook his head, hearing what she was saying but not able to accept it. Not when she didn't know the full story.

'The first year I raced in Elite One, the press got hold of my father's debt history. They decimated him in the press, painting him as a con man. And it was my fault. My press officer at the time advised me to play upon my parents' working-class roots to my advantage. So I gave an interview, waxing lyrical about how my father had scrimped and saved to pay for all my karting expenses when I was a kid. I had no idea that he had taken money from Peter Liang to pay off a bad debt.'

He shook his head, hating himself all over again for his naivety.

'After Peter Liang had stepped in and cleared my father's debts he told me that I raced for *him* now. He was starting his own Elite One team in Singapore—the first one that had ever been created there. He wanted to win a championship and he knew Julian wouldn't be the one to do it for him. He wanted me. I didn't realise for a very long time that it had likely all been orchestrated from the beginning. I had raced with Julian as a kid. I knew his father well. I knew that he could be ruthless. His father liked me, but when the time came and he asked me to sign on to their team I said no. I wanted to enter an Elite One team on my own merit.'

'That's why you never talk about your involvement in the technical side of things? Your business interests? Because you don't want the press to use it against you?'

'Exactly. I've learned that if I give them nothing, they get nothing.'

'Yes, but hiding yourself like that all the time... Trusting no one and working yourself to the bone... That can't have been easy.'

'Spoken like someone who has direct experience?'

She dipped her head, a small smile spreading across her lips. 'You always see far too much of me, don't you?'

'I don't understand how others can look away.'

She inhaled sharply, attempting a weak laugh, but he saw the shiver of unease in her eyes. He didn't want his truth to make her uneasy...he didn't want to push too hard... But when she spoke to him like this he felt his ability to refrain weaken more and more.

'We'd better get going or Astrid will probably have me retrieved by the police.'

'I hope I've helped you a little,' she said quietly. 'I don't want this trip to be in vain. I already feel like my appearance here is cramping your style somehow. I know you're probably used to a more high-flying, fun-loving type of trip when you're in your home city, so please don't change anything on my account.'

He stood up, reaching down a hand to pull her from the sofa.

'You are not an inconvenience, Isabel O'Sullivan. You

are my fake girlfriend. And you will be treated to a grand tour of the city in a style that befits your position.'

She laughed aloud at his formal tone, and the sound carried him through the rest of the afternoon's meetings, where he took her advice and tried his best to lower his mask just a little.

It turned out it wasn't as hard as he'd thought to be honest—to a certain point. He would never give unfettered access to the press. He was not a fool. But he didn't have to pretend that he was something he was not either.

He saw Isabel smiling as he gave detailed answers about the new technology that Verdant was engineering for the next season. And when they asked about his mystery lady he gestured to her, seated at the back, where she was fully prepared and accompanied by Astrid.

But when Astrid announced that his appearance was obligatory at a foam party that night, at a well-known rooftop nightclub, he drew the line.

Isabel's eyes were red-rimmed, which gave him a direct insight into how hard she was working to conceal her exhaustion. His working schedule over the past two decades, and his experience of switching seamlessly between time zones while remaining fully alert and able to perform, had given him stamina. But Isabel didn't have that to fall back on. So when Astrid suggested that Isabel get dolled up and attend the event with him, Grayson put his foot down.

He escorted her personally back to his home and ignored the flicker of unease in his gut as she bade him a weary goodnight.

CHAPTER ELEVEN

IZZY AWOKE TO the dawn light filtering in through the floor-to-ceiling windows. Or at least she assumed that it was the dawn light. But in fact when she took a quick glance at her phone it turned out to be almost midday.

Jumping from her bed, she rushed out into the hallway and listened for sounds of Grayson, only to find the house completely silent. He had told her he didn't employ a large staff when he was in town, preferring to have maximum privacy.

When she looked at her phone properly, it was to find a text from him.

Got in late and had to leave early for the track. The kitchen is fully stocked. G x

She analysed the tiny x on her phone screen for much too long, wondering if it had been a mistake. Wondering if he automatically signed off that way with everyone in a text. His email sign-off hadn't ever included any tiny kiss symbols…but then again maybe it wasn't meant to signify a kiss at all. Because why would it?

She looked down at her bare feet and realised she'd been unconsciously pacing the length of the open-plan living room area while staring at her phone like an angst-ridden teen. With a deep breath, she sent back her reply, apologising for sleeping late, thanking him and wishing him luck—with no kiss. Then she stared at both messages some more, knowing that she needed to put her phone away and go in search of food.

She could go for a swim. Or maybe spend the day reading. There was no rule to say they had to spend every waking hour together.

Still, she couldn't help one more quick look at his social media accounts, just to see what he had got up to the night before.

It appeared he had attended the foam party, as planned, and then Grayson had stayed alone for the musical act that had followed—a 'famous' DJ Izzy had never heard of.

She clicked through a series of photos tagged with Grayson's name, telling herself that it wasn't snooping because technically it was public knowledge. Image after image showed him flanked by beautiful women in bikinis who seemed to be removing his shirt as the crowd around them became more and more submerged in thick white foam.

She zoomed in on the images—then froze at the wave of unbridled possession coursing through her body. With one decisive click she closed the app and placed her device face-down on the counter.

This was his life, she reminded herself. He was doing nothing wrong by attending a party and dancing. He had promised her that they would remain exclusive for the purpose of their arrangement, and she trusted him in that promise. But still… Old feelings resurfaced, from a time when she had been weaker and more fragile. A time when she had trusted someone at his word and been proved wrong in the worst way.

Grayson's Singaporean villa was part modern home, part work of art. A beautiful infinity pool bracketed the house, surrounded by tall trees that offered maximum shade and privacy. She remembered being here for a barbecue when Astrid had attended the Singapore Elite One *premio* during the year she had been Luca's nanny. She had been just as amazed by the house then as she was now. It was an architectural masterpiece of wood and glass that you couldn't help but be awestruck by. The pool and outdoor areas had been landscaped with care, providing the perfect entertaining space for its wealthy host and his many parties filled with many beautiful guests.

A thought struck her, and she pushed it away just as quickly. It was none of her business how many other women Grayson had brought here. Just as it would be none of her business once their time together had come to an end. The sooner she realised that, the better. She was beginning to feel possessive over him in a way that could only spell disaster for them both.

Refusing to wallow, she took action, responding to a series of client emails and updating Eve on her trip so far. It was still night-time in Ireland, so she didn't call her friend, knowing that she was likely still riding the high of her new baby with her beautiful wife. She was happy for Eve, she truly was. Her friend had had her share of heartbreaks in the past too. But she knew that she would have to tell her the truth soon about what exactly was going on between her and Grayson.

A part of her knew that the reason she had held off on telling her so far was because Eve knew her so well. Eve had been there when Izzy had kissed her very first boyfriend and declared her undying love for him, right in the middle of the street like a fool. She'd seen Izzy at her worst, when her short-lived marriage had been revealed as a farce, and she'd been right there to pick up the pieces.

But that was another time, she reminded herself. The old Izzy might have been tempted to do something so silly as to imagine a true future with a man like Grayson, simply because he'd given her the very best, most attentive lovemaking she'd ever experienced and made her feel like the most beautiful woman in the world. But the new Izzy knew better than to try to sow the seeds of romance where they would never bloom. The new Izzy was learning to enjoy sex with Grayson for what it was, and to look forward to the life they would create from their passion.

Once she was pregnant, and the physical part of their relationship was done, she would come clean to her best friend. But until then she would keep herself grounded.

When Grayson finally returned from race practice he was already running late for their meeting with Astrid and Luca for lunch at their hotel. When he emerged from his bathroom with wet hair, wearing a simple gold-coloured polo shirt and loose ivory trousers, Izzy fought not to stare.

He started to update her on how the new car they were testing was working out on the track, stopping himself when he began to throw out terms like *downforce* and *vortices* and obviously noticed her eyes beginning to glaze over a little.

Then he asked about her work, and she realised that he never glazed over when she talked about her designs. In fact he always remembered specific details, like how she was working on a few proposals for upcoming projects with a big publisher for some jobs that she really hoped she would get. She mentally reminded herself to try to learn a little more about G-forces and tyre compounds.

But mostly the conversation between them felt stilted—as if they were trying to force a friendly vibe that had never truly come easily to either of them in the past. That realisation weighed heavily upon her as they rode side by side in the elevator to Astrid's penthouse suite.

'Falco Roux must be throwing around the big bucks if they can afford to put their PR manager in a place like this,' Izzy said, and whistled as the elevator opened onto a large open-air apartment that had its very own pool built into the terrace.

'Tristan Falco likes to flash his cash, that's for sure,' said Grayson.

'You say that as though you have direct experience?' Izzy raised one brow. She noticed that he looked away quickly at that comment.

'That's one way to put it.' He laughed. 'Another way is to say that he offered me a ridiculous amount of money to cancel my retirement and accept another two-year contract with the team.'

Izzy froze at the realisation that his retirement might possibly not be the permanent thing she'd thought it was. 'That seems…a little over the top.'

'That is the perfect phrase to describe Tristan Falco.'

'Were you tempted?' she asked, feigning nonchalance.

He looked away, giving her the briefest glimpse of an expression that confirmed the answer was undoubtedly yes. He'd been tempted to go back to Elite One racing. Maybe he still was.

Their conversation was interrupted by the fast thump of feet and a loud screech as Luca caught sight of them from his position in the pool and launched himself away from his mother, climbing out and running straight for them, leaving a river of water in his wake along the non-slip terrace tiles.

Grayson caught the youngster as he came barrelling into his legs, not seeming to mind that he became instantly soaked in the process. Luca grinned, then caught sight of Izzy and frowned.

'You're probably a little surprised to see me here, eh?' Izzy said softly, taking care to keep just a little distance between herself and the boy, in case he felt overwhelmed by her sudden reappearance.

In the end, she needn't have bothered being careful at all, for Luca launched himself bodily from his uncle's arms and collapsed directly against her chest. She buried her face in the boy's soft, springy curls and inhaled his familiar baby shampoo scent.

The lump in her throat turned into a full-blown rock that she could no longer hold down, and Grayson met her gaze just as a single tear escaped onto her cheek. He reached out, wiping the tear away with a look so sincere it melted her heart anew.

Astrid appeared from the kitchen, dressed casually in jeans and a T-shirt. 'Luca Lewis—what did I tell you about launching yourself at people like that? You are not a rocket.'

The little boy answered his mother by launching himself once again, this time onto the floor, before pulling on Grayson's hand and urging him out towards the pool he had just emerged from. Grayson chuckled, shucking off his outer clothes before performing a very impressive cannonball into the water.

Astrid sighed heavily. 'There's no hope of getting him out of there now.'

'Are you talking about the overexcited little boy…or Luca?'

They both laughed at the joke, and Astrid guided her into the modern living area, where she had prepared a table full of finger foods and refreshments.

'I thought the baby years were hard… Nothing could have prepared me for the ferocious fours and fives.'

'Ah, yes, the ferocious fours and fives.' Izzy smiled. 'Not to be undersold by the fury of the terrible twos and torturous threes.'

'He couldn't read when he was three. But now I get sternly worded letters when I displease him.'

'He's reading and writing already?'

Astrid looked out towards the pool, a serious expression momentarily tightening her usually neutral features. 'He reads and writes, but he doesn't talk much yet. His teacher wants us to go for another assessment.'

Izzy looked to where the little boy had emerged from the pool and was taking another running jump back in. The toddler version of Luca she'd known had always been very high-energy, fiercely intelligent and wise beyond his years, but equally prone to challenging moments that had at times felt like a little more than the average toddler tantrums. She had noticed the quirky behaviours that Astrid had mentioned, and she could see how they might stand in his way in the more formal setting of a seated classroom.

'And how are you feeling about that?' she asked, taking a seat beside her former boss in the way she had often done before in the evenings after Luca's bedtime, when they were both free to relax. They had forged a tentative friendship during those evening conversations, she recalled. That was one of the things she had missed most of all.

'Truthfully? I'm feeling thoroughly out of my depth.' Astrid sighed. 'But I'd do anything if it meant helping him.'

'That's exactly what I would expect you to say.' Izzy smiled. 'He's a great kid, and he's very lucky to have a wonderful mother who is ready to do whatever he needs to thrive.'

'You always did know exactly what to say. So, this thing with Grayson... Am I correct in saying that it feels...serious?'

Guilt churned in Izzy's stomach. It just didn't feel right, keeping Grayson's closest friend out of the loop—not when they planned to have Astrid be a part of their baby's life too.

Before she knew it, she found herself talking. She told Astrid the truth—or at least a pared back version of the truth. That she and Grayson had decided to have a baby together, and co-parent platonically, and this 'relationship' was simply a ruse to set the stage for safety from the press once they'd actually brought a child into the mix.

A tense silence followed, until Astrid began to chuckle softly.

'God, I bet he actually believes that it's fake too.' Astrid took a long sip of her wine and looked out towards the pool. 'Let me tell you one thing I know for certain about Grayson Koh. The man is the worst actor I have ever met.'

Izzy sat up a little straighter. 'But it's the truth. We came here specifically to pretend we're dating. It's part of our arrangement.'

'So you're telling me there have been no sparks between you while you actively aim to create a child in the traditional sense?' Astrid raised a brow, smiling widely when Izzy avoided her knowing gaze. 'That's exactly what I thought.'

'We have good chemistry, sure. But that's not enough.'

'There is more than chemistry between you two. I saw the way he looked at you from the moment you started working for me. When he told me not to renew your contract, to guide you instead in pursuit of your illustration talents... I don't know why I didn't make sure that was what you wanted before I let you go. He seemed so certain it was what you needed. Believe me, I was furious when he finally admitted to me that he'd wanted to be free to pursue you.'

Izzy was shocked. 'He said that?'

Astrid nodded. 'Izzy, he was smitten, for goodness' sake. You should have seen the look on his face when he found out you were going to Bali with Julian. He even drove to the marina to try and stop you... But you should probably be hearing all this from him.'

Izzy tried to keep a straight face when Luca and Grayson came barrelling into the room before she could press Astrid for more details. She remained calm as they all sat together to eat, but inside her mind was a riot of emotion.

Had he really wanted to stop her going that day she'd left with Julian? Had he really stopped Astrid renewing her contract as some kind of misguided way to give them a chance at being together? It had still been a truly inappropriate move, but knowing he hadn't actually set out to have her fired because he didn't like or approve of her...

She wondered what else she had assumed wrongly about him.

Playing the role of Grayson Koh's adoring girlfriend came a little too easily to her, Izzy discovered as she spent yet another day on the arm of the most charming and attentive boyfriend on the planet.

They had started their day at the official Legends racing weekend launch, where Grayson and a panel of other
drivers talked about the goals of the historic event, as well
as the personal charities they were supporting. It turned
out that Grayson's charity of choice, the Boost Academy,
was one that he had started himself years ago, to combat
inequality in motorsport.

She could feel his passion as he outlined the many issues that stood in the way of true equality in Elite One,
focusing on the costs involved for aspiring racers and how
many talented young people were forced to walk away
from their dreams due to significant financial barriers
and discrimination.

She knew that had very nearly been Grayson's own experience, and the price he had wound up paying to get his
place on the grid was significant. To think that he was purposefully paying that forward by giving others the chance
to succeed without any expectation of repayment brought
a tear to her eye. She found herself with a newfound understanding of this man who had been doing so much for
a very long time with no expectation of praise.

After the launch event they attended a youth race run
by the Boost Academy, followed by a lunch where Izzy
met a whole host of students past and present who had already benefited from the globally run academy's tutelage
and efforts. She watched Grayson laugh and joke with the
young drivers, each of whom looked at him with complete
awe and admiration, and she could see once again how
easy he was around children.

For a man nicknamed the Golden Lion, effortlessly
dominant both off the track and on it, he immediately
turned into a playful pussycat around youngsters. He had
a gentle side that he rarely showed in public, so driven was

he to win all the time and to hold his cards close to his chest whilst he did so. But he had always shown it around her, she realised. Even when she'd been his godson's nanny and he had been trying to ignore her.

She had contemplated asking him about what Astrid had divulged the day before, but she wasn't quite sure how to word it.

Hey, Grayson, did you plan to pursue things with me before I ruined everything and eloped with your best friend?

Even if he had been interested in her back then, she knew it would only ever have been for a brief fling, to explore the physical attraction between them. Grayson didn't do relationships, and he most definitely didn't do commitment and before her disastrous marriage that had been all she'd ever wanted.

Still, being the main focus of Grayson's magnetically charming attentions throughout the day was fast taking its toll, and she was increasingly having to remind herself that this was all an act. He touched her at almost every moment, and when he wasn't touching her he was looking at her with that dark, brooding gaze of his.

To any onlookers he'd certainly appear besotted. But of course Izzy knew that he wasn't holding her hand under the table and whispering terrible jokes into her ear because he wanted to. He was simply playing his part—just as she was.

When the lunch wound to a close, and they'd waved goodbye to the Boost Academy management team, she contemplated faking a headache, just so that she could hide in her bedroom for the rest of the night and catch her breath.

But Grayson, completely oblivious to her inner turmoil,

announced that he had taken the afternoon off so that they could do some sightseeing.

With two pairs of dark sunglasses and a discreet guard trailing them a few paces behind, they walked the footpath along the banks of the bay with ease, while Izzy tried desperately to focus on the sights and not the man beside her.

The area around the Marina Bay racetrack boasted views of the most famous sights in Singapore, including the Supertree grove in the gardens by the bay. From a distance, in the afternoon sun, she thought the structures weren't quite as imposing as the pictures she'd viewed online.

'The light show is truly spectacular,' Grayson told her. 'But I'm sure you've seen that before.'

'It was one of the few things I missed out on, actually. Luca was always in bed by that time.' She looked towards the opposite side of the bay, where the grove of manmade trees stood tall. She was not quite ready to give up their time alone just yet. 'Do you think we could stay to watch it?'

'I'm sorry, we have dinner with the Verdant team, followed by another prominent sponsor event.' He winced.

Izzy quickly brushed off her suggestion, easing them away from the subject by asking questions about the Singapore Merlion as they walked towards the famous statue that stood watch over the bay.

Grayson played tour guide as they walked, pointing out small details about the buildings and bridges they passed as only a local could. She loved every small snippet he shared about growing up here, storing away each tiny nugget of information about his childhood as though it might prove useful in understanding the man he was now.

They walked until her feet ached and her stomach began

to rumble, and Grayson finally suggested they stop to eat at one of his favourite places in the city, a street food centre in the central business district, which boasted stall after stall of authentic fare.

He closed his eyes as he ate, and the word he growled was one she'd heard often since arriving. It had thus far evaded her attempts at learning some simplified Mandarin basics from an audio app on her phone.

'Does that mean it's tasty?' she asked, noting how the corner of his mouth rose a little at her question.

'*Shiok?* It's usually used when food is good.' He reached over, stealing a dumpling from her plate with a smirk. 'But it's also kind of a catch-all word for something pleasurable. Winning a race can be *shiok*, just as a great kiss can be.'

His eyes met hers across the table with meaning, and she felt a blush creep up from her chest all the way to her eyebrows as she murmured, 'Seeing the city with you today was also *shiok*.'

'I'm glad.' He smiled, his hand reaching to cover hers on the small white table.

All around them voices hummed, and she was aware of the bodyguard sitting a few tables away, but for the most part it felt like the most intimate they'd been with one another since leaving Ireland. Like a tiny moment of peace. Then there was a flash nearby, and they both looked up to see a group of teenage boys approaching them, with phones and Elite One memorabilia in tow.

More followed, and Grayson apologised to her as he switched into famous racing driver mode, graciously signing a few items and posing for photos before the bodyguard guided them to a car.

He seemed reserved and brooding as they travelled back to his home, where they had yet another quick turn-around to get ready for the evening events. She knew that his schedule was booked up for the next couple of nights, and then she was scheduled to return to Ireland, but she didn't mind. She was pretty sure he'd rescheduled his day today, to go sightseeing with her.

But maybe the simmering tension between them was all in her mind, and he was quietly relieved that they hadn't been physical since that one night in Ireland? Maybe he had already begun to regret blurring those lines?

She was here to make things easier for both of them in the long run, and yet it felt as if with every moment they spent together she was only complicating things more.

CHAPTER TWELVE

GRAYSON LOUNGED ON a low sofa in the hotel suite he'd booked for the night, waiting as the styling team finished performing whatever magic Isabel had asked them to do. She didn't need magic. Truthfully, he would have been happy having her on his arm in her jeans and black boots if it meant having her smile in his direction again.

She'd been different these last few days, since they'd left Ireland. Sure, his schedule was hectic, and he hadn't made her very comfortable, considering most of their time in public had been spent with him taking every possible chance to touch her and play the adoring boyfriend.

The press adored their fairy-tale love story. Astrid had made a point of telling him that every moment she could. Both he and the Legends event had been trending on social media for three days in a row. For a man who had given so little of himself to the public over the past twenty years, in an effort to shield his supposed deficits, it appeared this more human side of him was infinitely more saleable.

He'd been inundated with requests for and interest in the new Verdant models, and also in him—including a documentary proposal from a major television company. Unveiling the real Grayson Koh beneath his mask of indifference was apparently a big sell in the motorsport world.

More of a sell than his shield of ruthless cool had ever been. And he had Isabel to thank for that revelation.

It was the greatest irony, though, that showing the real him to the world meant being fake with the one person whose attention he craved more than any other.

If he had thought that having Isabel in his bed had been torture, it was nothing compared to playing her loving, attentive partner over these past few days. It hadn't been hard at all to appear infatuated with her as they'd attended the various sponsors' events and played tourist around the city in between. But in private she seemed cool, and even a little distant at times, retreating to her room to work on her latest commissions and retiring to bed early.

His plan to seduce her back into his bed seemed to have been foiled at every turn, between his hectic schedule and her determination to hold him at a distance. But this evening's Legends gala ball at the iconic Marina Bay Hotel was to be the penultimate event of the week, followed only by the big race tomorrow night.

He had spent most of today practising, and completing the qualifying laps that would decide everyone's starting position on the grid. It had felt so natural, sliding back into the driver's cockpit, his racing suit and gloves fitting him like a second skin as he'd gripped the wheel in his hands. But even after he had qualified in pole position, surrounded by the comforting sight of his old Falco Roux crew, all he'd been able to think about was returning to Isabel.

She consumed his thoughts—much as she had in that first year, when he'd been unable to stop himself from seeking her out. For a man who'd always prided himself on control and discipline, he'd been unable to resist the lure of even the briefest stolen snapshot of time in her presence.

The problem was, as he'd learned then and as he still knew to be true now, the more time with her he allowed himself, the more he craved. It was a dangerous thing, allowing himself the illusion of having her as his own.

The sound of wheeled cases and clothes racks moved along the hall as the styling team appeared in a flurry of chatter, and Grayson thanked them all before they hurried on to their next appointments. When he turned back, Isabel stood in the centre of the room, looking like every filthy fantasy he'd ever had come to life.

The rich teal-coloured concoction of shimmering fabric hugged her hourglass curves like a second skin, showcasing her ample breasts with a plunging neckline. But his favourite part was the deep slit on one side of the skirt that went up to mid-thigh.

He didn't speak for a long moment, simply looking his fill as his heart…and other parts of his anatomy…threatened to burst through his tuxedo.

'I'm guessing this is a good silence?' she asked, giving him a slow twirl that showed off the low back of her dress.

'This is a breathtaking, awestruck, give-me-a-moment-to-drink-you-in kind of silence,' he said, fighting off the wave of nerves that had suddenly made him feel tongue-tied.

She looked radiant, but the smile on her face was what had struck him speechless. It was the kind of smile she'd given him long ago, when they had first met.

The gown suited her to perfection. It was sexy, and edgy, and the rich tone complemented the colours of the delicate tattoos that adorned her back. He'd bet she'd chosen to wear her hair up in a sleek ponytail style for exactly that reason.

'You're extra charming this evening.' She smiled, walking beside him towards the floor-length mirrors that bracketed the private elevator. 'You know what I'm going to ask for right now, though, don't you?' She smirked.

Please, please let it be something X-rated.

'What?' he asked, his throat dry, and she popped one curvaceous hip, revealing the gloriously thick length of one pale thigh.

'Let's take a selfie together!' She waved her phone, positioning them both at a flattering angle in front of the mirror and fussing as she angled her camera towards their reflection.

'You know, technically, a selfie is when the camera is pointed towards—'

She pressed one artfully manicured fingertip to his lips. 'Hush with your cranky technicalities. Do as you're told and give me that million-dollar smoulder of yours.'

He did as he was told, facing their reflection and trying not to linger on the sight of them both side by side, his midnight-blue tuxedo jacket acting as the perfect partner to her gown. They looked good together. Too good. They looked as if they fitted perfectly.

He tried to ignore the tightness in his stomach as they stepped into the plush golden interior of the lift while Izzy excitedly tapped on her phone screen and mumbled something about Astrid getting her money's worth this week.

He wanted nothing more than to touch her again. To have her touch him for real. But outside of the few stolen caresses he'd managed during their public appearances, neither of them had made that first move. Their agreement still stood, and it wouldn't be long before she would be back in his bed once more. But it wasn't enough. He was beginning to realise that it probably never would be.

He wanted what they'd had for that brief window of time

in her little cottage, when she'd fallen asleep in his arms and he had lain awake, listening to the rain fall outside the windows. That night, much like this one, he'd been awash with a riot of emotions he'd had no idea how to begin untangling. Perhaps that was why, when she had suggested they pretend to be a couple and yet refrain from any repeat rule-breaking, he hadn't contradicted her. Because the alternative was telling her that he wanted her to desire him—not just for their agreement but for *him*.

More and more he found himself dwelling on how things would be when she finally fell pregnant and they moved on to the platonic co-parenting phase of their contract.

Even entertaining the idea of being platonic with her... It made rage and loss build in his gut. He wasn't good enough to have her—he knew that. But what if at some point in the near future someone else decided that they were?

She'd said that she would never have dated again and had children the traditional way, but life could be unpredictable. In taking himself out of the running, he was leaving her out in the open for anyone else to snatch up.

And that was completely unacceptable.

He couldn't simplify it or brush it off by thinking if he couldn't have her no one could. No. He was the kind of selfish bastard who simply wanted her all for himself, and he was fast running out of ways to talk himself out of it.

As though sensing the dangerous nature of his thoughts, Isabel took a tiny step backwards, putting even more distance between them. His eyes narrowed on her. On impulse, he reached out and pressed the emergency stop button. The floor beneath them vibrated as they came to a smooth stop, and a small blinking red light came on above their heads.

'What are you doing?' She frowned, reaching to remove his hand.

'Being spontaneous.'

'But we're already running late,' she said, her eyes widening as he stepped closer, bracketing her with his arms on either side of her head.

'Our captive audience can wait,' he growled, his eyes not leaving hers. 'I cannot.'

Her mouth dropped open a little, and the delicate pulse at her throat was visibly thrumming as she looked down, as if realising just how little space separated them.

He catalogued all these reactions, running them against what he already knew of her tells, and came to one glorious deduction. In this moment she was not pretending to be indifferent to him, and nor was she afraid. Far from it. She was...excited. There was no crowd here to appease. No audience. Just as he needed it to be if he was to say these next words aloud.

'You're running from me again, Isabel,' he said softly, reaching up to cup her jaw with one hand.

She inhaled sharply at his touch, but this time she did not look away. Thank goodness. Because he didn't think he could bear it. He needed her eyes on him. Her hands on him.

'I'm right here...' she breathed.

'You are...and we're going to talk.' He forced himself not to pounce, not to claim her as he craved. Not before she said the words he wanted to hear. 'Be honest with me, Isabel...have you not missed my touch at all?'

She frowned, looking past him. 'Our deal doesn't start up again for another few days. We said we'd keep things normal outside of...those days.'

'*You* said that. I, however, thought I was quite clear on where I stood in that regard. I need you to know that if this had been about what *I* wanted...you would never have left my bed.'

'You don't actually mean that. Not when you have crowds of beautiful half-naked women lusting after you.'

'Ah…you saw the foam party photos.'

He had hated every moment of that ridiculous event, but he had been forced to stand and pose with dancers for the press and various social media influencers as part of his sponsorship commitments for the upcoming race.

'I didn't think this through,' she said. 'This part of your life. I feel like I'm cramping your style.'

'We discussed exclusivity and I stand by my commitments. Not just for our agreement, but because the idea that I'd have any interest in some stranger throwing her clothing at me when I can barely think straight for wanting *you* is laughable. I spent most of my practice session today fantasising about our next window…of how I might convince you to extend it to a week instead of three nights. Maybe even two.'

'I may as well just take up residence in your bed at that rate.'

'Yes,' he said simply, watching her cheeks turn that beautiful shade of pink he loved so much.

He had coveted her blushes, not getting nearly enough of them since they'd begun this ruse.

No longer would he go without them.

'Grayson, what exactly are you saying?' she asked, her voice a small whisper.

'I'm saying yes. Yes to you taking up residence in my bed. No more pretending, Isabel. I'm done with taking these small pieces of you and expecting satisfaction. I crave you and I want it all.'

Her mouth formed the most delicious little O and, damn it, weak as he was, he leaned in and stole her next exhalation of breath with a kiss, before pulling swiftly back.

'Sorry, I couldn't resist. You don't have to answer me right now. I understand that you have your hang-ups—'

Whatever he'd been about to say next was swallowed up by Isabel's perfectly painted red lips as she launched herself at him in a kiss to end all other kisses. She tasted like sweet plums and spice, her tongue sliding against his own without any of the nerves she'd shown before. She was a goddess, and he was utterly at her mercy. Her hands gripped his hair, her soft weight pushing him back against the wall of the elevator, pinning him in place.

'What is this, hmm?' he murmured against her lips.

'This is me answering you,' she said roughly, deepening the kiss until only the sound of their laboured breathing filled the elevator.

The sound of a low beep permeated the air, and it took Grayson a moment to realise that it was coming from the emergency call panel. Placing his finger upon Isabel's lips, he pressed the button and briefly addressed the concierge on the other end.

'Did you seriously just offer that man an inordinate amount of money to give us ten minutes alone in here?' Isabel's husky whisper turned into a gasp as Grayson's lips trailed down the side of her neck.

'Believe me, I'd have asked for two hours if I could.'

He gripped her waist, swapping their positions so that she was pinned and at his mercy. He only had ten minutes, and he didn't intend to waste a single moment with discussion. Without breaking eye contact, he sank down slowly to his knees.

Izzy felt all rational thought leave her as Grayson's strong hands bracketed her thighs and spread her dress wide. A flimsy scrap of lace was all that separated them. She leaned her head back against the elevator wall and silently thanked her stylist for selecting a gown made of some magical kind of ultra-fitted stretch material that required no supportive garments beneath. She didn't think she could have managed a straight face if he'd needed to forcibly extract her from her underwear in order to do whatever it was he had planned.

With one deft flick of his fingers her knickers were in his pocket and his mouth was delving hungrily between her thighs. The act felt both crude and impossibly tender as he framed her sex with one hand, reaching the other up to twine his fingers with hers.

She felt too exposed, too open to him in so many ways. But just when she was about to tell him to stop, he hooked one thumb behind her thigh and raised it to rest upon his strong shoulders. The position was scandalously erotic, and made it utterly impossible for her to hold on to the tiny scrap of control she'd been clinging to any longer. With every sweep of his tongue against her she felt herself tighten, careening down a runway of pleasure that Grayson alone was in charge of.

She was not the one in control here, and she didn't think she truly wanted to be. And that was a revelation.

Trusting him to get her there, to keep her safe in this tiny pocket of time… It gave her a strength and confidence she didn't know she'd been searching for. She clutched at every part of him she could reach—his hair, the nape of his neck. She leaned into his dominant strength and held on for dear life as the strongest orgasm she'd ever experienced crested, sending glorious waves of pleasure through her very core.

Her legs trembled, but Grayson was right there holding

her as she came back to her senses, a sinful smile on his lips as he stared up at her.

He was still on his knees, and he made no move to stand right away. He simply held her for a moment, his hands circling her hips and his face pressed against the softness of her stomach. Then he stood, staring down at her with a look of dark possession that sent skitters of excitement and trepidation through her.

In the back of her mind she knew that she was hurtling faster than she had ever anticipated towards falling for this man. Maybe she was fooling herself to think she hadn't already been halfway there from the moment they'd met. She wanted him more than he could know. He'd said he craved her, but he had no idea of the depth of feeling coursing through her in this moment.

'I want you inside me,' she whispered, pulling him close against her.

He shook his head, his fingers smoothing her errant hair away from her face. 'Not yet.'

Not yet? She frowned, wondering what exactly that meant. But of course... Reality returned, and she realised that they still stood in the lift. Probably rapidly approaching the end of their ten-minute window and thus risking discovery. Public indecency was not something taken lightly in this part of the world, and she could hardly believe that they had taken it this far, even with Grayson's assurance of privacy.

'Isabel, look at me,' he commanded, waiting until her gaze met his. 'Don't for a second think that I didn't mean anything I just said. I meant all of it. When I make love to you again, I want complete certainty between us. Do you understand?'

'Yes, I... I think so.'

Her mind was racing, muddled in the aftermath of the destruction he'd just wrought upon her control. Everything was going so fast...but she felt happy. It was slightly terrifying, but she felt as if something truly cataclysmic had occurred in the last ten minutes.

He helped her put her dress to rights, smoothing down the folds all the way to her feet with a tenderness and attention to detail that tightened her chest. He always took care of her, she realised with clarity. From the very beginning he had done all those tiny things that she so often overlooked doing for herself. She had spent so much of her life just surviving that small comforts seemed to bypass her attention completely.

He moved to press the emergency button once more, and the lift began to move again.

Far too soon they had reached the foyer, and the doors opened to reveal them to the crowd of guests and the few select photographers who were allowed to attend.

Grayson took her by the hand, guiding her to where a small gathering of people with familiar faces stood. Nina Roux wore a glamorous red ballgown and was in avid conversation with Astrid, who wore an equally stunning sheath of gold sequinned silk.

'I'm going to leave you for a moment, but I'll be right back,' Grayson said, pressing a kiss to the inside of her wrist before letting her hand drop. 'I just have something I need to do.'

Izzy watched as he moved away, towards the private elevator they'd just exited. 'But, Grayson, where are you—?'

Her words were swallowed by the crowd, and she could do nothing but watch as the doors of the lift slid shut and he disappeared from her view.

'What on earth is that lovestruck fool up to now?' Astrid mused softly beside her.

Izzy tried not to let her nerves get to her as minutes passed and Grayson didn't reappear. All too soon they were being called into the sprawling event space on the Skydeck, where wildflowers decorated every surface. It felt like walking into an enchanted forest, with the music pumping from the speakers below their feet seeming somehow ethereal.

It wasn't long before she was left on her own on the edge of the balcony as the others scurried off to their duties. They had a purpose here, while she… Well, she tried not to think too negatively about how very small and out of place she felt.

Grayson wasn't lovestruck over her—not really. Was he?

She needed to go and find him and ask him for herself.

Downing the last of her drink, she made her way through the crowd with as much calm and poise as she could muster. She wasn't running away, she told herself. She was running *to* him.

She emerged back into the foyer, the now-empty space feeling cavernous and cold without the throng of guests that had filled it before. But it wasn't empty. A man stood nearby A man with a face she had only ever seen once before, on a day that had left scars on her confidence that she'd fought hard to heal.

Peter Liang. Julian's father.

CHAPTER THIRTEEN

'I HEARD YOU'D found yourself a new target,' the old man croaked, his voice just as thin and reedy as she remembered.

Isabel stood frozen in place, her hand still braced on the handle of the door she'd just come through.

She'd known that by coming here she would have to face the Liang family eventually, but she hadn't been prepared for it tonight. She hadn't been prepared to be alone when it happened, either.

Her words seemed stuck in her throat, her ability to fight back trapped beneath a layer of ice. For all her talk about finding her power and rebuilding her life, she'd still never quite mastered the art of conflict. But here, in this grand hotel, there was nowhere to run without causing a scene. So she decided she had nothing to lose.

She had long thought about what she might say if she ever saw any of her late husband's family again. How she might lay to rest the burden of guilt she had carried over how his life had come to an end. This was her opportunity.

'I had hoped to see you while I was here,' she lied, planting her feet and inhaling a sharp breath. 'If only to tell you how utterly disappointed I am.'

'You're disappointed?' He laughed. 'Is that supposed to make me feel something?'

'Oh, no, I wouldn't say anything is capable of doing that, Mr Liang,' she said neutrally. 'Not a man who treats his children like pawns. Julian may not have been perfect, but he didn't deserve the way you treated him. And as for Grayson…'

The old man smiled, looking over her shoulder. 'Ah, yes, please do champion your new lover to me. Some pretty tears might even earn you some diamonds if you start now.'

Isabel looked behind her to see Grayson emerging from the lift, his expression swiftly tightening into alarm as he realised who was with her.

She vaguely processed the sight of Grayson storming in front of her, his voice tight as the two men began arguing in their native tongue. She had never managed to learn more than a select few words, but judging by the increasingly tight line of Peter Liang's lips whatever Grayson had to say was not pleasant.

Not a moment too soon, Grayson turned to her and ushered her back through the doors to where the gala was now in full swing. Humid fragrant air filled her lungs and the music chased away all the unpleasantness of the past few moments.

'Are you okay?' Grayson asked softly, his nostrils still slightly flared with anger.

'I'm fine. I wanted to speak with him…to say how I felt. And I did.' She exhaled a long, steady breath. 'The real question is are *you* okay? That sounded like it got pretty heated.'

'That is not how I planned for tonight to go. I didn't think he would be attending, considering his own team has gone bust and he's had to pull all his funding from the Singapore Elite One race. That's what we argued over, mostly.'

'And about me?' she offered.

'I don't care what he thinks about me, and I told him as much. But I told him that if he so much as attempts to upset you ever again, I will buy everything he owns from under him.'

Izzy tried not to be shocked at the vehemence in his voice, but she could see that he meant it. She could see that he would defend her in this against anyone who dared to draw attention to their mismatched pairing. But deep down a small part of her wondered if that was right. If perhaps they would always be up against all those comments that painted her as an opportunist.

Her uncertainty followed her as Grayson was called away to attend to his duties as one of the hosts. But before he walked away he kissed her, right in the middle of the dance floor, much to the delight of the crowd around them. As she smiled up at him on stage she knew she couldn't deny it any longer. She was deeply, madly in love with this gorgeous man.

But she felt as if she'd decided to stay safe, only to climb back out onto the precipice all over again now. She knew that Grayson would never truly love her as she needed him to, nor want to be a family with her for real, so stepping into this in-between life with him was dangerous to her heart. As was getting close to his friends.

Because that was what they had always been, wasn't it?
His friends. Not hers.

Sure, she had Astrid and Luca now, but what if they decided she wasn't good enough for Grayson and abandoned her? Only it wouldn't just be her—it would be an innocent baby in the middle of it all. She knew how intoxicating it felt to be enfolded into their big racing family, and how cold it had been in contrast once she'd been cast out.

Logically, she knew she was being irrational, but she

couldn't stop those feelings from bubbling up to the surface like oil, coating all her fragile hope with fear. She could hardly smile, and her limbs felt numb as Grayson began to give a speech about the various charities that would benefit from the Legends race.

He was effortlessly charming, and she knew that while he might technically be retired, this would always be his world. He belonged here. But she didn't, and she had been fooling herself to think that their great chemistry in bed was enough to change that.

She had been prepared to have a baby with him—to co-parent and have nice, tidy boundaries. Control. Temporary visits she could walk away from when their time was up. But now she'd gone and fallen for him and everything had changed. She'd already begun to lose herself in the illusion that this fantasy might have a happy ending, when he had always been up-front about the fact that it never could. He wasn't a happily-ever-after kind of guy.

Just pull it off.

She bit down hard on her lip, repeating the mantra that had always got her through much worse times than this. With Astrid by her side, she had to turn her face away and choke down her tears. She knew she couldn't stay here. She had always known. And there was no sense in prolonging the inevitable because it would only hurt more.

She had to pull off the sticking plaster—fast and clean.

She had hoped that once the formal part of the gala had drawn to a close she might be able to convince Grayson to take her back to the suite. She knew that this was a conversation best had in private. But he'd suggested that they take a walk, said that he had something special planned...

She was powerless to resist the chance for even one more hour spent living in the fantasy.

She wasn't entirely sure what she planned to say to him—only knew she had to tell him that they couldn't do this for real. She had no guarantee that he would want to keep to their arrangement either. She was risking so much... But the alternative was more than she could bear.

Everything felt like too much, and with every step that she took, following him across the narrow bridge that separated the hotel from the beautifully ornate gardens that made Singapore so very famous, she felt her body grow tight with trepidation. They were going into the gardens they hadn't been able to stay in before, because of all his commitments.

'Surely this place is closed at this time of the night?' she asked, as Grayson guided her along a polished stone pathway towards the world-famous Supertrees Grove.

'I made a special request. It pays to be the country's only championship-winning Elite One driver sometimes.' He winked, looking lighter than she had seen him all week.

'This is beautiful,' she said, looking up to where the man-made 'trees' were lit up in pinks and yellows and purples. The sky seemed to glitter around them, the colours touching her skin and illuminating the fabric of her dress like a tapestry.

When she looked back at Grayson, he had a strange expression on his face.

'You've been happy with me this past week here, yes?' he asked. 'I hope that I've come to know you well enough to know when you're happy.'

'Of course I've been happy.' She looked out at the skyline, at the beauty of their surroundings, but still inside she felt a chasm open within her. 'Grayson... I think that sometimes we tend to idealise situations because we really want them to work...'

'Are we talking about me here, or you?' he asked.

'Maybe just me...' She swallowed past the lump in her throat. 'I don't know... All I know is that we are far too different. We have very different visions of our future, which is why we entered into this agreement. We both agreed that our situation would work best from a distance.'

'But what if it isn't best?' he said softly, reaching out to take her hand in his. 'You look so beautiful right now. But your beauty isn't the only thing that has me in your thrall. It's everything about you...'

She shook her head, pain lancing her chest with every word. 'Grayson, I—'

'Please, just let me get this out first. Just let me...'

He inhaled a sharp breath, reaching into his tuxedo pocket and pulling out a small velvet box. Time slowed as he met her eyes with a heart-melting smile, popping the box open to reveal a glittering diamond ring.

'I said I wanted you to be certain of what I want the next time we made love, so I decided that I'd make myself as clear as possible.'

Izzy watched with a mixture of awe and horror as Grayson dropped to his knees before her for the second time that evening.

Grayson stared up at Isabel's shocked face and instantly knew that he had made a mistake.

Silence fell between them, but still he remained frozen in place, hoping that she was simply taken by surprise. That any moment now she would laugh and fall into his arms, shouting the one little word he needed to hear.

But she didn't laugh. Nor did she speak.

When he looked closer, he realised that her bottom lip was quivering and she was beginning to cry. Somewhere along the line he had misread the signs, overlooked something crucial, and now they were careening off-track.

He stood up quickly, gripping her hands in his, hating how cold they felt.

'This went differently in my mind… I won't lie.' He'd aimed for a joking tone, but his voice came out just as strained as he felt.

Still she didn't respond.

'Isabel, I mean this. I want us to be married. I want us to raise our child together, as a family.'

She closed her eyes, shaking her head softly, as though his words were breaking her heart—which made absolutely no sense.

'Damn you,' she whispered, the words escaping on a hiss of pain. 'I was prepared to do all this alone, and then you walked into my life and made me start to hope.'

'Hope is good,' he urged.

'Not when the thing I had been hoping for was…' She opened her eyes. 'You told me how you felt about marriage once—or have you forgotten? You told me years ago that the only way you could abide the institution would be if there were no emotions involved. "Just sex and finances." I believe those were your words. You've told me you crave me…but I've done something so much worse. I've somehow gone and fallen in love with you.'

He felt her admission like a punch to the chest, stopping his heart and then starting it up all over again. He held her tighter to him, refusing to let her go. She wouldn't run from him this time—not when he had waited years to have her.

But then he felt the certainty within him that he deserved such a glorious gift wane—just for a split second. He froze, and time stretched out as her eyelashes fluttered and lowered to a close.

One moment of hesitation—that was all it took for Isabel's trust in him to vanish completely. He saw it in her face as her expression crumpled.

She tried to pull herself free from his grip but he held on tight, gathering her more closely into the circle of his arms. The lights that sparkled pink and purple above them now shimmered upon the tears that fell freely down her cheeks. Tears that somehow he had caused, with his inability to trust in himself.

But the right words wouldn't quite come.

'I... I adore you, Isabel,' he stammered. 'You must know that.'

'Must I?' She sniffed, successfully pulling away from him this time. 'Because from what you've told me, you've only ever seen marriage as a cold, meaningless union. The fact that you've decided to pursue it with me tells me everything I need to know.'

He closed his eyes, cursing his past self for being so cynical and his present self for being so damned obtuse. 'There is nothing cold about how I feel for you.'

'I know. And that makes it so much worse. Marrying each other would be a huge risk, Grayson. And it's simply not one I'm prepared to take. Not when we can stick to our original plan and avoid the drama and the heartbreak.'

'Maybe I've gone about this the wrong way... We should go home and talk.'

'It's not my home, Grayson. I have my home. I had everything in my life settled just the way I wanted it. And then...'

'I came along and ruined everything?' he suggested.

'Don't put words in my mouth. I am not saying that our

time together has been a waste. Or that it has had no effect on me, or that I wish it had never happened. I am unbelievably happy that it happened, and that I got to experience what it feels like to be the focus of your attention.'

'But that's how it can be always. That's how it will be if you just give us a chance.'

She shook her head sadly. 'I can't marry you, Grayson.'

He felt her words like a weight in his chest as she slowly took a step backwards. Her jaw was tight, her lips set in a grim line, and he could see that she truly believed the words she spoke.

On some primal level he wanted nothing more than to throw her over his shoulder and take her back to his bed, where he would work on convincing her otherwise. He would show her just how very alike they were in all the ways that mattered, and just how wonderful their life together could be if she gave in.

But another part of him asked if he wanted what was best for her or if he simply wanted her at all costs. If he convinced her to marry him, to stay with him here in Singapore, she'd have to sell her house and change all her plans just to fit in with his world. Because that was how it would have to be. He had a busy lifestyle that took him all around the world, and his plans frequently changed at the last minute. He was often exhausted, and he barely had time for social occasions, never mind the demands of being a part of a committed relationship. Wasn't that why his last one had failed?

Did he want her badly enough to force her into his world if he couldn't make her happy? Was that love? Or would the true act of love be letting her go and giving her the gift of the secure home and quiet lifestyle that she could only have without him?

CHAPTER FOURTEEN

GRAYSON COMPLETED HIS warm-up laps, trying and failing to feel the familiar pre-race hum of anticipation in his veins. Drivers on the track often compared a good relationship with their car to sex. Compatibility, connection, trust, feel… A poor feel for a car could have the best driver sliding around the track like a rookie, but a good feel…it made everything seamless. Hyperfocus kicked in and you felt unstoppable, as if you were flying on land.

Making love with Isabel was like that.

Seamless. Right.

So much for his pre-race calming rituals. He had never felt as wound up in his entire career, and it had nothing to do with the race and everything to do with the fact that Isabel was running late and likely wouldn't make it to the garage before the race began. Also, she had called Astrid to pass along that message and not him. Sure, the garage was technically a mobile-phone-free area, but did she know that?

He tried not to let his mind run wild with the possibility that she had made her decision to end things and was already on her way back to Ireland. After a few hours of fitful sleep he'd left the hotel before she woke—a necessity, to avoid sliding into bed alongside her to rehash his points from the night before. He knew her well enough by now to realise that would only send her running away faster.

The more he thought over his rash proposal, the more he realised what a mistake it had been. He had been selfish, wanting to keep her with him by any means possible. He had pushed away her worries that they were too different, but now he'd calmed down he could see things from her perspective. She had told him how important it was for her to lay down roots and commit herself to parenthood, and he had told her that he wasn't cut out to be a full-time family man. That his career was number one.

Was it any wonder she doubted him?

He closed his eyes, wondering how on earth he had got everything so wrong. She loved him. She trusted him with the role of her child's father, but not with her heart. And why would she trust him with that most precious commodity when he had all but told her he would never love her?

He'd believed the words when he'd originally spoken them, not seeing a world where he would ever willingly enter into marriage with romantic notions. He could never have predicted the speed with which he would become a lovesick fool for a chaotic blonde tornado full of colour and joy.

But then again, wasn't that why he had sent her running away all those years ago? Hadn't he admitted that he felt that connection and pushed her away because of it?

He slammed his hand down hard on the wheel, watching as the engineers moved off the track.

'Grayson, she's here.'

It took him a moment to realise that one of his engineers was alerting him to Isabel's arrival, as he'd requested.

'Put her on.'

A small commotion could be heard amongst the familiar

sounds of equipment and voices and the music pulsing for the crowds as they awaited the race to begin. Thankfully his team didn't question their driver's very unconventional request, and within thirty seconds, Isabel's breathless and slightly awkward *'Hey...'* graced his ears.

'Hey, yourself,' he said, feeling the tension of the silence between them for a breath. He despised this tension, and if he'd been with her in person he'd have done his best to dispel it as quickly as possible. As it was, he could only show her how he felt. 'Can you see me on the monitor?'

'Is that...is that one of my designs on your helmet?'

'Yes. I had it made years ago.' He smiled at the memory of finding a drawing she'd made for Luca left at the Falco Roux garage one time. 'I needed it with me today. I should have known back then that things were never going to be simple between us. I know you're surrounded by musty old men right now, who are probably highly entertained by all this, but I need you to know that I'm sorry I tried to rush things. But I'm not sorry for what I said last night. I meant every word.'

A voice cut across them as comms came in from various officials, announcing the clearing of the track.

He cleared his throat, realising his time was up, but needing to know that when this race was done she would be right there waiting for him. 'Sounds like I've got to go.'

'Yes.'

'You said that you can't marry me, and I will try and respect that... But you can't ask me to stop hoping that I haven't completely messed this up. I would walk away from this race right now just to hear you tell me you love me again.'

'Grayson, I... I'll be here waiting for you. I promise.'

It wasn't quite the profession of love he'd hoped for,

but it was a start. Maybe that was what they needed—a fresh start.

The sound of the engines all around him permeated his thoughts, reminding him that he was here to perform a job. He had a charity relying on him, and fans waiting for the dramatic show he always delivered. He focused on his breathing as he felt the familiar thrum of his engine and heard the shouts of the crowd.

He wouldn't let Isabel return to Ireland without pleading his case one more time, but first he would focus on winning this race.

Izzy swore she could feel the heat of more than a dozen gazes focused on her as she took a step back from the pit wall and shakily handed the headset back to the head engineer.

The man had a rosy tint to his cheeks as he gave her a knowing nod. The rest of the team purposefully gave her some space, and got back to work communicating with Grayson as his engine roared to life and the race began.

She made a beeline for the bathroom at the rear of the garage, not really caring where she ended up, just needing to be alone for a moment. Knowing that Grayson would be driving at high speed in rainy conditions had already had her nerves in a knot as she'd rushed to make it for the start of the race, but after that conversation her stomach was in a knot for a whole other reason.

Was she running away?

If she knew one thing about herself, it was that she felt the most discomfort when she was making connections with people. She didn't need a degree in psychology to know why. A lifetime of inconsistency and let-downs and abandonment had led to her developing a thicker skin than most. Perhaps even a kind of armour that she encased herself within. Had she made a mistake, disregarding his proposal the night before? Had she projected feelings onto him that were more hers than his?

She was so tired of holding herself at a distance all the time. It didn't feel like protection or comfort. Around Grayson she felt in every second she was with him that she was holding up a weight that he was already helping her to support. When she needed him, he was there. And when he messed up he tried to make it better by *being* better, not just making empty promises. He sought her out, and he saw her far too clearly...over-defensiveness and all.

Even after she had rejected his beautiful proposal the night before and practically run from him, hiding in her bedroom all night in floods of tears, he had still worried about her when she hadn't turned up. He had been sitting in the cockpit of an Elite One racing car, his favourite place in the whole world after months away from it, and he'd wanted to talk to *her*.

She stared at her own reflection in the bathroom mirror, feeling a bubble of emotion burst upwards through her chest. But it wasn't a sob that escaped her lips, it was a laugh. A laugh at her own foolishness and at his ridiculously romantic confession to her and the entire pit team. The man had no shame and arrogance to burn...it was what she loved most about him.

There was very little about him that she didn't like—that was what had always drawn her to him. Even though she knew his reputation on the track and in the tabloids, the Grayson that she had spent those snapshots of time with had been everything she had ever wanted. As if someone had drawn together everything that she might need in a partner to feel whole and wrapped it up in one gorgeous, brooding package.

She took a deep breath, and then another, hardly believing the direction her thoughts had taken. It felt like whiplash—she had been so certain the night before, so steadfast in her reasoning that they would never work as a couple.

The rain had never been this bad on the Singapore track in all the years Grayson had driven it. It fell in heavy sheets, and the track glistened like ice as he worked to keep his pace. His skill on a wet track was unmatched, and if this had been a usual Elite One race such conditions would have likely given him full advantage.

But this wasn't a usual race—in so many ways. From the moment he had set off, after lights out, part of his mind had continued to wander to the woman he knew stood in the garage, watching him.

He was keenly aware of that fact as he took each corner at speed, as he felt the give of his tyres on the track, every time edging closer to losing control, just on the precipice. And as he ended his first lap, knowing he still had countless more to go, he knew that at some point over the past weeks with Isabel he had been irrevocably changed.

He turned another hairpin bend just at the moment when the backmarker hit the wall and careened into a full spinning flip, coming towards him...

All he could think about was how sorry he was not to have told her he loved her.

CHAPTER FIFTEEN

IZZY FELT THE energy in the garage shift even before the sound of screeching tyres echoed in the distance. Everyone froze in place as they watched the action unfold on the multiple monitors that were spread across the wall. Cars spinning in stunning HD focus filled each screen at different angles, multiplying the sick knot twisting in her solar plexus.

All she could tell was that one driver had taken a turn too fast, lost control, and created an incident that had sent multiple other cars spinning. She struggled to make out each of the vehicles in the rain, trying to see which driver's helmet was the same colour as Grayson's. Which one had *his* name emblazoned on the side panel.

She was nudged to the side-lines as members of the Falco Roux team began to confer in multiple languages she couldn't understand, watching and analysing as much as they could. She knew that this was their job, that unlike her they actually knew what to look for to see if their teammate was okay. They had headsets connecting them to Grayson's car directly, as well as to the marshals and stewards on the scene…

Heels sounded down the corridor at the rear of the garage and she had never felt such relief flood through her as when she saw Astrid's frantic form burst through the doorway. She had been upstairs, schmoozing with upper management and the sponsors of the event. Izzy had been invited to sit up there as well, but she had told Astrid she needed to be down here to support Grayson.

Now, she almost laughed out loud at how utterly ridiculous that idea was. She was powerless to do anything at all right now, other than wait and try to keep out of the way.

Astrid didn't speak, simply held her hand. Both of them were looking towards the monitors in a silent plea. After a few moments there was a noticeable exhalation of breath from the professionals in the room. Izzy sat to attention as the team principal announced loudly in English that all the drivers involved in the collision were okay and that both of the Falco Roux drivers were on their way back to the garage while a large amount of debris on the track was cleared.

'We're looking at a restart, everyone,' the team principal told them, and then began listing a barrage of technical instructions that sent everyone into action.

Izzy felt her body go into shutdown after the adrenaline rush, dropping her face into her hands as a few silent sobs burst free from her chest.

He was okay.

She focused on watching the monitor that currently showed a British driver being escorted to an ambulance as he waved a hand to the crowd, to show he was okay. It was no use. She still felt as if her heart was about to thump right out of her chest.

She heard the roar of the Falco Roux cars coming to a stop behind her, but couldn't quite bring herself to stand. She felt foolish because of how utterly shaken she was, compared with these people who were so experienced with all the drama and unpredictability of Elite One.

She looked up to see Grayson's broad figure emerging out of the cockpit of his car.

'What are you doing?' the team principal roared, 'You're in pole position—this isn't the time for a bath-room break, Grayson.'

'It's a restart—they can wait.'

The crew parted as Grayson traversed the length of the garage with no more than a few purposeful strides, the visor of his helmet pulled upwards to reveal the full intensity of his gaze upon one person.

Her.

He looked like a warrior returning from battle as he undid the clasp underneath his helmet and pulled it off. His jet-black hair was wet with the sweat that dripped down along his per-fectly chiselled jaw. His mouth was set in a grim line as he came to a stop in front of her, cursing softly under his breath.

'Look at you. You're as white as a sheet.'

His hand rose up to cup her jaw so tenderly, in contrast with the wild expression in his gaze. The team principal once again called for him to return to his car, but Grayson ignored him. His eyes remained fixed on hers in a look so anguished it took her breath away.

'Listen to them,' she said quickly, keenly aware of all the eyes upon them. 'You have a race to finish. Honestly, I'm fine.'

'Are you?' he asked, his eyes seeing far too much as usual. 'Because I'm not.'

'You're hurt?'

She felt a fresh wave of alarm shoot through her as she scanned his body for signs of bleeding, reflexively reach-ing out a hand to run it along the side of his ribs.

He closed his eyes, inhaling a deep breath at the contact.

'Oh, my God, you *are* hurt.'

She tried to pull her hand back, only to have him pin it in place in the spot directly over his heart.

'Not hurt. But not okay,' he said roughly, his tone so far from the smooth, confident, arrogant voice that he had used over the radio. 'Do you have any idea how many times in my career I've been in a situation like that, or even worse? More than I can count. I'm known for thriving on the chaos. My mind clears to nothing but winning, my reflexes kick in, and I use the adrenaline as fuel. I don't allow myself to feel fear.'

Izzy inhaled a shuddering breath. He had told her before that he rarely felt nerves in the car, but right now his hand shook just a little over hers, and she could feel the frantic thumping of his heart against her fingertips.

'Isabel… I saw that crash happening ahead…coming right at me…and for the first time in my entire career I didn't think about winning. All I could think about was you.' He leaned in, his damp forehead pressing against hers as he fought to get his breathing under control. 'I could see your face so clearly in my mind…and I realised winning meant nothing to me compared to being able to walk back in here to you.'

'This is your *job*, Grayson. I understand the risks and I'm here to cheer you on. Whether it's just for today or if you decide to go back into Elite One. I would never stand in the way of your dream.'

'I know you wouldn't. And I adore you all the more for it. But that's the thing. I don't think this is my dream any more. Only one thing has made me feel right in a long time, and I'm holding her in my arms.'

She closed her eyes, the impact of his words hitting her squarely in the chest. Had anyone ever said anything like that to her in her entire life? Had anyone ever quite literally dropped everything to run to her, just to see that she was okay?

'But if you don't go back to the car you're going to lose the race. You love winning.'

'Nowhere near as much as I love you, Isabel O'Sullivan.' He took her face in his hands, brown eyes blazing bronze with the force of his words. 'I messed up last night. You have no idea how many times I've gone over that proposal in my head and wished that I'd gone about it differently. But once I want something I get tunnel vision…and you have become my entire focus. Not just creating a baby with you… You—yourself. I told you that my career has always been front and centre and always would be… And I truly believed that. I truly believed that I wanted to have a child at a distance, so that it wouldn't have too much of an effect on my vision for motorsport. My own ego astounds me even now. To think that I could ever have been so utterly blind. And even once I realised that I was falling for you I still held back. I still tried to hold on to what I believed I was, letting you believe that you would only ever get a part of me. But being with you these past few weeks has reawakened all of those old feelings that made me push you away before, simply because they terrified me. I wasn't ready for you then. I was too selfish. I probably still am too selfish…'

'You are the most unselfish man I have ever known,' she told him. 'You have done nothing but make me feel safe and secure and loved…even though I didn't recognise it for what it was. I'm sorry that I tried to push you away.'

'Does that mean that you're done with doing that?'

'I can't promise that I won't feel insecure from time to time—wounds like mine don't really disappear—but I'm ready to try. I've had the dress rehearsal this past week, and now I'm ready to be loved by you for real.'

'Haven't you realised yet? It was always real.'

He gathered her in his arms, his lips claiming hers in a kiss so scorching hot that she heard quite a few whoops and cheers coming from their audience. Grayson pulled back for a second, framing her face with his hands as he looked down at her, love and adoration quite literally beaming from him. Then he turned to his teammate.

'Nina, go and win that race for Falco Roux, like I know you can.'

Nina Roux's eyes shone brightly through the gap in her visor before she gave a single-hand salute and sped out into the pit lane to restart the race.

After that Grayson didn't wait very long, taking her by the hand and practically pulling her through the corridors and paths of the Elite One paddock towards his luxurious private dressing room.

'But Grayson...what about winning?' Izzy asked breathlessly as he slammed the door behind them and began frantically undressing them both.

'You think I'd waste a moment out there when the best prize I've ever won is right here?' He leaned in to capture another scorching kiss.

She paused, smirking. 'If I'm the best prize you've ever won...would that make me your trophy wife?'

'Funny.' He laughed, but then his expression turned serious. 'Have you changed your mind about marrying me? Because I don't have the ring—'

'I don't need a ring, Grayson. I just need you.'

He pulled her into his arms. 'I told myself that you deserved better than the chaotic life I can give you... But while I don't know if I'll ever feel like I truly deserve your love I'm going to take it. And I'm going to do my best to show you how much I love you every single day.'

And then he kissed her again...a kiss filled with the promise of for ever.

EPILOGUE

'IF YOU SLOW down any more we'll be driving backwards!' Izzy laughed as her husband took yet another hairpin bend in the country road at a snail's pace.

'I'm taking appropriate safety measures for the rain,' he grumbled. 'And for your nausea.'

'My nausea is behaving itself this morning.' She smiled, patting a hand on her still soft belly, where their baby was growing nicely. 'But if we keep going at this pace I may faint from hunger.'

'We have one pitstop to make before we get to brunch,' he said, his jaw ticking again in that terse way it did when he was nervous.

What was he up to?

'I'll push for max speed while we're on the straight here, shall I?' He smirked, flipping the gear shift of the car just the way she liked.

'Copy that, Grayson. Push, push.' She gave him her best Elite One radio voice.

He'd recently made good on his promise to do filthy things to her atop one of the cars in a darkened garage after the Brazilian Grand Prix, before taking them home to Ireland for a much-needed winter break. They'd had their first Christmas dinner in her tiny cottage with Eve and her wife Moira and their daughter as their honorary guests.

The rain was coming down more heavily now—pretty typical for Ireland in January—and she was grateful that he wasn't as speed-hungry in his day-to-day life as he had been on the track. Despite being married to one of the world's smoothest racing drivers, she hadn't been allowed to set foot in any of his supercars. He had all but packed them away in the basement of the Swiss chalet, joking that he would see them again in eighteen years.

He was ridiculously excited about the baby, buying all the newest gadgets and suggesting the most outlandish names he could think of every chance he could get. The idea that they had almost done this separately…it was unthinkable. Making love with Grayson had been life-changing…but being loved by him every day was everything.

They came to a stop at the side of the road and Izzy frowned at the sight of a very deserted, very brunch-less field. 'What exactly are you up to?'

'You'll have to follow me to find out.'

She did, getting her canvas sneakers soaked in the process, which prompted her husband's instant grumbling. Despite his having bought her no fewer than five new pairs of increasingly expensive boots she still insisted on wearing her old favourites from time to time.

'Happy anniversary.' He smiled.

Izzy raised her eyebrows, looking around for some sign of what was going on here. 'It's not our first wedding anniversary for another five months.'

'Not that anniversary.' He offered his elbow, holding her steady as she stepped across the hilly terrain.

'Oh…' she said as realisation dawned. She'd entirely lost track of the weeks since the nausea had stopped and the tiredness had begun. 'Is that today?'

'It is.' Grayson smiled as he stepped behind her, holding her close against his chest. 'Happy Platonic Baby-Making Deal Day.'

She smiled at the warmth of him holding her, and at the reminder of the day that felt like a lifetime ago. The day that had begun with her waking up and thinking that all her perfect plans had been ruined and had ended with her in the arms of the man who would become the closest thing to home she had ever felt.

'Hmm…so how is the whole platonic part going for you?' she asked.

'Best business deal of my life.'

'You know, some people have first date anniversaries…'

'Those people sound very boring. Some people have Paris—we have a Swiss fertility clinic mix-up.'

'You were so frazzled.' She laughed.

'You'd have been frazzled too if you'd just realised you wanted the very thing you'd always said you didn't.' He kissed her again, harder this time. 'And then you came along and ruined all my playboy plans.'

'Oh, I remember strict bachelor Grayson…he was such a cranky man.'

'He was misunderstood,' Grayson chided. 'Not surprising, considering he refers to himself in the third person. Who knew one freak snowstorm was all it would take to change everything.'

'For the better, I hope?'

'The best. And now, with this next chapter coming our way…' He rubbed the soft skin beneath her belly button with tender care. 'I've decided it's time for us both to step out of our comfort zones even more. What do you say, Goldilocks? Are you ready to be brave with me?'

'I know that I'm not the most outdoorsy type, but I don't

think I need a pep talk to agree to a picnic.' She smiled—
then realised his jaw was ticking again.

'We're not here for a picnic. Have you any idea where
we are?'

Izzy looked around again at the rolling green hills,
trying to find a landmark. 'Pretty sure we're in a field,
babe...'

'It's ten acres of land, waiting for someone to build
their dream home on it. Our home, if we go ahead with the
sale.' He pulled a rolled-up piece of paper from his jacket
pocket, smoothing it out. 'This is just a blueprint. I've told
the architect that you'll have the final say...'

Izzy looked at the blueprint and felt her throat tighten
painfully. It was a house. Her house. The one she'd told
him about on what she'd thought was their last snowy
night together a lifetime ago. As a child she'd drawn that
square-fronted homestead over and over again, like a mantra, dreaming that one day she might actually get to stay
in one place. He'd remembered it all. Every detail. Even
the red front door.

She closed her eyes, her fragile hormones not strong
enough to withstand the wave of emotion that swept
through her, crumpling her face as the tears began to fall.
But she didn't hold in her tears—not with Grayson. She
let them out freely, burying her face in the safety of her
husband's warm neck as she processed the beauty of his
plans for their future.

For a while Grayson was powerless to do anything but
stand still and shelter Isabel's sobbing form in his arms.
He'd spent the past two months sourcing the perfect location for them to lay down roots, while also reorganising
his greatly reduced schedule for the following year. But

still he knew how sensitive his wife was about the possibility of leaving her first home—the one she had found and fixed up and made her own against all the odds.

He'd prepared himself to allow her whatever reaction came naturally, but seeing her so visibly undone tightened the ever-present knot that had taken hold of his lungs.

'I'm sorry for the tears…' Her voice was barely more than a whisper, her cheek still firmly buried in the layers of his coat as she hiccupped between words.

'Don't apologise, my love. You don't have to say anything at all if it's too much.'

She inhaled a deep breath and sighed, but it wasn't until she lightly thumped her fist against his chest and began to chuckle at her own emotional outburst that he felt the tight bands release his chest.

He framed Isabel's face in his hands, wiping away the last of her tears as she smiled up at him. 'I know we can make our home anywhere,' he said softly. 'But if we want to get serious about our other plans for the future I thought we should get started on settling in a home that would better suit a growing family.'

The little two-bedroom cottage she'd bought had been the perfect part-time home base over the past year, as they'd split their time between Ireland and Grayson's international travel schedule. And it was a perfect size for their soon-to-be family of three. But they had recently decided that adoption was something they both wanted to do too, when the time was right.

'This place is the size of a small county.' She chuckled. 'Exactly how many children are you planning for us to have?'

'As many as you'll let me.' He smirked.

'Let's just focus on this one for now.' She laid one hand

across her stomach, cradling the place where their child grew steadily.

'As far as gifts go…is it too much?' he asked.

'It's *entirely* too much, and I absolutely love it,' she said, reaching up on tiptoe to press her lips to his jaw. 'I love you, no matter where we live. But building our own home together here and filling it with love…it's my dream come true.'

'*You* are my dream come true, Isabel O' Sullivan.'

She grinned, her cheeks turning a bright rosy pink. 'You need to stop saying these things. I'm already one step away from climbing you like a tree at every moment.'

'Well, we *are* in a field.' Grayson moved his lips along the soft shell of her ear, his voice a sultry whisper. 'How about I stand very still and you show off those climbing skills?'

'I was hoping you'd say that.'

No matter how many times he kissed this beautiful woman, every time felt just as explosive and all-consuming as the first. Her hands wrapped around his neck, scorching his skin and holding him close as she commanded and demanded from him. He gathered the firm, luscious swells of her behind in his hands and pulled her up against the hard ridge of his erection, growling when she moaned into his mouth.

He was vaguely aware that they were in a muddy field, and that it had begun to drizzle with rain again, but for once he was too happy to care about the details. Their kiss was one of pure need, filled with joy and passion for the life they were creating together, both inside and all around them. Desire vibrated along his nerve-endings, igniting the passion that never seemed too far away when they were together, and spurring him on to claim her body completely in the way he knew best.

But then the wind stilled for a brief moment, allowing just enough silence for the low, growling protest of Isabel's stomach to be heard.

'I think your climbing will have to wait until after brunch.' He smirked, letting out a full laugh at the resulting pout that transformed her kiss-swollen lips.

'Okay, but promise me we'll come back.'

'We're going to be here quite a lot, I'd imagine. As I'm self-appointed project manager. I can't guarantee it will be ready before the baby arrives...but I think I'm going to enjoy the challenge of trying.'

They walked hand in hand back across the rolling green landscape that was to become their family home, and Grayson felt peace wash over him with every tiny drop of rain that landed upon his skin. He loved the temperamental Irish weather just as much as he loved his chaotic wife and the way she never did anything he expected.

'Are you seriously going to try to build an entire house in six months?' she asked, chewing on her lower lip. 'Is that not quite fast?'

'Darling, most of our relationship has been fast.'

'I wouldn't change a thing about our fast track to happy-ever-after,' she said, and smiled, twirling into his arms for another kiss.

* * * * *

WEDDING NIGHT
IN THE KING'S BED

CAITLIN CREWS

MILLS & BOON

CHAPTER ONE

"YOU DON'T HAVE to marry him," Helene Archibald's cousin, best friend, and maid of honor said urgently—and unsolicited—as they stood together in the antechamber of the cathedral.

Outside the small yet ornate little room there were the sounds of organs and a great many people and a grand regal destiny besides, but here there was only the two of them. And Helene's astonishingly prodigious bridal train, pouring all over the old stone floor in a slithering cascade of elegant ivory fabric. Not to mention what had to be every flower in the whole of the Kingdom of Fiammetta, which had been nestled high in the Alps between Italy and France since the Dark Ages, as if to scoff at the frigid January weather with every bright and fragile blossom.

Her cousin, perhaps emboldened by the way her voice echoed between them and the flowers and the dour religious iconography on the stout old walls, carried on with a certain resolute passion. "Who cares if he's a whole king? I'll spirit you away myself."

Helene found this sweet, and unnecessary, but found herself questioning the logistics of the claim all the same. "Would we run off by foot? Down all the closed-off streets monitored by the palace guards and, last I checked, crowded with well-wishers?" She considered, and thinking about an exit strategy she didn't actually want was a nice change from standing about, heart rate alarmingly high, waiting to rush out into the main part of the church so she could then…walk. Very, very slowly up an acre or two of aisle to marry a man who was indeed *a whole king* in front of a crowd both in person and via all the cameras. "And if we somehow made it through, what would we do then? Dressed like this, no less. Would we clamber up the side of the nearest mountain and hope we could slide on our backsides all the way into France?" She gave the endless train a bit of a fluff so that it slithered out even farther across the stones. "In fairness, this might make an excellent slide. Assuming we chose the right mountain, that is. I hear some of these peaks on the Italian side are quite treacherous."

Faith, lovely and loyal Faith, puffed herself up as if prepared to take off in an immediate sprint for the white-capped hills when, until today, Helene could not recall her soft and sweet cousin committing to anything more physically taxing than a saunter down to a sunny beach to lounge about beneath an umbrella. "Only say the word, Helene. I mean it."

"I know you do," Helene assured her. The organ music out in the main part of the cathedral began to climb and swell, soaking in through the walls. There was a sudden uptick in the sounds of muffled coughs and shuffling feet from the hundreds of elite and important guests. She imagined the King himself was already there, standing at the head of the aisle as if the flying buttresses had been arranged to highlight his glory, not God's. They might have been, at that. She smiled, though inside her body, hidden away as it was in yards upon yards of white silk and ivory lace, something darker and deeper…*hummed*. "But I think

I might as well go through with it, don't you? Since everyone has gone to all this bother?"

"I hope that is one of your charmless jokes, Helene," said her father, then, closing the door to the rest of the cathedral that she hadn't heard him open. With his usual fastidious precision. Then he merely stood there, pinning her with that cold glare of his. "Of course you're *going through with it*. This is your wedding to the King of Fiammetta, for the love of all that is holy. It does not require *thought*."

What Helene wanted to say was, *Not for you, Papa, I know.*

But she had long since decided that there was no point arguing with her father. Herbert Marcel Archibald was slim like a wire, always vibrating with outrage and insult. There was nothing fruitful to be gained in debating him on any topic. The last time she had attempted it had been before her lovely, happy, bright beacon of a mother had died.

After Mama had gone, there was nothing to argue about. Helene did not expect her father to *see* her, much less *know* her, and he had not pretended to attempt either one. Instead, he had made his expectations for her excessively clear: she was to make a brilliant marriage, as, indeed, her own mother had done with him. Helene was to carry on this tradition of marrying up. She was to excel in all things so she might make herself nothing short of a shiny prize for him to barter away, the better to bolster his own wealth and consequence, as Archibalds had been doing for generations.

Helene had not exactly been thrilled with this fate, having harbored her share of dreams in which she imagined herself, variously, as an astronaut, a judge, and a mermaid. But she'd remembered the stories her graceful, warm mother had told her. Stories of princesses and castles. Fairy tales and happy endings that came from things like arranged marriages—much nicer to contemplate than the age-old games men like her father preferred to play.

She liked to remind herself that she could have rebelled, if she wished. Helene could have turned her back on her father and all his demands, but whenever the urge to do that rose up in her, she reminded herself that Mama never had. That she had stayed with Herbert and despite the obvious chill, had claimed she was happy.

I am safe and cared for, Helene had heard her mother tell Faith's mother, her sister, long ago. *Not all of us are made for passion. Some of us bloom more quietly.*

Helene had decided, then and there, that if she could bloom as her mother had, that would be a life well spent indeed.

And it had certainly been a frosty half a decade since the cold fall day they'd laid her beloved Mama to rest, but Helene liked to remind herself that she'd *chosen* to stay with her father. To submit to his demands and expectations. To do the things she knew her own mother had done, in her time, and how bad could all that cold civility be, really? She'd grown up watching her parents *freeze* at each other, and her mother had called that a kind of blooming.

She'd started to consider herself an icy little rose.

Just say the word, Faith mouthed at her now.

Because *her* parents had married for love. Something they could do, Helene knew, because her own mother—as eldest daughter—had not.

"Come, Helene," Herbert snapped at her, as if the ceremony was something he could do on his own. As if she was keeping him from *his* wedding.

"Yes, Papa," she murmured, as she always did, shooting a smile Faith's way.

And thought about her mother, who would have loved this day no matter how it came about. A cathedral. A kingdom.

An honest-to-God *king*.

Mama would have thought this was nothing short of a festival of blooming.

Helene took her father's impatient arm, and let Faith tuck her away behind the overtly traditional veil no one had asked her if she wanted to wear. Herbert then led her, with all possible ostentation, to the great doors of the cathedral proper, where the King's royal guard stood with expressions of great solemnity.

No one checked in with her. No one asked if *she* was ready.

Helene told herself that was likely because she *exuded* readiness, as was expected.

The guards waited for a signal from the palace aide dressed in finery that managed to look as capable as it did chic, who cocked her head toward what Helene knew by now was an earpiece. The aide spoke softly.

Inside the main part of the cathedral, the organ music swelled anew, into a piece of music that sounded so ornate it made Helene's bones seem to ache inside her skin—or perhaps, she chided herself with a lot less of the drama she knew her father had always disliked in her mother, it was simply a draft from the cold winter's day outside.

But when Helene thought of her mother's most loved stories, the ones she had told time and again that were the most magical of all, she sighed a little. Quietly, there beneath her veil where no one could hear her. And decided to believe it was the music.

The aide pressed a manicured finger to her ear and nodded at the guards, then smiled by rote at Herbert. Over

Helene's swaddled form, making it clear that she was the person here with the least significance.

Or, perhaps, she had been identified as the one least likely to complain.

Faith murmured something that sounded like *Ready when you are*, which Helene decided to pretend was about the wedding and not escaping it. She waited a breath, then another, and then moved in front of Helene only when Herbert made a huffing sound, accepting the bouquet the palace aide handed her as she slipped in one of the smaller doors to start down the aisle.

The music carried on, a tumbling, soaring symphony that twined with the humming inside of Helene and made every part of her...electric.

Then the great doors were hauled open. The crowd within rose, turned to look at her, and she settled in for a nice long think about...well. Everything that had led her here.

To this cathedral halfway up a mountain in a tiny kingdom that alpine dreams were made of. Where she had lied by omission to her beloved cousin, because she'd allowed Faith to believe that she was being forced into this marriage. It was easier to pretend that she was. Because Helene wasn't sure she had the vocabulary to explain what had happened to her to make her a far more willing participant than Faith was likely to imagine possible...

Besides, it was a very long walk down the cathedral's main aisle. So long that Helene couldn't really make out *which* figure down there at the end was the man who was the real star of this show today. There was a scrum of finery blocking the view and the bishop himself looked resplendent, and yet she somehow doubted that her august groom would *blend*.

Her groom. The King of Fiammetta himself. One

Later, she would curl up with Helene in the
spin out the most fantastic stories about how
riage would be a wondrous thing, no m
Papa imagined. That she and her d
have adventures and slay drago
balls, and live a happy and gl

But when it turned out th
lovely, then objectively
Herbert had gotten g
turned out to be c
sive Swiss boa
man sent his
that she
about
trul

Gianluca, more an *immensity* than

That thing inside her that she thought was him, or his, *hummed* all the more.

Marrying advantageously, and always ambitiously, was the single task of an heiress, her father had told her. Over and over again. Back when she was small he had talked quite openly about the consolidation of hereditary assets—the usual estate or two—and the way in which that could, if done well, create an upgrade in his own, personal status as well as hers. Which ought to have been her primary goal, clearly. Her mother would catch Helene's eye across the long, polished table where children were permitted to appear only if silent, her bright eyes brimming with laughter.

nursery and
             w Helene's mar-
          atter what her silly
        ashing prince would
      ns, dance at marvelous
     orious and magical life.
    at Helene was going to be first
   pretty, then really quite beautiful,
  reedy. Especially when Helene had
 ever as well, locked away in her exclu-
rding school where a certain sort of rich
daughter if he wanted to be absolutely certain
could have no personal life he did not know all
There was no sneaking out of the Institut. It was a
y lovely prison, set behind high walls and surrounded
by guards, where there were never more than ten girls in
each year and all of them were earmarked by others for
the sort of lives that took place in hushed, elegant castles
of one sort or another the world over.

There wasn't much to do but study, take classes, and
dream of Prince Charmings they were not allowed to meet
without familial oversight.

Helene had always considered herself lucky that her father actually let her finish her education, which was not
the case for many of her schoolmates. Plus the extra finishing year that the school was famous for—because, it
was whispered, certain monarchs who married for love
had made use of the Institut's *finishing* when their scandalously lower-brow queens needed a quick gloss-up.

She'd graduated in full just before her twentieth birthday and had expected her father to put her directly on the
auction block—figuratively, she hoped. She had antici-

pated a heap of tedious social engagements under her father's watchful eye, where she would have to not only be effortlessly charming as was expected from a graduate of the Institut and the Archibald heiress, but suffer her father's commentary on whether or not he thought she'd hit the notes he wished for her to hit.

In truth, she hadn't been sure that she would make it through a week like that, much less the entire summer season her father had been threatening her with when he'd installed her in his summer estate in Provence that year. The men he had in mind for her were all wealthy and titled and Helene and Faith had texted back and forth about them, tracking them all across the internet, and trying their best to turn their evident flaws—from mistresses to gambling to the kind of partying that never ended well and so on—into charming quirks.

Because it was easier to make it all a game. It was almost fun that way.

Or we could run away, Faith would say, as if she had anything to run from herself, with parents who adored and indulged her. *I think I would make a* smashing *artist in some charmingly bohemian city somewhere, living off my wits and my* creative energy.

I believe, Helene would reply, *that you are thinking of Broadway musicals, not reality.*

And while it was true that reality felt a bit heavier on this side of graduation, with actual candidates for her glorious marriage apparently queueing up across Europe, Helene was still resolved to go through with it. Because her father was not a warm man. This she had always known. But if this was the only way she could show her love to him—the only way she knew how to honor her mother now that she was gone and certainly the only way he could receive it, *if* he could receive it at all—she rather thought it was the least she could do.

She, too, could bloom quietly. Safe and cared for, in a very particular way, as she had been all her life. It was only that her mother had managed to make it seem brighter—but then, Helene could do that too. When she was settled in with the man her father chose for her.

But then, one day, the royal messenger had appeared.

In person, before the first party, where Helene had been expected to make her marriageable debut. He had arrived ostentatiously and had proclaimed the good news: Helene had—by what means, he did not specify—managed to secure the notice of the grand and notably great King of Fiammetta himself, who would very much like to meet her.

It had not been an invitation.

My God, girl, Herbert had seethed at her that very evening, beside himself with notions of crowns and consequence run amok. *If you ruin this, I shall never forgive you.*

Helene had not felt there was anything to be won by pointing out that she had not ruined anything yet. That she had been all that was good and obedient, all her life, so much so that Herbert really ought to have been under the impression that she was biddable.

That he was not, she could admit, pleased her. It must mean that her real self lurked *just there* no matter how diffident and obliging she attempted to act in his presence.

Accepting the King's kind invitation that wasn't an invitation at all had been an involved process.

Helene had met with a succession of aides, each of whom had arrived with a new agenda and different versions of combative interview styles wrapped up in deadly courtesy. They had seen her alone and with her father. She had been required to surrender all her devices with a list of all her passwords to anything a person might wish to access online. She had been called upon to account for what seemed like her every last movement since she was a child.

Usually they already knew the answers themselves, but wanted to see what she would say.

You texted your cousin about our last meeting. The most ferociously correct of all the aides had confronted her one day, about a month into the process. *You told her, if I recall it correctly, that you were beginning to suspect that the King might not, in fact, exist. Is that not so?*

I did text that, Helene had agreed, and had been glad her father was not present. He would not have liked the appalled way the woman had gazed at her. He would have forbidden her from contacting Faith, possibly ever again, given he had never cared much for Helene's mother's family anyway. Helene had laughed without meaning to. *But can you blame me?*

The King himself had descended the next day.

She almost tripped, here in the cathedral, as she recalled it. She wasn't sure how she kept from sprawling out in an inelegant heap right there with the eyes of the Kingdom upon her—though perhaps her father's grip on her had something to do with it.

Helene let him guide her along. And let herself think back to that June morning that still stood out so clearly to her, marking a *before* and an *after*.

Kings did not simply *turn up* in places, not even when they were attempting to go incognito. So while it was true that he had *descended* upon her father's tidy château, there had been some small bit of notice. Another messenger had appeared that morning, followed swiftly by an advance team who had treated her father's estate to a sweeping security review even though several other similar reviews had already been undertaken.

While the King's security secured the perimeter of the property, again, Herbert had leaped at the chance to direct Helene in how she needed to behave on such a momentous occasion. He had conferred with both the palace aides and his own staff to curate the perfect introductory scene.

No detail was beneath his notice.

He sent Helene back to her rooms three different times because he felt her hair was first inappropriate, then wanton, and then again, too casual. He was only satisfied when her long, usually wavy, dark brown hair was tamed into submission and woven into a loose French braid that he deemed neither too casual nor too sophisticated, both *kisses of death*.

Her outfit was subjected to the same scrutiny. And if Helene had learned anything in her time at the Institut, it was not to ask perfectly reasonable questions of unreasonable people. Like, for example, shouldn't she simply present *herself* to the King? Given that it was she who had caught his notice? It was certainly not down to her father's machinations—Herbert had never dared imagine *royalty* might be within his reach.

Ladies, she had been taught again and again, did not lower themselves to argue. They endured with dignity and then, when it was time, they *encouraged* their way toward different outcomes.

Meaning, she bit her tongue. She changed as directed into these trousers and then that gown. She exchanged bold accessories for subtle hints. She scrubbed off this round of cosmetics and started anew, time and again, until her father deemed what she wore suitable enough.

How funny, Helene thought now as she measured one

step, then the next, that she couldn't remember any longer what that final outfit had been. Every time she thought she'd come round to the final choice, she remembered instead that her father had ordered her to change it. Or that one of the palace aides had lifted a brow at the sight of it, which her father had taken to mean regal disdain from afar.

What she remembered distinctly was that she had never felt less like herself when she'd been ordered, at last, to go and wait in one of the drawing rooms where she was directed to arrange herself artfully on the settee. Her father would greet His Majesty, she was informed, and then they would all sit down for a bit of a chat. Perhaps there would be a drink, depending on what sort of man this king was, and then Herbert would excuse himself.

And I trust that you will behave as you ought, her father had barked at her, right there in front of the King's advance team and the entirety of his own household staff. *When in doubt, smile and remain silent.*

She'd sat in the chosen drawing room, practicing. She and the other girls in her year at the Institut had actually held a contest to see who had the most *enigmatic smile* of the lot, because they all knew full well that the right one could be used as a weapon. Sadly, Helene had never mastered the art. There was too much hope and too many fairy tales in her smile.

In that she was her mother's daughter.

And she'd grown rather cross with herself as she waited, because she was actually getting nervous. Helene had not understood why *she* should be nervous about some man she didn't even know and might very well never lay eyes upon again. It didn't matter if he was a king or one of her father's business associates. It was all the same to her, wasn't it.

What she chose to believe, then and always, was that her real job was to make certain that she followed her mother's directives as best she could. Meaning that no matter the situation, she was to look for the magic. She was to find the marvel in the thing, and no matter if it was decidedly un-marvelous.

And if there are no Prince Charmings to be found? she'd asked, presciently, she thought. *What will I do then?*

You'll look deep and you'll find him, her sweet mother had replied, squeezing her hand tight. *I have no doubt,* mon chou.

Nervousness didn't help anything, she decided then, and she'd gotten up from her decorative position on the settee her father had indicated. She'd moved over to the great doors, done in a mullioned glass that opened up over one of the château's many patios. This one in particular let out to her mother's garden.

That was not why her father had chosen it, Helene knew. He had chosen it because all of the art on the walls were recognizable masterpieces. Herbert did like to show off.

Helene had opened up the doors and stepped outside, breathing in the sweet summer air. She'd walked over to the edge of the patio, glanced back over her shoulder, and had decided she had plenty of time to pad down the stairs, breathe deep of her mother's favorite flowers, and collect herself.

Blooming lavender made her feel safe again. Hints of rosemary made her smile. And the first flush of the summer roses felt like the sort of happy-ever-afters her mother had always loved best.

Helene had breathed deep.

And when she turned around again, prepared to start

back in and arrange herself artfully, silently, and dutifully once more, he was there.

She had squatted down to get a really deep breath—or ten—of her favorite fragrance, a mixture of all those hints of herbs and flowers that reminded her so strongly of her mother, and so he had seemed tall enough to block out the sky itself. Helene had stopped breathing. Her throat had gone almost painfully dry. At the same time, there was a sudden deep and thudding thing that nearly knocked her back on her behind into the dirt—

And it took her far too long to understand it was her own heart.

She gazed up at him, all the way up at him, and deep inside her—low and insistent—that humming thing took root.

He made her shake from the inside out.

She did not ask it was really him. She knew him at once, without question. She had seen the photographs of him that his own staff had presented her, and the many pictures of him that littered the internet, but Helene knew she would have recognized him all the same.

Because he stood there at the top of the patio stairs as if he expected nothing else than to find women—if not everyone, everywhere—writhing about in the dirt at his feet.

As if they often did exactly that.

Helene knew full well that they did. She'd seen the pictures. He was, according to many sources, the most eligible man in the world.

And for a moment there, she couldn't decide if she ought to throw herself face down on the dirt before him or not, because every lesson she had ever learned about comportment and elegant manners at the Institut seemed to have deserted her entirely.

There was nothing of *her* left. There was only that humming. There was only him, the actual king, and somehow, one single stray thought: that this man was not the least bit photogenic.

He was widely held to be handsome. She'd thought so herself when she'd studied the many pictures of him and had even harbored a thought or two—that she would deny if asked, because it seemed silly and unseemly at once—that perhaps this whole arranged marriage deal might not be as terrible as she'd imagined because of this handsomeness.

Perhaps he would be wretched, she'd told herself, but at least he would be pleasant to look at. For Helene was astonished to discover that, if anything, every photograph she'd ever seen of Gianluca San Felice, King of Fiammetta, made him look ugly.

That was the effect of his stark, stern, overwhelming male beauty. It was so much *more* in person. It was like a force field.

He struck her like a natural disaster. A storm of epic proportions.

That was the sort of *beautiful* this man was.

Helene was not certain how she withstood the first sight of him. She had stood up, somehow, though her body had not felt like her own. She'd felt sunburned, suddenly, as if she'd been out in the summer sun for hours instead of mere moments. As if it had roasted her very bones.

The cold, German-accented voice of the Institut headmistress made itself known inside her then, counting out seconds like a metronome. And she remembered, almost too late, to drop into the appropriate curtsy one typically offered at the sight of royalty.

Helene was grateful, in a way she never had been before, for the headmistress's insistence that they practice these things again and again and again. She was grateful that her body did what it had practiced so many times with ease, as if it was all muscle memory, because it gave her time to figure out how to breathe again. How to keep herself from toppling over. How to try her best to wrestle with that bizarre sunburn that seemed as prickly and hot on the inside as it was on her skin.

"Rise," the King ordered her softly enough, but with evident command, and she did.

And then, for an endless, airless moment, he simply studied her.

That prickling sensation got worse. Or better, maybe. In any case, it was more and it washed over her, changing her as it went. Shifting things she hadn't known were there, or moveable. There were too many competing urges inside her, then. She'd wanted to say something smart to impress him. She'd wanted to prove, with a few carefully chosen words, that she was so much more than whatever he'd seen in whatever dossier he'd received on her. That she wasn't her father, who she understood was not a man that other men admired.

She was *this close* to announcing to this impossibly compelling man, this *king*, that she was a whole person, brimming with contradictions and obsessions and marvelous, secret bits that she hardly knew herself.

But she didn't dare.

In a few moments I am going to go around to the front of this château and make my official entrance, he told her. Eventually. He did not smile, but she felt the urge to smile back at him as if he had. *But you see, I have learned that it behooves me to take a sneak peek first at whatever woman I am set to meet.*

She started to speak, then remembered that he was no ordinary man. He was a king and there was etiquette for all interactions between kings and commoners, and for all she knew this was a trap.

But his eyes were so dark, like the middle of the longest night, and they gleamed. *You may speak freely. After all, I am the one lurking about in your garden, am I not?*

She knew better than to take him at his word. Not entirely. This was a game, and obviously one he had played before. But she did not remain silent, either. *What is it you're hoping to find?* she asked. *When you take these* sneak peeks *of yours?*

It is hugely instructive, he replied, easily enough that she realized, with a certain dizzy sensation, that he could be charming. This immensity of a man who stood before her so easily, so used was he to being gazed up at in this manner. *Often the house is in disarray, or too clean, like a crime scene of some kind. Often the woman I am to meet is barking unhinged orders at servants, screaming at everyone she sees, and otherwise behaving in a manner she would not if she knew I was watching.*

Forgive me, Helene had said. *But I am given to understand that a great many royal personages often behave in precisely this manner.*

It had been a risky gambit. She'd waited for him to draw himself up in umbrage and affront, and march away, having crossed her off his list. And she'd wondered what had possessed her when it surely would have been easier to simply murmur something inoffensive instead.

Perhaps she had even been holding her breath.

Though she forgot about that—and everything else—when he smiled.

If his gaze was night, his smile was a whole, bright summer, and as he beamed it down at her she saw entirely too much. That he was a man, a mortal, and more—that he could indeed make a woman a fine husband, if he chose. And then, in a rush of heat and wonder and something sharp, like need, she saw the kind of future she hadn't dared imagine for herself unfurl before her. A hand to hold quietly, in the back of a car, no words required. Dancing with her head tipped back and his smile all the music she needed. Laughter, and children, and rooms they made sing with the force of all the things they were to each other—

All of that as he gazed down at her, that smile such a bit of unexpected magic that she rather thought the deep black night of his eyes was shot through with stars.

A great many royal personages are appalling human beings, he'd said, the smile in his voice now too, like dawn breaking over a new day, all of it laced with the very things she'd just seen stampede through her. *Why do you imagine I have come to look for this behavior in advance? I know it too well and wish to avoid it, at all costs.*

I'm sorry to disappoint you, she replied, and her smile felt reckless. But it was impossible to contain. *I suppose I could soundly abuse the plants, if I liked, but I doubt if I did that they would bloom as they do. This was my mother's garden and I tended it with her when I was small. The fragrance of the things she planted makes me happy. That's all.*

His smile faded, but what took its place was more complicated. More…considering. *And this is what you wished? To be happy, today of all days?*

This is what I wish every day, Helene corrected him, still smiling, though she dropped her gaze to the shoots of lavender and ran her fingertips down the buds. *It is not always achievable, I grant you.*

It occurred to her that could be taken as a slight, but he'd still been looking at her in that narrow manner, as if she was a calculation he needed to solve. *And if I told you that I do not believe in happiness?* His tone was light.

We must all believe in something, Your Majesty. Surely.

I believe in duty, Miss Archibald.

My mother used to say that we must plant flowers wherever we can make them grow, instead of waiting for flowers to bloom. Duty is what you make of it, in other words.

He'd studied her for another moment, and she had never felt anything like the weight of his gaze. The intensity of his attention. The heat of him, like his very own sun.

That prickling within her seemed to melt into the humming until it was all one thing, shivering and hot, a beautiful tornado. It tore through her, laying waste to whoever she'd been before, so sudden and so devastating that she wasn't sure if she'd drawn a single breath since the moment she'd looked up and seen him there.

King Gianluca inclined his head, and some odd sort of light or other gleamed then, in the encompassing darkness of his gaze.

I look forward to meeting you, Miss Archibald, he said in his commanding way, and then he turned and strode back around the side of the house. Taking the air and the blue sky and the gold and purple of Provence with him.

For a moment she'd stood there, dazed. She wasn't sure if she'd imagined the whole thing—but then her body was moving of its own accord again. It carried her back up the stairs, into through the same mullioned glass doors to settle herself on that delicate settee as if she was still the same person she'd been before she'd gone out into the garden.

As if she could ever be the same again, seared straight through as she was.

It had seemed a lifetime, though she supposed it could as easily have been mere moments, before her father's voice could be heard in the hall outside. Before the palace aides found their way inside, and then, with great fanfare, announced His Royal Majesty, King Gianluca of Fiammetta himself.

Helene rose, then sank into the curtsy that was expected of her—no matter that she had already performed this mark of respect outside, he had acted as if that meeting was to be kept between them, surely—and when she rose, he was smiling directly at her once again.

Not the same smile. This one was a slight curve of his hard, stern lips and no more, but Helene had known all the same. She had known, at that very moment, that she was going to marry him. That she would marry him and that whole future she could see sweeping out before her would be hers.

It was sweeping through her now, here in the cathedral at last. It had carried her along through the rest of the summer, walks in that garden and visits in her father's parlors, that smile of his so rare and unpredictable and yet world-changing every time. It had buoyed her during her father's lectures and critiques that grew more scathing in the lead-up to the actual proposal, such as it was, involving as it did meetings with her father and staff and stacks of contracts to sign and too much attention given to the few words he said to her personally, where everyone else could hear, that smile she'd come to think of as hers turned to stars in his gaze.

Stars and a smile, that was what she'd held on to that fall, as her life turned inside out and she became the property of the palace, trotted out for photo opportunities at events both grand and humble. The King's date for another royal's wedding abroad. Or a seemingly casual walk together on a crisp afternoon in Fiammetta, caught by engineered "happenstance" and plastered across every gossip rag in existence.

They had never been truly alone, and so she'd taken that smile and their imagined future and the stars in his dark night gaze with her to bed, curled around them like pillows she could shape to hold her as she wished, and dreamed about what was to come.

And when she lifted her gaze toward the end of the aisle once more, she found him standing there at last.

Resplendent and self-possessed, and even more shockingly magnetic than she'd remembered, when she'd last seen him the night before during a highly photographed celebratory dinner.

His dark black gaze seemed to hold fast on her as she moved down the aisle and as it did, it kicked off a new lightning storm within her even as it settled her, somehow, in the same breath.

There had to be another mile to walk, at the least, but Helene scarcely noticed.

All she could feel was him. That gaze. That storm inside her. She trembled, and knew her father felt it where their arms were linked because the crook of his elbow tightened around her hand, and the look he shot at her was more of a shout.

It confused her for a moment. But then she realized. Herbert thought she was having second thoughts.

When nothing could be further from the truth.

Because this was the secret she hadn't told even Faith. That there wasn't a single part of her, inside or out, that did not wish to marry this man. And he could have been anyone. It had nothing to do with kings or crowns, thrones or settlements. She didn't care about any of that.

She would have married Gianluca San Felice no matter who he was.

Because when he looked at her, her entire body blazed into life. When he took her hand in his, she felt thick and wet between her legs, and silly straight through. He made her breasts ache. He made her want to press herself against him, again and again, and try out the things she'd only read in books.

Her cousin might not have approved of this marriage, but Helene had known that it was what she wanted back on the first day she'd met Gianluca. It felt like an inevitability, something necessary—not a choice. A lightning bolt from above and she had no choice but to meet it head-on or let it burn her to ash.

Though this felt a lot like both.

After an eternity, her father delivered her to the head of the aisle, passing off his daughter to this king who claimed her.

Gianluca took her hand and everything in her ignited, the way it always did. That hum became a roar, and wound itself into a delirious tangle everywhere it touched.

And then everything became that tangle. That rush of heat and wonder.

That glorious future dancing before her, stars and his smile, the things that would be only theirs when they were finally alone together.

That humming within her only expanded as the ceremony began, until it was her turn to speak and she could not simply shout out her joy at this union the way she wanted to do. She had to sound elegant enough for a king. Sophisticated enough to become his queen.

She repeated what the bishop said, and then, finally, it was time. Gianluca slid a ring on her finger to match the diamond solitaire he'd put there a few months before. His mouth so stern, his dark eyes so deep.

And there were only two words to say, but Helene meant them with every part of her aching, needy body, and the whole of her soul.

"I do," she whispered.

Then he lifted the veil and kissed her for the very first time, making her his wife.

And teaching her how precious little she knew about fire.

CHAPTER TWO

IT WAS NOT until Gianluca, the King of Fiammetta whether he liked it or not, sat at the high table set aside for the royal couple's use while the spectacularly elegant reception went on all around him, that he allowed himself to think about anything save his duty.

In any detail, that was.

Because he needed to think only of his duty and that had proven surprisingly difficult when Helene—now his *wife*—was around.

He found he was deeply wary of precisely how difficult it had become, even today, when his marriage had always been an inevitability. It had only been a question of *when* and *who* and he had never tried, like some men in his position, to shirk his responsibilities in that area. On the contrary, Gianluca had been attempting to find the perfect queen for his kingdom ever since his father's death some ten years before had catapulted the matter of Gianluca's marriage from a hypothetical *someone, someday* to a priority.

But despite his attention to the task, the proper wife—and queen—had remained outside his grasp. Until now.

Until Helene, who was not afraid of the dirt or of saying things to him others would not dare. Until Helene, who had a certain earthy appeal that had him very nearly ready to toss this whole party out the front doors of the palace so he could explore it all he liked—

Yet that was one of the details he was *not* going to think about. Not quite yet.

Because unlike his parents, he had taken his time seeking out the right woman for the job—and he had no illusions on that score. He might flatter himself that being his wife might be a position any woman would aspire to, but being Queen of Fiammetta was a job. A thankless career, in many ways, with no promotions and no deviations, though there were a few perks along the way. He needed to make certain that he knew what he was getting into with any woman put forward for the position. He had studied the hopefuls who had been trotted out for his approval and he had only made this choice after digging, deep, into all there was to know about Helene Archibald—now Her Majesty the Queen of Fiammetta, for good or ill.

She was out there in the sea of people before him, talking with that cousin of hers while all the self-important people in his kingdom studied her, looking for flaws—when there were none. Helene was as poised as she was beautiful, gracious to all who came to bestow their well wishes upon her even when it was clear that they were poking around for gossip fodder, and kept sliding looks in his direction.

Always fully cognizant of precisely where he was in the ballroom at any given time.

He was inclined to think this marriage might be more than good. It might just be the best decision he'd made yet.

But he did not gaze at her the way he wished to do. Because he did not intend to make his marriage the talking point of his reign, as his father had done, not even tonight. He would not allow it.

Gianluca had long practice in hiding his true thoughts behind a neutral expression, and he was glad of it now. Because he didn't like to think about his parents too much. Not if it could be avoided. There were the darker, private moments he had half convinced himself were merely nightmares he'd had as a child—but he did not permit himself to dig into *that*. What he did not care for, and what offended him still, was the stain that their overly publicized antics had left on this kingdom. And because of that stain, the weight he felt upon him at all times to prove himself nothing like the pair of them.

He would never allow any queen of his to behave as his own mother had, making a mockery of her vows and dragging the crown through the mud. Parading the private business of the palace out into the public eye and making certain it stayed there in some twisted, misguided bid for revenge because—as far as Gianluca could discern—her *feelings had been hurt*.

And if the feelings he recalled most vividly from his childhood had been vile and unsettling, alarming and often frightening—

But no. That was a story his mother told, when surely, if it had been as bad as all that, she would not have stayed. The truth, then and now, was that she was addicted to the drama. And the attention she could wring from it all.

He checked himself then because too many eyes were upon him now, as always. He inclined his head toward a pack of diplomats. He gave his public version of a smile to a set of his distant cousins. But he did not beckon anyone to approach him and thus no one dared.

Not even the loathsome Lady Anselma, one of his mother's boon companions, who had made herself a tidy little cottage industry over the years as his mother's "unnamed source from within the palace." He smiled, as he knew he must, but Gianluca had no use for her or the rest of the many Dowager Queen Elettra apologists in the Kingdom, forever making up excuses for his mother's actions and trying them out one after the next when the previous one failed to garner enough sympathy. As it always did, eventually.

He knew all the excuses by heart. They claimed she had been too young when she'd married King Alvize a few months shy of her nineteenth birthday, when Gianluca had already been in the military at the same age—an adult in every sense of the term and expected to act accordingly. Elettra had been an adult who had been perfectly capable of competing in her beloved dressage circles at the highest levels. *The Champion Queen*, they had called her when she'd won the highest medal in the sport six months before she'd been elevated to the Fiammettan throne.

No one had ever suggested she was too young or too foolish to compete at that level.

They claimed she hadn't known any better, which Gianluca had never understood. For it was made perfectly clear in the wedding vows themselves. Were her supporters truly claiming that an aristocratic young champion gold medalist…could not comprehend a set of wedding vows? One either followed them or did not, but they were not *confusing*.

Surely his mother's behavior made her character plain. It always had for him.

His favorite—which was to say, the least persuasive argument, to his mind—was that his own father was to blame for the betrayals that had been practiced upon him. Sometimes he remembered those stormy nights inside the King and Queen's apartments, when he'd hid from the shouting—but he knew, now, that his father's reactions had been warranted. Because there were always the endless stories of his father's first great love, the Lady Lorenza, who had been promised to another and raised by a man who kept *his* vows to his daughter's betrothed. No matter that Lorenza had dallied with the King before her official engagement.

Not to mention, it was accepted fact that Alvize and Lorenza had consummated their feelings in a scorching affair that had rendered the tabloids breathless with speculation that Alvize might reverse centuries of Fiammettan tradition by marrying her.

When everyone knew that it was written in the law of the Kingdom that the King must marry a virgin bride.

His mother was the one who had accused his father for the sake of that drama she craved, he thought now, firmly, as he always did. When she was the one who had sinned.

Gianluca had no sympathy for anyone involved. His mother had been a disaster but his father had been the King and should have handled her better, he thought now, gazing out at the many luminaries who graced the great hall of the palace tonight. Lady Lorenza and his mother were among them, of course, because *he* upheld the traditions and expectations and customs of his position. No matter what.

He could not help but reflect, as he had many times before, that his father had known perfectly well what the rules were. They had been made abundantly clear to Alvize in the same way they had been imparted upon Gianluca when he was still a small child. The many palace tutors whose job it was to see to it that the young kings knew their own traditions made certain of it.

What Gianluca could not get past was one simple truth:

if his father had intended to marry the woman he seemingly loved so deeply, then he should not have let himself get so carried away with her. Even if the so-called scorching affair had been perfectly innocent in private, which Gianluca doubted, his father should have made certain the tabloids never got wind of his attachment to the Lady Lorenza in the first place. If he had been swept away by her, as everyone seemed to think, he should have dedicated himself to negotiations with not only his beloved's father, but the match she'd been meant to make all along.

That he had not done so, to Gianluca's mind, meant that he had not been quite as madly in love as everyone liked to pretend. While either excusing him or demonizing him.

And yet he had knowingly walked wide-eyed into his own destruction, because he'd chosen a woman like Elettra, who craved attention above all things. She could have been in no doubt that Alvize's affections were engaged elsewhere, though she still claimed she had not known of the King's very famous love affair until after the wedding. And it did not matter to Elettra that the object of her husband's supposed affections was married to another by then, and was, by all accounts, faithful to him.

What mattered to Elettra was that *she* was not the center of the King's attention, then or ever, and so she had acted out.

Again and again and again.

She had made no secret of her affairs. She'd thrown them not only in her husband's face, but had made sure that her exploits were tabloid fodder at all times. She sent out her minions to keep her name forever in the press, forever stoking that same fire, forever embarrassing the palace, forever carrying on in full view of all of Europe and the whole of the world besides.

Elettra thought she was thereby punishing the King.

And Gianluca could not say whether that had worked, because his father's emotions had always been hidden in public, but volatile in the palace. And this particular topic had been one his father had declared off-limits when Gianluca had still been an adolescent—unless Alvize was the one raging about it.

The people, meanwhile, had chosen sides in the streets and otherwise told poll after poll that they would prefer a lot less of a soap opera from their monarchy.

What Gianluca did know, however, was that he was the one who had to clean up the mess they'd left behind after his father's death. His parents' scandals were now his problem. Not that he could recall his father, in the whole of his lifetime, ever indicating that he was aware his only son and heir would be left to handle the fallout of the soap opera he'd let play on.

His mother, on the other hand, knew all too well. She was here tonight on sufferance.

Yet Gianluca was not particularly surprised that his mother had somehow failed to get the message he knew full well must have been delivered to her by every aide in the palace and half of the royal guard. Because there was a ripple in the crowd below the raised dais where he sat and there she was. As perhaps he should have expected. Marching right up to him as if she had that right. As if he did not normally make certain she was kept from his sight.

But then, Elettra knew that he would not behave with anything but the utmost courtesy in front of all these people and his proper new bride. She was counting on it.

Gianluca disliked that she was right.

"Will you not rise to greet your own mother?" she asked with a merry sort of laugh that they both knew would look like a bit of maternal devotion, as if the two of them were close. "On your wedding day?"

"Your invitation was all the greeting I intend to give, Madam," he replied icily, though he had to keep the affront from his expression as she helped herself to the chair reserved for his new bride and sat in it. With, again, a familiarity that they both knew would send any number of false messages to the avidly watching throng.

This was another reason Gianluca did not trust her. She was much too good at these games while his father had too often seemed a victim to his own temper.

"The new queen seems like a lovely girl," Elettra said quietly. "But does she know, truly, what she is in for with you? This heart of stone you carry in your chest might crush you both. Not to mention your unwillingness to forgive. You cannot think these will serve you well now you are wed."

"Have you come to give me marital advice?"

She had the grace to wince, however faintly. "I do not offer advice, Gianluca. How could I? Still, you might learn from my example."

"But here's the difference, Madam," Gianluca said, leaning closer to her with a faint smile that would be read as possibly affectionate from afar. He hoped. No doubt reading the truth of his feelings, his personal aide started forward, but Gianluca stopped the man with the barest shake of his head. "My bride will not betray me. She is not you."

And he was well used to his mother's performances by now. The way she tipped her head back as if struck. The way she let her shoulders sag, making herself the very picture of despair for one, single beat before rallying again... But then, she had always been an accomplished actress.

And he knew full well he was not the audience to whom she played.

She liked a crowd, did Elettra.

"My bride does not require your concern, Madam," he said, and rose then, ending the conversation before Elettra could up the ante. "You and she will have no relationship. I see no reason to let you poison the well, simply because you find yourself bored once again."

"I haven't even met the girl," his mother protested.

Gianluca inclined his head with his polished smile on display for all to see. "By design."

He left her there at the table, making his way through his own ballroom and nodding to all those who bowed before him as he passed—taking care to look like the merry groom he rather thought he actually was, all things considered.

Not that he had much experience with merriment.

He blamed his parents for that, too. And try though he did to put Elettra from his mind, he could not understand why his mother still, after all these years, pretended she did not understand how things were done. Or that he was not going to indulge her displays like his father had—something she should have picked up a long while ago, because he had not exactly hidden his criticisms of her even before his father's death. What she should have done tonight was express her gratitude that he had allowed her to attend this wedding at all.

Instead she spoke of his *stone heart.* As if, were that the case, she had not rolled that boulder there herself.

But he caught sight of Helene and thrust all thoughts of the Dowager Queen aside. He made his way toward his bride, who was now in the clutches of her own questionable father, as the grasping little man steered her around the room like a prize bit of horseflesh that he intended to use to open as many doors as he could.

For some men's ambition only grew through their children.

Gianluca knew a lot about that, too.

A hush fell over the little group as he approached, though he noted that it was Helene's father who was the last to take note that the King himself had appeared.

"If I may claim my queen," Gianluca said, quietly enough. But when he spoke, his words created a kind of ripple of reaction. As if he had shouted when he had not. He was used to this effect, so he used it to take Helene's hand and draw her to him.

And he liked very much the way she came to him, that smile all over her face and her steps so light, her lovely eyes fixed to his.

Gianluca was not his father. He was not in love with another woman. He was not in love at all, of course—though he did not mind if the watching crowd thought otherwise. Or even if Helene did, as a sheltered girl likely might in her situation. He had found himself averse to the very notion of love from a young age, so often did his parents bandy it about the palace, hurling it at each other as if the word itself was a weapon.

At the same time, he could not deny that he had liked Helene from the start.

All the options that had been presented to him over the past ten years had been beautiful. He supposed that was a prerequisite when a man was a king. But he had found that most of the beautiful women offered to him were the same sort of beautiful that had nothing to do with their specific looks. They had all been cold. Icy, even. They would, each and every one of them, have looked lovely at his side. They would all have complemented him in their own ways and he imagined that would have been pleasing enough.

But Helene made him…hungry.

He took her hand now, aware that it was cool to the touch but then heated, quickly. He could see that same fire in her cheeks, and watched, fascinated, as it turned the skin of her neck a faint peach hue.

And he remembered standing outside on a summer's morning in France, catching sight of her for the first time. The way she gazed up at him from where she crouched down with surprising elegance to stroke a sprig of lavender in a simple shift dress that only drew attention to her lush beauty.

She had looked at him with a kind of stunned longing, as if he was a wish fulfilled.

When she could not possibly have expected him to appear as he had. They never did. Most of them had never seen him at all before they were formally introduced and never knew that he had seen them first, unguarded.

Helene was no ice queen, no cardboard cutout. She was not yet another exquisitely blue-blooded heiress whose looks vaguely resembled that of an Afghan hound no matter what her coloring might have been. Her father had all the charisma of a pillar of salt, but Helene herself had been something of a revelation.

What shocked him was that, all these months later, she still was.

Her mouth was wide and generous and if she were the sort of woman to paint her lips crimson and wear a dress that made love to her curves, he had no doubt that she could bring whole populations of men to their knees. That she *could*, but did not, only added to her mystique.

Helene's eyes were wide and large and a deep, velvety shade of brown ringed in gold. Her hair was thick and dark and waved languorously down her back tonight, half of it twisted into something breathtakingly elegant at the back of her head to better accentuate the tiara he had presented her from the family collection.

Gianluca had not known until he'd seen her in that garden, all curves and that mouth, how deeply he had longed, the whole of his life, to get his hands on a figure like hers.

It made everything feel…fraught.

He had always thought of his wedding night as one more simple expression of his duty to the crown. Gianluca had always hoped to find a suitable bride with whom that duty would not be a chore, but that was as far as his thinking on the matter had ever gone. Mostly he had been focused on making sure any queen of his had not only a spotless reputation, but was self-possessed enough that he need not fear she would follow in his mother's footsteps.

And yet tonight, he found that all he could think about when he let himself consider the fact of his marriage was the marital bed.

It was unseemly.

He knew too well where *feelings* led.

But no matter what might have surged about within him, Gianluca was a king, not some callow youth, so he pulled her into his arms as the party arranged itself around them to create space on the dance floor.

The orchestra immediately shifted to accommodate him, as was only right and proper, but Gianluca lost all interest in what was going on around them. Because she was his wife. His queen. And she was lush and she was curvy, and yet she was as light in his arms as if she had trained in ballet all these years when he knew full well she had not.

"Are you enjoying the party?" he asked, as if he was a lesser man with no conversational skills whatever.

And he watched, captivated despite himself, as her eyes lit up with laughter. All she did was incline her head, ever so slightly. "I can hardly say that I don't like it, can I?" That gleam seemed to intensify, as if it was inside him, too. "It would be churlish. After all, this is meant to be my party as well, isn't it?"

Gianluca had wanted to *like* his wife. He had not planned to find her *quite* so fascinating. It was making it difficult to be kind, but distant, as intended.

Because he would not litter his rule with the personal explosions that had so marked his father's.

"You can feel anything you like," he said, with perhaps more severity than necessary when they were waltzing about the royal ballroom. On their wedding night.

But she did not react the way another woman might have. He had the sense of her laughter all around him, yet the only place it appeared was her gaze. "As long as I am not so ill-mannered as to say it out loud, which, of course, no daughter of my father would ever dream of doing. I understand, Your Majesty."

"We are married now, Helene." He was not sure he could remember if he'd actually tasted her name on his mouth before. Had he? Certainly not when she was his. He found himself pulling her closer than was strictly encouraged, if one's manners were as scrupulous and above reproach as his had always been before now. "Surely you can call me by my name. When we are alone."

Another wave of laughter, yet she did not laugh. But the gold in her eyes seemed to get brighter by the moment. "Does this count as alone? Here in the middle of the crowded ballroom?" But then she smiled as she relented. *"Gianluca."*

And it took Gianluca a few moments to realize that what moved in him then was pure satisfaction. For what else could it be, this stampeding glory of a feeling that washed through him, head to toe?

He had done it.

Despite everything, he had made certain that the sins of his parents would stop with them. He had drawn a line under their nonsense at last—and there was no point dragging old nightmares into the light. No questioning if it was really nonsense, not all these years after his father's death. It was easier to think of the soap opera aspect and make sure he did not succumb to such behavior himself. And it was not that he had doubted that he would succeed, because of course he'd expected he would. Nonetheless, that this particular task had been dealt with at last pleased him.

That she was such a delight pleased him more.

And it was also possible that simply holding this new queen in his arms pleased him most of all—because he had succeeded, he assured himself. That was the only thing that mattered to him.

He had spent a series of not unpleasant hours with her in Provence, watched from varying distances by his people and hers, and they had talked of all the things strangers talk about—weather and small things, anecdotes and reminiscences, all in service of taking the measure of each other.

It had been far more entertaining than he'd expected.

Once he'd proposed, naturally, there had been little time or need for private moments. The presentation of a potential new queen to his people had required a focused strategy, the better to get the sort of photo opportunities that would allow every citizen of his kingdom to feel as if they knew Helene in the short few months they had to get used to her.

Gianluca knew that it was the fashion these days for royal men such as himself to date out in the open whenever possible, thus allowing the public to speculate about the worthiness of each and every woman seen on his arm. And then to offer unsolicited opinions about whether or not the woman in question was prepared to take on the job, as if he was not perfectly capable of judging such things himself.

But Gianluca was not modern. Not like that. The old ways were what had kept his family on the throne of Fiammetta for many centuries. What was good enough for the first of his name was good enough for him, as he always liked to say. He would have had the words tattooed into his skin, but that felt redundant. Those words were who he was.

His grandparents had gotten to know each other when they were already married, and really only once they had a baby on the way. If then. Gianluca smiled at the thought, because he could hear the way his grandmother would have said the words herself. She had never been one for too much *mawkish intimacy*, as she would have called it. She had famously preferred distance and her own company. And given that she and his grandfather had ruled the nation through turmoil aplenty for some fifty years, none of it emanating from their marriage, how could Gianluca not look to them as his guides?

But as he gazed around the ballroom, pleased that he had crossed this particular thorny issue off of his list, his eyes caught on the one person at the party who seemed to have no issue whatsoever scowling.

Directly at him, the King of Fiammetta, when no one else would dare.

"Is your cousin well?" he asked his bride.

This time, her laugh was audible. "Faith is perfectly well. Just rather...protective."

"Do you require protection?" he asked, and there was something, then, in the space between them. He could not say he knew what it was. He could not say he liked it.

It had something to do with her small, elegant hand in his, skin to skin. It was the memory of standing at the altar and peeling back her veil, then pressing his mouth to hers for the very first time.

That moment poked at him, and Gianluca didn't like that, either. He had congratulated himself at length on not touching her at all in the lead-up to their wedding. It was a long road between untouched and no longer a virgin, of course, but he had not taken so much as a step along it.

He had been certain that he had made that choice simply because it was the right one. He had felt morally superior.

Then he had kissed her, standing at the front of the cathedral for all to see, and he had the lowering thought that perhaps the real truth was that he hadn't dared kiss her in private.

Because she was far too potent, and kissing her packed a hard punch.

Gianluca had the most astonishing thought then, and again now. He actually wondered if he'd kept himself from touching her all this time because he knew that once he started, he wouldn't stop.

As if he was a slave to his own desires the way his parents had been.

It was insupportable.

"It's more that my cousin intends to marry for different reasons," Helene was saying, with charming diplomacy. "She has a different take on the enterprise, that's all, and is not certain that she can fully support how we are going about it."

"The history of the world is filled with examples of marriages like ours," he told her, perhaps more repressively that he might have done had he not been questioning himself in real time. "It is not until recently that such arrangements were viewed with suspicion instead of acceptance."

"But were they happy?" Helene smiled when his gaze came to hers, perhaps too sharply. "I am, naturally, transported with nothing short of joy, Your Majesty. Gianluca," she amended as his brows drew together. "It is my cousin who worries that if a couple does not start in a state of tested and true happiness that they can only find themselves miserable."

"Your cousin sounds silly," he replied matter-of-factly. "For even a few moments of research instead of reckless feelings would make it clear to her that when it comes to stability, arranged marriages are more successful. Precisely because the union is not based on such odd notions as happiness or romantic attachment. And our union, Helene, must last. It must stand all tests, of time and trial alike."

He lowered his voice as he said that, lest anyone overhear and imagine there was already trouble, but Helene only nodded.

"I remember what you told me in Provence. No scandals. No separations. One smooth, unified front at all times, forever." She held his gaze as she said that. "I agreed to those terms."

She had. They had been walking in a field of gold and purple and the sun had seemed to seal the bargain they were making, so solemnly, out where they were nothing but a woman and a man. He could not have said why the way her cousin looked at him got under his skin.

He could not recall ever being quite so prickly before. He could not say he cared for it.

As other couples took to the floor when the music changed, and he was once again called upon to perform for his public, Gianluca found himself questioning that moment over and over.

As if it mattered far more than it should.

And as if he really ought to have been paying closer attention to why it felt that way—

But finally, after an eternity of duty, it was time for him to take hold of his bride and leave the reception behind.

Like everything else about this very public wedding, there were stages to the departure. Everything had to be properly photographed, recorded, and disseminated to the papers, the news shows, and all the rest of the industries that fed like parasites off of his position. A ruler should not be a celebrity, to Gianluca's mind, but that was a battle that had been lost long ago.

But soon enough, the necessary steps had all been taken and he and Helene waved for the last time from the balcony of the palace.

And then, at long last, retreated within.

Though they were not alone.

His usual aides surrounded him as they walked, and he nodded along as they filled him in on things that had happened during this long day of celebration that required his comment or signature or merely his attention. When they arrived at the King and Queen's apartments, half of the entourage peeled away and took Helene with them, so that they might prepare her for the next part of the evening.

As was tradition.

Yet there was something in him that wanted to stop them. That wanted to dismiss all the staff, and carry his own wife into his own bedchamber, then strip her out of that gown of hers with his own hands—

But that was not how things were done. And he was not going to start making up his own rules now. That would spit in the face of all he'd attempted to do since he'd taken the throne and, sooner or later, make him no better than the people he least admired.

So he allowed her to be borne off without him, little as he liked it. Then he tried his best to focus on the things his staff were telling him as he strode into his rooms, casting off his own wedding garments as he went.

But focus did not seem to be available to him. Not today.

And it was a relief to dismiss them soon after, so that he could stand there in nothing but his shirtsleeves and his trousers low on his hips, allowing himself a small bit of liquor that he had decided was permissible long ago.

It was one more thing he would not deviate from now, no matter the provocation.

The Fiammettan Royal Palace was a standing pageant of its own history, much of it starring Gianluca's own family. He had grown up here. He had played in all of these rooms, even when instructed not to, and so he knew exactly which doors separated him and his wife now. He could even guess which rooms her aides were moving her through. Readying the new queen for the King's royal pleasure.

And he was glad, then, that he had taken this moment to himself, because there was a howling thing in him— that brazen hunger—that he was just as happy to keep to himself. So that he might wrestle it under control here, alone, when no one might suspect it lurked within him.

So that he could pretend it did not.

He and Helene had talked about their wedding night, obliquely. He was well aware that in some marriages like theirs, sex was not assumed. That it was something to be worked up to, or perhaps suffered through when necessary.

But he had walked with Helene on a late summer evening out in the garden her mother had planted and had seen the way she'd blushed when she'd nodded and said that all things considered, she was perfectly happy to do things the traditional way.

His mouth went dry even now, remembering it.

Gianluca told himself it was perfectly reasonable to wish to enjoy this particular part of his duty. For he would execute it either way. If he had found himself a woman who flinched at his touch, well, they were both lucky that they lived in a time where intimate touch was not necessary to build the required bloodline a king needed.

But he did not think that was going to be an issue.

When he heard that faint tap at the door at last, and then the sound of it opening, he waited for one beat, then another. He heard her quick, light feet in the hall, yet still he stayed still, his eyes out a window he hadn't looked through once tonight.

Almost as if he was not entirely sure what his response would be.

Or if he could control it, more like—

But then he stopped trying. He turned.

And she stood before him at last.

His wife. His queen.

His Helene.

They'd taken down her hair so that it waved riotously over her shoulders, but still did not conceal the fact that they'd been left bare. That she wore another bit of soft white, but this one cascaded from tiny straps all the way to the floor and was just transparent enough. Just enough, so he saw the hint of the ripe swell of her breasts and got his first taste of the curve of her hips.

One taste was all it took when her eyes were so wide and so gold, and the smile that she aimed at him seemed to resonate deep within him.

He crossed to Helene and finally took his bride into his arms, then fastened his mouth to hers.

This time, there was no one watching them, so Gianluca stopped pretending that he could control any of this.

And so he let himself go.

CHAPTER THREE

THERE WAS NOTHING in the stretch of Helene's life, quietly blooming or not, that could have prepared her for the look on Gianluca's face just then.

Her heart seemed to simply stop, there in her chest, then beat so hard she thought it might knock her flat.

This man who had always seemed so ruthlessly controlled, so stern and so deliberate in all he said and did looked nothing short of...undone.

She barely had time to suck in a small gulp of air before he was there before her and then his hands were on her.

Then his mouth descended to hers.

And then everything caught fire.

And the press of his mouth to hers in the cathedral had shifted things inside her. It had made her wonder ever since if she could handle this, him. It had winnowed all the way through her and then pooled between her legs, so that she'd spent the whole of their reception feeling outside herself, swollen with the need she understood in theory but had never experienced before. Not like this. Not with the memory of those firm lips against hers crowding into her, washing over her, making her question everything.

But now there was no question.

There was only the sleek fire of his mouth on hers and the way he licked his way between her lips, so that one fire became another, the heat building on itself and shaking through her to become another kind of humming all its own.

Louder. Better.

In the Institut, they'd been given all kinds of classes on how best they should treat the loss of their virginities, given that their innocence was likely to be a matter of barter in the marriages girls who grew up there were likely to take part in. They did not shy away from such topics at the school, though, it had to be said, they also did not advertise that particular subject matter much outside the Institut's walls.

Even if you feel overwhelmed, you must lean into it, they'd been advised, in one way or another, by their teachers. *For it is up to you to find your own pleasure, ladies. Whether it is offered to you or not.*

All the girls in Helene's year had been resolute when discussing it amongst themselves. If pleasure was theirs to find, then find it they would. They all read enough. Watched enough. They all knew that what they'd been told was only too true and they would have to assume and then proceed as if it was up to them—

But it had never occurred to Helene that she might find herself in a scenario where locating her own pleasure was not required.

Because *pleasure* was far too tame a word to describe what crested within her, over and over, as Gianluca kissed her. As, again and again, he angled his head to take the kiss deeper.

As if, were it up to him, he might eat her whole.

Everything in her shuddered into the wildest sort of delight at that notion.

Just as quickly, everything seemed to spin around on

itself, and it took her a moment to comprehend that he was lifting her from the floor. Something he did so easily and without a pause in the way he was kissing her that it sent another humming thing swirling around inside of her. She leaned into it, still wild over his kisses, and chasing his mouth with her own. Learning with every slide of his tongue, every angle, and even the faint scrape of his teeth.

He set her down on what she assumed was the bed, though she didn't bother to look. All she knew was that he'd set her *apart* from him and, accordingly, she made a soft noise of sorrow.

But it changed into something else halfway through, because she'd never seen him look like this. Gianluca's dark night eyes were a mad heat, and his stern, aristocratic face was changed, somehow. As if he could feel the same wildfire that was eating her alive.

As if it had carved its way into him, too, making him look something like cruel, stark and needy.

Something else she could feel within her, a kind of beckoning.

He moved to stand between her legs, and then reached down, smoothing his heavy palms over her hair, and then, with a look of intense concentration on his face, he set about the task of *learning* her.

Helene could think of nothing else to call it. It was as if he was committing her to memory with his fingers, his hands. And then, as if he wished to make her feel turned inside out, and scalding hot besides, with that mouth of his, too. He started at one temple and eased his way all over her face. Brows, cheekbones. Her nose. Her eyelids.

Then he took his time learning his way along her neck, finding his way to her breasts through the sheer material gown they'd given her to wear. The gown she'd thought made her look silly, a gothic virgin from another age who ought to be chased down a hallway with a candle in her hand—but she had sighed happily when she moved in it, because it was softer than a dream and felt like caresses all over her skin.

Though she understood quickly now that she had no idea what caresses were meant to feel like.

Because Gianluca was a revelation.

He did not make any attempt to lift her gown or find his way beneath it. What he did was urge her back so that she lay against the coverlet, sprawled before him. Her whole body shook with every breath she took, while he took his time.

And lit her up.

Gianluca found her navel, the jut of her hip, and then trailed heat over the top of her most private triangle. He glanced up at her then, only the touch of that vast night, and she braced herself—or she surrendered herself—but he only grazed that wet, hot center between her legs as he worked all the way down to her feet.

Leaving her limp and wild and unable to do anything but *shake*. And then, when he reversed direction and started making his way back up, he pulled the gown along with him.

And Helene lost herself entirely.

She simply…poured herself into him.

Into his mouth, arching her back or thrusting her hips forward, whatever he demanded. Whatever felt good, then better, then better still.

He took his time, moving all the way back up to her face again to kiss her all over again. Until it was almost hard to remember that she was naked and in his arms—

But only *almost*.

Gianluca pulled back and seemed to study her once more, and Helene felt that like a touch all its own. But he did not speak. He looked at her, his face as stark and as wild as she felt, before flipping her over and making his way back down the length of her body once more.

This time, when he made it back up again, Helene was shuddering. Sobbing. Clenching her fingers into the coverlet below her, making fists, writhing—so outside herself she wasn't sure, if asked, she would even know where she was.

Nor did she care as long as this man, her husband, was right here with her, working his rough and tender magic.

He left her for a moment and Helene was so dazed with pleasure and longing that all she could do was lie there, her face pressed against the bed, able to do nothing at all but pant. Her head was spinning. Every nerve ending in her body was *exulting*—

The Gianluca's hands were on her again. And that was even better, because when he pulled her to him she discovered to her great wonder and delight that he was naked too.

And she wanted nothing more than to celebrate this madness, this astonishing and all-consuming wildfire that felt as good as it burned, so she did her best to mimic what he had done to her.

She tried to follow the bold, breathtakingly masculine lines of his body. She explored the flat planes of his chest. She tested the heavy slabs of muscle along with the deep ridges carved into his abdomen, and she savored every taste of him. Faintly salty, his skin smooth and rough in turn, and these unprecedented acts made a new heat move within her.

And then, when she reached it, the jut of his maleness was huge and hot and it made her feel like whimpering.

With a need she had never felt before.

She reached out, not sure if she wished to wrap her hands around the length of him, or maybe follow a darker, hungrier urge to lean forward and put her mouth on him—

But he didn't let her choose.

Instead, Gianluca tipped her back against the soft bed and crawled his way up the length of her body once more. Until he was beside her, stretched out so that she could see almost all of him at a glance.

And for a moment, she felt almost overwhelmed at the sight of him. Of *all* of him.

Because he was so perfect. And because it all seemed so different from what she'd imagined, but was still perfect. There was no question in her mind about that, either.

Gianluca was long and lean, made of a great many muscles, sleek and heavy. She'd never thought too much about the state of a man's chest, but now she found that his consumed her attention entirely. She was fascinated by the dusting of dark hair there and the way it felt against her body when she rubbed herself against him. The way it made a new and darker flame lick all over her.

As if she'd been made for the sheer physicality of this thing they were doing. As if deep within, all along, there had been this need to wrap her naked body around his— only his—so they could rub together like tinder and see what sparked.

He didn't speak. There was something almost stricken about the way Gianluca looked at her as he reached down between them, found the place where she ached for him the most, and drew his fingers through all that heat.

She felt something break inside her, but broken was better still, and so she shook against him as her thighs clenched of their own accord around his questing hand.

He let out a dark, male sound that Helene had never heard before—and yet knew, somehow, was approval. Then he pressed deeper, as if he knew perfectly well that every time he did, a great wave of sensation washed all over her.

He did this again and again, until she felt something rush at her, hot and dark and *his*, until it burst through her and made her cry out.

Then he was rolling her beneath him, holding her thighs apart with his own hips. His dark gaze was all she could see when she opened her eyes, and she didn't look away as he reached down between their bodies to fit the great blunt head of his manhood against her softest heat.

Helene was a chaotic blaze, too wild to bear. She caught her breath. She found herself dragging her lower lip between her teeth as if that might help her survive this. Gianluca's dark night gaze seemed like it was a part of her, as if it was already deep inside her, as slowly—so very slowly—he began to press himself into her.

"You are too big," she whispered, and there it was again, the flash of that smile of his.

"Have patience, *mia regina*," Gianluca murmured in a low voice, as if his throat was too rough for words.

But he was too big. He really was, and Helene couldn't see how *patience* would help any. There was no way he could fit—

Still he pressed in deep, then deeper still.

She threw back her head and tried to ride it through, the stretching, the pressing. She was so soft and the fire inside her was so bright, and all of these things felt as if they were braided together.

As if it was all meant to be this way, the flames burning hot on one side, and the press of pain on the other, yet somehow working together. So that somehow all of it was wildfire and wonder, and she arched into him, surrendering herself to the grip of it. To the inevitability of the way he slid in, so deep, until she felt him kiss up against the very depths of her.

It was as if everything she was, everything inside her, *rippled.*

And then shattered.

And the shattering was its own kind of dance, its own slick and sweet marvel, a wonder all its own. Too magic and too wild for her to do anything but let it take her.

Over and over.

The way he did as he thrust within her, again and again and again.

So that when she fell back into herself anew, returned from all the shattering, that was all she knew.

Once. Twice.

Until she broke apart once again, so completely that she was little more than a shooting star off there in the cosmos—

But she heard Gianluca's voice, his wild cry of need and wonder as he came with her, and she thought she could stay like that, scattered out there in the stars, forever.

Particularly if he was with her.

She wasn't sure she would ever come back to her own body again, and when she did it felt wrong. As if she was not meant to be solid like this, separated from him in the indignity of flesh and bone.

Not when they could shine. Not when she knew they could dance like that, out where galaxies collided.

It took her a long while to understand how she was even lying there on her side, curled up next to the blazing hot body of the man she'd married. The man she barely knew.

The man whose addictive taste she had in her mouth, even then.

There were no lights on in this great room of his, but there was a fire dancing in the grate, and she liked the way the firelight moved over his skin and hers. As if it was keeping them connected the way no small part of her felt they were meant to be.

Always.

Just as they had been out there in the stars he sometimes carried in his eyes.

But the longer Helene lay there, the more she found herself going over what they'd just done again and again in her mind, so that her heart began to pound all over again. She had been taught repeatedly that it was always best to allow oneself to be led so that one could more easily adapt to whatever might befall her, but surely that didn't apply to *this*. She was lying there, laid out like the grandest sort of meal, and the man had made her his queen. If rank had its privileges, surely she did not need to deny herself ever again.

So Helene shifted, pushing herself up on her hands so she could look down at the King, her husband, there beside her. He lay there with one arm thrown over his eyes, as if he knew the firelight danced over all the lines of his body and made him into art.

And she had found him gorgeous from the start, there was no denying it. But he seemed something more like *celestial* to her now. She leaned down over him, smiling as her hair found him before she did. She let her soft, dark waves trail across the skin of his chest, as if she was using it like a tool.

Because she was following wherever this mad pleasure led, and more, because he liked it. He began making the most fascinating sound, low in the back of his throat, that made that abundantly plain.

Helene pressed her lips to the pulse she found, beating in time with hers, at the base of his neck. And then she simply gave herself over to that beat. To the longing inside of her.

To the magic of this, and every new marvel she uncovered along the way.

She found the corded tendons in his neck entrancing. She followed them down to his collarbone, lost herself for some while in that shoulder and the underarm he was presenting to her with his arm in that upthrust position. And better yet, his bicep.

After a while, she felt drawn to his chest again, and shivered, because she could remember so clearly how all those hair-roughened muscles had felt against the tips of her breasts. She could feel it again now, as if her body was preparing itself.

But that gave her an idea, so she leaned in and found his nipple, teasing it with her tongue until she heard that growl once more.

And then, more exciting still, she felt the way his big, strong hands clenched deep in her hair.

Helene charted her own course down the length of his torso, eventually realizing that she was following the arrow of dark hair that led to that most mysterious part of him. The lower she went, lavishing attention on ridges and thick muscles alike, the more that part of him stirred.

And by the time she got there, he was hard again. And Helene still couldn't quite believe she'd taken all of that, all of *him*, inside of her.

She wanted that again. But first she wanted to kiss her way around the base of his proud length, taking in all the ways he was so different from her. And then, following that urge she'd had before, and remembering all those books she'd read in secret over the years, she licked her way over the velvety tip of his shaft.

That made him make those sounds again, so she did it again. Then again.

Then she leaned in closer and took him in her mouth as best she could. And this time, when his hands clenched deep into her hair, it very nearly hurt in the most surprisingly thrilling way—

But he wasn't stopping her.

On the contrary, he was keeping her there, right where she most wished to stay.

And as he did, he began to tell her precisely what to do.

His voice was low and certain, a current of dark, hot glory that wound around her and into her and held her tight as surely as his hands did, still sunk deep into the waves of her hair.

Helene thought she'd never felt more alive than she did now, with his hands on her and that male part of him surging over her tongue as if every single part of her was finally working precisely as it should.

And she had been taught to eat the finest foods. Drink the most exclusive wines. She'd been trained to have an exquisite palate, but none of that tasted like anything to her. There was only the taste of him. The sheer, dizzying, hot and hard *taste*—

Gianluca groaned out his release, then, and flooded her mouth, and that taste took her over—far better and hotter, saltier and more *him* than before.

For a moment, all she could hear was the sawing of his breathing, raw and loud. It took her long moments to recognize that she was trembling everywhere, her heart drumming wild in her chest, and she was once more slick and hot between her legs.

When he moved, she thought he might be about to do something about that. Instead, he rolled from the bed and looked back at her, the firelight making him seem almost soft, almost kind, though he did not taste like either.

He said nothing. He only bent down and swept her up into his arms.

Helene thought then that she would let him carry her anywhere. She trusted him completely. She let her head fall to his shoulder and watched him, not wherever they were going. He was a view that she imagined she would never tire of.

What a sweet magic this was that she would not need to try.

It took her a moment to understand where they were when he set her down on her feet, and she had to bite back a smile, as it seemed so incongruous to her that a mighty king did something as prosaic as reach into the great glass enclosure before them to turn on the water for his own shower.

Like anyone else.

Gianluca pulled her in with him, picked up a whisper-soft cloth, and stood her on one of the benches as he tended to her. He washed every part of her with the same focus and intensity, until the washing itself became a sensual pageant all its own.

Until Helene had her head tipped back, eyes nearly closed, as he began to use his hands instead.

She gasped a bit as he lifted her up. Then more as he pressed her against the side of the great shower enclosure, then hoisted her higher still, until she had no choice but to wrap her thighs around his neck and then reach out to grip the nearest showerhead—because he was gripping her bottom in his hard hands while he used that devastating mouth of his to lick his way deep between her legs.

And for a long while after that, it was all shooting stars and sheer delight.

She came apart again and again, riding his tongue and the sweet torment of his jaw and that *focus*. Then he slid her down the length of his sleek, wet body until he could thrust himself deep within her once again.

Only when they were both limp and hoarse did he slide them both down to sit on the floor of the shower together. The hot water pounded all around them, but the sound of his thundering heart beneath her ear was louder by far. Helene closed her eyes and let her head fall to his shoulder, thinking she might slip off into sleep and stay there for half a lifetime or so.

She still felt that way, sleepy and dreaming, as he toweled her off and carried her back out to the bed. She was barely aware of it when he tucked her in, then sprawled out beside her, but there was a small part of her that resented that her first night with a man was occurring *right then* and she was too spent to truly experience it...

But Helene woke up quickly enough sometime much later when he pulled her on top of him in the dark and taught her new ways to break apart and burn.

When she woke up again, there was light outside the windows and she was alone in the wide bed. She stretched where she lay, feeling new and intriguing twinges in all the different parts of her body. And she was smiling as she sat up, then finally looked around the King's grand bedchamber, which had clearly been decorated to announce precisely who lived here. It was an impressive sweep of art, sculpture, ancient furniture, and the sort of resonant colors that she had learned in school were meant to softly underscore power and might.

It wasn't until she tottered off to the bathroom, blushed at the sight of that shower enclosure, then walked back into the bedroom that she realized the windows were doors that let out onto a balcony. And more, that there was a figure out there in what had to be a rather bitter January cold.

Gianluca.

She pulled one of the quilts that had ended up in a heap on the floor around her like a cape, and pushed her way out through the door. Alpine air bit at her, in a harsh rush, and her breath deserted her. She could see it.

Her husband stood as if he could not feel the cold, but at least he was dressed. He stared out at the view of his kingdom, nestled there before them in the long, narrow valley that was the heart and soul of Fiammetta, and all Helene could think was, *This is the life we get to live.*

She opened her mouth to say it to him, too, but something in his stillness stopped her.

Gianluca did not turn around to greet her. And somehow, she felt that everywhere. Like a bit of foreboding.

Maybe more than a bit.

And when he did turn, it was as cold as the air around them and with far more bite.

Even before he spoke.

"I thought that the rules were clear from the start, Helene," Gianluca said, and his voice made the cold winter morning so high up this mountain feel balmy in comparison. His black eyes seemed fathomless. There was no star in sight. "You were supposed to be a virgin."

CHAPTER FOUR

HELENE WAS EVEN more beautiful with the morning light pouring all over her, making her eyes sparkle and her cheeks get pinker in the mountain air. She looked regal, standing there in nothing but a quilt that looked as if she might be wearing royal robes. She was picture-perfect.

She was beautiful, she was the Queen of Fiammetta, and she was a liar.

How had he missed all the signs? The way her mouth dropped open now, the way his mother's always did when it was convenient. Her eyes going wide, as if she was in shock.

How had he married his mother when he had gone to such great lengths to make that impossible?

Helene opened her mouth, then closed it. Then she tried again. "What?"

Gianluca shook his head. "Is that the best you can come up with? I felt certain you were far more imaginative."

He had woken in something as close to a panic as he had ever felt. He had bolted upright in his bed, rumpled and still warm. And he had stared down at the woman sleeping there beside him, his wife and queen, curled up like the very picture of innocence.

But the entire night that they had spent together suggested otherwise.

Had he dreamed that unpleasant truth? Or was it simply that he woke with that longing for her heavy in him all over again when that was not like him? He had always been as measured in his bed as anywhere else in his life. Not for Gianluca the tyrannies of emotional involvement with anyone, for hadn't he witnessed, personally, where it all led?

He knew that misery all too well.

Images he knew were not nightmares, not quite, rolled through him. His mother claiming her favorite stage, loud sobs and the destruction of hapless objects while his father raged at her, in his insulting, belittling way—

All while Gianluca tried his best to disappear, right where he stood.

He had vowed he would never ransom off his reason to his emotions. He knew too well where it led.

Do yourself a favor, his father had sneered at him once, over a sea of shattered things that Elettra had hurled at him in one of the private salons. *Find a queen who does not simply aspire to the crown, but knows how to wear it.*

Gianluca thought he'd chosen so astutely. He had not rushed. He had done his research. And still this had happened.

Surely no innocent could have participated the way she had last night. It defied all reason.

When he had first awoken he had tried to find a reason. Any reason at all, but he couldn't convince himself that the woman who had taken him so enthusiastically so many times was not only a technical virgin, but *untouched.*

At first he had felt a deep rage that he could not fully identify. It did not seem clean and righteous like the fury he had always felt toward his parents. It had taken him some time before he'd understood. This was betrayal.

And then the rage made sense, much more sense than that yearning that had sat on him so heavily.

It was, for a few scant moments, even a kind of *relief.*

That was what got him up and out of the bed. He'd paced around the bedchamber as the new day dawned, trying to think his way into a solution for what had happened here. Her betrayal.

He kept repeating that to himself. *Her betrayal.*

But no matter how he tried to think around it, the damage was done. He had married her. He had claimed her as his queen in front of the whole kingdom.

She had not only made him a liar, she had seen to it that he was now participating in an unlawful activity. He, the King. He, Gianluca San Felice, who had long prided himself on his unimpeachable character—the antidote to his parents.

He had to assume that this had been her plan all along. And so, even though it had not been fully dawn, he'd woken up his aide and demanded that her background be investigated. Again. And far more comprehensively.

"As you wish, Your Majesty," his aide had said. "But our initial investigation was remarkably thorough."

"Not thorough enough," Gianluca had retorted.

And then, because he refused to act as if *he* could not control his temper when that had never been an issue for him before now, he'd taken himself out of the bedroom where his beautiful, treacherous wife slept on. He stalked through his apartments until he reached the room set apart for his personal gym. He threw quite a lot of weight around and then he put in a great many miles.

All of that and yet he felt that great betrayal claw at him all over again at the sight of her.

"Step inside," he ordered her, when all she did was gape

at him. "Unless it is part of your plan to experience hypothermia when you have only just managed to lie your way into the crown of Fiammetta."

"My plan? Did you say I *lied*?"

She sounded baffled. And he studied her, because she had fooled him. He, who prided himself on his ability to take the measure of any person he encountered at a glance. He, who had always been praised for his cool head and his ability to cut through so much of the pomp and drama that surrounded Fiammettan politics.

Gianluca had come to stand out here in the cold because there was nothing like a high alpine winter to clear the head. And he had decided that the fault must have been in that longing he'd felt for her. She must have known. She must have discovered his trick of taking a first, unobserved look and played on it.

This woman had managed to manipulate him, something he would have sworn—he *had* sworn—could not be done.

Even now he could not believe how credible she seemed. How utterly believable. She walked back inside, then began to shiver as if it was only then, back in the warmth of the bedchamber, that she'd realized how cold she'd really been. It was a fine little detail that he might have thought proved her innocence on any other morning.

But he had been here all of last night. He had been lost in her, completely out of his head with that driving, impossible lust, and she had met him at every kiss, every thrust.

Gianluca knew better, little as he wanted to.

She went and stood near the fire that was not quite banked, keeping her back to it as if she did not dare turn her back to him.

"I don't understand what you're talking about," she said

when all he could do was glare at her, trying to see *into* her. Her voice was even. *Careful.*

He had the fleeting notion that she was speaking to him as if she expected him to explode and was attempting to minimize the damage. She was *managing* him. Gianluca would have objected to that, too, but he also could feel that he was the most unsettled he had ever been.

Though he did not *explode* the way both of his parents always had.

He folded his arms over his chest and made certain that his voice was as frigid as the weather outside. "It is an ancient law," he bit out. "Outsiders are forever calling this law archaic, but the truth of the matter is that it brought peace to this kingdom when all the rest of Europe was at war. For many, many centuries. The Kings of Fiammetta learned that marrying virgins was not simply culturally smiled upon, particularly in our less enlightened periods, but kept everything neat and clean, with no need for the sorts of wars that might crop up in other scenarios. Situations in which, for example, enemies or aspirants to the throne might call into question the precision and accuracy of an heir's paternity."

"Thank you."

She didn't sound as if she was offended. Or even particularly upset. She certainly didn't act like she'd been caught out. If anything, she still seemed baffled. He would not like to play poker with her, Gianluca thought bitterly.

Helene continued in that same quiet manner of hers that had lured him in the first place. "I'm actually familiar with the laws of Fiammetta, to some extent. I thought you knew that the palace made certain I was tutored in the intricacies of your country's traditions and a great many of its laws since almost the moment you proposed."

"The virginity of the Fiammettan queen is of paramount importance," he growled at her, sounding nothing at all like his usual composed self, and he blamed her for that, too. "For a great many reasons, not least among them being that the fact you lied means that I have now unwittingly broken the law. You may not care what is right and what is wrong, Helene, but I must assure you that I do. I cannot make the laws if I break them so cavalierly."

She pulled that quilt tighter around her. Her hair was a mess, falling wildly where it would, but it was his mess. He had raked his fingers through her wavy dark hair so many times he could feel the heat of her in the indentations on his palms. He could smell the scent of the shampoo she used. And he hated that despite his fury, he wanted her.

Oh, how he wanted her.

He was hard, achingly so, and having sampled her throughout the night only seemed to make that worse. Because he knew. He wanted to pull her to him. He wanted to throw that quilt to the floor and lay her down on it, then explore her all over again with the daylight washing over her. He wanted to feed her, wash her again, and stay inside her for a week.

For a start.

Gianluca did not understand how a man as civilized as he had always been could turn into such a monster. He had watched his father lose this battle. He had been collateral damage.

He thought, again, of how hard he had worked to disappear—to fade into the walls, the brocaded chairs. How he had done his best to hide in plain sight so that as his parents warred and shouted and threw their missiles at each other, he would not draw fire.

It had not always worked.

And yet here he was.

He supposed he should find a way to be grateful that it was in bringing him to this state that she'd given herself away...but he did not feel anything like *grateful*.

"I don't think I'm following you," Helene said after a moment, and it was some small comfort that her voice was *slightly* less serene. "Is this...? Are you suggesting that I... wasn't a virgin last night?"

The bitter laugh that burst from him then offended him, horrified him, *appalled* him to the core. Because he recognized the sound. Had he not heard his own father make it a thousand times throughout his childhood?

Was this how the war zone began? Was he even now wheeling in the artillery?

His ribs hurt and yet that laugh still hung in the air of the room between them. And he could not seem to keep himself from throwing more words after that sound, as if to make sure he laid down enough cover fire. "Are you suggesting that you were? After that performance? Please spare me the act, Helene. It's too late now."

"Performance?" Her mouth opened, then closed. "You thought that I...? That it was...a *performance*?"

She seemed to sway slightly on her feet, and though he wanted to reach out to steady her, he could not trust himself to touch her. Not when he knew she was naked, and all he needed to do was unwrap her like the most delectable gift...

Where is your vaunted control now? he demanded of himself, but he had no answer.

"Gianluca." Helene was whispering now. "I can't understand any of this."

"You gave yourself away," he said softly, and even though he knew better, he closed the distance between them.

And he didn't mean to touch her, because surely he should not even *wish* to touch her, but without his meaning to reach out at all his hands were smoothing over her hair.

Almost tenderly.

Though he did not feel anything like tender. "You gave yourself away again and again."

She frowned, and swallowing seemed to take her a moment. "What is it you think I have done?"

He made himself drop his hand, but he could not seem to step back. He, who had long considered his will stronger than iron, *could not* do it. And all she did was gaze back at him as if he was the one hurting *her.* "I will find the truth. You must know this. I will dig up your lovers, one after the next, if it takes me a lifetime."

"My lovers?" She sounded as if she wanted to laugh, but didn't. Instead she searched his face, her eyes as gold-tipped as he remembered, and how was that fair? Surely he could have imagined at least that. "What lovers do you imagine I have taken? And when would I have enjoyed these trysts? Everyone knows what the Institut is like."

Helene pulled in a breath as if this conversation was upsetting her—but he could not let himself be pulled in by this act of hers. Not again. He could not let her continue to deceive him. He did not yet know what he was going to do about the initial deception that had made him as much of a liar as she was, tainted as he must be by his association with her if anyone were ever to know.

"Maybe you actually don't know what the Institut is like," she corrected herself when he didn't speak. "So I'll tell you. Even if I had wanted a battalion of lovers, there were none to be found. There were guards, but they were never allowed inside the buildings where the students reside. And even if they bypassed the rules, they would regret it, as we are monitored night and day. Your country is not the only place in the world obsessed with something as silly as virginity."

"You think it's silly." Gianluca leaped on her words as if they were evidence. A smoking gun she'd thrown down in the middle of the floor. "Is this why you chose to deceive me? You thought you could trick me and the whole of my country besides because you think our ways are *silly*?"

Helene blew out a breath and closed her eyes for a moment. But only for a moment. Just long enough for Gianluca to start talking himself into reaching out for her once more, as if that might shift the weight of this betrayal inside him. If the great ball of it, dread and shame alike, might ease if she helped him hold it—

But that was a new, terrible madness.

He was very nearly delighted when she opened her eyes again and focused on him, though he found himself less pleased that there was something like the light of battle there. As if she'd found something within her, something resolute.

Not that heavy wedge of concrete she'd left in him.

"I have not deceived you in anything," Helene said, distinctly. But then she wavered, there as he watched, and he couldn't stand that either. That was how his hands ended up on her shoulders. There was an acre of fluffy down stuffing between his palm and her skin. It was the same as not touching her. "But if I had… How was it—exactly— that you decided I was lying to you?"

Gianluca could not let go of her, no matter how many times he ordered himself to do so at once. It infuriated him.

He was Gianluca San Felice. His parents had proven themselves unworthy of the roles they'd held, but he had always been made better. Stronger. He had always had the utmost faith in his righteousness above all things.

And yet this woman seemed to cast some spell upon him that made him question the fundamental truths of who he was. She made him wonder if he even cared about those things when he more than *cared*. He had built back the trust of his people by being, always, nothing short of a paragon.

Not a saint. He would never call himself that, but he did his level best to get as close as a man of flesh and blood could.

He told himself to step back, but he didn't.

Proving once and for all how saintly he was not.

And so, instead, he drew his fingertips down one side of her lying face, still marveling at the silken heat of her soft skin. At that generous mouth of hers that had pleasured him so intently that he was sure he could still feel the scalding hot clasp of sweet seduction on the hardest part of him...

Damn the woman to hell.

"You are meant to be untouched, untried," he gritted out at her. "Instead, last night made it obvious in every possible way that you have been put through your paces in a great many beds before mine."

And then he didn't have to worry about whether or not he could stop touching her, because Helene jerked herself back and out of his grasp. "I beg your pardon. *Put through my paces?* First of all, slut-shaming does not look good on any man, especially not a king. Second, I'm not a horse. What I am and always have been is an avid reader with an excellent imagination. I'm sorry if my enthusiasm offended you. I'm sure that will never be an issue again."

For reasons he couldn't fathom, Gianluca hated the fact

that there was distance between them, even though he knew it was better that way. Even though he should have taken a kind of refuge in the fact that she dared speak to him like this, suggesting that *he* was the one at fault.

It was an outrage, and perhaps that was why he moved closer to her, curling one hand to cup the nape of her neck. He pulled her to him once more. "Your enthusiasm was overdone, Helene."

"Or perhaps the great King has never met an enthusiastic woman before," she shot back with a hint of temper that shocked him, coming from her. "Is that the kind of man you are, Gianluca?"

"Have you no conscience at all?" His voice was low, then. Soft. Deadly. "I took you into that shower expecting that I would have to wash your virgin's blood from your thighs, but there was none. How do you explain this?"

"My deepest apologies," she said, her dark eyes narrowing with another helping of that temper that he would have sworn had been bred out of her long ago. "I didn't realize that the expectation was that we would wave stained bedsheets from the ramparts of the royal palace. I regret to inform you that hymen is not a conscience, despite a great many fevered fantasies, most of them male. And I have ridden far too many horses in my time to expect that there be much to mine, anyway." She leaned in as if about to tell him a secret, but mockingly, and he should have hated this arch version of her. He should have, but he did not. "Fun fact, that doesn't mean I lost my virginity to a horse. Something I would have thought did not need clarification, but then, this has been a deeply surprising morning already."

There was a part of him that wanted to believe her.

Desperately, in fact.

But Gianluca had already seen a game like this unfold. He'd been raised in the middle of it, forever used as a scapegoat, as ammunition, and even, on occasion, as straight cannon fodder.

He took a step back. Then another. "Virgins do not behave as you did."

And he thought that landed on her like a blow, because she jerked, quickly. Then held herself still.

It felt like a blow and he should have gloried in it, but instead it made him feel small. It made that heavy weight in him seem to press down harder.

"And you're the expert on virgins, are you?" Helene's voice was cooler now, more distant. But her eyes flashed even hotter. "Because it seemed pretty clear that you're not one yourself."

"What clued you in? Was it, perhaps, a certain level of enthusiasm that made it clear it was not my first time?"

"This is an unproductive argument." And though Helene's voice was not precisely even, she lifted her chin and stood her ground. Under other circumstances, he might have admired it. "If you require proof, I can't give it to you. It seems silly to me that you have a law on the books but no way to ensure compliance one way or the other. I'm afraid you're simply going to have to believe me."

"What I believe," he said, and then he was moving toward her once more, as if he could not control himself at all. As if he'd lost that ability entirely at some point last night. "What I *know* is that you are a liar. You deceived me, utterly. And I may not know how you did it, but I will find out. It is not only your lovers I will uncover but your objectives. And you can be sure that whatever they might be, you will not achieve them."

He was close enough now to see the way her eyes flashed. And worse still, to smell himself on her skin.

That need, that *hunger*, nearly ate him whole.

"What if you're too late?" she threw back at him, sounding very nearly reckless, another thing he would have said she was incapable of. "What if the whole of my objective was to be your queen. Now what?"

He growled something at her, not certain he even managed to form words. But it didn't matter, because Helene—who he would have said had no temper to speak of—seem consumed with it now. She pushed herself closer to him, gripping that quilt around her like a set of royal robes.

"Will you divorce me, Gianluca? Call for an annulment? What if, even now, your child is within me? Will you be the first divorced, single father king to ever sit on the Fiammettan throne? Will your ancestors rise from their graves in protest?"

"Don't tempt me."

"Then why wait?" She turned and made to sweep toward the door. "Let's tell the world right now. Gentle subjects, we consummated the royal marriage, but it was too… *enthusiastic,* so the Queen must clearly be a whore." She threw a scathing sort of look over her shoulder, but it only made her more beautiful. It only made him harder. It only *hurt.* "Would you like to announce it to the populace or shall I?"

And he did not know if she tripped over her own quilt or if he was reaching out for her anyway, but one thing and another, Helene was in his arms.

Where some part of him insisted she belonged. Even now.

And nothing had changed, even though everything had.

She was sleek and glorious, lush and magic.

He could not stop himself. He was not sure he wished to try.

And she looked at him as if she wanted to murder him, but she pressed her mouth to his instead.

As if they had always been at war.

As if they always would be.

As if a war like this was his true birthright.

They came together in a fury, there on the floor of his bedchamber, that quilt and his clothes only pushed aside so he might thrust inside her again and again and again.

But he couldn't tell if she cried out or he did when that wildfire between them burned them whole.

Only that both of them were lost.

CHAPTER FIVE

AT FIRST HELENE thought that it would be all right.

They would have to talk it all through, of course. They would have to unpack whatever it was that had made him hurl accusations at her like that, and it would likely be an unpleasant discussion given how raw he seemed.

But she was, at heart, an optimist.

After all, she'd been raised on a steady diet of fairy tales.

And as they lay there in a pile of his clothes, sprawled out across that quilt, she tried to focus her gaze on the ceiling far above, festooned with near-operatic moldings. She felt she could relate to the feeling of a good aria, as she tried to catch her breath.

She told herself that *surely* it wouldn't feel even better than it had before—and last night had been truly spectacular—if it was all going to go horribly wrong.

But it turned out that she was wrong about that. Because even though she'd managed her father's moods for most of her life, she wasn't prepared for Gianluca.

"Are you ready to—" she began when he stirred beside her, then stuttered over the rest of her sentence when he pinned her with that dark gaze of his. "T-talk now?"

"About what?" he asked, though the question was clearly rhetorical. "What else can be said about this travesty?"

Maybe, she admitted to herself privately, the trouble here was that she wasn't used to feeling quite so vulnerable.

Gianluca stormed away, leaving the *travesty* that was her behind. Naked and reeling and on a quilt on the floor, still trying to find meaning in the moldings. Helene sat up gingerly, not sure that she'd expected something quite so swift and overpowering and brutally, wonderfully sensual.

Then again, she also hadn't expected to be called a liar who had broken Fiammettan law because she had enjoyed her wedding night.

"A subject they really should have covered at the Institut," she said out loud, mostly to see if she could still speak—or if that lump in her throat that she was trying to pretend wasn't growing had taken over entirely.

She climbed up off the floor. Then it took some doing to pull up that quilt after her and wrap it around herself once again. But she could hear her mother's cheerful voice in her head.

"But of course we do the hard things the same way we do the easy, mon chou. *One step at a time, that is all. One little step and then the next."*

Helene thought that it was possible that if she allowed herself to stop going one step at a time, that terrible vulnerability that yawned open inside her might consume her, and she had no idea what might become of her then. Because she had planned for so many different outcomes, but not this one.

She had not expected to like him so much. She had not expected to *want* to throw herself into this marriage the way she had. It had all seemed *charmed,* if she was honest with herself now. As if her mother had been looking after her all this time and had sent her a King Charming to make good on all those happy-ever-after stories she'd told when Helene was little.

Maybe Helene should have remembered that the focus of an Institut graduate was never happiness, but harmony.

They weren't the same thing at all.

That yawning thing inside her seemed to get bigger and heavier, and she really was afraid that if she gave in to it, it would never stop. So she took a moment and tied her hair back from her face, knotting it on the back of her head. She took a few moments to search around for the nightgown she'd worn so briefly last night.

She made herself breathe. In. Out. Again.

And she had only just settled herself in one of the chairs by the fire, no longer naked and marginally calmer, when the doors were flung open and a set of palace aides streamed in.

Her aides, Helene realized belatedly. The same group of women who had dressed her last night, though that felt like a lifetime ago now. They came in and swept her out of the King's bedchamber, chattering happily.

"The day is fine and bright, if cold," one said in French. "Surely this must be in celebration of our new Queen!"

"What a romantic wedding!" cried another in Italian. "The King and the Queen were all that is elegant and beautiful—all the papers are swooning!"

"It has even been picked up all the way in America," said another in German. "They had to show the location of Fiammetta on a map, naturally, but this does not take away from the fact your special day received international notice, Your Majesty."

Helene was surprised to find this all a comfort, as she was not called upon to respond in any way. They marched her off the way she'd come, down that long hall that snaked along an interior wall of this part of the palace for the sole purpose of letting the King and Queen come and go from each other's apartments as they chose. Or did not choose.

It was possible, Helene thought, that she might stick a chair in front of her side of the door forevermore.

Though no matter how entertaining it was to think such a thing, she knew she wouldn't.

"There's a bath drawn and waiting, Your Majesty," one of the women said. "We've taken the liberty of sprinkling in some soothing herbs. A lovely soak might be just the thing."

"That sounds perfect," Helene murmured.

And it was indeed a lovely soak in an epic sort of tub could have held a family or two, placed advantageously in a set of windows that looked out across the whole of the Fiammettan mountain valley. A place she'd expected to call home. And now...

Somehow, *home* wasn't the word that came to mind.

When she was pickled straight through she got out of the bath, expecting the staff to descend upon her once more. She imagined all kinds of things they could do now. Perhaps march her off somewhere, having packed up all her things, so she could be divorced? Or arrested? Or whatever it was Gianluca thought was going to happen now that he'd decided she was a liar and a travesty.

But instead they led her into one of the smaller rooms, bright with the winter sun, where she ate a solitary breakfast. And rather hated herself for it, all things considered. Because surely, after what happened between her and Gianluca, she should have had no appetite whatsoever. She should have been wan and pale, better suited to a fainting couch than the hearty meal—*"A great favorite of the field hands, Your Majesty,"* one of the aides told her when she asked for more coffee and a second helping of sausages—that she tucked into as if she hadn't eaten in weeks.

Though she hadn't, really. There had been too many dress fittings and too much nervous fussing on the part of her father and too many dire warnings about appearing in photos and appearing on television and how Helene was going to have to get used to thinking about the end result on film, not what she might see in a mirror. That had rather dulled her appetite.

Then, of course, there'd been a great deal of physical activity last night, and none of it—despite what Gianluca seemed to think—anything she was used to at all. That would make anyone hungry, she thought.

"And if I'm soon to be kicked out of the Kingdom, I might as well build up my strength," she told herself. Particularly if it involved going over those towering mountains into Italy.

But she couldn't eat forever. And by the time the afternoon rolled around, she had napped and showered again and had a huge lunch, and found herself…bored silly.

Something that had never occurred to her before, in all her life, because there had always been an inescapable *thing* bearing down on her. Her mother's sickness and death. Her father's ambitions. Her inevitable graduation from school that would mean it was time for her to actually do the things Herbert had talked about all her life.

But now she'd done all those things. She'd actually thought yesterday that she'd won some kind of lottery. She'd been so *proud* that she'd managed to make all the things she'd dreaded, but had been resolved to do anyway, work for her.

"You know what pride goes before," she muttered to

herself after her sixteenth turn through the Queen's apartments.

They were expansive and luxurious. She had rooms for everything and anything. Her own gym, her own media room, a selection of salons and lounges, studies, an office, a small kitchen should she wish to have things on hand rather than having to ring down to the palace kitchens, her own library, two separate art galleries, a balcony that it was too cold to investigate fully. It was far nicer than any other place she'd ever stayed.

But she was antsy and filled with dread, which meant she couldn't concentrate on anything. And she didn't want to sit still—that way could only lead her to that pit of vulnerability and something too much like despair deep within.

Better to call it *boredom* and *do something* about it.

Happily, Helene knew a thing or two about the Fiammettan palace that was now her new home, because she'd been taken on a great many official tours of the place. First when she'd visited here after she and Gianluca were engaged, and then, as the wedding drew closer, when she'd lived in one of the royal residences on the palace grounds and her tutors had used the palace's many riches as a part of their lessons.

That meant that she knew that in addition to the grand library that was sometimes open to the public and better resembled a ballroom than a place of quiet study, there were any number of smaller libraries placed here and there in the palace's many wings. As if various royals in the past had felt it was beneath them to walk to the larger, more centralized library and so had created their own.

Fiammettans, Helene had discovered, liked to have more than one of everything. More than one official language. More than one city that called itself the capital of the Kingdom, depending on the season. Just like there was more than one door that led out of every room in every official building in the Kingdom.

Including, she discovered, the Queen's rooms.

It really did pay to nose about, trying every door. Including the one that she knew led into that shared hallway between her rooms and Gianluca's rooms, which she was somehow unsurprised to find locked.

Against her.

For a moment she stood there, staring at the door handle, while that yawning thing inside her seemed to swallow her whole—but no.

It wasn't going to be a locked door that was the end of her. She refused.

At first Helene thought that perhaps this meant he'd locked her in, effectively putting her under palace arrest, but soon after she found the door that opened up into the hallway from the Queen's little kitchen and it opened easily enough.

By this point, happily, she was no longer dressed in a quilt pulled from a bed or a nightgown that she never wanted to lay eyes on again. One of the things her aides had showed her in her daze this morning was her own vast wardrobe. Room after room of it. All of her own clothes, imported from her father's house, and then entire sets of pieces she'd never seen before.

Gifts for you, Your Majesty, her aide had said with shining eyes.

From the King, who loves me so much? Helene had asked.

And had only smiled serenely when the woman looked at her curiously, suggesting that Helene's tone had been a touch too sharp.

In any case, she been able to ignore any *gifts* and dress herself instead in her favorite pair of jeans, the ballet flats that never failed to make her feel both comfortable and elegant at once, and an extremely cozy sweater that held her like the hug she desperately needed.

If there was a dress code for royal travesties, someone was going to have to tell her so.

Helene was out the door and out wandering the halls of the greater palace complex before she realized how strange it felt to be walking around this place dressed the way she had dressed any number of days at the Institut, or in her father's house, back when she had felt that achieving a feeling of not actively hating her life was the best Herbert Archibald's daughter ever *could* feel.

Then she had met Gianluca.

She had imagined a whole other universe of potential feelings all summer long.

And she had married a king, become a queen, and been accused of being a deceitful whore all in the course of the last twenty-four hours.

Yet here she was. Hair twisted back out of her way, her favorite clothes on, and all on her own, again.

Helene told herself, repeatedly, that this should feel like a comfort.

All the comforts of home, in fact.

The other good news about having married the King was that she been given access to her mobile phone again. She suspected it was monitored, but that was what was so funny about all of this. In the sense of not being funny at all. She didn't really care if Gianluca read every text she'd ever sent anyone. What was he going to find?

She really was exactly as innocent she claimed to be.

And she really did watch that many videos of cats doing cattish things.

Helene texted Faith as she walked, taking a picture of herself in front of an instantly recognizable painting as punctuation.

Her cousin's reply was immediate.

I beg your pardon, Your Majesty. Dutch Masters and kings? The world really is your oyster.

And for the first time in her life, Helene did not text Faith a full recounting of the night before. She did not tell her cousin what she was actually thinking or feeling. In fact, as she stood there staring down at the screen of her mobile, she felt the strangest feeling creep over her, twining with that knot of vulnerability that seemed to pulse deep within.

It was the headmistress in her head once again. *Remember, ladies,* she had said in that crisp manner of hers. *The ideal wife does not share her marital troubles with all and sundry. She is never a source for unscrupulous journalists and she does not take even her closest friends into her confidence on matters pertaining to the private things that go on between men and women, no matter her station. Why?*

Because she has already been bought and sold once already? one of Helene's more bitter classmates, who was not expecting happy ever anything, had replied.

Madame had only smiled in that flinty manner she did so well. *Perhaps, Georgianna. But also because part of her power lies in how she protects her marriage. Men, you see, are so good at making declarations about what it is they want, what it is they demand. They bluster, they*

bloviate, and in many ways, we must accommodate them.
But it is the woman who is the bellwether, like it or not.
How she behaves sets the stage for how the world will treat
not only her, but the marriage that entirely too many will
believe is within her purview to change as she wishes.

Everyone in Helene's year had dissected that particular
nugget and called it utter crap.

But now Helene stood there in the Royal Palace of Fiammetta, her mobile in her hand and her cousin right there
on the other end of the text. She could say anything she
liked. Faith would believe her no matter what she said,
even if it wasn't true. Faith would immediately come in,
guns blazing—whether only via text or actually at the palace gates depended on what Helene told her.

Helene knew this without having to type a word.

Or…she could protect her fragile, likely fractured relationship with Gianluca instead.

She sent her cousin a string of emojis that said nothing
at all, then slipped her mobile into her back pocket before
she could ask herself why.

It wasn't until she'd located what likely qualified as one
of the so-called "pocket libraries"—though it was large
and featured a great many window seats that let in the
snow as it began to fall—that she understood that it wasn't
the headmistress's discussion of various kinds of subser-
vience that made her want to protect this.

Whatever *this* was.

It was her mother.

Her lovely Mama, who had maintained until the end
that she was happy. She had insisted on it. And she had
never, to Helene's knowledge, *ever* told another soul about
the things Herbert did that an objective observer might
find unkind.

She had even defended him to Helene herself.

Why didn't you marry a Prince Charming? Helene had asked, artlessly enough, when she was too young to know better.

Her mother had held her there, snug in her lap, and so it was only now in retrospect that Helene thought that the smile she'd given then was sad.

But I did, mon chou, she had said. *That is the thing about Prince Charmings, you see. Sometimes it is only their chosen princess who can see them for who they truly are. Don't you worry. You'll know.*

Looking back, Helene did not think her mother truly believed that Herbert was any kind of Prince Charming. But she had protected him anyway.

He had kept her, clothed her, allowed her as much time with her child as she wished, and then he had cared for her when she fell ill. He had protected her, too, in his way.

And Helene did not have it in her to do otherwise.

Or perhaps, she thought later, when she'd found her way back to her rooms with an armful of books so the staff could dress her for a dinner she had assumed she'd be taking on her own, that wasn't the truth. Perhaps the truth was that she was a coward. That she had not wished to face her cousin's reaction if she told Faith what had really happened.

Perhaps she was afraid that a marriage—or her marriage, at any rate—was a fragile thing. And that that telling others the truth of what happened inside it could tear it asunder.

But then she was marched through that previously locked door and down the hall into the King's rooms to find herself in Gianluca's private dining chamber. And she rather thought that if there was going to be any sundering, he would do it himself.

He greeted her with sharp, frigid courtesy, dismissed his staff, and then gazed at her as if she was a specimen beneath the microscope that had gone unexpectedly viral.

"I've spent the day considering my options," he told her.

"That bodes well," she replied, which was not the way she had been taught to handle such situations, but there was only so much she could be expected to do. She laced her fingers together in front of her, wishing she had pushed back a bit more when the women had selected the dress she was wearing. It was far too voluminous. It felt like another wedding gown all over again and even though it was certainly not a virginal white, it made her feel…

Well. Too many things and none she liked.

Gianluca stood there by the great windows that let the mountains in, staring at her, and she had the faint notion that if she took her seat he would take his as well, but she didn't. She stared back at him, wondering where that man she thought she was getting to know had gone.

Or how he could read her so wrongly.

She supposed the silver lining in this was, the knot in the deepest part of her aside, that she couldn't feel the sort of shame and horror she supposed she ought to, because it was *that* ridiculous. No man had ever touched her but him. Yet he believed she was as dissipated as the nefarious, likely made-up women the headmistress had always thundered at them to heed as terrible warnings.

Helene almost wished she really had been out there, sewing wild oats with abandon, if she was going to be punished for it either way.

"You have put me in a terrible position and I will never forgive you for it," Gianluca said in that low, cold voice of his. And that might have been a body blow. If she was guilty. "If I divorce or annul you there is not only the fact that I would be forced to share the fact that you inadvertently made me break the law, I would break even more traditions by ruling while divorced. I would appear weak and easily fooled. None of these are options. We will concentrate on the things we can control. We will get you with child."

Helene might actually have flinched. "Excuse me?"

Gianluca did not appear to notice her reaction. "This is what you promised me, Helene. Is it not bad enough that you lied about the part that is actually required by ancient law? Will you now cast aside every other vow you took as well? Will you attempt to undercut my reign with the scandals and tantrums that have sunk many other monarchies in these modern times?"

She could hardly breathe. "And if I do?"

"You will not have that opportunity." He looked grim. But also something like…pleased, she thought. As if he wanted the chance to issue these threats. As if that allowed him the control he clearly wanted so badly. "My grandmother cherished her isolation, and thus built herself a small castle halfway to the Italian border, accessible only by helicopter or a very sturdy mule. It has no contact with the outside world. Know, with every part of you that imagined it was wise to lie to me, that I will think nothing of stashing you there if I must. That I will always do whatever I must to protect this kingdom."

Helene made herself sigh a bit, as if none of this was really affecting her, when that wasn't at all true. But she suddenly thought that she would rather die than let him *see* her. "That sounds a lot like a high school reunion, if I'm honest."

He stared at her for a small eternity. Maybe two. "Do you think this is a joke, Helene? Because let me assure you in the strongest possible terms that it is not."

"I can see that."

And then it took her a moment to realize that the reason her throat felt so strange was because there was a lump in it again, larger than before. And her eyes felt scratchy, as if she'd been hollowed out. Worst of all, that knot in her took up its own sort of humming, and it made her want to do something completely out of character.

Like fall to the floor and sob.

We do the hard things the same way we do the easy, she thought.

And then Helene swept forward in her absurdly over-size gown and seated herself at the place set for her at the table—on a diagonal from the table's head, which it did not take a great chess master to realize was set for the King—and settled herself into place with what she hoped was every appearance of total serenity.

She'd learned that from her mother, too. That when in doubt, simple rituals could carry an awkward moment and were often far more effective than engaging in a scene.

Though as she sat there, her hands folded in her lap, pretending not to sneak glances at him from beneath her demurely lowered eyelids, she had the distinct impression that he might have preferred a scene, after all.

That this was him, throwing one.

There was something in her that wanted to rise to meet it, the way she'd met every touch, every caress, every moan last night.

But everything in her balked at that.

And this wasn't anything she'd been taught. It was something deeper. Some feminine intuition that was all hers, whispering that if she behaved the wanton in this, too, it would prove his point to him.

More, that Gianluca wanted her to do exactly that.

Helene had no intention whatsoever of doing that work on his behalf.

She was aware of him—too aware of him—but still she sat, engaged in what had been known in the Institut as quiet domestic warfare. The province, according to their teachers, of every powerful woman who could not claim the spotlight herself.

If one must be the power behind the throne, Madame liked to say, *it behooves one to know how to wield it to its best effect.*

And that almost made Helene smile. For there had been no point in any of her schooling in how to be *the most aristocratic of all* that it had ever occurred to her that she would end up anywhere near a *real* throne. Just as she hadn't anticipated getting on the wrong side of her new husband so quickly. Surely she had to have set some kind of record.

She thought that his glare intensified when he finally took his seat, likely because she had permitted her lips to curve in wry amusement.

She thought he might lay into her then, but he didn't. Their meal was served with the exquisite perfection that she had come to understand he required in all things. It was not until all the staff withdrew, leaving them to enjoy their food, that he spoke again.

"Just so we're clear," he said forbiddingly, and when he looked at her it *hurt*, "I remain as allergic to even the hint of scandal as ever. There can be no whispers. No rumors. I will know precisely where to look if any appear."

"Happily," she said, attacking her first course with

gusto as if she was too hungry to pay any attention to him, "I haven't the slightest idea how to set about starting a rumor. I was taught many things in the course of my schooling, but never that."

He picked up his fork too, but only fiddled with it, that brooding glare hard on hers. The more he glared, the less it hurt. Or so she told herself. Bracingly.

"You've picked up many things indeed," he said, his insinuation unpleasant. Deliberately, she knew. "And I cannot pretend that I have reached any place of equanimity about the deception you have committed against crown and kingdom."

"My sins are vast indeed."

That black gaze of his darkened further, without the faintest hint of starshine. "All I can tell you in the meantime is what we will do to mitigate this crisis."

She did not ask what that was. Instead she allowed the sound of their cutlery against their plates to make a bit of music.

"If we are to sit in such baleful silence at each meal," she said after this went on some while, "and assuming that we will be taking our meals together, which I realize isn't at all certain given your opinion on my character as that would put anyone off their food—"

"This will obviously be viewed as something of a honeymoon phase," he said darkly, as if Helene was personally responsible for such wedding traditions. To add to her list of sins. "Even though we will not take any sort of holiday, we must behave like newlyweds." When she only slid a look his way, he set his fork down and leaned back in his chair. "In other words, yes. We will be taking our meals together. We will have a heavy slate of engagements to introduce ourselves as a working couple to the whole of the Kingdom, and assuming you manage to not embarrass yourself or the crown, you may even have your own. But I suggest you remember that it is nothing but a pantomime. You are on borrowed time."

Helene waved a hand. "Yes, yes. You will have your revenge." It made her feel strong, she could admit, to come so close to laughing when nothing was funny. She thought she had never understood her mother more, for what could be more infuriating to a man who *wanted* to cause upset than...not to seem the least upset? She smiled at Gianluca. "In the meantime, however, it would be so much more pleasant to have a bit of music while we eat, don't you think? To cover up the echoing silence and seething recrimination between us."

"I imagine we will have something," he told her in that same dark way that made her wish, despite herself, that all of this was the way she'd imagined it might be last night. "You can be certain of that."

"Marvelous," she said brightly, tucking into her second course. "In the meantime, I believe you mentioned crisis management. Which involves me playing the role of broodmare, does it not?"

When he laughed, then, it was a dark, grim sort of sound that nevertheless set off explosions and wildfires all over her body. As if, no matter what, they were connected now. They were connected intimately, so that even a laugh like that winnowed all the way down her spine.

Then settled there, spreading until it hummed deep between her legs.

And the only shame Helene felt was that it didn't matter that he thought her a liar. It didn't matter to her body at all. She felt swollen with need, aching with it. Even if, at the same time, she had the distinct urge to take one of the forks lined up so prettily beside her plate and stab him with it.

She didn't know how she could feel so many things at one time for the same person. She didn't even *like* the man very much right now and yet she knew that if he reached over and put his hands on her again, she would melt into his arms. At once.

"You act as if providing heirs to the throne was not your primary purpose all along." Gianluca lifted a brow. "Or were you somehow under the impression that the King of Fiammetta went about looking for a bride with certain requirements for sport?"

Once again, something inside Helene shifted. She couldn't tell what she felt, then. She only knew that it was dangerous. That it seemed entirely too likely to tear her apart.

Steps, she reminded herself. And the only step available to her was to breathe.

And to stay very still, so none of the things inside her *erupted*.

"This is not a love match, Helene," the man who had been inside her in too many ways to count growled at her. "For which I can only count myself endlessly grateful. The good news is that there is no longer any reason whatever to pretend otherwise."

He pushed back from the table then, standing up so swiftly that she was caught first by the grace in the way he moved. And she knew him on a far more intimate level now. But there was also that lurching sort of hope that bloomed in her immediately, because some part of her clearly wished that he would reach for her after all—

But instead, he stalked from the room, as if he could not bear another moment in her presence.

Leaving behind the sort of bone-deep silence that she doubted very much any music could cover at all.

So there was nothing to do but sit there, staring down at her plate, whispering words that seemed to rebound back at her.

"I wasn't pretending," she said, because something in her felt as if it might break into pieces if she didn't say it.

She said it again, then again, to the plate before her and the mountains that pressed in from the night outside.

But it didn't make her feel any better when she did.

CHAPTER SIX

HELENE DIDN'T KNOW a whole lot about typical honeymoons, that having been considered low on the priority list of marital concerns across the board, but she did feel fairly certain that most people did not spend it in as much of a deep freeze as she and Gianluca did.

A deep freeze that had nothing to do with the typically blizzard-like conditions outside, that was.

While the snow fell—and fell and fell—the palace was toasty and warm. Fiammettans were well used to their excessively cold winters and Helene's astonishment at the snow that built up on her balcony rail each morning only made her aides laugh.

This was how she knew that what she viewed as entirely too much winter weather was perfectly normal to them.

She tried to tell herself that the same was true of her marriage. It wasn't as if she had a host of friends who were also queens who she could ask, so for all she knew, this was bog-standard behavior for kings of all kinds.

Helene assured herself it was.

That, too, was comforting. In its way. Since for all his talk of *broodmares*, Gianluca did not touch her that way again. She tried to tell herself it was a *welcome reprieve*, but she knew that was exactly the kind of lie he had already accused her of telling him.

Because every night, her usual staff would walk her back to her bedroom from the King's private dining room and then assist her in undressing herself, as if walking and undressing were activities that suddenly required a team effort now that she had married a king. She supposed it was to remind her that everything she did could be scrutinized, and thus she had better act the part.

As if she had ever *not* acted appropriately in the whole of her life—but then, that was his contention, wasn't it?

What it meant was that it was only when Helene crawled into the Queen's stout and imposing four-poster bed and lay there, staring at the elegantly embellished paneled ceiling, that she could really replay their wedding night.

Over and over and over again.

And admit to herself that it did not feel much like a reprieve at all that he had taken that away from her. That wonder and heat. That soaring, life-altering delight.

It felt like cruelty.

But that was the nighttime. The first few *days* of their so-called honeymoon, ever cognizant of the fact they were under scrutiny from the palace staff and the typical tabloid spies within, Gianluca insisted—coldly—that they do the kinds of things they had done while courting.

Quote marks implied.

They took walks in the palace gardens, every day the weather was clear enough. When it was not, they toured the palace galleries. They made polite conversation, as if they were very distant strangers. Breathless accounts of these moments made their way into the papers and if they ventured outside, usually with a picture to match.

"I thought you wanted there to be no discussion of anything we do in the papers," Helene said on one of these promenades across the snow-cleared pathways under which, she knew from photographs, glorious flowerbeds waited for spring.

Gianluca shot her a glimmering sort of look as he kept pace with her, in a manner she knew too well the public interpreted as him *hanging on her every word*. "That is not realistic. And that being so, I prefer to offer them the content I wish to see rather than having them dig up things on their own."

Though he made that sound as if there was a great wealth of digging to be done, and all of it to expose her.

She endeavored to ignore that. "There have been a great many pieces about the Royal Family since our wedding. Takes on history from various viewpoints. I'm enjoying them all, though I keep reading references to your father's *moods* that seem to be nearly in code—"

"Helene." And he was still *glimmering* at her, so she was the only one who could see that he was not hanging on her words. He wanted them to stop. Now. "Unless you see that an article came directly from the palace, you can assume that it is fiction."

Helene only smiled noncommittally, gazed at the snowbanks, and kept her questions to herself for the rest of their walk.

At least these forced interactions were mercifully brief. Perhaps an hour each day of pantomime, and otherwise, Helene was given the run of the palace libraries to do as she would. And it wasn't that spending her days eating marvelous food, reading books, and going on walks—with or without the company of a brooding, furious male—was torture in any real sense. She knew that. In many ways, it was the life she'd always dreamed she might have, having digested every possible version of *Beauty and the Beast* ever made.

It was only that everything felt so *fraught*. And she

couldn't help but think this was all a lot of tiptoeing around land mines while hoping for the best.

Instead of worrying about the inevitable explosion, she dedicated herself to the task of answering her own questions. There were very few papers or magazines allowed in the palace, so she scoured the libraries for primary sources when it came to the Royal Family in general and former King Alvize in particular.

Because she couldn't help but think that the key to Gianluca, and his wild reaction to their wedding night, was caught up somehow in those *moods* everyone seemed to know about but no one dared mention directly.

She didn't find much, but what she discovered was that if the staff saw her curled up in armchairs with stacks of old books, no one questioned what she was reading online.

After a week or so had passed, her aides woke her up one morning to announce that it was time she took on her expected royal duties. This meant they shuffled her between tutors again, so that she might learn everything there was to learn about the Kingdom. And more, the historic role of the Queen.

Or rather, the spouse of the monarch, for Fiammetta had enjoyed three queens in its time. One had maintained what was considered a perfect marriage to a man who was perfectly happy to loom about in the background, assisting the throne, which her tutors told her was the sort of marriage Helene should view as her guide. The second queen had ruled only a few short years and had been married to the Prince of a neighboring land, but had died without issue. Throwing the Kingdom into chaos, according to her tutor, who had waxed on about the war that had raged for many years after that short-lived queen's death, as various would-be heirs vied to take their place on the throne.

"This is the one who interests me," Helene said, smiling winningly at her tutor while tapping her finger on the picture of the third queen, who had married as she had been ordered to do. And then, when her prince turned out to have his own aspirations for the throne—and wasn't above a plot or two to get his way—had first had him imprisoned, then assassinated. "It's a bit of a lovely bedtime story to tell the children, isn't it?"

"Your Majesty is very droll," her tutor replied.

Quelling.

But she was curious, not droll. Because all these lessons about historical queens made her think more about the only other queen she knew—from a distance. That being the Dowager Queen Elettra, about whom Gianluca had nothing at all to say. He refused to discuss her.

That left Helene no recourse but a forensic examination of the tabloids. She enlisted Faith's help, claiming she wished only to get to know the way her new family was portrayed over time in the popular imagination.

Faith was only too happy to dedicate herself to the task of tracking down chatrooms and message boards and vitriolic social media threads, but it all painted the same picture. Yes, King Alvize had been a touch moody—if the "palace insider" reports were true, and always in private—but everyone agreed that Queen Elettra's whorish ways *drove him to it*.

It was that word *whorish* that Helene couldn't seem to let go of. It was the universality of the response to Elettra, which she knew by now had to be a specific and deliberate campaign. And not one that benefited the woman in question.

After all, Helene knew a thing or two about being called a whore.

One night, as they departed the palace in the royal motorcade with flags flying, she opted to regale Gianluca with the entire bloody story of his ancestress, the assassin, whom history unfairly called *the Killer Queen*. "She had good reason to do what she did, if you think about it."

"He was the King and she plotted against him, Helene. I think you'll find that's more commonly known as treason."

"He was plotting against her first," she argued. Then smiled when Gianluca raised that brow of his at her. "And you know what they say."

"Be careful who you marry?"

She smiled wider. "Play stupid games, win stupid prizes."

He did not speak to her directly again that night unless it was necessary.

Oh, he put on an act. It was humbling, really, to see how good he was at acting. It made her question every single moment she'd spent in his presence. Had it *all* been an act? Helene had been so certain that despite their circumstances, and despite the arrangements that had to be made for a man in his position—not to mention, the arrangements her father had always intended to make for her no matter if a king turned up or not—there had still been something between them.

The way he had smiled at her, surely, had been real.

If rare.

She was still holding on to that.

"You did well enough," he pronounced on the way home from the gala, the two of them tucked away again in the dark backseat of the limousine. "It is heartening to see that I can depend on you to play the appropriate role. If nothing else."

"I'm very well trained," Helene agreed. Mildly enough. "You should direct any and all compliments to the Institut, however, as this is their entire purpose for existing."

"If I were you," he said, in that dark-night-of-the-soul sort of voice of his that she wished did not make her ache, "I would not be so flippant. I have no reason to think that any of the things I was led to believe about you are true, do I?"

She turned to him as the motorcade sped through the narrow streets of the old city, all cleared in advance to make way for the King and Queen. "I don't think you're in a position to speak on such matters when it turns out that you, apparently, could be an award-winning actor. If I didn't know any better, I would have thought that you were desperately in love with me tonight."

Helene shouldn't have said it like that. That was clear the moment the words cleared her lips, because the look on his face changed. It became darker, deadlier. Or perhaps it was simply that she felt it as it thudded through her, then seemed to squat there inside, a thorny, pulsing thing she really didn't want to look at too closely.

Because she also didn't want to think about the way it had *felt*, circling around a glittering gala on this man's arm, too aware of the way he looked at her. As if he was the besotted yet capable king she'd imagined he would be.

It had been too easy to believe, for a few hours, that they hadn't taken this bizarre turn.

"What you must understand, Helene, is that I will always give my people what they want," he told her. And every word felt like a knife. Like a blade he was specifically aiming directly at her, each syllable precisely uttered to pierce her poor heart.

She made herself smile anyway. "And you think that's what they want? An act?"

"I know what they don't want. My parents' endless operatics, each and every salacious headline making a mockery of the duty they were called upon to perform for this kingdom. My people want a love story, and they will receive one." His gaze made her heart feel even more perforated. "No matter what I have to do."

"It will be a tender love story indeed," she replied, and did not shrink from that gaze, no matter how she might wish to, "and will seem especially so when I am carted off to a mountaintop prison, without my children, to live out my days in isolation."

But Gianluca smiled, and not in the way that made everything around her feel like an endless summer. This was a cruel crook of his lips, nothing more. "You must have more faith in the palace's ability to spin a story, Helene. When they are finished, the Kingdom will rejoice. They will tell the story as if it is our very own Fiammettan fairy tale. Watch and see."

"I believe the palace can spin anything," she replied quietly, and had to take what satisfaction she could from the way his lips pressed together.

That night, she lay in her bed while her body still ached in all these new ways that he had taught her, then taken away from her. He was pretending to love her in public. She was pretending she didn't care that he despised her in private.

And none of that helped with this ache at all.

It was possible that nothing ever would.

Once the tears started, they didn't stop.

Helene sobbed. She sobbed until her head hurt almost as much as her heart. And when she staggered into her bathroom suite, all the mirrors and marble reflected back her own red eyes and swollen face, and she thought, *At least I finally look the way I feel.*

But that was so tragic it made her laugh at herself, and

she ran cold water over her wrists for a while until she calmed. Then wet a cloth so she could press it to her eyes.

And when she'd gotten the swelling down a bit, she went back out into the bedroom and wrapped herself in her favorite cloud-like throw that was always folded so neatly over the chair near the fire. She wrapped herself in it, sighing at the touch of warm cashmere against her skin, and then moved over to the windows she could curl up in the window seat and press her face to the cold glass.

It was still January. It was breathtakingly cold. Earlier tonight, as she'd stood outside so briefly to go in and out of the palace and the gala wrapped in warm things, she'd felt the sharp alpine air cut all the way through her. She'd taken a deep, shuddery breath each time, as if she was afraid it would be too cold for her lungs to work.

That was what she felt like now, gazing out at the bright lights of the long, narrow valley that made up the bulk of this kingdom. This kingdom that was now hers, whether the King liked her or not.

And Helene had always considered herself something of an indomitable spirit, but tonight, the self-pity took hold. Hard. Because she had only been said indomitable spirit because she'd always hoped, deep down, that things would end well.

She'd trusted that they would, no matter how they appeared.

But now…was this really what her life was going to be like? This…fakeness in public followed by so much darkness in private? Part of her wanted to get up immediately, snatch up her mobile, and beg Faith to come break her out of here after all.

She considered it logically, and for a long time. It would never work, for a number of reasons. First of all, her cousin was loyal and true, but she was no match for the royal guard. And even if she somehow managed to get into the palace, there was no way she was going to abscond with the Queen. Besides, even if Helene attempted to trick her way out of this, she doubted Gianluca was going to let her traipse off on some kind of holiday anytime soon.

Did queens even take holidays?

And in any case, it wouldn't solve anything. Even if she did run away. Helene and Faith could ski on their bottoms all the way into Italy and set themselves up in a lovely *pensione*, and it wouldn't make her any less the new Queen of Fiammetta. It wouldn't solve her marriage. It wouldn't do anything but give Gianluca more proof, somehow, that she was this person he thought she was. A liar who would also run away from him, thereby causing an even bigger scandal.

Still, she stayed where she was for a long while, her forehead against the glass and her breath a little more ragged that she wanted to admit even to herself. And slowly, that great tide of tears and despair seemed to ebb away.

Helene wrapped herself tighter in her cozy throw and angled herself away from the window, so that the winter cold was no longer pressing into her skin. She pressed her fingers to her eyes, blew out a breath, and then straightened her shoulders.

The truth was, she had spent the entirety of her life learning how to manage a man who never acted as if he cared for her at all. Herbert had been a marvelous training ground in that regard. She had watched her mother do it, then she had done it. And while she couldn't claim that she had actually pleased the man, because he couldn't be pleased at all and certainly not by her, the situation she found herself in here in Fiammetta was nothing new.

The specifics might be different, and more personal, but it was the same old game.

If she looked at it that way, the only problem she was currently having was that the cold marriage she'd imagined she would escape turned out to be the one she was in, after all.

And the real trouble was that they'd had that wedding night. So now she knew. She *knew*.

Helene was certain that she could handle the rest of it. The tragedy was that her body had other ideas.

Even now, sobbing her eyes out and plotting foolish escapes from captivity, she could feel that insistent heat between her legs. That slickness that whispered dangerous things to her. That she should get up and try the door to the King's bedchamber. And upon discovering it locked, as she thought she would, why not head out into the hall and find a different way in? Or better yet, go outside, and see if she could make it along the wintry balcony that separated his room from hers?

She'd always thought that the best-case scenario would involve civility by day and a friendly, businesslike approach at night. She'd hoped that she wouldn't find whatever husband she ended up with physically repulsive, but even if she did, she'd hoped they could at least both behave with a certain amount of kindness. And everyone claimed that children were their own reward, so she was looking forward to that, too.

It had never occurred to her that she, born and raised to be a peacekeeper no matter her own feelings, could find herself in a situation like this.

Helene thought there must be something wrong with her, because all of her schooling had led her to believe that the most anyone could hope for when it came to marital relations was something pleasant. Perhaps gentle laughter might be involved, and a certain closeness.

Not this.

Not the enduring sensation that she'd been hollowed out by her own desire, left raw and unfinished, and possibly deformed by the things she wanted.

The good news was that it seemed as if Gianluca was so focused on what he believed to be her deception that he hadn't noticed.

Helene sighed a little bit and ran her hands over her hair. She had been trained to deal with her marriage. She would deal with her marriage, come what may.

But she wasn't her mother. She was not the sort of flower that could make do with any old soil and bloom prettily, on demand. Look what had already happened, and all she'd done was marry as expected.

She was going to have to choose a different sort of blooming altogether.

Helene turned that over, again and again, and what she kept coming back to was the enduring ache inside her.

And the sure knowledge that no matter what Gianluca pretended now, he had been as bowled over by their night together as she had been. As she still was.

Maybe, she thought then, frowning at the cold glass and the world beyond, she was going about this all wrong.

Maybe it was time to stop playing his game and start playing her own.

"Besides," she murmured, her breath fogging against the windowpane, "it's not as if he can hate me *more,* is it?"

So she might as well try to get at least some of what she wanted out of this.

And maybe the prizes wouldn't be quite so stupid after all.

CHAPTER SEVEN

SOME WEEKS LATER, Gianluca found himself standing in the midst of another gala.

He couldn't have said what it was in aid of. He couldn't recall how many engagements he'd had this week. He'd forgotten everything his staff had whispered in his ear about the various dignitaries and such promenading about before him.

Because the only thing he could seem to concentrate on for any length of time was Helene.

Especially when they did events like this, where he could watch the way she charmed every person who crossed her path without even seeming to try.

"You look displeased, my king," she murmured through her serene smile when they took to the dance floor, always dancing for those few first moments before others joined them.

Though Gianluca never noticed the others.

"I am ruminating on your ability to hide the fangs I know you carry," he said, but rather too late, because it was difficult not to get lost in all the ways she shone. "Right there behind that smile."

Helene did not look abashed. If anything, her smile grew brighter. "Fangs? How marvelous. Unless what you're telling me is that my dentistry needs work?"

Gianluca wanted to laugh, but controlled himself. Because he still couldn't believe that he had been taken in by the very sort of woman he had vowed to avoid. A woman like his own mother.

Women like Elettra, his father had told him on his deathbed, *hide in plain sight. A viper waiting to strike when you least expect it.*

Yet his viper made cracks about dentistry, right here in the middle of a ballroom, and what was he meant to do with that?

There was nothing to do, he knew, but dance.

As if this wasn't a game they played, but something real.

She had taken to her royal duties far too easily, he thought when the dancing was finished and they moved once more to the endless rounds of meeting and greeting the subjects who paid to attend galas like this for the chance to have a few moments of conversation.

So easily and so well, he couldn't help but think as she dazzled the whole of the group before them, that it was tempting to ask himself what might have been. If she had been who she'd seemed to be on those summer walks in Provence.

He knew that was not a helpful line of thought.

But she acquitted herself beautifully at every engagement. She was charming, interesting, and the papers swooned daily not only over what they called the *royal romance* but the many ways their new queen epitomized all that a Fiammettan woman should be.

She was elegant. Poised. She was sophisticated enough to host a formal dinner consisting of heads of state and diplomats from afar, but down-to-earth enough to make everyone laugh, put everyone at ease, and make certain that no one at her table ever felt out of place.

And as many times as he told himself that it was that school she'd gone to, renowned as it was for turning out perfect hostesses just like this, Gianluca was well aware that there was something special about Helene.

Fangs, he told himself darkly as the night wore on. *Stuck deep beneath your ribs.*

It was no wonder he couldn't seem to catch a full breath in her presence.

Later, when he had given the expected speech and they were sitting in the back of the car yet again, inching back toward the palace, she turned to him.

Gianluca expected barbs of some kind, no doubt involving those fangs she pretended she didn't know she had.

He braced himself, because it was only a matter of time. Now he'd made it clear that she wouldn't get her way, things between them would evolve the way his parents' relationship had. He expected that she would strike out at him, becoming more and more bitter by the day. The only upside was that he knew precisely where that led.

And precisely where he intended to put her, no matter how she sparkled in public.

But instead, Helene smiled at him.

In that pretty way of hers that made the gold in her eyes glow all the brighter, without the faintest hint of a fang in sight.

"It's going to be hard to act the broodmare if there's no breeding," she said.

And the shock of that went through him like an electric charge. "I beg your pardon?"

Gianluca couldn't have heard her right. He was sure he hadn't. He spent entirely too much time as it was replaying their wedding night on an endless loop in his head. And recalling those wild, hot hours filled him with a hard, edgy hunger that had him up and pacing, then trying to beat it out of himself in his workout room, to no avail.

But he knew women like this. He'd been raised by one. He had expected that once he'd uncovered her game, she would never indicate that she even knew what sex was unless she could use it against him. He'd expected her to dole it out, playing carrot and stick, and he'd assured himself that he would simply refuse to engage in her games.

This had to be a game—but he was too busy thinking about *breeding* with every last part of his instantly too-hot body to figure out what her goal was in playing it.

"My apologies," Helene said, in that particularly dry voice she used when she was being polite, but sharp.

Fang-sharp, he told himself.

"I keep forgetting that you are a king and perhaps don't muck about in the stables like some. You clearly don't understand how this works. If you want heirs, Gianluca, I'm afraid you will have to fight past your disgust for my deceitful ways and take me to your bed once again."

And there were so many things he could have said to that. He had the uncharacteristic urge to defend himself. To make it clear what it was he had distaste for and dampen whatever this was, because it couldn't be good—

But instead, it was as if his body took control of him. It was as if he became a different man.

Right there in the back of the royal limousine.

And he found he enjoyed it far more than he should have when her eyes widened. When her lips formed a perfect *oh* as he leaned toward her.

"We don't need a bed, *mia regina*," he growled at her. "I have told you this already, have I not? I always give my people what they want. Always."

And he proved it.

Then and there, while the motorcade made its way back up the hill to the royal palace.

When they got out of the car Helene was red-cheeked, her hair a mess, and yet she managed to march back to the royal apartments as if daring anyone to look at her sideways, with that elegance that was a part of her.

As if she was a true queen, something in him whispered.

And it was good to have that reminder, he told himself later—having restricted himself to his quarters, alone. Because he dared not take her twice again in one evening.

He already knew what that was like, and where it led.

Still, he assured himself as he stood in his shower in the small hours of that same night, letting the cold water pound down upon him to no great effect, it was useful to remember that no matter how elegant she seemed at this gala or that function, no matter how sophisticated a queen she might appear, she was still a supposed virgin.

The one who had gone so wild on their wedding night that she'd made it clear she could not be any such thing, and then she'd gone ahead and compounded that error in the car tonight.

For he had tugged her to him, then into his lap.

And the moment they'd touched, it was as if they'd both been burned alive.

The flames *exploded* when he kissed her. When she kissed him back.

The conflagration grew between them, bigger, and yet bigger still—and after he helped himself to the long hem of that gown she wore, pushing the fabric up to her hips, he reached down to free himself and found her hands were already there.

"Mia regina," he had growled, and told himself it was a factual statement, that was all. *My queen.*

When she'd sunk herself down upon him, he had clenched his hands tight to grip her hips, because it was a process. She was so tight, so soft. And there was something mesmerizing about the way she fought to take the whole of his length.

Something almost unbearably hot.

It was when she'd managed to take all of him within her—shifting, bearing down, and then retreating to start again—that she let out a deep sort of sigh. She closed her eyes for a moment, as if *savoring him.*

Gianluca would never know how he had not lost control of himself entirely.

But she opened her eyes again. And then, holding his gaze as if she was the one who told the truth and always had—like a challenge—she had ridden them both to a mad, galloping finish.

He should not have second-guessed himself. She proved herself a liar every time they made contact. A wise man would not have been fooled a second time, no matter how excellent her training.

But his body didn't care if she told the truth or not, it only wanted more of her.

When the morning dawned, Gianluca redoubled his efforts to dig into her past. People never hid their sins as well as they imagined they did, so he knew he would uncover the real story about how she'd spent the past few years soon enough.

Yet in the meantime, he unlatched that door between their bedrooms and congratulated himself on persevering. Because, of course, he did this entirely for the bloodline.

Let her imagine he was the sort of man she could manipulate into abandoning his plans, if she liked. That changed nothing. She could brood about it up in his grandmother's retreat of stone and silence.

He was doing his duty, as he had always done. And as he would do again, when she bore him children and they were old enough to live without her.

"And what age is that, exactly, Gianluca?" Helene asked one night, in her mild way that he no longer quite believed. Because he could hear the edge beneath it now, that she hid beneath her lovely manners, and her cultured tones. "The age at which children are only too happy to live without their mothers?"

He had, for no reason at all, reiterated his precise plans for her. It had nothing to do with the fact that they had turned to each other when they walked into the royal apartments tonight, that he'd waved away his staff with a dismissive hand, or that he'd then carried her bodily to his bed. It had no relation to what followed from there, or to the fact that now they lay on the soft rug before the fire, both of them naked and gleaming with the force of their exertions.

All three times.

Helene sounded almost lazy as she asked him that question, and one thing he knew now about Helene was that she was in no way lazy.

"I was sent to boarding school when I was six years old," he said abruptly.

And he expected some sort of arch response, but all she did was prop herself up on one elbow. She raked the mess he'd made of her hair back from her face, then regarded him solemnly. "Six years old?"

Gianluca had the strangest urge toward defensiveness, then, when nothing could have made less sense to him. What did he have to be defensive about? He had been a crown prince, not a regular boy. Royal personages such as himself had been sent off to boarding school at young ages as long as boarding schools had existed.

"Some of my classmates began their education even earlier," he said, in freezing tones, and he would have sat up, perhaps removed himself from his conversation entirely, but he felt that would be more telling.

He did not want to tell her anything. Not about himself.

Especially not when a more layered version of the truth was that, despite his loneliness, he had often found school a reprieve from the dread and calamity of this palace. He had counted the days until he could return, no longer relegated to be as invisible as the furniture or a handy bit of cannon fodder.

Gianluca was appalled that he even *thought* such things. There was no possibility that he would *say* them. To anyone.

And certainly not her.

She was frowning at him as if what he said *hurt* her. "That doesn't sound like an education at all. It sounds like daycare. Or proper full-time care, I suppose."

"I'm deeply surprised by this attitude, Helene."

He did rise then. Gianluca stalked over to the bedside table, where he rang to have a light selection of food brought up, as he found himself famished.

It was no doubt his hunger that was affecting his mood.

When he was finished placing his order, he expected to find that Helene might have wrapped herself in something, but instead she stayed where she was.

Wholly naked, stretched out before the fire like every fantasy he had ever had, brought to vibrant and alluring life.

It was the lushness of her curves. It was the dark waves of her hair that spilled all over her, dancing this way and that and making her more sensual every time she breathed. It was her eyes of melting brown and brilliant gold that made him—the King of Fiammetta, who bowed to no one—feel as if he was to prove himself to her.

Or for her, something in him whispered, but it was a voice he refused take on board.

He pretended he could not recognize it.

"You spent a great many years of your life in boarding school," he said, frowning at her because it was that or go to her again, to try once more to slake his unquenchable thirst for this woman. "And you credit your education for the ability to execute your duties as Queen in the way that you do. I would imagine you would exult in allowing your children to follow much the same path toward excellence."

He did not choose to recognize the way his pulse seemed to rush in him. He told himself it was a simple physical reaction, nothing more. Chemicals, that was all. Nothing he needed to consider any more closely than not—especially not when all he could see was that solemn gaze she aimed his way.

"I was sent to boarding school after my mother died," Helene said softly. But he was learning, too, that when her voice was soft, it did not make her weak. Or lessen the blow of anything she might be saying. And he did not like the fact that he knew such things. They made him wonder who she really was, this woman he had married under false pretenses that he still could not prove. "I was twelve. And all things considered, I would have preferred to have my mother."

"Children are not meant to stay forever with their parents," Gianluca gritted out, as if this was a fight he needed to win *right now*. As if this was about him instead of their hypothetical children.

"But they are expected stay for some while, surely. Or why bother having them at all? You could as easily adopt a few stray orphans off the street when they hit eighteen and they wouldn't know the difference."

Gianluca let out a deep sort of breath. "Your father is, at best, a minor noble. Mostly because of shrewd investments. By which I mean that you, though an heiress of gentle breeding, are not of noble blood."

"I don't recall ever claiming that my blood was blue." The look of something like a wicked amusement passed over her face, making the way she was lounging there seem to grab at him, until he was not at all certain that he was capable of keeping his distance. But he forced himself to stand fast. "I know you must have known this before you ever set eyes on me. I've met every member of your staff by now, Gianluca. They are remarkably thorough."

He did not scowl. That would suggest a bigger reaction than he was having. "Bloodlines are of paramount importance when it is those very bloodlines that determine succession to a throne. Don't pretend you don't know this very well, please."

Helene sat up then and she took her time with it. She stretched like a cat and it was too much. It seemed to punch straight through his chest.

Like a knife, he told himself as he dug his palm against the sudden, searing ache.

The woman was a killer and he was letting her have her way.

But he did nothing as she got to her feet in that same, seemingly languid way she did everything, and then helped herself to one of the silk wrappers that his staff had taken to leaving in his rooms and hers now that there were no locked doors between them. Once she'd belted it and was covered in the finest silk, she drifted closer to him. He thought she might come to him, but instead she perched herself on the end of the bed, as if continuing a fascinating discussion.

When he was certain he had been trying to end it.

She looked entirely too serene. "Do you ever think about the fact that throughout all the ages past, no one could actually tell?"

"I do not know what you mean." Though he had an inkling.

"There are no paternity tests. There were just…regular people storming about, pretending their feelings were facts. On some level, how can you possibly know what your bloodline is or isn't?"

"Is this how you think you will convince me of your innocence?" he asked, his voice barely above a whisper.

And most people would cringe at that. Bow their heads in shame, at the very least.

But all Helene did was shrug.

Insolently.

"I think it's the guilty who run around trying to get others to buy their story." And if anything, if possible, she looked even *more* at ease. "I feel no need to prove my innocence. I know it to be true. I'm the one who's lived every day of my life, after all. I would know if I had accidentally collected a selection of lovers, but then again, so too would your staff. Funnily enough, I think they've come up empty-handed too. Why do you think that is?"

And he could have raged about her offhandedness. He could have made certain she knew that he wasn't giving up and that he was in fact tracking down every stray lead. He could have put his mouth on hers and quelled her insolence at the source—

But instead, there was a faint knock on the door that indicated the arrival of the food he'd ordered.

Gianluca told himself that was a relief.

Just as he told himself that he was not succumbing to temptation, but merely making certain that he had as many opportunities as possible to get her pregnant as quickly as he could, so this torture might end.

That was why she fell asleep in his bed that night, the way she had been doing with some regularity by now. Even though it was something he'd vowed to himself he would never allow again.

Over the following days, he reviewed his staff's findings, not best pleased to find that she was right. They had found nothing. Everything she said about her past was easily verifiable. If she was hiding something, it was so well hidden only she knew about it.

"And of course, sire," his personal aide said in a tone stripped of even the faintest hint of any inflection, "a secret is only really a secret if no one else knows it. And if that's the case here, it's unlikely that it's a secret anyone else could tell. Which is a victory, is it not?"

For he had told them that he wanted to make certain no one could ever step forward with any so-called secrets from the Queen's past. He'd intimated that there might have been some cause for worry, so that they would look harder.

Instead he was left with something far worse than any confirmation of the sins he knew she'd committed.

And that was his urge to believe her.

But he knew better.

To underscore that some days later—or to remind himself of what was truly at stake here—he gritted his teeth and took his least favorite walk of all. He had watched his queen charm the better part of Europe. He had proven himself unable to keep any promise to himself when it came to erecting boundaries between them. He was disastrously close to becoming a version of his father, and that could not stand.

And so he took himself out one of the small, hidden doors at the rear of the palace. He crossed the wintry grounds, winding his way through the ancient cottages and chapels and ruins of old castles until he could present himself to the guards who stood before the farthest cottage, closest to the stables without actually being a part of them.

It was a bitterly cold February day. Sullen snow fell insistently from low, gray clouds, with winds from the tops of the surrounding mountains sharp enough to draw blood.

Adequate preparation for an interaction with Elettra, to his mind.

He nodded to the guards and was instantly admitted, and though he immediately wished he had not come at all, he walked through to get this done.

"To what do I owe this unimaginable honor, Your Majesty?" asked his mother as she rose from the seat where she waited for him in her lovely drawing room, sketching a perfectly appropriate curtsy that still somehow managed to scrape at him, as if she was mocking him. "When your secretary called and ordered me to clear the afternoon, I could hardly believe my ears. The King of Fiammetta? Polluting the very shades of the dower house?"

Gianluca ignored all that. He would ignore his mother entirely if he could, and he usually did, but he had come here to speak to her. Ignoring her would be a waste of time.

He looked around this room that he had entered only a handful of times before. If he remembered right, while his grandmother had still been alive. And though the furnishings were very much the same, they were brighter than he recalled. Happier.

As if his mother liked to let in the light, when there was light to let in.

He didn't like how that sat in him, like a hint he ought to take.

Just as he didn't like the fact that most of the pictures on her mantel were not of her with various celebrities, as one would expect from such a dedicated attention-seeker as Elettra.

Instead, they were all of him.

There was even the official wedding photo that had been released worldwide, showing Gianluca and Helene gazing at each other as they exited the cathedral. He did not wish to investigate why it was he didn't like that picture here, either.

"I did not come here to fence words with you, Madam," he told her with as much formality as he could muster.

Elettra sighed as if he'd said something provocative, then sank back down on the nearest settee, where she set about pouring out hot cups of tea. When Gianluca was certain she must remember he could not abide the stuff.

"Afternoon tea is not, strictly speaking, a Fiammettan ritual, though we have adopted it," his mother told him, and he felt some great storm inside him, though he refused to acknowledge it.

He wanted no part of it, but there was something about her voice. Gianluca had the strangest memory then that he rejected almost at once, certain it was far more likely to be an invention of that six-year-old child who had cried himself to sleep every night in that school where he'd been sent. Something he had never admitted to another living soul.

Gianluca had learned to tell himself that he was merely imagining things. That he had no memories of his childhood. That his mother had certainly never gathered him onto her lap, and read to him.

That she had never told him stories or taken his little hand in hers to walk with him around the palace, telling him made-up names for things that he absolutely did not remember today, damn it.

She was still going on about tea. "It was when one of your great-grandfathers procured himself an Englishwoman for a queen. She brought the wonderful tradition of afternoon tea in the British style with her when she came here, and so there have been Fiammettan tea shops ever since. Do you not remember? I used to take you there—"

"I have always hated tea," he told her, sternly.

But Elettra did not seem dismayed. She merely set down a teacup in his direction, then sat back with her own and sipped at it.

It made him want to shout, though he restrained himself.

"And here I thought you wanted to meet with me so we could debate, once again, whether we prefer scones or crumpets," she murmured.

He wanted to dismiss that as a kind of foolishness too, but Gianluca found that it hit him strangely. His mouth almost watered. He could almost taste the scones he loved so much, though he did not associate them with his mother. Still, it was true that he indulged himself from time to time, in the privacy of his own quarters.

"How many lovers did you take when you were married to my father, the late King?" he asked icily instead.

And his reward, such as it was, was the slight widening in his mother's eyes, dark like his. She set her teacup down in the saucer she held with a click, then placed them both on the table before her. He thought that it took her a moment or so to raise her gaze to his, but when she did, her expression was smooth and unreadable, the way it always was.

"I wonder," Elettra said quietly, "what would become of us, you and I, if just once we stopped playing these games." He said nothing, and her lips curved into something sad. "If you and I stopped having arguments with people who are no longer in the room."

"Is it an argument?" He watched her closely. "Or is it that I find myself wondering, from time to time, if I have been less merciful with you than I should. If perhaps I should look to my benevolence in my dealings with you and revise my impressions. So I ask again, how many lovers did you take? And of them, how many did you leak to the press yourself?"

Elettra folded her hands in her lap and sat there with a dignity that enraged him, as certainly she did not deserve it. Surely her own sins should have precluded her from even the faintest shred of dignity, assumed or otherwise.

Yet somehow, without changing her expression, she managed to make it clear that he had disappointed her once again.

Gianluca did not sit taller, as he had half a mind to do at that—some deep-seated vestige of the child he must once have been. Instead, he relaxed as he stood, and leaned against the mantel, his back to all those pictures of himself through the ages.

"Come now. You had so much to say in all of those interviews, one after the next, each one a nail in the coffin not only of your marriage, but of our people's trust in their leaders." He shook his head. "Not once did it occur to you that you were leaving me to clean up after you. A king in name only, because in truth I am a janitor, forever trailing after you and attempting to make your trash disappear."

Elettra's eyes flashed. "How poetic, darling," she said. "I didn't know you had it in you."

And yet he felt as if something was lost when all she did was pick up her tea once more.

"I must thank you." He straightened from the mantel and affected his own bow, deep enough to be mocking. "You are, as ever, precisely as I expected you to be."

"You're so discerning," his mother murmured, as if in agreement. "And in no way afflicted by confirmation bias, my son and king."

"I'm certain you've cast yourself the victim of your own crimes," he said, but he was already heading for the door. "Thank you for reminding me why I keep you separate from everything that matters."

It was good that he'd come here. She was his past, but also his future if he did not handle this terrible attraction to his own queen, herself a proven liar as well.

He hated that he'd needed the reminder.

And he told himself that he was dismissing her once again as he pushed his way back outside into a day gone grayer, colder.

But he heard her parting shot anyway.

And with that laugh of hers that made it all the more damaging, hitting him right between the shoulder blades.

"Because, of course, the King of Fiammetta could never be wrong. By definition. Just like your father, is that not so?"

CHAPTER EIGHT

FAITH MESSAGED ONE MORNING, some two months into Helene's marriage.

Why did I have to read about the fact that you met my most favorite singer in all the world in a tabloid magazine?

Then she devolved into shouting by text.

YOU KNOW HOW MUCH I LOVE HIM!

Helene dutifully texted back a full play-by-play of her interaction with the singer in question, and even indulged in the sort of silly, make-believe gossip she and her cousin had enjoyed in the past. Where they made up a wild speculation about people they would never meet, and then treated it as fact. Helene thought that was the least she could do, having actually met the man.

While she left her cousin satisfied that Faith, and Faith alone, was the one true love of a rather odd young man she was unlikely to ever meet, the exchange left Helene unsettled.

The feeling followed her through a day of her usual duties. A morning of classes and correspondence, because it was her office that was responsible for sending out cards for all manner of occasions to the Fiammettan subjects. And because it offered her a way to ask her aides about all kinds of subjects that interested her after, like the previous king and queen. And the day's headlines, chock-full of palace intrigue.

She wrote cards, asked questions, and listened not only to what her staff said—but what they didn't.

"My mother always said that any man must know trouble, whether in a crown or in a quarry," one of her aides said in German after one of Helene's leading questions about Gianluca's parents.

"Heavy is the head," another replied in French, with significant looks all around.

This was standard. They would deny if asked—Helene had tried—but none of her staff cared for the former king. And they were all of them staunch royalists, or they wouldn't be here, tending to her.

She tucked that away with all of the other details that she hoped she could weave into some kind of tapestry that, one day, she could look at and make sense of her husband at last.

Every day she got a little closer. She was sure of it.

But for some reason, over the last ten days or so, she'd begun to find all of it, all the waiting and weaving…exhausting.

And today when she was free, instead of taking her usual walk in the palace gardens—which she did no matter what the weather or Gianluca's desire for photo opportunities, though those were fewer now that they were seen together so often at events—Helene headed down to her favorite library instead.

Outside there was another snowstorm brewing, this one extreme enough that even the natives had raised a brow or two in concern. Helene sat by the fire, and for once, didn't find herself a few books to read. Not today. Somehow, she wasn't quite in the mood.

Instead, she found herself gazing into the fire, and trying to reason through why it was that a perfectly normal exchange with her cousin this morning had left her feeling so…bereft.

And the answer didn't take long, but still, it seemed a bit longer than it should have. The way everything did lately.

She was stuck in a gloomy marriage she couldn't escape if she wanted to, so that giggling about make-believe relationships her cousin wasn't having seemed like a reprieve.

Though even as she thought that, she knew that the true problem with her marriage was that it wasn't *gloomy* at all.

On the contrary.

Everything with Gianluca was white hot and *wild*.

And to her astonishment, there was no getting used to him. There was no reaching a saturation point. Every time he touched her it was better than the time before. Every time they came together, no matter where they came together, it was as if it was the first time. And the last time.

It was that epic. It was that unbearably beautiful.

It was that catastrophic.

Because the truth was, Helene thought as she watched the dancing flames of the fire before her, she really did want those fairy tales. The ones her mother had told her when she was a girl. The ones she and Faith created for each other about pop singers who fancied themselves ambassadors to the world, and anyone else who took their fancy. She wanted all those stories. She wanted to be an old woman who could look wisely at young girls like the ones at her luncheon today and tell them that it was all worth waiting for, whatever perfect fairy tale they carried within them, because it would happen.

If they believed. And if they let it come.

And sometimes *letting it come* took too long, so a woman did what she needed to do to prod a man along.

It wasn't that she defied Gianluca. Not outwardly.

But she used the weapons she had.

Without mercy.

She had to believe that if she could only show him how, he might come around to her way of seeing things. And that maybe if she showed him who she really was, in bed and out, he would finally believe her.

And maybe then she would get to see that smile of his again.

That practical girl inside her, who had thought she could march into a frigid marriage with a total stranger only to fall in love at first sight, wasn't so sure. Because she might believe in fairy tales, but now she knew too well that even when something seemed to be moving in that direction, it could turn out to hinge entirely on an innocence she could not prove. And that he would not believe.

No matter how many times he called her *mia regina* and made her sob out his name in reply.

"In other words," she muttered into the fire, "you're doomed."

Helene woke sometime later, surprised to find she'd drifted off into a very uncharacteristic nap. But there was no time to worry over it, because while she and Gianluca had no outside engagements tonight, her aides had come to ready her for one of their private dinners in their palace apartments. The dinners Gianluca insisted on, because, she thought, it made him imagine they were more civilized

than they were afterward, in his bed. Or hers. Or wherever they found themselves in a set of apartments with so
very many rooms.

And though she might think differently in the aftermath, Helene could find nothing *gloomy* about spending
time with her husband.

It was the way Gianluca waited for her each evening.
He stood there looking resplendent as always, even though
their private dinners were meant to be casual. He usually
wore only a shirt and trousers, while she liked her jeans
and something pretty on top.

But there was never any doubt that he was the King, no
matter what he wore.

Or didn't.

He was there before the windows, so that the lights of
this beautiful kingdom glittered behind him through the
storm. Sometimes she thought she saw the same lights in
his dark night gaze, the way they'd been there that first
night.

Before everything changed.

And maybe that unexpected nap still had its claws in
her, because her usual jolting reaction to the sight of him
didn't seem to translate into the lightheartedness she liked
to use at dinners like this. If only to confound him.

It hadn't occurred to her that *not* doing it would confound him too.

Halfway through the meal he sat back in his seat and
eyed her even more closely than usual. "Are you unwell?"

"Not to my knowledge," she replied, frowning at him.
"Why?"

He studied her frown, making Helene wonder if she'd
never actually *frowned* at him before now. Surely not.

"You do not seem your normal self."

And this was clearly true, because she shot back, "I didn't realize you knew what that was, Gianluca."

And she expected him to glower, but to her surprise, he tipped his wineglass in her direction. "Fair enough."

And Helene felt...listless and yet half frenzied, all at once. She had the urge to leap up from her chair and *do something*. Dance down the length of the table, for example, kicking the fine china to and fro and watching it shatter. Whatever it took to break all these unspoken rules they followed these days.

That they would have these excruciatingly civilized dinners, then tear each other apart after dessert. But never, ever, both at once.

It was always the same sequence of events and while it was true that they knew each other intimately, in ways she hadn't known one person could know another, what did it mean? She knew the precise shape of that tender place between his ear and the sideburn he kept trimmed short, and how it fit her fingertip when she stroked him there. She knew the entire vocabulary of his moans and groans and how to make them into a kind of song as she took her time with him. She knew his scents, his tastes, and the shape their bodies made together when they were both asleep.

And she knew every thread of the tapestry she was building, every color and weight of each story she read or heard, all leading her closer to him. Everyone she encountered added to it. Everyone they met contributed a tale about his parents or him, and she thought that really, she was the reigning expert on King Gianluca.

Save him.

But he wouldn't discuss it.

And tonight she was tired of quietly weaving.

"Tell me," she demanded without any preamble, "one happy memory from your childhood. Can you do that?"

"Do I appear to you to be riddled with childhood wounds, Helene?"

And on another night she might have made an elegant sort of demurral and waved that away. Tonight she only sat back in her chair, held his gaze, and raised a challenging brow instead.

Because she knew the answer—that there was not one part of him that childhood hadn't touched, warped, even ruined—but she also knew he would likely get up and leave if she shared her learned opinion that he was, in fact, a *walking* wound from the things that had happened to him during his childhood.

He let out one of those laughs of his, short and sharp, more a surprised bark than anything else. And she rather thought that he would storm off, though he hadn't done that in some while…but he didn't.

Instead, he looked at her as if he was trying to see beneath her skin, and she became aware of too many things all at once.

That everything was *different* tonight, or she was. She could feel too much, as if the Vivaldi that played gently in the background was winding its way in and around her body instead of simply filling the air.

And she felt *desperate* straight through, when that was the most absurd feeling of all. She was a queen. Sitting in a king's private dining room, in the palace they shared, eating another feast prepared by the finest chefs in all of Europe, according to her husband. She was listening to classical music while making awkward, yet polite, conversation about charity events and current issues.

There was nothing *desperate* about this.

So maybe it was her.

"My father was always quite busy with matters of state, appropriately," Gianluca said into the messiness swirling around inside her, and even though moments before—seconds before—Helene had wanted to kick off her shoes and dance on the tabletop, she was suddenly riveted by him. Gazing at him, just there on the other side of this corner of the long table they shared, as if she had no intention of ever looking away again. "I was left in the care of tutors and nannies and the like. But at night, a woman would come into the nursery, take me in her lap, and read me a nighttime story. Every story was…a different world. I suppose even a prince in a castle liked the idea of imagining himself somewhere else."

He looked very nearly defensive then, and she felt almost breathless, as if the slightest move on her part would ruin everything and break whatever fragile thread this was between them, suddenly.

Because, for once, Gianluca did not look serious or betrayed. For a moment, she could almost see the little boy he must have been. Before they'd sent him away from here to whatever dire boarding school took in six-year-olds. When that smile she might not have seen too often, but could recall perfectly, wasn't so rare.

"My mother used to read to me too," she said.

But it was the wrong thing to say. She could see it in the way his brows drew together. "I didn't say it was my mother."

She blinked. "You said it was a woman, and it sounded as if it wasn't a nanny or a tutor…?"

"I have long since left escapist fiction behind, I'm afraid." He sounded curt. Dark. "That's what happens as a person grows up. There's no time for such stories when there are so many real-world things to consider instead."

"I don't think you could say anything I would disagree with more." But she smiled a little as she said it, because she knew, somehow, that he was remarkably vulnerable just now. She just knew. "I think that human beings need stories. We need to engage our imagination or we are doomed to lose ourselves."

"In what? Reality?" He shook his head. "That is not doom. That is life."

"But if you can't imagine yourself out of a bad reality, what will become of you?" she countered. "And what better way to train for that than reading stories?"

"Is your reality so heinous, Helene?"

She could see that he hadn't moved, not even a millimeter, and yet she felt as if he had. As if he'd stood up, then loomed over her, crowding into her space and taking over her senses.

"I didn't say it was. That doesn't change how I feel about the necessity of stories, Gianluca. Fairy tales teach people how to *be* people."

"Some stories are necessary," he gritted out, as if they were in a desperate fight that he needed to win. "The story of the Kingdom, that all its subjects can share in. These specific beliefs we all must live by to do so in relative peace with the hope of prosperity. But you are speaking of something else. When surely you should know that the purpose of such tales was never singing seafood and dancing candelabras. The first fairy tales were no doubt told over the fires of yore as morality tales. Warnings, not love stories. Making them something else not only takes their power, it steals your own."

"Or," Helene returned with precious little hold on her

hard-won charm, "they are just good stories, no matter what you use them for."

"At heart, they are lies." Gianluca's voice was harsh and unequivocal. "And I cannot abide lies."

"What sort of lies do you mean?" she asked softly, carefully, because she had woven that tapestry so carefully and so steadily and now she was tugging on its threads. And she couldn't seem to stop, not now that she could see a glimpse of the real Gianluca shining through. Not even though she knew that she was risking everything here. And worse, risking hurting him in the process. "Like the one where you pretend that the only happy memory you can draw up from your childhood involves a random servant? I think both you and I know that's not the case."

"Damn you," he growled at her.

And then he really did rise from his chair. And he really was looming over hers, with a look on his face that she'd never seen before.

As if the ice she'd cracked was him.

Then Gianluca was hauling her up, slamming his mouth to hers, and breaking all of his own rules.

She half expected him to shove all the china out of his way, onto the hard floor, but he was still Gianluca. He lifted her up into his arms, dragging her thighs around his waist, and carried her down to the far end of the table, where the table was not covered in dishes and he could lay her out like a feast.

And then he proceeded to eat her alive.

And it was different this time. There was something *different*, as if both of them were naked in ways they never had been before. As if they were both too raw to do anything but show themselves, and Helene couldn't understand that entirely, but everything in her was open to this, whatever it was.

To him, however he came to her.

Especially when it was as if they had revealed themselves tonight in ways so new there was nothing to do but imprint on each other with every touch. With every hard, deep kiss. With the way he dug his hands into her hair, then tipped back her face as if he could make a whole meal out of her mouth alone.

He really did try, and Helene tried back.

But it didn't last, because every time they built a fire, a new one raged, and they seemed unable to do anything but throw gas on each.

Her hands were busy and shaky at his waist. She ripped his shirt off, heedless of the buttons that popped off and hit the floor. Because it was necessary, more necessary than breath, to put her mouth on the glory of his bare chest and then to trace with her hands that arrow of dark hair that led her right where she wanted to go.

He didn't let her get there. Not this time. He muttered something she didn't understand, though it seemed to fill her all the same.

Then his hands were at the hem of her shirt, pulling it up and off. He made a low noise of deep male approval at the site of the frilly, lacy thing she wore beneath, but then he pushed it up and out of his way. Then he took that off of her too.

Gianluca drew one proud nipple into his mouth, making another low sort of noise when she arched into him, giving him better access. And delivering herself directly into the carnal delight of that hot, clever mouth of his.

Helene could do nothing, then, but surrender. As he

went on and on, teasing her and taunting her, until she was begging him. Pleading with him.

Until he bent her back against the table, slid his hand down beneath her waistband, and palmed her wet heat at last.

Then he played her like some kind of classical instrument, making her a part of the symphony that soared all around them, as he slowly, expertly, tore her apart.

Once. Then again.

And then, while she shook and sobbed, Gianluca pulled the rest of her clothes off. He kicked off his own, and then, with a glorious ferocity, slammed his way into her.

He folded up her legs between them so she was wide open, completely his. No barriers, no control, nothing but the way he thrust deep, again and again.

Helene opened her eyes, gripping his shoulders as he braced himself above her. She held his gaze as he slammed into her and made her bloom with each thrust, shoving the heavy, antique table across the floor.

It should have been a kind of madness, but it was something else.

Because his eyes were on hers and she could see those stars again.

And Helene knew she wasn't the only one who understood that there was something profound in this moment. That despite themselves, they had moved into a different place.

That this was the kind of prize she had only hoped she'd find when she'd decided that she wouldn't hide from him. When she'd decided that she would fight for the both of them whether he wanted to help her or not.

This was what she won—the glory of it built high— and she hurtled over the edge once more. And when she floated back again, he was still inside her, huge and hard.

But this time, he lowered himself against her, drawing her legs around his waist.

And then, keeping that gaze of his locked on hers, Gianluca went slow.

Time spun out and lost all meaning.

Helene clung to him, but even as she did, she felt as if she was inside him as he was inside her. As if they were both a part of the same thing, wrapped up tight like this. Made new every time he found himself inside her.

Sanctified here, together.

Something broke over her that wasn't another shattering, not yet. Helene shifted, reaching up to cup his dark, stern face between her palms. And he looked even more austere now, the stark lines of desire making him seem something like cruel, when she knew he wasn't. Not really.

No matter how he liked to pretend, because there was this.

A cruel man could not make love.

Maybe this was the truth she'd been looking for all along, because it settled in her now like sunlight. As if it was a fact she had always known.

"Your problem," she whispered, because there were other things she knew, "is that deep down, you trusted me all along."

She watched her words wash over him, then through him. And then become a part of that same pure sunlight as he roared out his release, flooding her and sending her catapulting over that edge once more.

Into nothing but the brightest light.

And for a long time after that, neither one of them could move.

When he did, he pulled her up so she was sitting there with her legs dangling off the table, dazed.

But, something in her whispered, *defiant, too.*

Maybe that was what the truth did. Or better still, speaking it out loud.

Gianluca gazed down at her, his face stern.

"I wish I could believe you," he told her, his voice gravelly. Rough. "Just as I wish I could believe those fairy stories my mother read me." He reached over to trace the line of her lips with his thumb, as if he couldn't help himself. Yet in those night sky eyes of his, Helene saw only dark. "But I don't."

And she was both unsurprised and deeply shocked that he walked away and left her there.

She put her clothes back on, carefully, as if she was hurt when she wasn't. Maybe she wished she was, as then she might have something to tend to. Instead she set the dining room to rights and only then, having hidden the evidence from any staff members who hadn't heard the table moving, did she wander out. Then make her way back to her own bedroom, where she curled herself up in a ball and wished that she could cry.

Instead, she lay awake until late, wishing she didn't feel as if all the skin had been flayed from her bones.

And the next morning she woke up to Faith's monthly complaints about how wretched she felt, because she and Helene usually felt the same sort of wretched at the same time. She started typing back—

Then stopped.

Helene sat straight up in her bed, and even though she hadn't slept well, too caught up in dark eyes filled with stars, then not, and all the things they hadn't said that had flowed between them last night and left her *flayed* and *raw*, she was filled with a wild energy.

A certainty, more like.

She scrolled through the calendar on her phone. She started counting back on her fingers, to double-check.

But she already knew.

She thought of her listlessness. How outside her own skin she felt. How raw she was lately. How incapable of the simplest things, when she'd used to pride herself in taking refuge in perfect dinner table conversation.

It was no fairy tale that she had been here two months and had been both having sex and doing nothing to protect herself from its consequences that whole time. She hadn't had a period since some two weeks before her wedding.

That was truth. That was reality.

And she knew.

Helene sat there on the high bed, her hands over the belly she'd never really given much thought to before. Did she already feel some kind of thickening? She'd thought that was simply all the rich food she ate now that there was no wedding gown to model for half the world...

But it wasn't the food.

Helene was pregnant.

She was *pregnant*.

And it was as if a kind of floodgate burst open, then.

Because once she accepted what a missed period indicated, when she had never missed a period in her life, it was as if everything else fell into place.

She felt kind of wild clarity that she'd never felt before.

And there was a peace in it, too.

Because there was absolutely no way in hell that she was letting her child grow up like this.

There would be no boarding schools at six years old.

There would be no chilly parents, tearing strips off of each other for the child to hear.

She had loved her mother, she would always love her

mother, but Helene had no desire whatsoever to *become* her. And she knew, because she'd tried.

While it was always possible that her parents had a different relationship behind closed doors, Helene had no intention of showing her children weakness or acceptance in the face of cruelty.

And she had no intention of becoming *his* parents, either.

She would not raise a child who would pretend not to remember whether or not his own mother had read them stories.

Her children would not grow up the way that he had. Or the way that she had, either.

Gianluca had been right when he'd said that she was not of the sort of aristocratic blood that he was. Her people had fought across the ages for every scrap of what they had. They had not had palaces to retreat into or armies to carry their banners. They had done it all themselves.

And she, Helene Archibald San Felice, the Queen of Fiammetta, would do no less.

Starting now.

CHAPTER NINE

AT FIRST GIANLUCA thought that Helene was having the same sort of hangover that he was after that night. When things had become entirely too raw between them, in ways he wasn't sure he wanted to analyze.

Nor could.

On the surface they carried on as they had been. They had a full roster of royal engagements and neither one of them was the sort to scrimp on such things. He might not trust her, as he had said. But he did know her to be a hard worker in that sense.

Is that the character of a liar? came that voice again, and again he ignored it.

Tonight they were at yet another formal event. And Gianluca, who prided himself on knowing as many details as possible about everything that went on in his kingdom, in his name, and with all the charities that he spearheaded, had completely forgotten what this event was even *for.*

He was beginning to wonder if he had overcommitted to this charity circuit of his, all of it calculated to prove to his people that he was a far better king than his father had ever been.

That his reign would be filled only with positive things, and as few negative things as possible.

But it had been easier to focus on such things when he wasn't married. When there wasn't Helene.

Because liar or not, he would far rather spend an evening with her, alone.

She told him happy little stories of her time in that boarding school she'd gone to, making the whole thing sound like a sparkling adventure when he knew full well it was one of the most restrictive schools in existence. She told him stories about her late mother and growing up in that château in Provence, where, in her telling, it was always a sunny day in summer and even Herbert was an entertaining character, in his way.

Gianluca even liked it when she argued with him, in that understated way she had. As if, could she only prod him gently enough, he would realize the error of his ways and happily see her side of things.

And she did it all so adroitly that sometimes, he almost did.

But his father had taught him well what liars women were. And how could he have believed otherwise when a man so grand, so captivated by his own magnificence, had declared such things? Had shouted them? Had overturned tables as punctuation?

Something in him hitched at that memory, but he shoved it aside with the ease of long practice.

Women lied. Especially when they claimed otherwise. And though Helene had fooled him well—she had revealed herself on their wedding night. Much as he might wish that she hadn't. Much as, some nights, he lay with her curled around him and wished he could forget it.

The truth was the truth whether he liked it or not.

Because if it wasn't, then he would not need to watch himself so carefully when he was around her. He would not have to fight so hard to contain this wild addiction to her. To let it out only when they were alone and he could make sure not to say anything he would regret, by filling his mouth with her instead.

These were all things he would prefer to do back at the palace, he admitted tonight. Instead of having been dragged into some tedious conversation with other world leaders that had nothing to do with governing and everything to do with the photo opportunity.

Gianluca was sick unto his soul of *photo opportunities* in place of reality.

Though he did not intend to delve into why that was. Not tonight.

He looked for his queen instead.

As ever, Helene was not hard to find. She was too bright, too astonishingly lush, in a sea of Afghan hound sameness. There were a great many glittering jewels on a great many aristocratic necks in this elaborate mountainside venue tonight, but there was only one gleaming queen.

And she was his.

Gianluca was so enchanted by her, the way he did not like to admit he always was, that it took him a long moment to recognize the woman she was speaking to. The two of them stood close together over by a set of the voluptuous orchids that were serving as the better part of the decor for this gala.

He had to blink to be certain, but there was no mistake. Helene was deep in conversation with none other than the Lady Lorenza, his father's infamous first lover.

There was no reason for a chill to go through him, as if he was looking at some kind of ghost.

No reason at all, and yet he started moving through the crowd at once, hardly noticing how easily it parted before him. And as he moved, he accepted the unpalatable truth that Helene was the only person he had ever encountered who made him feel that he was some kind of a fool.

It was always something.

There was always some hint that she was outmaneuvering him when that should have been impossible. He was the King of Fiammetta and she was a sheltered girl who'd been raised to marry a rich man. To contribute her lovely genes to a set of predetermined bloodlines, and no, he did not care to think too closely about the comments she'd made about the provenance of those bloodlines.

As he moved across the gala floor, Gianluca entertained the possibility that Helene really was that girl, bright and sparkling perhaps, but without the ulterior motives. That girl might very well have found herself speaking to the Lady Lorenza who, despite her past with King Alvize, had ever since lived an entirely blameless life. Gianluca had seen her earlier in the evening, here at the charity gala with her own son—who despite much speculation in the press, bore an unmistakable resemblance to her husband and not to the former king. And there were a thousand reasons why the Queen of Fiammetta might speak to one of the Kingdom's aristocrats.

But, somehow, Gianluca knew none of those were Helene's reason tonight. Not only because he knew that she was not as naïve as she might pretend. That even if he had somehow misread the situation on his wedding night—an impossibility—there was the fact that the girls who came out of the Institut were taught how to function as weapons, not merely wives.

It was why he'd asked to meet her in the first place.

More fool you, he thought darkly.

He closed the distance between him and his wife and

as he did, it was Lady Lorenza who saw him coming. And in so doing, confirmed what Gianluca already thought, by putting up her hand as if to stop whatever Helene was saying to her.

When Helene looked over her shoulder to see him there, Gianluca thought she should have looked guilty. With her sins all over her face, for once.

Instead, the look on her face was rather more speculative. Gianluca did not like it.

He found himself perilously close to a scowl, right here in public, but caught himself at the last moment and merely took Helene's arm.

Then inclined his head toward Lady Lorenza as she curtsied before him.

"It is a pleasure to see you, as always," he said, with great formality.

"It is an honor, Your Majesty," she replied, with her usual faultless manners.

It all made his jaw hurt, this sharp game of courtesy, and he ordered himself to unclench it. There was nothing objectionable about this woman, he told himself, not for the first time. She could not be blamed for having dated the young King Alvize. But Gianluca also knew that every second he spent in her presence led to tabloid whispers, unsubstantiated rumors, and a resurgence of all the old nonsense he liked to think dead and buried.

And suddenly he had the strangest memory. Of being all of seventeen and at a party a great deal like this one. He had come across Lorenza there, and they had talked politely, about nothing in particular that he could recall. Had she not been *the infamous Lady Lorenza*, he doubted he would have remembered the interaction at all.

But *Like father like son!* the tabloids had blared.

Gianluca might have laughed the whole thing off, so absurd was the very notion that anything untoward might ever have happened between them—much less when he was a teenager—but his father had gone into a terrifying black rage.

He didn't like to think about the things that had happened then. The things his father had said. And done.

And worse, threatened to do.

Gianluca avoided Lorenza as much as possible without being impolite, even though his father had been dead a decade.

He made his excuses now as he steered Helene away from her.

"That was rude." Helene's voice was very pleasant and pitched so that only he could hear what she said. Anyone else would take it for far happier conversation. "She and I were speaking."

"You and she have nothing to speak about."

"All anyone ever talks about when it comes to Lady Lorenza is your father. Did you know that she's actually an incredibly interesting woman in her own right?"

"I cannot imagine that you're going to tell me anything I don't already know. But what I can tell you, what you should know above all else, is that this is not a topic I wish to discuss. Ever."

Helene carried on as if she hadn't heard him. "After she finished with your father, she went to school. Back to school. Whereupon she got numerous degrees in anthropology and now spends her time either on digs or at the offices of the University of Fiammetta, where she is also a professor. Her son has followed in her footsteps, and though he teaches at a rival university, they have managed to fund a fair few digs together. Her daughter teaches literature at one of the colleges here in the city. They are a very brainy, learned, academic family, including her husband, who has something of a mad scientist bent and, while not swanning about being an aristocrat, invents things in his spare time."

Gianluca could not stop dead in the middle of the floor the way he would have liked to do. That would give all the gossips something else to chew upon, and they would. With relish. So instead, he pulled her along with him until he could steer her outside, where braziers had been set out in the renovated castle's courtyard to cut the chill of the winter night. Once there, his guards quickly cleared the space of the inevitable trysts and smokers so that he and the Queen could have a moment alone.

He hoped this would seem romantic to the audience watching them from within.

And to help with that, he turned his back to the glass doors and windows so anyone gawking would see only Helene. "I cannot imagine what makes you think I wish to know the details about that woman's family. Or anything else concerning her." He bit that out, not sure he liked his words any better when he could see them puff in the air before him. But that didn't make them any less true. "The Lady Lorenza is not an appropriate person for you to be seen talking to, Helen. Surely you must know this."

"She didn't do anything wrong." Helene's gaze seemed particularly intense, there beneath the glow of the artificial heat, and he found himself moving closer to her. To block her from anyone watching, he assured himself. That was all. "Do you know why she broke things off with your father?"

Gianluca did not understand why she was continuing with this line of discussion when he had made it clear that it displeased him. "She has always stated that she found the media coverage entirely too intense."

"I'm sure that's part of it. There's no denying that it's all a bit mad. The paparazzi can take the most intrusive pictures, then say anything they like, and there's no recourse." Helene frowned, suddenly. "Just yesterday I read an unhinged story about us. You apparently have a secret mistress stashed away on the palace grounds who you visit in secret, right under my nose. You are your father, naturally, and I am being cast as prudish yet also angelic, as if they haven't quite worked out what character I'll be playing."

He did nothing to control his scowl then. "You shouldn't be reading that trash. It's forbidden in the palace for a reason."

"I hate to break this to you, Gianluca, but there is such a thing as the internet." She shrugged as if she didn't see the look on his face. "Besides, my cousin Faith and I have an ongoing competition to see which one of us can find the most outrageous tabloid article about me. Some days, it's a draw. But my point is, that's not why Lady Lorenza broke up with your father."

Gianluca couldn't navigate the shifts in this conversation. He couldn't—or he didn't want to. He wasn't certain there was a difference.

He felt, again, that he was out of his depth. He, who had only yesterday navigated his way without incident through a thorny political issue that the more serious papers had felt certain would take him at least twice as long, and would likely end in failure. In every other area of his life he not only considered himself well prepared, but fully capable of steering events to the conclusions he preferred.

And in this case, he once again had the strangest sensation. Strange, but familiar over the course of these last couple of months. Despite the familiarity, it took him long moments to realize it was him feeling like some kind of fool.

Again.

He had never felt like this before this woman had entered his life, and he had no wish to feel it again. But it did not go away as she stared back at him. And when he said nothing, she continued.

"She said that in some ways, your father was lovely," Helene told him. And everything inside of him was on high alert, warning him that he wasn't going to like whatever she was about to say. Or perhaps it was that something in him knew it would be one more of these explosions she was far too good at doling out. He wanted to tell her to stop, but he worried that would seem like a weakness. And worse, that she wouldn't. Especially as her expression shifted into *compassion*. "But only if he wasn't crossed. Get on his bad side, however, and he could be vindictive. Petty. She said he had a nasty temper."

He did not want to hear this. He could not hear this. There was no point digging up a dead man—much less that temper of his that Gianluca had long believed had been saved for his family alone.

Because it was unthinkable that anyone else might know of those black rages.

If they did—if anyone did—then everything his family was, everything *he was*, could be no more than another lie.

He ran a hand through his hair and hated that he was betraying his own agitation. "And you believe that I am the person to whom you should repeat this bit of fantasy? From a woman discarded by a king?"

There was too much of that compassion, all over her. "Why would she lie?"

It would have been different if Helene had seemed in-sistent. If she had poked or prodded in some way. If she had treated this like some kind of a grand exposé. Instead, she sounded...

Not sad. Not quite. Rather as if she felt sorry for him, and Gianluca would obviously have taken immediate ex-ception to such an outrage, but having never experienced it before, he found that the best he could do was stand there, wondering why it felt so much like a heart attack.

"If she wished to profit off such claims, she would have done so many years ago, in the wake of her actual relation-ship with your father," Helene pointed out when he did not reply, sounding quite reasonable. "She would have made a tremendous amount of money. She said she had people at her door night and day, bothering her parents and chas-ing her friends. While she was dating your father and then twice as many after. She could easily have dined out on her stories of dating the King for years. Instead she said nothing. And her reward was finding herself cast as a participant in a love triangle she had never taken part in."

"Why are we standing here in the cold, litigating an-cient history?" Gianluca demanded. "I lived through the aftermath of this, Helene. I do not need a primer."

"You never speak much about your father, did you know that?" When he glared at her, she smiled, though her gaze remained direct and solemn. "Lady Lorenza didn't wish to speak about him either. Do you know what she told me?"

"I do not."

One of the reasons this woman was so confounding was that she ignored him completely when she chose. As she did now. "She told me, with a sincerity that made her voice shake, that her relationship with your father had been a whirlwind. So wildly intense that she'd never quite known where she stood. She'd never known if she truly loved him or if she was swept up in his insistence that *he* loved *her*. And he was the King!"

"You might be surprised how little some women find themselves in awe of kings," Gianluca said darkly. "It is the scourge of modernity."

She acknowledged that with the faintest smile, but kept going. "But she found that breaking up with him felt like a relief, not a disaster, no matter the carrying-on in the gossip columns. And then she finally met her husband, who she'd been promised to when she was young but had not met as an adult. She said that the moment she did, that she had ever imagined that a royal three-ring circus—her words—could have anything to do with her was a joke. Because it seems that she and her husband have been quietly and completely in love with each other since first sight."

"Did you read this in one of your fairy stories?"

"Where I didn't read it was in the tabloids, where she was cast as a villain at best. And it certainly didn't stop your father from trying to involve her in his games."

Gianluca was rapidly reaching his limit. "My father did not play games, Helene. If you wish to muck about in other people's history, I suggest you get your facts straight."

"He didn't need to play games when he had the tabloids to do it for him," Helene said softly. "And look. He's been dead for ten years and now you do it too."

And that, Gianluca decided, was his breaking point.

That was *enough*—

But he was the King of Fiammetta, so he certainly could not break in public. He could not let the things that roared inside of him out.

He did the next best thing, bowing curtly to his queen and then ushering her back inside, so they could finish out the rest of this formal evening without becoming the only story that would be told about the event.

Later they sat in the car on the way back to the palace the way they always did, and he knew that he was not alone in thinking of the many times by now that he had closed the distance between them. Or she had. The many times they had found their way beneath each other's formal clothes to find the truth about themselves beneath.

Or *a* truth, he amended.

And that was not the way this night was going to go.

Not when he couldn't get the things she'd said about his father out of his head.

When they got to their apartments, she turned toward her own rooms and he did not stop her. But he didn't go to his bedchamber either. He dismissed his staff, finding his way to one of his private studies where he was drawn, unerringly, to a framed old picture he kept on the wall.

It was a famous photograph, one that had been published all over the world. It showed the young, vibrant King Alvize playing with his young son one summer afternoon in the palace gardens. Queen Elettra sat behind them, laughing happily in the sunlight.

A vision of a happy family, everyone had agreed. Everyone so beautiful, so covered in joy, so perfect in every way.

But it was all a lie.

One he had been telling himself ever since.

Though he had to have been only five years old, Gianluca could still remember that afternoon clearly, though he rarely allowed himself to stick his fingers in that particular wound. He didn't remember this moment, captured forever on film. But here, tonight, he let himself remember his mother flirting with the photographer— or rather, that his father had accused her of flirting later.

From those actual, long-ago moments in the sun, what he remembered most was the terrifying force of his father's attention. And the agony he had felt to perform perfectly for the man, lest it be his fault that Alvize's good mood go away.

As it so often was.

It was not a good memory, that photograph.

Yet he had chosen to keep it where he could see it, always, though he hadn't allowed himself to really think about that day in years.

And it was only now, standing here after one more confounding evening with his own queen, that Gianluca questioned himself. He was forced to wonder if the reason he held on to this photograph, and kept it displayed where he would see it often, wasn't for any sense of nostalgia as he imagined others might think.

As he had convinced himself he felt.

Because he kept hoping that if he looked at this picture long enough, he would forget what had actually happened between the people in that photo and instead see what everyone else did.

Or what he had hoped they did.

A happy family. A sweet moment. A light so bright that winter could never come again. No rain, no snow, not even the faintest shadow.

He made a low noise that he didn't recognize as himself. Then he wheeled around, making his way almost blindly to the door that connected his apartments to Helene's. The hallway was too long. There were too many rooms.

He didn't *recognize* himself and that was impossible.

Because he knew who he was. The whole world had known who he was before he'd drawn his first breath. He had been born to his role and there was nothing else.

Surely there could be nothing else.

He found her sitting at the vanity in her dressing room, taking down her hair. She had dismissed her staff too, as she usually did, so used was she to fending for herself.

Tonight he was glad of it. He walked up behind her, watching the shifting emotions as they played through the gold in her gaze, the softness of her wide mouth.

The graveness of her expression.

"Gianluca," she began.

"You have said quite enough tonight, *mia regina*," he said, and it, too, was someone else's voice, rough and raw.

Helene swiveled around on her seat as he drew close, and that suited him. He went down before her and ran his hand up her legs and over her thighs, urging them apart as he moved to kneel between them.

She whispered his name again, but he could feel the heat of her.

When he leaned in, he could smell her, too. The hint of the perfume she used and beneath it, far more potent, that scent that was only hers. That scent that made his mouth water and his sex ache.

He shifted her, tilting her hips up so he could drape her knees over his shoulders and spread her wide for him.

Like dessert.

She did not bother with undergarments any longer, because they only ever got in the way, and Gianluca was glad of it.

As he did not want to think. He did not want to interrogate the strange things he felt, or wonder why it was that he had locked them away inside himself all this time. Too many unwieldly truths. Too many intensities he did not wish to face.

He did not understand how she had managed to find the key to all these things.

But he didn't want to *think*, he wanted to *feel*.

Instead, he could hold her rounded bottom in his hands. He could get his mouth into all that silky heat, that sweet delirium, that he thought about more often than he should. In places where his thoughts should have been far away from such private matters.

But he was here now. He licked his way into her and that roar of longing and relief soared in him. He lifted her off the vanity so he could lay her out on the floor. So he could really dedicate himself to what he was doing and so when she thrashed beneath him, as she began to do quickly, she would not knock over anything or hurt herself in any way.

Gianluca did not choose to question himself.

He did not ask why it was he settled down, took his time, and ignored the demands of his own body as he made her sob and moan beneath him. As he took her to that edge, and teased her there, again and again.

Too many times to count.

When he could take no more, and she had tears tracking down the sides of her face from the force of the many times she'd come apart, he finally freed only the hungriest part of himself. He pressed himself to her, working his way inside her.

She was still a tight fit. She was always a tight fit, no matter how many times he made her buck and sob, and something caught at him—

But he couldn't hold on to it, because she was so soft, so scalding hot, and it was all he could do to thrust into her, over and over, until there was a hitch in her breathing again.

Until she was lifting her hips to his and arching up against him all over again.

Until she shattered once more, and took him with her.

And it took them both some time to find themselves again, lying in an inelegant heap on the floor of her dressing room.

"Do you have more to share with me?" Gianluca asked her, lifting a brow at her disheveled state, her hair a mess and every part of her flushed. "Tabloid stories, perhaps?"

And when all Helene could do was laugh, he carried her to the bedroom and started all over again.

Gianluca congratulated himself in the following days for finally understanding that there was only way to handle his wife. The more orgasms he gave her, the less she seemed to feel the urge to say such provocative things to him.

And if there was a part of him that missed the way she challenged him, he dismissed it.

Because this was better, surely.

This was what he'd wanted all along.

He might have actually found his footing in this marriage.

He assured himself that, finally, he had.

But one night, after they hosted a party in one of the palace's private rooms, Gianluca stayed afterward to talk with some of the guests a bit more privately so that they could hammer out a delicate arrangement that would leave the crown out of a particular business issue.

He expected it to take some while, but was thrilled when he was able to wrap it up and tie it in a bow quickly.

Because while Gianluca had only and ever been a creature of duty, forever in service to the crown, he was learning to resent it when those duties took him away from his wife.

And from wielding those tools he had finally learned how to use properly.

Yet when he let himself into the Queen's apartments, Helene wasn't there. He headed back to his own rooms, assuming he might find her in his bed instead. But she was not there either.

He walked out to the guards who waited at the entrance to the King and Queen's apartments, for none could pass without their knowledge.

"I'm looking for the Queen," he said.

And then, to his astonishment, he watched members of his own guard exchange a look, and then...not answer their king immediately.

One stared at the ground. The other stared straight ahead.

Gianluca felt a kind of storm in him, first a hint of far-off thunder. "I beg your pardon. Was I unclear? Where is the Queen?"

The guard with his head up cleared his throat. "My most abject apologies, Your Majesty. But the Queen expressly commanded us to keep silent about her whereabouts."

Gianluca merely raised a brow. He did not point out that his wishes superseded all others, always.

He did not have to. If he *did* have to, then perhaps it was time he abdicated.

But sure enough, all he needed to do was stare. The man let out a long sigh, the other one groaned, and they confessed.

And that was how Gianluca found himself stalking through the palace, then out into the rear gardens. He crossed the sprawling palace complex with what felt like murderous steps, hardly noticing the cold night, until he found himself at the door to the dower cottage once more.

He did not permit the guard to announce him.

Instead, he moved in a seething silence into the house, following the sound of voices he knew only too well.

And there he found them, sitting close together on the settee. With all those pictures on the mantel arrayed above them, another set of carefully curated lies.

His mother was dressed, suggesting this visit was no surprise though it was after midnight. And his own treacherous queen had not bothered to change from dinner, so it was tempting to imagine this was formal, the two of them talking the way that they were…

Except they were clasping each other's hands as if they were friends, and Gianluca felt something in him tear open at the sight.

He told himself it was betrayal.

"What," he bit out, and perhaps he enjoyed the way they both jolted a little too much at the sound of his voice, "in the name of all that is holy is going on here?"

His mother looked instantly defiant, but that was typical Elettra. He would deal with her later. He kept his gaze on Helene, expecting to see a look of guilt on her lovely, lying face.

But he did not.

Instead, if she was still startled by his sudden appearance, she didn't show it. All she did was shift so she could train that gold-tipped gaze of hers on him.

"What does it look like?" she asked, with that unimpeachable serenity of hers that might very well be what put him in his grave, no abdication required. "I decided it was high time I met my mother-in-law."

CHAPTER TEN

HELENE COULD FEEL the older woman's hands trembling in hers, so she didn't let go. Instead, she held on tight—but she didn't take her eyes off her husband.

Who she thought was the most stubborn man she'd ever met, and she'd grown up under the foot of a man who had redefined the term *single-minded.*

"And before you tell me that I have nothing to talk about with my own mother-in-law," she continued, because she by now could read the kinds of storms that moved through his gaze, "I'll thank you to allow me to decide such things on my own. It isn't up to you."

"When will you understand?" Gianluca's voice was almost soft, and she knew that meant he was at his most dangerous. "It is all up to me. This is my kingdom, Helene. I was born to rule it. My word is law. Which is likely to prove that to you?"

"Be cruel to me if you must, Gianluca," his mother said then. She shifted so that she could put an arm around her daughter-in-law's shoulders. "Don't turn yourself into a bully. Hasn't he already taken enough?"

Helene was absurdly touched by that. She had first come to see Elettra not long after she'd initially realized she was pregnant.

My dear, Elettra had said when Helene had snuck over

to see her, *you must not know my son very well if you think that there is any way to ingratiate yourself to him through me.*

I'm trying to ingratiate myself to you, Your Majesty, Helene had replied, with a perfect curtsy. *And much as I'd like to be friends, I have a deeper purpose.*

She had not announced that she intended to get to the truth of things. Still, Elettra nodded as if she knew. And they had enjoyed an afternoon tea, which happened to be Helene's most favorite meal of all.

The boarding school I went to took tea very seriously, she'd told Gianluca's mother. *We were in Switzerland, and the headmistress was quite ferociously German, but she told us all that a great deal of the world was arranged around a proper British tea service. The feminine part of the world, I mean. And it was a language she insisted we learn, if only because calling for a tea service during the middle of an unpleasant discussion gives everyone something to do. And therefore can shift the discussion to something more pleasant automatically.*

There is a reason, Elettra had said with a murmur, *that the British were so good at holding on to their empire for a time.*

Helene did not think that colonialism was predicated on tea, but she also did not intend to argue with the Dowager Queen of Fiammetta.

So instead, she and this wary, watchful, beautiful woman whose son looked almost exactly like her, sipped at their Darjeeling. They nibbled at cunning petit fours and did not have to choose between scones and crumpets—the way Elettra suggested Gianluca had always done—for both were on offer.

And as she'd risen to leave, Elettra had studied her teacup as if it held all the wisdom of the world.

Do you make my son happy? she'd asked. And then she'd looked up, with a smile. *It is not that I think he is particularly capable of happiness. It is more that I'm wondering if you've managed to convince him that he could be. That it is even remotely possible.*

Helene had shrugged helplessly. *I don't know,* she had said honestly.

They had met twice more after that, and while each visit was pleasant, they started doing a bit of digging, Elettra and Helene. Some comparing of notes. And Helene had intended to raise the subject of his mother with Gianluca.

Eventually.

She couldn't say she was sorry that he had appeared here tonight. No matter how thunderous he looked.

And that was putting it mildly.

"You will not speak of my father, Madam," Gianluca bit out, that black glare of his on Elettra.

Helene did not think it through. She stood, as if prepared to put her body between Gianluca and Elettra if necessary. And she knew the instant she did it that he would not take to it kindly.

He did not. His eyes widened in affront.

"This is your mother, Gianluca," she reminded her husband. "How is it you have managed to forget that?"

As he took a step toward her, Helene felt her heart catch in her chest. Because the lie she believed least was that he was as cold and as remote as he sometimes behaved.

She knew different. She'd *felt* different.

This was the man who'd become her lover.

This was the man who was still obsessed with the absurd notion that she had lied about her innocence—but who she sometimes caught looking at her with a very nearly soft expression on his face when he thought she was asleep.

Maybe she was putting too much stock in those moments. Maybe she wanted them to mean something they didn't, a necklace of connected baubles, little threads for a tapestry only she would ever see.

Helene had to believe otherwise.

She had to, for her own heart—and for her child.

"I never forget my mother," Gianluca told her darkly. "I never forget her betrayals. The mockery she made of her position, of the crown, and of everything else I hold dear. I do not need you to wade into matters that do not concern you and make them more complicated."

But Helene did not back down, because she could see beneath that darkness. She could see the hurt in him. She could feel it like an ache in her own bones. She thought of a little boy who believed what he was told, because he had no reason not to, and she hurt, too. "I can think of very little that concerns me more."

"I will deal with you later," Gianluca told Helene, though his gaze shifted to Elettra. "My mother and I need to refresh our memories."

Elettra stood, then, and somehow Helene knew that she was the only one here who saw the way the other woman trembled. And also how she hid it.

She met and held her son's gaze. "My memory is perfectly clear," she told him.

And every single thing Helene had ever learned urged her to sit down. To do as she was told. To retreat in the moment, so she might live to fight another day. To bend, choose silence, and utilize softness as a weapon.

Helene had always been so good at these things.

But she was carrying a baby. She was going to be a mother.

She could not live with herself if she did not fight for the life she wanted. The life her child deserved.

Because what good was the magic she and Gianluca made between them if everything else was poisoned? And though she had intended to simply prove, over time, that she could not be the liar he believed her to be—through her character, through her works, through the way she loved him—she felt as if she was running out of that time now. For there was no way she could bring a child into the world when her own husband truly believed that, at heart, she was a liar.

She knew it started here, in this quiet little cottage, where another woman branded a liar and a cheat had waited all this time. Not always out of sight. Not always quietly. Not always according to the principles Helene felt certain Elettra knew as well as she did, when it came to handling powerful men and highly weighted marriages.

"Do you know what I asked your mother?" Helene began.

Gianluca let out that bitter laugh of his. "I shudder to think."

"She asked me a question no one has thought to ask me in a very long while," Elettra said, and she looked almost wistful. "And for once I felt I could truly answer."

"I don't understand the purpose of this," Gianluca thundered then, as if the storm in him had spilled over. "Is it not enough that I allow you both to live here, insulated from the lies you have told and the damage you've done? What more is it that you want?"

It was not clear which woman he was speaking to, Helene saw.

Which was the problem.

"I asked your mother if she really had cheated on your father," Helene said quietly, well aware that the words made Gianluca jerk as if she'd kicked him in the gut.

And it was hard not to go to him, but she couldn't. She wouldn't. This was her chance to carve out a better life for all of them here...if only he would let himself see it.

"Not why. Not how. Not, *what could you be thinking?* and so on." Elettra laughed, and the sound coming from her was not bitter at all. "I was stunned. In thirty years, no one has ever doubted that I am guilty as charged, in every possible way."

"Because you are." Gianluca's voice was so low. His eyes were so dark.

Helene still stood between the two of them, and she lifted a hand as if extending it toward Gianluca.

She did not expect him to take it. But it still cut that he didn't.

"But what if there was a deeper lie?" she asked him, and shook her head at the look of something like bewilderment on her face. "I couldn't get the things Lady Lorenza told me out of my mind. The things she did not want to say about your father's character, and how that, juxtaposed with a happy life she leads outside of the spotlight, made me wonder. And I started to think about what it is that lies do. How they can transform everything."

"Do you need a lesson in this?" Gianluca demanded, but he did not sound like himself. He sounded...torn.

She had to hope it was enough.

"I am a walking object lesson in this, Gianluca," Helene replied. "But first, imagine this. A young girl marries an overwhelmingly powerful man. He is older than her, the king of everything, and he quickly makes it clear that he will only tolerate the strictest possible control on her at all times. As if she is little more than a trophy. All his, to do with as he wishes."

Gianluca ran his hands over his face. "Is this one of your fairy tales, Helene?" He dropped his hands and eyed his mother. "Do you think this version of events will work?"

"The thing about tabloids," Helene said softly, before Elettra could snap back at her son, "is that they don't have anything interesting to say about people who find happiness and quiet lives on the other side of the glare. So why would they continually drag Lorenza into all those stories about King Alvize and his marriage? Unless, of course, someone far more powerful than an ex-girlfriend who made no attempt at any point to capitalize on her relationship to the crown, was feeding it to them?"

Gianluca's dark gaze moved to Elettra, then back to Helene, as hard as a fist. "What are you saying?"

She thought he might know, but she kept going anyway. "Imagine Lorenza was less the great love of your father's life, and more the only person who had ever dared defy him. Would he want revenge? That was the second question I asked your mother."

Helene glanced at Elettra, who swallowed. Hard. But she did not back down.

"One night," the older woman said, "your father was in one of his moods. You remember how he was." And Helene thought that Gianluca's silence then said more than any protestation could have. "One of the aides told me it was because Lorenza had announced her pregnancy. Alvize did not like this. He was ranting and raving, and I was all of twenty. Heavily pregnant myself, with his heir, and I thought I'd heard quite enough of the Lady Lorenza to last me a lifetime." A shadow crossed her face, as if she was looking in a very old mirror. "I suggested that he was jealous. I pointed out that she couldn't make it any plainer that she'd moved on."

Gianluca let out a sigh that told Helene that all the inferences she'd made about his father, about his family, were true.

Elettra looked down for a moment. "That was unwise. But I didn't learn my lesson. He made me sorry enough that night, but I got to thinking in the way that angry young girls do. He'd hurt my feelings and I thought I could hurt his, too." She lifted her head, and Helene saw her son in the way she held herself. "Maybe what I needed was a little leverage. Maybe I needed him to think that I was something he could lose too. Maybe then he would treat me with a little more respect."

Gianluca muttered something beneath his breath. Helene held hers.

"Your grandmother was still alive, and while she and I never had a bond as some do, she had told me very early in my marriage that she had never known a man who did not benefit from imagining there was some competition." She smiled when Gianluca made another dark, low noise. "So one time, when he was raging on about Lorenza and how it was obvious to anyone who looked that she was living her life *at* him, I asked if he would show the same interest in me if I ever decided to break up with him. Or, in the way of so many royals, not break up with him at all, but move on all the same."

Gianluca looked shaken. "You did not say this."

Elettra held her son's gaze. "I did."

"That was a remarkably foolish thing to do." And Gianluca sounded as close to stricken as Helene had ever heard him.

"Did you ever wonder why a man with your father's temper, raging down the palace, somehow sat idly by while his wife betrayed him so publicly and repeatedly?" When Elettra laughed this time, it was a brittle sound. "When I woke up, it was to discover that he had knocked me out cold in two ways. The first with a backhand. And the second with the papers. The stories of my first affair were all over the papers."

Gianluca flinched as if he'd taken a blow himself. He was breathing too heavily, ghosts in his eyes, and a dawning, horrible new knowledge. "While you were pregnant. With me."

Elettra nodded slowly. Deliberately. "And then, my darling son, he had a weapon. One he could use as he pleased. When I spoke out, or dared defend myself. When I misbehaved or when you did—every time, he invented a new lover. I lost count. And for good measure, he made certain to suggest that, perhaps, Lorenza's son was his too. That Lorenza was part of the triangle that existed only in his head. I'm sure he hoped that, at the very least, he could wreck her marriage as well."

Helene moved toward Gianluca then, putting a hand on his arm that he did not seem to feel, too lost was he in the past.

"You are not to blame for believing this," she told him fiercely. "You had no reason not to. He was your father. He was the King. From everything I've heard, he was terrifying."

"And charming," Elettra said, her voice thick. "He could be so charming, out in public. That was what made you imagine he wasn't a monster. But then we would come home and he would be hideous to me and unkind to you too, and I didn't know what else to do. I knew he would never let you leave. So I stayed. And then he died and I still stayed, even though you did not want me near, because I could not bear to leave you. I still can't."

Helene watched something wash over Gianluca then, like a body blow. And there was the distinct sheen of vulnerability in his gaze when he looked at her. Anguish. Despair.

But then, just as quickly, it was shuttered again.

He took a step back. He shook his head once, then again. "No," he said, very distinctly. "These are lies upon lies upon lies. I will not let you drown me in the swamp of yours, Madam."

Though Helene was not certain whether he spoke to her, or his mother.

And then it didn't matter. "You have outstayed your welcome," he threw at his mother.

She only sighed as she sat again, looking smaller than before. "Like father, like son," she murmured.

It was a blow, and it landed. For a moment Gianluca looked as if it might take him down—

But he shook it off.

Then he was taking Helene by the arm, and she let him because she knew what he apparently did not—which was that there was no going back from this moment. There was no pretending that the whole of his life, and all of his beliefs about his family, weren't stacked precariously on the lies and petty jealousies of a very small man on his big throne.

She waited until they were out in the middle palace complex, with gardens on all sides, the late winter night above them, and no guards nearby to hear.

"It's surprising that you claim to be so allergic to lies," she began.

"Yet you keep on spinning them," he ground out.

Helene stopped walking, and Gianluca whirled so he could face her. And she thought he looked nothing like himself tonight. He looked as close to disheveled as she'd ever seen him. His eyes were wild. His face was twisted.

This should have scared her. But it didn't.

Gianluca didn't scare her at all.

That wasn't to say he couldn't break her heart. That he hadn't already. That he wouldn't again. But she didn't *fear* him.

His own mother had not been able to say the same about the King she'd been married to.

"Why are you so sure that I lied to you on our wedding night?" Helene demanded of him now, out here in the dark and the cold. With no trace of her usual calm, her hard-won ease and grace. There was no room for that now. "What is your evidence? Or is it just you have always been taught that women are liars?"

"It has nothing to do with what I have or haven't been taught," he threw at her. "It is as simple as this, Helene. Every time I touch you, every time I go near you at all, you burst into flame. What virgin does this?"

"This virgin," she shot back at him. And she did not shrink. She did not dip her head or avert her eyes. Tonight she was done with strategy, with waiting for the right moment. What moments were left? This was her life. This was her child's whole world they were discussing, whether he knew it or not. "This woman, who has been in love with you since the very first moment she set eyes on you, and not because you're a king. You could have been the gardener, for all I cared. I looked up, you were there, and everything changed. I burst into flames every time you touch me because of the fire between us. It's *ours*, Gianluca."

He looked wild, but she couldn't stop.

"I have never touched another man," she told him, as if they were standing at another altar. But this one was far more critical. "I have no interest in other men. And no, I can't prove that. Just as your poor mother couldn't prove to anyone that she was the innocent victim of your father's schemes. The same way poor Lady Lorenza couldn't either. Deep down, Gianluca, I think you know this already."

He made a sound that was more animal than man. He speared his fingers into his hair and wrenched himself away, turning from her—but he only walked one step, then two.

She thought that when he spoke again he would sound as unsteady as she felt, but he didn't.

Helene would never know how he didn't when she wasn't sure her own heart would ever be the same.

"Do you think I will wait to send you away?" he asked in that voice of his that was all soft fury. "You are a disruptive presence. I will not allow it. I will pack you off to my grandmother's mountain retreat at dawn."

"No," Helene said.

She didn't plan it. The word simply slipped out, shocking her with its power.

Perhaps it shouldn't have shocked her. After all, it was the only word the Institut had always forbid them to use. They were taught to go under, over, or through.

The point of being obliging, the teachers would always tell them, *is to appear so even when you're being nothing of the kind.*

It is your appearance of meekness that is your greatest weapon, the headmistress had told them, time and again.

But out here in the dark, with clouds scudding across the waxing moon, Helene stopped being meek.

She stopped worrying about weapons.

Because she already had one and he didn't even know it. It was high time he did.

"No?" Gianluca repeated, as if he'd never heard the word before. "I don't recall asking for your permission."

"I'm pregnant, Gianluca," she told him, and she did nothing to soften the blow of those words. She did nothing to cushion him or protect him. This was not the time for softness. "And that means a great many things, but most of all this. You have to decide what kind of life your child is going to have. You have to decide what kind of family you are going to give him or her."

She thought he said her name, but she wasn't finished.

Helene drifted closer to him, tipped her head back, and looked him in the eye. "Starting right now."

CHAPTER ELEVEN

SHE COULD NOT have said anything that could have cut him in half more neatly.

Gianluca stared down at her, feeling as if he'd fallen from some great height and landed hard on his back, knocking the wind straight out of him.

This time, it was far more than the usual unsteadiness in Helene's presence.

This time it felt like a mortal wound.

He could hear her breathing, or maybe it was him, his own wind kind of stalling deep inside him. He felt a kind of sundering, deep within.

He could think of no other word for it.

He wanted to reach out and pull Helene close. He wanted to sink down onto his knees before her, put his hands on that belly he knew so well, yet had not sensed any changes in.

He wanted to make it clear to her, however he could, that he had no intention of being the kind of father his own had been—

But he did not do any one of those things.

Because wasn't he on track to being *exactly* like his father?

And tonight, as the clouds danced across the moon, he couldn't pretend his father was the innocent victim any longer. He couldn't pretend he hadn't spent most of his adult life tamping down on the memories that he'd long ago decided could not possibly help him.

His father had been cold and distant, violent on bad days, and then he had been dead.

When there were others around, he had been handsome and awe-inspiring. He had seemed everything a king and a father should have been—but it had never lasted.

Hoping it might had been almost as bad as weathering one of Alvize's rages.

Gianluca had learned how to hide. He had escaped to school. He had stopped *hoping*. When he finished school, he dedicated himself to a life of preparation for the crown. He made himself a beacon of duty.

He made himself the man he'd wished his father really had been.

Anything to be someone other than that terrified small boy.

Anything to be something besides a victim.

Because if he was a victim, then it was far more possible that his mother was, too.

His mother, who had stuck around. Who had never hidden away, nor run. Elettra had instead remained seemingly unapologetic. She had never corrected the record. She had never explained.

Gianluca had thought it was defiance—he had wanted to believe it was—but out here in the cold tonight, it seemed a lot more like dignity.

And after tonight, he was going to have to face the fact that while he knew his father all too well, he knew his own mother not at all.

It all seemed to jumble around inside of him. Mothers and fathers. Children. Helene, who was simply waiting in that way of hers. Not quite so maddeningly serene tonight, but watching him closely—as if she already knew exactly what would happen inside him in the face of her announcement.

He suspected she might.

She was his queen. His wife.

She was going to be the mother of his child.

The child that he had declared he would treat precisely as he had been treated. When he'd said that, he'd been focused on his work. How he'd turned out. What had become of him, not how it had felt.

But tonight he could remember that scared little boy who had wanted only his mother.

And whatever it was that had come asunder inside of him before broke apart even further now.

Gianluca took a step back, then another. He was aware that he was staggering like a drunk man, but he could not seem to stop himself.

"Helene," he managed to grit out. "Helene, *mia regina*, I do not think you understand…"

But when he stepped back again, she came forward. She came straight to him as if she was sure that he would welcome her easily.

As if he had not been keeping her at arm's distance from the start.

He thought of what she'd said to him here, that she'd had the courage to say it when he had not. That they had looked at each other in a garden in Provence, the smell of lavender in the air and bees buzzing lazily as they would, and everything had changed.

They had changed, and theirs were not the sort of lives that allowed for such things.

There had been no place to put something so overwhelming. So mad and wild and intense.

"I had to keep you in your proper place." He would never know how he forced those words free from the constriction in his chest, his throat. And he could hear how it sounded, there in the cool night air in the shadow of the palace. "I don't mean that in the way you think I do."

"Then tell me what you mean," she said quietly.

Gianluca blew out a breath, as if that would help. Or loosen his chest enough to speak, anyway. "My father, who I wanted very badly to think of as a good man, called me into the throne room and told me how the world works. I was ten. Looking back, I do not think this was because he was seized with the urge to parent his only child. I believe it was because he thought he could leverage me against my mother."

And it wasn't lost on him that the word *mother* sounded thick and little used on his tongue.

Because it was.

Helene moved closer, keeping that gaze of hers so steady on his. As if all he really needed to do was follow the gold there, brighter than the moon. "He explained to me that the King especially must keep everything partitioned. And I'm not sure I thought much of him as a man, though I wished I could, but I thought he was a decent king. And after his death, when my mother seemed to get more and more erratic by the day—"

He stopped himself. Because everything inside him was spinning around and around, and he could not be certain he knew anything. Not even what he would have said, only a few hours ago, was the inevitability of Elettra's lust for the spotlight.

Because it was possible—it was more than just *possible*—that it had never been that at all.

"I think you can grieve people in a variety of ways," Helene said quietly. "And not all of them are palatable to others. I don't know why we think they should be."

Gianluca tried his best to focus. Not on his mother's grief, but on the things he needed to say to this woman. His wife and queen.

This woman who would make him a father.

"I was sure that I could handle you," he told her then, his voice low and rough, not cultured at all. "I told myself that the connection between us was simply...icing on the cake. Instead of what it really was."

She nodded, solemnly, and did not pretend that she didn't know exactly what he meant.

"And then, on our wedding night, it was all too much." He raked his hands through his hair again. "I thought I could control that, too. I needed to control everything, Helene, and when I couldn't, I seized on the only possible explanation I could find for why everything between us was..."

He couldn't find the right word.

But she could. She gazed at him, all solemn gold and a kind of certainty that made his heart thud against his ribs. "Magic."

Gianluca had no defense against her. Why had he ever imagined otherwise?

"And so instead of telling you that I was terribly afraid that I'd fallen in love, when the only thing I had ever seen was its death throes, I chose instead to accuse you. I worked for years to block my father's offense from my memory, because the truth is that he never loved anything. Not Lady Lorenza. Not my mother. And certainly not me."

"But your mother did," Helene whispered, as if she already knew this confession was so terrible, he had never admitted it even to himself. "She loved you no matter how horrible you were to her."

Something old and painful cracked inside of him. "She did."

"That's what mothers do," Helene told him, standing there before him as if she was impervious to the mountain air. "That's what my mother did. There were no public recriminations, not like here. But you've met my father. He was always a cold man. Before my mother died, commenting on his moods was like the weather, nothing more. After she died, I had to cater to those moods, and that was different. Because a parent who doesn't love you, or loves himself far more, allows for no imperfections. Every step put wrong is a mark against you and a stain upon their name. I learned to be spotless."

"It is as if you and I were raised by the same man," Gianluca said roughly, though the words still hurt. His throat was still too tight. Every bone in his body ached. And his ribs could not seem to contain his heart. "Though I find myself envious that you had the time you did with your mother. My father saw to it that I could not have even that. I was sent away to school so soon that I heard stories about my mother from my classmates, and so she was framed in my mind as the harlot he painted her to be, even then."

"I don't think I really understood until this moment," Helene whispered, "that my sweet mother spoke to me of fairy tales and Prince Charmings, not because she wanted to inure me to my fate, but because on some level she must have believed that she would be able to sway my father from his path." She pulled in a breath gone ragged. "Because it never occurred to me until now that fathers who truly love their daughters do not sell them for clout. Not even to kings."

And then with the weight of all of this clear and obvious between them, Gianluca sank at last to his knees.

When he reached for Helene, he found that she was crying. Tears rolled down her cheeks, and splashed on his fingers. This from a woman who he had never seen cry, not outside the bedroom.

"I did this to you," he said gruffly. "I have stolen your reserve."

"That is nothing but a mask I wear," she whispered, dashing her fingers across her eyes, though more tears followed all the same. "I don't think I knew until just recently that I could take it off."

And Gianluca thought of the day he had proposed to her. How he had come once again to that château in Provence, sweeping into the old house in all his state, with all his aides and staff. They had conducted the last of his talks with her father—all about money, naturally, not a word about his daughter's well-being or happiness—and then the many contracts had been signed, one after the next.

It had been a business meeting like any other.

Then they had all sat down to an excruciatingly formal lunch, where Helene ate nothing, her father made off-color jokes, and, at last, Gianluca had stood, inclined his head, and announced that it would please him greatly if she would consent to become the Queen of Fiammetta.

Tonight, he took her hands in his. He pulled her close so he could kiss each one, and then he circled her hips so he could lean in and place a kiss to her belly.

It felt like starting over.

So that was what he did.

"I believe you," he told her.

Gianluca did not think about kings, not his father nor himself. He thought about Helene. And whatever man he was, hidden beneath all that perfection he had imagined he could attain when what he wanted most was this.

To breathe a little while and hold her while he did it.

No wonder she had scared him so much he'd turned tyrant instead of facing that he, all along, was the problem between them. He was the lie.

"I think I always knew you did not lie to me, no matter what I tried to tell myself. For how could you be so perfect in every way, even in bed? I could not make sense of it. I've had my staff scouring all of Europe to uncover your deceit, yet they continue to come up empty. And I think that you are very wise, Helene. Far smarter than you sometimes let on. But I do not think that even you can escape the kind of scrutiny that I have given your past."

"That is all very logical," she said dryly. "I'm so pleased you had your reasons."

And as he knelt there on the cold ground, he felt a huge thing move in him. For a brief moment he thought that perhaps he was dying, after all—

But it was a laugh.

A deep, surging laugh from the deepest part of him.

He let it come. He threw back his head and let it out, and it felt good. Right.

Just like her.

"Is that a hint of temper I hear in your voice?" he asked Helene. "Are you, a graduate of the Institut and the Queen of Fiammetta…actually displaying your true thoughts to me?"

She wiped at her face again, seeming as shaken by the

sound of his laugh as he was. "It appears to be that kind of night."

Gianluca knew it was. So he pulled her down with him until they were both kneeling on the earth, as if he was trying to re-create the day they'd met. But better this time. More honest.

Maybe he was.

"This is our beginning, you and me," he told her intently. "For I have been a fool of epic proportions. Starting with the fact that I have never properly asked you to be my wife and tumbling on from there, so let me be perfectly clear, Helene. I have never been the same since the moment I saw you. I would never have said I believed in love at first sight, but I know that it can be nothing else. I would have told you that I have no idea what love might be, but you have showed me, haven't you?"

This was not a real question. She had. Every day, she had. She had not threatened him like his father. She had not challenged him to think the worst of her like his mother. She had simply loved him, and in so doing, unraveled him from the inside out.

He hadn't even realized she was doing it.

Gianluca smoothed his hand over her cheek, then let his fingers find their way into those wild, dark curls he adored. "You have weathered my disgraceful behavior. You had every reason to throw temper tantrums, break things, perhaps even leave me here in this kingdom of mine, but you did not. You stayed by my side. You listened to me speak ill of you with compassion. You have showed me, again and again, that love is far more complicated than I could have imagined. And far more beautiful. And so all I can hope is that I have the opportunity to prove to you that I can love you back, in the way that you deserve, and somehow make up for these things I've done to you."

"Just because you didn't see my reactions doesn't mean I didn't have them," Helene whispered, her tears still falling. "There was a part of me that wanted to leave. There was a part of me that wished, desperately, that I could hate you. There is always this thing in me that is a product of how I was raised and what I was taught, that urges me to make myself disappear in plain sight. To be obliging, reserved, and to live behind this mask of good manners even if it suffocates me."

"Promise me," he said, dark and intent, "*promise me* that you will leave that mask at our bedroom door. That, alone, you and I will not be a king and a queen, but a man and a woman."

"A husband," she whispered. "And a wife."

"I am so sorry, *mia regina*," he told her, from every part of him. "*Cuore mio*, my heart, I promise you that I will do everything within my power to make myself worthy of your forgiveness."

"Just love me," she whispered back. "And I will love you back. We will forgive each other whether we deserve it or not, and we will teach our child not only how to love, but how to be loved as we were not." And she leaned closer, her expression grave again, no matter that her eyes were still so wet. "But Gianluca, I will not be going away to any prison on a mountainside. And I will not send my baby away at the age of six. I don't imagine I will like it very much at sixteen."

"Helene, my wife, *mia amata*," he said, very seriously. "You must know that I was never going to send you away. I cannot exist without you. I do not wish to. And we will have as many children as you like, who you can tether to yourself if you so wish." He leaned forward then, and slowly, with great deliberation, began to kiss each and every tear from her cheeks. "I only ask that this tether does not extend into our bed."

"Of course not," she whispered back, her own laughter catching in her throat. "Whatever do you take me for?"

High above them, the clouds were finally gone. The moon beamed down, making the gardens they found themselves in glow silvery and bright.

It was not warm, so neither one of them removed their clothing. But he pulled her over his lap and she worked between them until she could take him inside her, and then they moved there, whispering their vows to each other as the long, dark night faded away all around them.

Again and again, they consecrated this new union, this new, true wedding.

And when the morning dawned, it was cold, but it was spring.

Gianluca and his wife rose together and breathed in the new day, the new season. They clasped their hands together, hung on tight, and walked back toward the palace. Because flowers weren't the only thing that could come back to life after a long, cold winter.

He looked down at this woman who he had given no reason to love him, no reason to trust him ever again, who had nonetheless placed not only her life, but the life of their child in his hands.

And Gianluca knew that no matter what came next, he would do his best to make certain that no winter was overtly long, that no deep freeze could not be melted, and that every summer was bright and bold enough to last them all the way through until the next one.

Because his Helene deserved to bloom.

CHAPTER TWELVE

THE FIRST THING Gianluca did was set about beginning the process of repairing his relationship with Elettra.

Their initial conversation, consisting mostly of apologies, was not long. And moving forward was not easy. It was, he discovered, less the repairing of a relationship and more the building of one. And it would have been only too easy to simply step back from this peace he was trying to weave.

But he didn't.

Because each time that happened, Helene was there, whispering to him of *tapestries*.

She was compassionate, understanding, and on the occasions—the very rare occasions, in his opinion—when he was entirely too bullheaded to listen to reason, prepared to fight him *for* him.

To shock him into listening to reason, if necessary.

He could not say he enjoyed it while it was happening, but in time, he came to depend upon her quiet reason and her willingness to challenge him when no one else would. Her acceptance of the intense emotions he tried to hide away, afraid who he would become if he was anything less than perfect.

And so, in time, he learned how to feel what he felt and express it, perhaps not immediately, but always appropriately.

Gianluca returned this favor by encouraging his reserved, masked paragon to show the world more of the Helene he knew, so that as the years passed, she became as well known for her laughter and her sense of humor as her good works and great dignity.

When it came to their children, she took him at his word that night. Their daughter was born with a head of dark hair, and his mother's gold-tipped eyes. And she was followed soon after by six more perfect, gold-eyed babies in rapid succession, because, as Helene would say to anyone who asked, she and Gianluca had always wished for siblings.

Their children, she laughed, would no doubt choose the opposite, after all the noise and joy and laughter.

But what they would not do was grow up cold and afraid, forced to be spotless, and uncertain whether or not they were loved beyond reason.

Her much-adored cousin Faith became the sister Gianluca never had. She married for love as Helene had said she would, but Helene—apparently not trusting that love would show up in time—arranged the meeting. She made sure that her cousin got to know none other than Lady Lorenza's aristocratic, anthropologist, academic son.

"I think they might have some things to talk about," she said.

And she was right.

Their eventual marriage had many knock-on effects, one of which was the fact that Lorenza and Elettra were finally forced to truly get to know each other, instead of merely reading about each other in the papers.

Not that either one admitted they did such a thing.

And having witnessed the kind of magic Helene was capable of kicking up in her wake, wherever she went, Gianluca was not the least bit surprised that soon enough, the women his father had tried so hard to destroy became the very best of friends.

Years later, when Elettra told him that she had been approached to write a tell-all memoir, but would never so disrespect the throne, he told her to go right ahead.

"My darling son, I cannot promise I will keep anyone safe," Elettra told him.

She still lived in the dower house, because she was forever a champion and she still loved to ride, and could not give up her access to the stables.

But he had long since gotten rid of the guard at her door.

"No one kept you safe," he said, and then, recalling a little boy on his mother's lap, he smiled. "You tell your story as you wish, Mammina."

When her book came out, exposing the truth about his father for all the world to see, Gianluca was first in line to buy it. And he made certain that it was captured on every camera in Fiammetta, so there could be no doubt where his sympathies lay.

For no longer did he feel he had to prove himself to his people. He did that every day. The proof was in his policies.

He made no promises whatsoever to be perfect, and he knew he wasn't. He could only rule as best he could, always keeping his people in the forefront of his mind, not his own concerns.

And this was what he told his daughter, the Crown Princess Angelica. He did not speak to her of compartments and partitions. He did not try to leverage her affection. She was a levelheaded girl, more like her mother than like him, and he told her things his father would never have said to him.

"You must reign with your heart," he told her. "But rule with your head."

"And what if those two things do not align?" Angelica asked, because, at sixteen she was a smart, serious girl who knew her own destiny, but had a mischievous streak that made him far happier than it should.

And her mother was only starting to come around to the idea that she might wish to go off and live her own life—or at least have a few years of school and horizon-building before getting down to her royal duties.

"But that is the point," he told this marvel of a girl that he and Helene had made together. "It is not your job to align them. It is to honor both in every decision you make."

That was what he strove to do.

And every night, he and the Queen would step into their rooms, and become…simply themselves. Gianluca and Helene, who loved each other and held each other, comforted each other and soothed each other's wounds.

Day after day, year after year.

They held hands in the backs of cars, no words necessary…on the occasions they did not use that backseat for other, hotter things. They danced at a great many formal events but they also danced when they were alone. She would tip her head back and her smile reminded him of summer in Provence, and she told him he was all the music she needed.

They laughed so much it hurt, they loved their children wildly, and every room in the whole of the palace sang with the force of all the things they were to each other.

"Like a fairy tale," he liked to tell her, his mouth at her ear.

"Because," his Helene said when they were both very old, still smiling at each other over sprigs of lavender and melodies only they could hear until they made their great-grandchildren groan, "happy ever after is just another way of saying…*us*."

* * * * *

COMING SOON!

We really hope you enjoyed reading this book.
If you're looking for more romance
be sure to head to the shops when
new books are available on

Thursday 15th
February

To see which titles are coming soon, please visit
millsandboon.co.uk/nextmonth

MILLS & BOON

MILLS & BOON®

Coming next month

CINDERELLA'S ONE-NIGHT BABY
Michelle Smart

Skimming her fingers up his arm, Gabrielle placed her palm on his chest.

He sucked in a breath. His grip on her hip tightened. The thuds of his heartbeat perfectly matched the thuds of her own.

Andrés was a strictly short-term relationship man. He wouldn't want more than she could give, and all she could give him was one night. It was all she could give to herself.

This was meant to be, she realised, staring even deeper into his eyes. It had been from the start. If she'd known he was single, she would have refused point blank to attend the party with him, would have spent the night alone in her tiny apartment unaware that he held the key to unlocking all the desires she'd kept buried so deep she'd hardly been aware they existed.

For this one night she could put those desires first, and do so with the sexiest man to roam the earth, the man who had the power to turn her to liquid without even touching her.

A man who wouldn't want anything more from her.

She moved her face closer. Their lips brushed like feathers. The heat of his breath filled her senses.

Continue reading
CINDERELLA'S ONE-NIGHT BABY
Michelle Smart

Available next month
millsandboon.co.uk

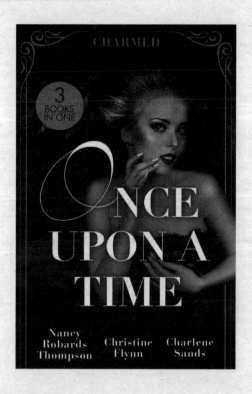

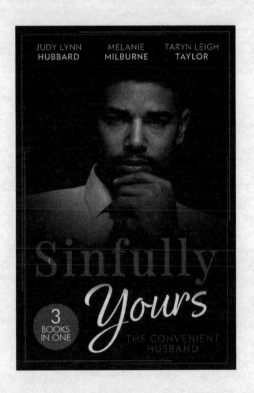

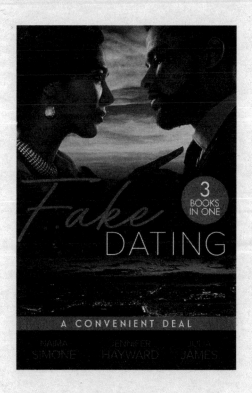

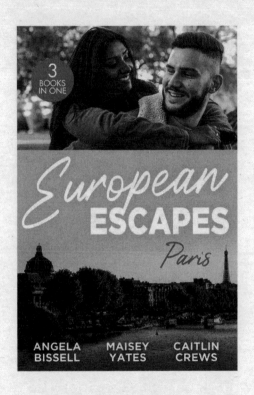

LET'S TALK

Romance

For exclusive extracts, competitions and special offers, find us online:

f MillsandBoon

X @MillsandBoon

⊙ @MillsandBoonUK

♪ @MillsandBoonUK

Get in touch on 01413 063 232

MILLS & BOON
A ROMANCE FOR EVERY READER

- **FREE** delivery direct to your door
- **EXCLUSIVE** offers every month
- **SAVE** up to 30% on pre-paid subscriptions

SUBSCRIBE AND SAVE

millsandboon.co.uk/Subscribe